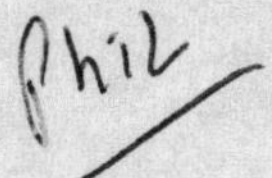

BUZZ

Also by Anders de la Motte

Game
Bubble

ANDERS DE LA MOTTE

Buzz

Translated from the Swedish by Neil Smith

This novel is entirely a work of fiction.
The names, characters and incidents portrayed in it are the work of the author's imagination. Any resemblance to actual persons, living or dead, events or localities is entirely coincidental.

Blue Door
An imprint of HarperCollins*Publishers*
77–85 Fulham Palace Road,
Hammersmith, London W6 8JB

First published in Great Britain by Blue Door 2013
1

Published by agreement with the Salomonsson Agency

A catalogue record for this book is available from the British Library

ISBN: 978-0-00-750029-1

Set in Minion by Palimpsest Book Production Limited,
Falkirk, Stirlingshire

Printed and bound in Great Britain by
Clays Ltd, St Ives plc

MIX
Paper from
responsible sources
FSC C007454

FSC™ is a non-profit international organisation established to promote the responsible management of the world's forests. Products carrying the FSC label are independently certified to assure consumers that they come from forests that are managed to meet the social, economic and ecological needs of present and future generations, and other controlled sources.

Find out more about HarperCollins and the environment at
www.harpercollins.co.uk/green

for Anette

My warmest thanks to all the Ants out there, without whose advice and achievements the Game could never have become a reality.

The Author

Buzz [b^z]
To leave, to get away from your current situation
Something that creates excitement, hype or a thrill!
A rush or feeling of energy, excitement, stimulation or slight intoxication
The verb used when posting something (mainly on Google buzz)
To clip, to cut, to shave, to remove, to mow
A method of obtaining immediate attention
Being overly and unnecessarily aggressive
A continuous noise, as of bees; a confused murmur, as of a general conversation in low tone
A whisper; a rumour or report spread secretly or cautiously
Making a call

www.wiktionary.org
www.dictionary.com
www.urbandictionary.com

'The speed of communication is wondrous to behold. It is also true that speed can multiply the distribution of information that we know to be untrue.'

Edward R. Morrow

'Nothing travels faster than light, with the possible exception of bad news, which follows its own rules.'

Douglas Adams

From: Mail Delivery Service
To: Badboy.128@hotmail.com
Subject: Delivery Status Notification
Date: 26 July, 23:44

Failed; 6.2.12.12 (rerouted)

Original message
From: badboy.128@hotmail.com
To: undisclosed recipients
Subject: the Game
Date: 26 July, 23.43

Dear newsdesk/TV station/blog

About four weeks ago I found a mobile phone on the train. A nice, shiny one – brushed steel with a glass touch-screen. It pulled me into a chain of events that came to an end out in Torshamnsgatan a few days ago, and I'd like to tell you about it.

My name is Henrik Pettersson, HP to my friends, and I'm 31 years old. (I don't really see what my age has got to do with anything, but you lot seem obsessed with how old people are, so there you go.)

By now the mention of Torshamnsgatan should have set a few alarm-bells ringing, seeing as that was where the bomb went off. The bomb that was actually intended for someone else entirely. (I'm not going to write their name, you know who I mean and you never know what sort of surveillance filter might pick up this email . . .)

Back to the mobile phone on the train:

It invited me to play an Alternate Reality Game, where the boundaries between fantasy and reality had been blurred. Little tasks you had to carry out, and film them with the phone at the same time. And those tasks earned you points, giving you a ranking on a high-score list, where your performance could be judged by people watching online. And you got money if you succeeded.

It all sounded cool, so I signed up pretty quickly.

But this particular Game turned out to be way more real than I had imagined.

And way more dangerous . . .

Try googling the weird shit that's been going on in the last few weeks!

That police car that crashed at Lindhagensplan, an abandoned house going up in flames out in Fjärdhundra, not to mention what happened to the royal procession in Kungsträdgården . . .

It's all linked to the Game.

And now you're wondering how I know that . . .

Easy – I was responsible for it all.

I got off on the buzz, the feeling that I had an admiring audience out there in cyberspace. Giving me cred for all the things I was doing. And like the sad little approval-junkie that I am, I let myself get dragged into it without protest. I shifted the boundary of what I thought was acceptable so far that I couldn't actually see it anymore. I even managed to harm those closest to me . . .

Pathetic, isn't it? How the hell could anyone do something like that, just to get a bit of public recognition? But take a look at yourselves. How many of you have got Facebook, Twitter or Instagram open in another window as you're reading this email? Running them as apps on your mobiles and checking them compulsively from the moment you wake up until you fall asleep? My guess is: all of you.

The whole damn lot of you.

So you're not exactly in a position to judge me!

I'm sure you'll do your job properly, so I might as well tell you now: I've got a sister, Rebecca Normén, she's a bodyguard with the Security Police. Yes, THAT Rebecca

Normén . . . You've probably written loads about her in the last few days. What with the medal and everything.

Becca's good at her job, she's a good bodyguard. A fucking good one, actually. Which isn't all that surprising, seeing as she's been in training her whole life, since we were little. She always looked after me. Except for one time when I stepped in and saved her life. Took a bullet for her.

But that's a long time ago now, we don't talk about it . . .

Somehow the Game Master managed to take advantage of our fucked-up relationship, and got me to subject Becca to things I'd rather forget.

She isn't involved in the Game, at least not the way I am. In fact she even doubts that the Game really exists. But like Verbal Kint says in The Usual Suspects:

The greatest trick the devil ever pulled was convincing the world he didn't exist.

Anyhow, I've given you enough, so get digging.

Check out who really owns that pile of ruins out on Torshamnsgatan. ACME Telecom Services Ltd is just a front. The set-up out there was used to control the Game. Collecting information, sending out tasks, and letting other people bet on the outcome.

Start by finding out what happened to

Erman, the IT genius who installed the servers. It's not a pretty story . . .

But once you've been dragged in there's no way out.

You're always playing the game!

Talk to my old BFF, Magnus Sandström, who almost had his computer shop burned out (but call him Farook or he'll get upset). Then throw in all the weird stuff that keeps happening. Computer systems that just shut down, sabotage, unexplained thefts. People vanishing – or being killed . . .

Put the pieces of the puzzle together, think big! Then even bigger!

You've got a lot of work ahead of you, but once you've got to the bottom of this you won't believe your eyes.

They've been playing for years, poor Erman told me. And I'm sure that's true.

Be careful – the Game Master's got eyes and ears everywhere, and will do everything in his power to stop you.

Dig deep, join the dots and – most important of all – don't trust anyone!

/HP

ps. Don't waste time trying to find me. I'm long gone by now. Somewhere no-one will ever find me.

Not even the Game Master.

This message did not reach its intended recipients.
It was rerouted and removed by the administrator on July 26 at 23:43

She had been awake just a few seconds when she realized that the man was behind her. Something told her that he had been standing there for a long time under the scorching sun while he waited for her to come round.

She had been dreaming about an al-ghourab – a scrawny little desert raven with shimmering, blue-tinged feathers that had been sitting not far from her on the sand. The bird had tilted its head and looked at her curiously with its peppercorn eyes, almost as if it was wondering what she was doing out there all on her own.

She didn't actually know if she had imagined it, or if a real raven had chosen to take a closer look at her inert body.

But, real or not, the bird was gone now – possibly scared off by the man's silent presence.

The man's return could mean only one thing.

Suddenly she was wide awake – her pulse was pounding against her eardrums.

She took a deep breath before slowly twisting her head to look in the man's direction.

The sun was reflecting off the object in his hand, blinding her and making her instinctively raise one arm to her sunburned forehead.

And at that moment she realized that the Game was over.

1

Neverlands

He was on her in two quick strides.

She didn't even have time to react before he had dragged her out of her chair. Her back was against the wall, one of his hands in an unshakeable stranglehold round her throat – so hard that the tips of her toes began to lift from the soft carpet – while he fumbled for the object on the table with the other.

There were gasps of horror from the other diners, a clatter of porcelain – but he didn't care. The lounge was on the sixth floor and it would be at least three minutes before the security staff got here. Three minutes were more than enough for him to do what he had to.

She was gurgling, desperately trying to ease his grip, but he tightened it further and felt her resistance drain away. In a matter of seconds the colour of her immaculately made-up face dropped from bright red to chalk white, suddenly matching her little pale suit.

Blonde businesswoman – my ass!

He released his grip enough to let a small amount of blood reach her brain. A sudden badly aimed kick at his crotch made him jerk, but she'd lost her shoe and without

Jimmy Choo's help the kick wasn't hard enough to make him loosen his grip. He tightened it again and pressed his face right next to hers. The terror in her eyes was oddly satisfying.

'How the fuck did you find me?' he hissed, holding the mobile up in front of her eyes. A shiny silvery object with a glass touch-screen.

Suddenly the phone burst into life. Out of reflex he held it further away from him, and to his surprise saw his own face reflected in the screen. Staring, bulging eyes, sweaty, bright-red face. The mobile must have a camera on the other side because when he moved his hand her terrified, pale face moved into shot. Beauty and the fucking beast, in podcast!

Totally fucking mad!

What the hell was he actually doing?

He was supposed to be a superhero, a saviour of worlds – but this? Attacking a woman? Had he really sunk so low?

He met her gaze again, but this time the fear in her eyes merely made him feel empty.

He wasn't himself.

He wasn't . . .

'Mr Andersen?'

'Hmm?!' HP came to with a start.

A little man in a uniform was standing next to his table, his soft voice just loud enough to drown out the soporific background noise of the lounge.

'Sorry to disturb you, sir. Your new room is ready.'

The man held out a small envelope containing a key-card.

'Room number 931, Mr Andersen: we've upgraded you to a junior suite. Your luggage is on its way up. I hope you continue to have a pleasant stay with us, and I can only apologize for the confusion regarding the change of room.'

The man bowed lightly and gently placed the envelope on the table.

'Can I get you a refill, sir?'

'No, thanks,' HP muttered, casting a red-eyed glance at the window table. Yep, the woman was still there, and beside her cup he could still see the little silvery rectangle that had made his imagination go mad.

He closed his eyes again, pinched the bridge of his nose and took several deep breaths.

Apart from the fact that the phone looked familiar, what evidence was there to suggest that they might have caught up with him?

He was on his umpteenth false passport, and none of them had the smallest connection with the previous ones. And he had put on a few kilos, a deep suntan and a long, fair hippie beard to match his even longer hair. He hadn't spoken Swedish for at least a year, not since he left Thailand. In other words, the risk of anyone being able to identify him was pretty fucking small, not to say microscopic. Apart from him, there wasn't a single soul in the whole world who knew where he was.

So your conclusion, Sherlock?

The phone had to be a coincidence. Almost all smartphones on the market looked pretty similar, most of them were probably made in the same Chinese sweatshops. Besides, this was hardly the first time he had imagined he had been found . . .

He'd lost count of the number of times he had panicked and escaped through rear exits and down fire-escapes to get away from imaginary pursuers.

Even if it had been a couple of months since his last dope-trip, his over-heated little brain still played tricks on him on a fairly regular basis, serving up ghosts in broad daylight, courtesy of the little grey men in the withdrawal department.

His lack of sleep was hardly making things any better.

He had just managed to nag his way to a more comfortable room, further away from the lifts.

But he already knew that wasn't going to help . . .

The woman whose phone it was showed no sign of picking it up.

Instead she was calmly sipping her coffee, glancing out at the sea, and didn't even seem to have noticed him. She was pretty fresh, forty-something, with her hair cut in a tight little bob. Jacket, trousers and low pumps. Now that he was looking more closely, he could see that she had her ankles crossed, and had slipped her heel out of one of her presumably extremely expensive shoes, and was dangling it rather absent-mindedly from her toes.

For some reason this casual act made him feel a bit calmer.

He took a deep breath through his nose and slowly let the air out through his mouth.

The whole of his dreamlike existence had, almost imperceptibly, changed its character and become something completely different.

Fourteen long months in exile. That was four more than he had spent locked up for killing his sister's violent boyfriend, and obviously in many ways a fuck of a lot nicer. Even so, the sense of restlessness was almost the same now, weirdly enough.

The nights were worst. Grass huts, youth hostels, airport hotels, or platinum palaces like this – it didn't really make much difference. His insomnia didn't seem to care about the weave-density of the sheets.

At the start of his tour he'd made sure he always had

company. He'd pulled numerous carefree backpack girls at campfire gatherings, all of them willing to party the night away.

Then, later on, when he was sick of the meaningless pillow-talk and beach-busker versions of 'Oooh baby it's a wild world', he had restricted himself to the pickings in the hotel bars.

But by now it was a long time since he had felt any real human intimacy.

Instead he was left having a doped-up wank to one of the stupid porn-films that his increasingly desensitized sex-drive demanded. Then a bit of lukewarm room-service grub while he surfed through the Thai knock-offs of blockbuster films until he slid into a state that was at least reminiscent of sleep. A grey fug where his imagination ran riot, exploring places he'd sooner forget.

He just had to accept that his dream-life was slowly going to . . .

Hell!

Even though she saw the automatic weapons before the cortege stopped, the smell that hit her when she first stepped from the car was so overpowering that Rebecca almost forgot about them for a couple of seconds.

It was a sweet, sickly pressure wave of scent from tightly packed bodies, rubbish, sewage and decay. She may have noticed the stench the day before when they checked the route, but it was considerably busier and hotter today and the heat seemed to have made the smell exponentially stronger.

The crowd quickly circled their drop-off point, as hundreds of agitated people pressed against the cordon of tape that had been put up to hold them back.

The soldiers exchanged nervous glances. Their hands

were hugging the barrels of their guns as they shuffled their feet anxiously on the red dirt.

There were six assault rifles, and the same number of soldiers in badly fitting, sweat-stained camouflage uniforms and scruffy boots. Their leader, a considerably better-dressed officer in mirrored sunglasses, waved at her to encourage her to offload her charge. His gun was still in its tight leg-holster along his right thigh, which meant seven weapons in total, not counting their own.

The officer's gestures became more impatient the longer she hesitated, but Rebecca ignored him. She remained standing with the car door open, while Karolina Modin, her driver, waited behind the wheel with the engine running.

She heard the doors of the car behind open and cast a quick glance over her shoulder. Göransson and Malmén were coming up behind her. Neither of the men said anything, but the expressions on their faces behind their sunglasses told her what they thought of the situation.

The crowd was getting noisier. The feeble plastic poles that were holding the cordon tape started to buckle as they pressed against it. Rebecca could make out a few random words in English.

Help us. No food, no doctor.

The soldier standing closest to her licked his lips nervously as he fingered the safety-catch of his rifle.

Click, click.

Safe, unsafe.

Not dangerous, dangerous.

A drop of sweat ran slowly down her spine.

Then another.

'Well, what are we waiting for, Normén?'

Gladh, the desiccated embassy counsellor, had evidently let himself out of the other side of the car and had come up behind her.

'The press are waiting, time to get going. We're already late.'

He reached for the handle of the rear door of the car to let the Minister for International Development out, but Rebecca beat him to it.

'Don't touch that door!' she snarled as she slapped the door window with the palm of her right hand.

The embassy counsellor kept hold of the handle, and for a few seconds they stood there exchanging hostile glances. Then Gladh let go, straightened up and, insulted, adjusted the knot of his tie.

'How long are you thinking of making us stand out here in the heat, Normén?' he whined, slightly too loudly, so that the minister would hear him through the tinted glass. 'Can't you see that these people are getting more agitated the longer we hesitate? They're waiting for us – for the minister, don't you understand that?'

Oh yes, she understood all right, but there was something about the whole situation that didn't feel right.

When they reconnoitred the site the day before they had been able to drive right up to the office of the refugee camp where the meeting was to take place. But today the road was blocked off two hundred metres from the building, even though she could see plenty of vehicles there already. Walking the minister two hundred metres through the crowd with six nervous government soldiers as their escort didn't feel like a particularly good idea.

Anyway, why so few?

The previous day the place had been crawling with soldiers, armoured vehicles and even a helicopter hovering above. The refugees had mostly stayed inside their flimsy little tents, hardly daring to come out.

But today the situation was suddenly the complete reverse.

'Come on, let's go! All is good, all is good . . .' the officer called, sunglasses flashing, waving eagerly at them to go over to him, while a couple of his soldiers made a feeble attempt to hold back the more eager members of the crowd pushing against the cordon. But still Rebecca hesitated. The sound of the mob was getting louder, yet she still imagined she could hear the metallic sound of the soldiers' safety-catches.

Almost like a second-hand counting down.

Click . . .

Click . . .

Click . . .

Unconsciously she moved her right hand to the pistol in the holster on her belt.

'We need to move now,' Gladh whined, and she noted the sudden fear in his voice.

Göransson and Malmén exchanged glances across the roof of the car.

'How do you want to do this, Normén?'

Her deputy was right. She had to make a decision.

Dangerous?

Not dangerous?

Make a decision, Normén!

Obviously she ought to open the door and let the minister out. But she still couldn't shake the feeling that something wasn't right – something more than just an agitated crowd, a blocked road and an embassy counsellor who needed the toilet.

The rubber handle of her pistol felt clammy against the palm of her hand.

Click . . .

Click . . .

Then suddenly she saw him. A man in the crowd to her right. He was dressed the same as all the screaming black people around him. A long white shirt, dark middle-eastern trousers and a length of cloth covering his head. But still he stood out, something about him . . .

To start with, he was calm. He wasn't shouting, he wasn't waving his fists or trying to get her attention.

Instead he was moving steadily forward, slipping calmly between his agitated brothers in misfortune, getting closer and closer.

The man was holding something in his hand and it took her several seconds to see what it was.

A plastic bag, and, to judge by its uniformly bright yellow colour, it was still too new to have been bleached by the sun and creased like everything else in the camp.

What was something as new and clean as that doing in the midst of all this overwhelming misery?

She shaded her eyes with her left hand and tried to focus her gaze. The bag kept moving in and out of her field of vision, hidden by the crowd only to reappear shortly afterwards in a small gap. Bright yellow, smooth, and definitely out of place.

For a moment she thought she could just make out a dark object at the bottom of it.

And suddenly her decision was made.

'Get back in!' she roared, glancing quickly at her two colleagues to make sure they'd understood her order.

'Get in at once, we're aborting!' she yelled at Malmén, who didn't seem to have heard her over the noise of the crowd.

At first her deputy didn't react, then he nodded curtly and signalled with his hand to the driver of the third car to reverse and clear their path.

'What the hell are you doing, Normén?!' the embassy counsellor shrieked, grabbing her right arm.

She shook him off easily.

'Inside the car, Gladh, unless you want to get left behind!' she snapped as she gestured to her driver to get ready to leave.

Gladh carried on shouting in her ear but she wasn't listening.

The man with the plastic bag had vanished but she was sure he was somewhere in the crowd – and that he was still heading towards them.

The Landcruiser behind them reversed a few metres, and without taking her eyes off the crowd she banged on the roof of the car to signal to Modin to follow suit.

Slowly their car began rolling backwards over the uneven road surface.

The passenger door was still wide-open, waiting for her to jump in.

At the same moment as the cortege began its retreat the noise of the crowd rose to a furious roar and the feeble cordon holding it back gave way.

The soldier closest to them didn't even have time to raise his gun before he was swallowed up by the mob.

In just a couple of seconds their car was surrounded. Hands banging on the bonnet and windscreen – tugging at her clothes, trying to pull her away from the open door.

She stumbled and for one panic-stricken moment thought she was about to fall.

Her pulse was racing as she struggled to pull herself free, but she was being attacked from all sides.

Hands were roaming over her belt, towards the pistol in her firmly clenched right hand. She smashed her left hand into someone's face, kneed another man in the crotch and rammed her head back towards a voice that was yelling in her ear, but her attackers were too numerous and she was likely to fall at any moment, and then everything would be over.

Suddenly the car jolted and the heavy door swung back, clearing enough of her attackers out of the way for Rebecca to be able to pull her right arm free and draw her pistol.

Barrel in the air, squeeze the trigger!

The weapon jerked in her hand – once, then several more times, and suddenly the roar switched from fury to fear and panic. And suddenly she was free. The people closest to her tried to flee and collided with others who were still pushing forward. Screams blended into the sound of bodies thudding together. She heard shots from directly in front of her. Short salvoes of automatic rifle fire, probably aimed directly into the crowd. A bullet buzzed past her head like an angry bee, but she hardly noticed it. Modin revved the engine and the spinning wheels threw up clouds of dust that quickly filled the whole of her field of vision with red fog.

The car began to pick up speed. She stumbled but eventually managed to grab hold of the swinging door. Her fingers were still clutching her trigger, the barrel pointing up at the sky.

The man came straight out of the cloud of dust. Right in front of the bonnet, maybe six, eight metres away. He leaped nimbly over the prostrate bodies and zigzagged through the fleeing crowd, heading straight for the car. He had one hand halfway out of the plastic bag. The object was clearly visible now.

Rebecca lowered the arm holding her pistol, trying to aim at his legs, but it was impossible to hold the gun steady. The car was speeding up, throwing up yet more red dust, then hit the front of the vehicle reversing behind them. The sudden stop sent the car door swinging back to hit Rebecca on the chin, and once again she almost fell. For a few seconds all she could see were stars and red fog.

When her vision cleared the revolver was pointing straight at her.

She was riding him like a bucking bronco.

Her perfect silicon breasts were bouncing in sync as she ground her hairless crotch against his pelvic bone. She had one hand on the frame of the bed and the other wound in a tight grip of his long hair, so hard that he could hear the roots groan as she pulled him to her. The heels of her shoes were digging painful grooves in the outside of his thighs.

But he really didn't give a shit, because the businesswoman was giving him the ride of his life.

He certainly wasn't an inexperienced pilot in the bedroom – quite the contrary! In fact he had always regarded himself as something of a Top Gun in that area.

But by God, could she fuck!

This year's Gonzo at the Adult Awards, with a double nomination for *Female Performer of the Year*. The experience was so intense that he had to keep reminding himself to breathe.

His groin began to twitch – the tension transmitted itself to the rest of his body as he tried in vain to think about something that would put him off. But it was impossible.

'I'm coming,' he gurgled in warning, but she made no attempt to get off. Instead she let go of the headboard, moved her hand down her back towards his groin, and, just as he started to come, she dug her nails into his scrotum. He thought he was dying! His orgasm was so intense that he arched his back as far as it would go, and, to judge by her screams, she was using his movements to her own advantage.

It took him several minutes to come to his senses again,

during which time she had rolled off him and lit a cigarette.

'Isn't this a non-smoking room?' was the first thing he managed to say when he regained the power of speech.

'Who are you – the smoking police?' she grinned, blowing a long plume of smoke towards the ceiling.

Quite. Who the fuck cared? What a total dweeb he could be sometimes!

'What . . . what's your name?' he stammered, in the absence of anything better to say.

'Anna – Anna Argos.'

She put the cigarette out in one of the glasses on the bedside table, then slid down the bed.

'Erm . . . nice to meet you, Anna.'

But she didn't answer. Her mouth was already fully occupied trying to wake the dead.

The gun was pointing straight at her, but Rebecca still couldn't move.

Her arms were hanging over the car door while her feet dragged on the ground rushing past below her. She was still clutching the pistol in her right hand, but because the whole of her bodyweight was resting on her lower arms, she couldn't move it more than a centimetre or so. She tried to get a foothold, so she could redistribute her weight and free up her pistol-arm.

But the running man had already raised his own gun and she realized she didn't have time. The dust was flying up from the car wheels, swirling round her and narrowing her field of vision to a red tunnel, until all she could see was the barrel of the shiny revolver at the far end. She waited for the shot.

But it didn't come.

The car suddenly lurched hard to the right, and the

force of the swerve was so great that it threw her halfway inside the vehicle. She got a grip on the seat, managed to brace one leg against the door pillar, and pulled herself in. The car continued to spin, the door slammed shut behind her and suddenly they had performed a 180-degree turn and were heading forward again, back down the road they had arrived on.

The dust from the Landcruiser's wheels billowed around them and Modin had to switch on the windscreen-wipers to see anything.

Rebecca spun round to try to get a glimpse of the man with the revolver through the rear window. She rested her arm on the back of the seat, ready to fire. Her eye was glued to the view along the barrel of the gun, her finger on the trigger . . .

But all she could see behind them was a swirling cloud of red dust that seemed to cover the whole world.

The refugee camp, the mob, the man with the revolver – everything just vanished. After only a couple of seconds it was as if they had never existed at all . . .

Modin was shouting something, and far away she heard the radio crackle, but her pulse was pounding so hard against her eardrums that she couldn't make out any of the words.

Everything around her seemed to be happening in slow motion. She could make out the tiniest details: the smell of the leather seats, the figures huddled on the back seat, Modin's jerky movements as she fought to keep the car on the road.

Her hands were clutching the pistol so tightly that her fingers were beginning to cramp.

The dust was still being whirled up by the airflow behind the car, forming long, hypnotic spirals that captured her attention and made it impossible to look away.

Then Modin must have hit a pothole, because for a few moments it felt as if they were flying, floating free, almost like in a dream.

A couple of milliseconds of weightlessness – then the car hit the ground again. Rebecca's back crashed down against one of the seats, the dreamlike sensation vanished and she was knocked back into reality again.

'Answer the radio!' Modin was shouting, and at the same moment Rebecca realized that her earpiece had fallen out and was dangling on her right shoulder. She quickly poked it back into her ear, lowered her gun and sank back onto the passenger seat.

'Is everyone okay, Normén, over?'

Malmén's voice sounded worried.

She twisted round to glance at her fellow passengers.

The minister and Gladh were huddled on either side of the back seat.

'Are you okay back there?'

No answer, but two chalk-white faces peered slowly up at her.

'Are you okay, Ann-Christin?'

Rebecca leaned back at an angle and prodded one of the minister's knees, which was at least enough to prompt a glassy nod in response.

'The minister's okay, we're returning to the villa,' she said as calmly as she could into the microphone, but the radio somehow seemed to reinforce the tremble in her voice.

'Understood,' Malmén replied curtly.

Rebecca suddenly realized she was still clutching her pistol with her right hand.

She loosened her grip, put the gun back in its holster, then slowly pulled the seatbelt on.

Her pulse had begun to slow down, the adrenalin kick

faded away and she could feel a vague sense of nausea rising in its place.

‘That was fucking close . . .’

Without taking her eyes from the road Modin nodded in response.

‘I thought I’d had it for a moment there, I don’t know why he didn’t shoot?’

Modin gave her quick sideways glance.

‘He probably didn’t have time to get his rifle out before they were on top of him.’

It took a couple of seconds before Rebecca understood.

‘No, no, not the soldier – I mean the man with the revolver.’

‘Who?’ Modin said, shooting her a questioning look.

Before she had time to answer, Gladh leaned forward and spoke into her left ear.

‘What the hell do you think you’re playing at, Normén?’ he hissed.

2

Flashback

'Hello?'

'Good evening, my friend. It is already evening with you, isn't it . . .? Is this a bad time to call?'

'No, no, not at all, I've been waiting for you to get in touch. I'm in position – is everything . . . ready?'

'Everything's ready.'

'What about . . .?'

'Like I said – everything's ready. The only question is: are you? The task is risky, so I can understand that you might be feeling doubtful . . . But the fact is that we can't do this without your help.'

'I'm ready – no problem!'

'Excellent!'

'So when do we get going?'

'Soon, my friend – very soon . . .'

'Darfur?'

'Hmm . . .'

'How long?'

'About a week for recon, four days with the minister, then a couple of days to finish off. Two weeks in total, I'd guess, depending a bit on whether I come home in the government plane or have to take a regular flight.'

He nodded, then looked down at the morning paper open in front of him.

'It's my job, Micke. You know that.'

'I know,' he muttered without looking up. 'But that doesn't mean I have to cheer every time you head off for some new dangerous location, especially when there are other options. So what's it going to be next time, Baghdad?'

More like Kabul, she almost said, but stopped herself before the words formed. She was planning to hold back that particular little surprise until she was sure it was her team that would be going.

'Look,' she said, then waited until he looked up. 'I am actually capable of taking care of myself, and besides, I like my job. We've already been through this whole idea of me doing something else, like working for your lot, so you know how I feel. How about showing a bit of support instead of this grouchy routine every morning?'

She held his gaze for a couple of seconds until, as usual, he backed down.

'Sure, sorry, I didn't mean to sound like an old woman . . .'

He folded the newspaper and put his hand over hers.

'Sorry, Becca, of course you need to go. Okay? The last thing you need is problems at home before a trip like this. I've just been having trouble sleeping, lots to do at work, you know . . .'

He looked at her with his puppy-dog eyes and she smiled back dutifully.

'Sure,' she muttered. 'No problem.'

His abrupt change of attitude ought to have cheered her up, but instead she mostly just felt disappointed.

Micke was a wonderful guy who never caused any

trouble, and who always backed down if they had different opinions. Good job, good general knowledge, sense of humour, all that . . . The dream prince, really, especially in comparison with her previous attachments.

But still she found herself regretting not throwing the Afghanistan trip in his face while she had the chance. Pouring a bit of petrol on the flames just to see what would happen. But good girls didn't do that sort of thing . . .

Besides, there wouldn't have been any point.

He might have sulked for another minute or so, but the end result would have been the same.

Big, sad, puppy-dog eyes and 'Sorry, Becca'.

For some reason that whole routine was starting to make her skin crawl and the idea of working for the same company as him held no appeal at all, even if the salary they were offering was almost *double* what she was getting now.

Sometimes she longed for the days when they only used to meet up for a bit of undemanding sex. He'd been more fun back then, more exciting somehow . . .

She grabbed part of the paper and started to leaf through it without much interest. He did the same for a few moments and she was left in peace with her thoughts.

She had everything she could wish for – and she still wasn't happy.

What was wrong with her?

There had been two million dollars, give or take a bit of loose change, in the Game's account when he cleared it out.

Admittedly, slightly less than he had expected at the start, but still more than enough to be able to live a comfortable life.

A fair bit of money had gone to certain people at the

banks that had helped him wipe away any trail, and some more had gone to the solicitor who had sorted things out for him back home. Paying off the mortgage on his flat, setting up one trust fund to take care of ongoing costs, and another to give the poor cop he almost managed to kill at Lindhagensplan a bit of money to compensate for his aches and pains. The newly established Special Police Foundation had awarded Inspector Hans Kruse a tax-free grant of a million kronor for bravery in the course of duty, and, for the same reason, his colleague Rebecca Normén had received an amount which almost exactly matched the amount owing on her mortgage with Handelsbanken.

Thanks to the solicitor all the documentation was 100% kosher, so neither of the recipients had thought to question their award. He also knew that his old friends Gustav 'the Goat' Boch and Farook 'Manga' Al-Hassan had each received a bulging envelope through their letterboxes, the contents of which more than made up for the cost of two wrecked mopeds and a fire-damaged shop.

After all his settlements and allowing for living expenses, about half of his haul remained.

A cool million dollars, stashed fucking well out of sight somewhere only he could find it. Not bad . . .

Four people in her team – three men and one woman.

There really ought to be more, but at the present time the supply of bodyguards was nowhere near enough to meet demand.

But anyway . . .

Four well-trained, experienced bodyguards who had worked together for a long time and who knew exactly how things were done. Even so, a new boss almost always introduced a note of uncertainty, all the more complicated because they had known each other for a while. No matter what anyone might say when asked, most people aren't especially fond of change. The problem with her group was that they had been without a boss for several months and that the group's deputy, David Malmén, had been expected to be appointed as the new boss.

The other three listened to him, and would have trouble accepting anyone else in command if he didn't. Groups with unofficial leaders never worked in the long run. She had seen that at first hand when she was training, as well as later in her career.

It would take both sensitivity and a firm hand if she was going to succeed. The margin for error was practically non-existent.

The flight had been wearing, three changes before they finally reached Khartoum.

A few nights in a hotel and a load of meetings to sort out the formalities.

The Sudanese authorities wanted to inspect everything – their weapons, communications equipment and bullet-proof vests. And all their papers had to be checked, stamped, double-checked and stamped again before they could pick up their vehicles and finally get going.

The further south they got, the more barren the landscape became. Dry red earth spread out around them, swirling up under their vehicles and finding its way into every gap, so that all their clothing and equipment ended up covered in a fine, crisp, pink skin.

Even though it was winter the heat was unbearable at times. Karolina Modin took care of the driving while she sat beside her in the boss's seat.

Bengt Esbjörnsson was driving the big vehicle that followed them, with their interpreter as a passenger.

Malmén and Göransson were going to be arriving in a couple of days with the minister in the government plane.

In the meantime she and the other two were supposed to check out the places they were due to visit.

She had put a fair amount of thought into the planning. She and Peter Göransson had trained together, and had worked together before, so she was fairly comfortable with him.

Malmén and Esbjörnsson got on well, so by splitting them up and hopefully getting a bit of time to talk to Modin as well, she would get the chance to refine the new hierarchy within the group. But she had to admit that her plan hadn't worked brilliantly so far . . .

Her decision to keep Malmén as her deputy hadn't been met with the acclaim she had expected. But perhaps that wasn't so strange. She hadn't really had much choice.

And the journey down hadn't exactly gone smoothly.

Esbjörnsson was a taciturn man from the far north of Sweden who didn't say more than he had to, and Karolina Modin kept to herself without being either unpleasant or particularly unfriendly.

Really the group should have had time to work together at home before being sent out into a live situation like this one, but her boss hadn't been willing to hear anything of that sort.

Superintendent Runeberg had interrupted her with a look that made her feel like a whining schoolkid. 'You wanted to be put in charge, Normén, so you're just going to have to grit your teeth and get on with it,' he'd told her.

They had picked up embassy counsellor Gladh in Khartoum, along with his assistant and their interpreter. It had only taken her a matter of seconds to read this particularly arrogant man, and unfortunately her fears had been proved right more or less immediately. The old duffer must have started work at the Foreign Ministry before she was born. She had never seen him dressed in anything but a pin-striped suit, tie and with a handkerchief tucked into his top pocket. The outfit only made him look even taller and skinnier, almost a caricature of himself, and on the few occasions that he deigned to talk to them his reverberant aristocratic southern-Swedish accent made it hard not to laugh.

Gladh had spent most of the return journey on the phone making complaints to his colleagues in the Foreign Ministry about how his staff could have made all the security arrangements with the Sudanese government instead of them bothering to fly in inexperienced Swedish police officers with no knowledge of the country or the culture. It also turned out that Gladh had a nephew in the police, and he declared that he 'knew a few things about the force', which, to judge from his tone of voice and the look on his face, clearly wasn't meant to be taken as anything positive.

The only good thing about the journey was that Karolina Modin seemed to share Rebecca's opinion of the embassy counsellor, and as the drive went on they exchanged ironic glances at some of the things he came out with.

Unfortunately Gladh wasn't stupid enough not to notice the looks on their faces, and the atmosphere inside the car had practically reached freezing-point by the time they arrived.

In marked contrast, Gladh's assistant, Håkan Berglund, was a pleasant man of about the same age as her, who made a few attempts to smooth over some of the worst of his boss's behaviour.

'Sixten is a bit old-school,' he said apologetically during their first after-work drink together. 'He's actually not a bad person, and I've learned a fair bit from working with him.'

Rebecca shrugged.

'He can behave however he likes, as long as you make it clear to him that I'm the one who decides where the minister goes and where she doesn't go, not Foreign Ministry protocol, okay?'

Berglund saluted her with his glass.

'Understood, Inspector. By the way, have I mentioned that I'm moving back to Stockholm in a couple of weeks . . .?' He gave her a warm smile, and it was more or less as she realized how much she liked his smile that she remembered that she'd forgotten to call home.

His life as a fugitive had started off pretty damn well.

First stop: his old friend Jesus's holiday flats in Thailand where he lazed about under the palm trees. Reliving happy memories of how he'd beaten the Game and made off with all their money.

But after a month or so he'd started to feel restless.

Hanging out in a hammock listening to the waves breaking sounded pretty fucking sweet when you talked about it – but for the rest of his life?

No fucking way!

Just like Caine the *Kung Fu* movie legend, he wasn't the type to settle down.

So he rented some wheels and spent a couple of weeks easy-riding before he got tired of the smell of exhaust fumes, a chafed arse and insects between his teeth.

Then he worked his way through the Philippines, Singapore and Bali before making his way Down Under.

He filled his days with tourist adventures – crocodile safaris, bungee jumps from bridges, swimming with sharks.

But *purchased experiences didn't count* – especially not after everything he had been through, so he tired of pre-packaged adventures and started to feel restless again, and decided to move on.

He had wondered about carrying on eastward, maybe all the way to the States, but he wasn't confident his fake identity would stand up at Immigration.

The passport was one thing, but fingerprints were harder to falsify and the Game Master was bound to have had him wiped off every database imaginable.

The thought of doing a stretch as a prison bitch in Alabama State was terrifying enough to make him park the dream of the US of A in the long-stay carpark.

Besides, all the constant drifting about was starting to get on his nerves.

The restlessness inside him seemed to grow exponentially, along with his insomnia.

More or less consciously, he slowly began to make his way north. He stopped off in India, spending several weeks doped up on the beach in Goa before he finally ended up here – in fucking Neverland.

Dubai is very cool, you will lurve it, my friend – mais bien sûr!

Note to self – never take travel advice from French queers with black AmEx cards, no matter how much Mary Jane they offer . . .

He'd already had more than his fill after OD'ing on the combined tourist attractions of the eastern hemisphere, and the whole of this make-believe country was pretty much as genuine as the name in his latest passport.

A façade, a soulless fucking surface without the faintest hint of any connection to its history – or reality either, come to that . . .

His new playmate Vincent had promised to meet up with him, but so far he hadn't heard a peep from him. At a guess the Frenchman and his posse were still lost in a cloud of smoke on the beach in Goa while he himself was languishing on this artificial island like some sort of luxury castaway. All he needed was a make-believe friend and he'd be home and dry.

Wonder if Armani make volleyballs . . .?

Fuck, this place could easily go twelve rounds with Vegas for the heavyweight title in tastelessness.

A few days ago he had heard a sunburned family with mum, dad and 2.1 kids talking Swedish a few tables away, and suddenly he felt like bursting into tears over his breakfast egg. It took him a couple of minutes to realize why.

Fuck, he was homesick!

For Sweden, Stockholm, Södermalm, his sister, Manga, the Goat, open-air singing at Skansen, 'eight carriages to Ropsten', *you fucking name it*!

But probably most of all – for himself.

Because even though he had pretty much everything your average Swede could ever want – money, freedom, and the bare minimum of responsibility – the bitter truth was that the only thing he really wanted was what he couldn't have.

To be HP again – *correction, the new, improved HP* – back in his own tiny little duck-pond.

The thought that he was doomed to drift around all the tourist hotels of Asia for the rest of his life until he could no longer remember his name was enough to make him seriously depressed.

He needed something, anything, that reminded him of who he really was, to make him feel even a tiny fucking bit alive again.

Not even the Kung Fu legend himself had been able to handle the vagabond lifestyle in the long run, and had ended up as a washed-up drag-queen in a hotel closet with the cord from a window-blind as his farewell necktie.

And who could blame him?

The government plane landed exactly according to schedule at the little airport of El-Fasher, the two jet engines whipping clouds of dust towards the waiting vehicles.

Apart from their own group, the UN's local representative was also there to meet the plane, and Rebecca had exchanged a few words with their security staff.

The door of the plane opened and Malmén looked out. Rebecca waved the all-clear to him and he nodded in response.

The Minister for International Development smiled at her in recognition as she came down the steps from the plane.

'Welcome to . . .' Rebecca began, but Gladh had already pushed between them.

'Welcome to Africa, Minister, I hope you had a good journey? Allow me to introduce the local representative of the United Nations, Mr Moon, and his deputy, Mrs Awaga. Our first stop, as you are doubtless already aware, Minister, will be the refugee camp at Dali where we will meet the Sudanese Interior Minister and the Governor of Darfur. After that we will continue to the children's home in Kaguro . . .'

Rebecca stepped aside and held the car door open for the minister, who obediently took her seat. Gladh went round the car and waited, but Rebecca ignored him. The minister was her charge, Gladh could take care of himself. Surely the old sod could manage to open a car door for himself?

A couple of minutes later they were ready to leave. The

minister and Gladh were in the car behind the first military jeep together with Rebecca and Karolina Modin. Esbjörnsson, Malmén and Göransson were immediately behind them in the Landcruiser, and the rest of the group was in a third car driven by a local driver. Then came the three UN vehicles and finally another jeep from the Sudanese military. All entirely according to plan.

Her mobile phone buzzed.

They were halfway to the refugee camp, nothing but desert savannah alongside the potholed dirt roads, so she couldn't see any reason not to check her inbox. It was actually pretty incredible that there was any signal out here in the middle of nowhere – but Africa was apparently the latest goldmine for mobile phone manufacturers.

Take good care of yourself, Becca – see you when you get home?

She smiled, then turned her head. In the back seat the minister and Gladh were still engaged in a discussion she had stopped listening to several minutes before.

Through the rear window she could just make out the vehicles following them, and the dark silhouettes of their passengers. From this distance it was impossible to tell which shadow was whose.

We'll see . . .

Just as she pressed send she noticed that Modin was looking at her.

'From home,' she said quickly, and Modin muttered something in reply.

She checked the time.

'Ten minutes to go,' she said into the radio-mic on her

wrist. She got a double click in her earpiece to indicate that Malmén had understood what she had said and had nothing to add.

Good.

But really she didn't need his approval. She had to get used to the fact that this was her team now, her four plus one.

The crowd of people was visible from a distance.

The military jeep out front had pulled off to the side and an arm waved them through, but unlike the day before the road leading up to the buildings was blocked off.

'Doesn't look like we're going to get any further,' she said, and Modin nodded.

'Change of plan,' she said into the mic on her wrist. 'The road's blocked so we're evidently going to have to walk the last bit. Esbjörnsson and Modin, wait with the cars unless you hear otherwise. Got that, over?'

'You don't think we might all be needed, it looks messy up ahead, over?'

Malmén's radio voice was clipped and abrupt, and she noticed Modin imperceptibly raising her head as if in expectation of her reply.

Rebecca took a deep breath.

Four plus one or four against one? It all depended on how she answered.

Malmén was an experienced bodyguard and he certainly had a point, but if she backed down now it would be clear to everyone who was the real boss of this group.

But if she slapped him down too firmly it might look like she felt threatened and that she wasn't going to listen to his ideas in future out of principle, however sensible they were. That sort of leadership was not only poor, but could even jeopardize the safety of the group.

Rebecca raised her left hand to her mouth, took a deep breath and pressed the broadcast button.

'I can see the way you're thinking, Malmén, but right now I'd prefer to be ready to leave. Esbjörnsson and Modin, stay in the vehicles for the time being. I'll make a new assessment before we unload. Over and out.'

The last three words marked a definite end to the exchange. Rebecca glanced at Modin, but she was sitting completely still, her expression unchanged.

They rolled into the small turning-circle and she opened the car door.

The first round appeared to have gone to her, but for some reason she got a feeling that the game had only just begun.

3

Foreplay

Pillars of Society forum
Posted: 6 November, 20:04
By: **MayBey**

The only truth is that everyone is lying . . .

This post has 20 comments

He really ought to be sleeping like a corpse. But not even a bout of sheet-wrestling of that calibre was enough to get him to sleep.

Oh well. He was pretty used to lying awake by now.

The woman beside him shifted in her sleep and he turned his head to look at her.

She was lying with her back to him and had kicked off enough of the covers to reveal half of her suntanned body.

So, Anna Argos – presumably from one of the posher parts of London to judge from her upper-class English.

He'd seen her down by the pool.

He had been lying there admiring her miniscule bikini

and wondering if he could be bothered to make a pass at her when she waved him over to her. The next moment he was rubbing suntan oil into the tattoo on her back, and ten minutes later, practically without any conversation at all, she was sitting astride his hips.

Isn't this a non-smoking room?

Christ, he was such a fucking dickhead . . .

He raised his head from the pillow to get a better look at Miss Argos. What he could see of her face was smooth as a baby's bottom, and probably just as natural as her tits. She'd tucked her blonde hair behind her ear and as he leaned over her he caught a glimpse of a little white scar behind her earlobe that confirmed his suspicions.

He slowly ran his finger over the back of her neck, continued across her shoulder and down her arm, then suddenly stopped at a dark little bruise that he hadn't noticed before. Curious, he ran his finger around it and carried on down her lower arm.

His touch made other similar marks begin to appear very faintly.

He turned his hand over. There were clear traces of flesh-coloured skin cream on his fingertip.

Carefully, and suddenly feeling uneasy, he leaned further forward to see the inside of her biceps.

'Are you still here?'

Anna was staring at him with a look that was anything but friendly.

'Er . . . yes,' he managed to say, sitting up.

'Then get the hell out, I don't remember asking you to stay – did I?'

'Er . . . No . . .'

Shit – he really did have the gift of the gab today.

Okay, so she didn't want to spend the morning curled up together – that was fine by him. He slid out of bed and started looking for his clothes, but evidently not quickly enough.

'Didn't you hear me? Get – the – fuck – out – of – here!'

She kicked out at him and managed a glancing blow to one of his buttocks.

'Okay, okay – take it easy!' he muttered as he hopped on one leg, trying to pull his bathing trunks on.

Two seconds later he slammed the door shut behind him.

Shit, what a fucking bitch!

What the hell was her problem?

But he already had the beginning of a theory . . .

The air was tense back at the embassy after Rebecca aborted the minister's visit with Sudan's refugee problem. The old villa was big, at least six hundred square metres if you counted both floors – yet the atmosphere still felt claustrophobic.

She would actually have preferred to evacuate at once, stuffing everyone and everything in the government plane and leaving immediately. But the plane had only recently landed and the pilots had used up all their flying time. They needed at least eight hours rest before they could fly again, which meant they'd have to wait until early the following morning. Assuming the authorities let them go, of course . . .

She was talking on the phone to her Sudanese liaison officer every ten minutes, and Runeberg every hour. The liaison officer was trying to persuade them to stay, claiming that the disorder was 'a regrettable incident' caused by troublemakers who wanted to disrupt the relationship between Sudan and Sweden, and that the Sudanese government could 'guarantee their safety'.

But he wasn't prepared to accept that there had been an assassin.

And he was hardly alone in that . . .

Upstairs Gladh was furious, roaring at his assistant, Håkan Berglund, and down the phone, so loudly that even the guards on the gate must have been able to hear him.

The minister, on the other hand, wasn't saying much. She had shut herself in her room and was letting her press secretary deal with everything.

'Ann-Christin is a little under the weather, she was travel-sick in the plane, and then with this . . .'

The press secretary nodded pointedly at Rebecca, and she could feel the other bodyguards looking at her.

'. . . attempted attack . . .' Rebecca filled in, in as steady a voice as she could muster. 'An unknown assailant armed with a revolver approaching our car with the intention of firing at it. Fortunately he failed and we got away. My job is to see that we all get home in one piece, as soon as possible.'

The press secretary nodded benevolently.

'And we're very grateful for that, Rebecca, we really are.'

The woman glanced at Gladh.

'It's just that an evacuation might send out . . . well . . . the wrong signals, if you understand what I mean?'

'No, I don't,' Rebecca said curtly.

Gladh flew up from his chair.

'We have an agenda, meetings – important people we've been working hard to arrange to see. The ambassador has staked his entire reputation on organizing this visit, and we're suddenly thinking of calling the whole thing off because of a little . . . disturbance?'

Gladh's face was pale, and he was firing out small drops of saliva.

'As far as I can see, the whole thing started when you,

Normén, decided that we should leave. Does anyone not share my opinion?'

He looked round the room, but no-one said anything.

Rebecca tried to catch Malmén's gaze but he was looking down at the floor, along with the others in the team, and Håkan Berglund obediently had his eyes on his master. She took a deep breath and tried to stay calm.

'I took the decision to withdraw because the situation was too risky. Things were radically different to how they were yesterday, and my judgement was that we couldn't proceed in a secure fashion. Aside from the general disturbance, surely the presence of the attacker proves that I was right?'

She looked at the others, but once again no-one would look her in the eye – no-one except Gladh.

'You mean the attacker that only you saw, Normén? Isn't it rather odd that no-one else noticed him, not your colleagues, and not those of us inside the vehicles? Doesn't that strike you as rather peculiar?'

He tilted his head to one side to emphasize his patronizing tone.

'Everything happened very quickly, there were loads of people and the dust was making it hard to see . . .' she began, but Gladh interrupted her.

'But surely your driver must have seen him? What was your name again? Modig?'

Karolina Modin looked up from the floor.

'Modin,' she said quietly.

'Yes, that was it . . . Well, Modin, did you see him, this assailant Normén describes, running towards the front of the car with a revolver aimed straight at us?'

Modin took a long look at Rebecca, then at Malmén, before replying.

'No, I didn't.'

'You didn't, you say, but your boss, who was right beside you, says she saw him clearly. Why do you think your stories don't match?'

Modin squirmed and she gave Malmén another long glance.

'I was mostly looking behind us, I was concentrating on reversing, so I didn't see much of what was going on in front of the car. There were people rushing about in all directions . . .'

'But a real-life attacker waving a big revolver, surely you should have noticed something like that? Or don't you learn that sort of thing when you're training to be a bodyguard?'

His patronizing tone was enough to make Rebecca want to strangle the miserable old bastard, but she restrained herself. No matter what Gladh thought he was getting from this discussion, the final word was still hers. She was going to win, the only question was how Gladh would react.

Modin muttered something in response and Gladh shifted his attention to the group's deputy leader.

'What about you, Malmén, that's your name, isn't it?'

'That's correct.'

'Did you see any assailant?'

'No, I didn't, but like Modin and my own driver, I was concentrating on what was happening in the other direction. And I was trying to get the vehicle behind us to get out of the way, which wasn't particularly easy . . .'

Gladh nodded and turned back towards Rebecca.

'As I said, what we appear to have here is a riot that was triggered by our own unplanned retreat, and a presumed assailant that only you saw, Normén. The matter is perfectly clear to me. There is no reason to break off this trip and the ambassador agrees with me. The Interior

Minister has promised us a full armed escort and we will continue as planned tomorrow morning.'

He looked around the group with satisfaction, as though the matter was settled.

'No, we won't,' Rebecca said firmly. 'You seem to be in some confusion about my role and authority here, Gladh. I have ultimate responsibility for the Minister and my team – not you, and not the ambassador. My decision is that we will return home as soon as it's light. If you don't like that, you're free to make a complaint to my boss, Superintendent Runeberg.'

She stood up and went out to the kitchen.

Over and out, you arrogant, scrawny little pen-pusher!

Four plus one.

That was how those marks were described on CSI.

Four fingers on the back of the arm and a thumb on the front. He'd seen them before, In Real Life . . .

He took a deep toke on the joint and held his breath for a few seconds before sending a column of sticky smoke up from the bed towards the smoke-detector in the ceiling.

Anna Argos had been really angry when she woke up, but for some reason he got the feeling that her morning tantrum had more to do with his discovery of the bruises than the fact that he was still in her bed.

He took another deep drag and sent another puff of liquorice towards the smoke-detector.

Just as before there was no response from the puck-like device stuck on the ceiling, which wasn't so odd considering that, like so many times before, he had carefully wrapped up the little killjoy with the complementary shower-cap he'd found in the bathroom.

He couldn't deny that Anna Argos has piqued his

curiosity – so much so that he actually almost forgot his little trip into emo-land.

Apart from the bruises there was something else that seemed a bit odd.

Anna was obviously a businesswoman, and people like that always kept their mobiles within arm's length.

He'd looked for her mobile while he was up in her suite. He checked every flat surface, both when she was dragging him to the bed and later, when she chucked him out. But he hadn't seen it anywhere.

Obviously that could be a complete coincidence – but in hindsight he couldn't shake the idea that she'd concealed her phone on purpose.

'Malmén!'

He stopped in the corridor and she signalled to him to come into her room.

Simultaneously she ended the phone-call she was in the middle of and gestured to him to sit down, but he remained standing.

'Make sure everything's packed. Swedeforce 24 has got permission to take off at 07.00, so we'll be setting off from here at 05.45.'

He nodded curtly. 'What about the cars?'

'We'll leave them at the airport. For all I care, Gladh and Berglund can drive them back to Khartoum if they don't want to come back to Stockholm with us.'

Malmén gave a wry smile and shrugged his shoulders.

'Well, it's your decision . . .'

'What the hell's that supposed to mean?'

The anger she had managed to keep under control up to now suddenly boiled over.

'Nothing, calm down!'

'I am calm!' she snapped. 'I just want to know what

you mean when you say it's *my decision*? You don't share my conclusion that we should evacuate? Don't you think there was an assailant either?'

'I was thinking about the cars, Normén, okay?'

She looked at him intently for a few seconds while she calmed down.

'Okay . . .'

It wasn't until he had left the room that she realized that Malmén hadn't answered her question.

The sound of the phone ringing made him drop his spliff.

He had dozed off and spent a few confused seconds fumbling on the floor to stop the cigarette from burning a hole in the carpet.

'Hello . . .?'

'Allo Thomas, this is Vincent speaking, how are you my friend?'

It took a few moments before his doped-up brain made the right connections.

Thomas was his latest alias – Thomas Andersen, from Trondheim in Norway. He'd been in prison with a small-time dealer from Bergen, and could gurgle enough of his incomprehensible Norwegian dialect to pass, even if they were celebrating their national day.

'Bonjour, Vincent, how's it going?'

'Good, very good. Sorry we haven't been in touch before, but we got a bit delayed in Goa. Had some trouble with the authorities, if you get my meaning . . .'

'Mmm . . .'

HP blew on the spliff to try to get it to burn better.

'Listen, Tommy, we're thinking of heading out into the desert tomorrow evening. Do a bit of rally driving, have a barbeque, smoke a hookah with the Bedouins. D'you want to come?'

He took a deep drag.

'Yeah!'

'Great, we'll pick you up around five. We've got plenty of room in the cars, so you're welcome to bring someone if you want to. À tout à l'heure!'

HP hung up and grinned up at the ceiling.

A mysterious woman, nocturnal adventures in the desert.

Secrets waiting to be uncovered . . .

For the first time in ages he almost felt alive again.

Game on!

4

Bad luck charm

Pillars of Society forum
Posted: 7 November, 15:09
By: **MayBey**

Sometimes you just have to make the best of things . . .

This post has 26 comments

The big vehicle lurched over the crown of the sand-dune, hanging in the air for a moment before it began to slide sideways down the slope. Powdery sand flew up over the windows and for a moment the inside of the car was almost completely dark. Then the 4x4 swung in the other direction, the sand was shaken off and the view cleared. The manoeuvre made all the passengers except HP burst out in rollercoaster whoops.

Twenty minutes of dune-rallying and he already felt like throwing up.

Hash and beer really weren't a very good warm-up combo for a desert safari. Fuck, he felt rough!

To make everything even worse, Vincent had squeezed him into the little seat right at the back, next to the bags, where both visibility and the lurching were at their worst. The Frenchman had put himself next to Anna A, who naturally spoke perfect French. The pair of them, plus the other Frenchman in the car, had chattered like polecats on acid almost the whole way out here, leaving HP feeling seriously excluded.

But he had at least managed to pick up a bit of it.

Evidently Miss Argos wasn't a Miss at all, but a Mrs, seeing as Vincent and the other bloke started calling her Madame.

He guessed divorced rather than widowed, especially considering her bitchy attitude.

And Madame certainly seemed to have plenty of money, to judge from her overblown suite in the hotel with its view of the Gulf, and her presumably absurdly expensive clothes. The hot little safari outfit she showed up in on the dot of five o'clock had been fairly remarkable.

Vincent had immediately switched on the charm, full-force. He kissed her hand and whipped out his flashy gold lighter the moment she held her cigarette in his direction.

All the smarming left HP feeling annoyed even before he had been stuffed into the luggage compartment, and things weren't made any better by the fact that Madame Argos appeared to be ignoring him.

The car in front dived into another valley and a few seconds later their car followed it. HP's stomach turned another somersault and suddenly he felt a familiar sensation creep through his body.

'Bag,' he groaned, and the other passengers grinned as they passed him the crumpled plastic bag they had already taken bets on.

1000 dirham, HP had time to think before filling the bag with the contents of his stomach.

Fucking expensive puke!

They stopped and he fell out of the door, stumbling a little distance away to heave some more. When his stomach finished cramping a few minutes later and he stumbled back towards the car, shamefaced and splattered with vomit, Anna Argos's mocking laughter told him that his vomit had cost him considerably more than the bet.

'Let's head straight for the Bedouin camp – no more hard driving, okay?'

The driver glanced at HP's chalk-white face in the rear-view mirror and merely nodded in reply. All the windows were open, the air-con was on full, but it was still impossible to escape the acrid smell emanating from his beard and clothes.

Anna leaned over and whispered something in Vincent's ear. HP could see her lips almost touching the lobe of the Frenchman's ear, and then they both burst into another peel of conspiratorial laughter.

No prizes for guessing who they were making fun of . . .

He made up his mind to ignore them and looked out of the side-window instead. The sun was slowly turning into a red ball on the horizon, and the shadows of the sand dunes were getting longer and longer. Far in the distance some dark birds were circling slowly. Round and round, above the same point in the desert sand.

Their movement was peculiarly restful – almost hypnotic – and for a short while it made him forget about the lurching motion of the car.

He didn't really know what he'd expected from the Bedouin camp. Maybe a few canvas tents and some scabby camels with BO? A decent dose of shabby, everyday desert life, just enough to keep the tourists happy? He should have known better. This was the land of excess, after all.

The camp was in a small hollow, about a dozen pavilions all facing into a circle, surrounded by a tall, closely-woven fence made of some straw-like material, presumably meant to protect against sandstorms. A number of telegraph poles with floodlights attached to them stuck up from the fence, and strings of coloured lamps and streamers hung between these. At the front of the compound the fence was replaced by a tall wall with two watchtowers and an open gate.

Everything had been made to look medieval, but to judge by the colour and condition of the buildings the camp must have been a fairly recent construction.

They parked the cars outside the wall and as they walked through the gate Arabic pop music began to blare out at them. In the open area at the centre of the camp there was a large wooden floor covered with Arabic rugs, and on these stood a number of low tables with cushions to sit on, with space for something like a hundred guests. The buildings he had seen as they were approaching turned out to be missing their fourth wall, and were open where they faced the centre of the camp. They contained even more seating areas, as well as a kitchen, a souvenir shop and a pavilion with water-pipes.

To put it mildly, the whole thing seemed rather absurd in the middle of the desert, almost like a mirage.

'*Salaam-aleikum*, welcome, welcome, my friends!' exclaimed a fat little man in Bedouin dress as he jogged over to meet them.

'You're early, dinner won't be for another hour or so, but you can spend the time buying souvenirs, riding quad-bikes, sand-surfing, riding camels or smoking shisha. If none of that appeals, then of course the bar is open for those of you who aren't Muslim.'

The man grinned and paused long enough for the laughter to die down.

'And if you'd like to freshen up, the bathrooms are over there.'

He gestured towards a barrack-like building at the edge of the camp, then gave HP a pointed look.

'The belly-dancing show starts at ten o'clock, I look forward to seeing you again and I hope you enjoy your stay with us!'

Even though HP just felt like slumping down on the cushions with a pipe of weed, he reluctantly decided to heed the man's advice and clean himself up.

As luck would have it, the toilet happened to have a hose with a showerhead attached, and, after plenty of acrobatic manoeuvring and a great deal of handwash, he managed to tidy himself up fairly reasonably.

He ditched his shirt in the nearest litterbin. It may have been tailor-made from Thai silk, but he was happy to sacrifice it if it meant he could regain a few crumbs of self-respect. In the souvenir shop he picked up a pink tourist t-shirt with a psychedelic Arabic pattern on it, then abdicated all responsibility and allowed the salesman to complete the look by winding a towel round his head.

When all this was done he went and sat on the cushions by one of the low tables, ordered a beer and waited for the others to finish playing outside in the sandpit.

Vincent and Anna didn't return until it was getting dark. They were walking close together, their bodies bumping and nudging together as they chatted confidentially in French.

He really shouldn't care. It wasn't like he was in love with her or anything – definitely not. But there were still some rules. Anna was his companion, he was the one who'd brought her along.

He could hardly avoid the looks of the others in the group. But his options were strictly limited. He was stuck out here in the desert, and, even if the stinging feeling of humiliation was turning more and more into a white-hot fury, there wasn't much he could do about it. Vincent was roughly the same height as him, but he was considerably more sinewy, and he definitely looked like he could take care of himself if he had to. Besides, the Frenchman had backup from his entire posse, so inviting him to take part in a bit of fight-club wasn't really a good idea.

Anyway, he himself was much more of a lover than a fighter . . .

No, all that remained was to pretend that he didn't care, try to get stoned and/or drunk as quickly as possible, and then get a ride on the first camel caravan out of here.

He decided to devote all his energy to this task, but instead he was dragged on to the dance floor by one of the French girls, who was far too attractive to turn down, and found himself belly-dancing along with close to seventy tourists.

Even though he was drunk, he felt unbelievably stupid. With a towel on his head, a tourist t-shirt and a fake smile, dancing the white man's overbite in a fake camp in a fake country. He probably looked even more ridiculous than he felt, if that was actually possible.

Anna and Vincent were dry-humping each other a couple of metres away. His thigh was stuck between hers, and she had her hands twined round the back of his neck as their hips rolled in time to the Arabic pop music.

The attractive French girl – whom he was obviously too drunk, too high and too ridiculous-looking to stand any chance with – danced off with her friends, so he made up his mind to weave back to the table and lubricate his self-pity with yet another beer.

The table was empty, they all seemed to be up on the dance-floor, but in amongst the glasses and plates he caught sight of something gold.

Vincent's blingy cigarette lighter.

Sweet!

He looked round, pretended to reach for a can of beer, then quickly snapped up the treasure. It felt cool and heavy in his hand, considerably more solid than his own trusty old Zippo.

It had to be solid gold, and just as surely the careless little frog-eater was bound to miss his golden trinket.

Maybe it was even an heirloom from his rich grandfather, something like that?

With a grin he slipped the lighter into his trouser pocket before standing up and heading off towards the toilet block.

Payback is a bitch, mothafucker!

The journey home was painless and they landed at Bromma just before four o'clock.

They were met by another security team who took over responsibility for the Minster for International Development, and shortly after that a minibus arrived to pick up her group. Ludvig Runeberg was sitting in the passenger seat in the front.

'Good to see you all back in one piece,' he said. 'Get your things in quickly, then we'll get back to Headquarters for you to hand in your equipment and have a debriefing. Doctor Anderberg is waiting . . .'

There was an opening in the fence at the back of the camp and HP stood for a moment at the bottom of the concrete steps leading to the toilets, gazing curiously out into the darkness.

It was actually a bit unnerving, making the comparison . . .

To one side of him he had the illuminated camp, with its flashing lights, music, food, drink and excess. On the other side – only a few metres away – darkness sprawled away from him. Mile after mile of sand and desert.

How long had they driven to get here?

It was hard to tell, the driver hadn't exactly taken the direct route, but he guessed at least two hours. How many hours would that be on foot? Six, eight? If you went in the right direction, of course. In fifty-degree heat with snakes and scorpions as your only company, it would be pretty easy to get it wrong. He wondered what it would feel like to be abandoned out there.

He couldn't help taking a few tentative steps out into the darkness.

The camp was in a slight hollow, but the light from all the lamps was enough for him to make out the top of the dune some way in front of him. He could see a lone shadow up there that he took to be a telegraph pole, and after a couple of seconds' hesitation he set off towards it.

As he got closer he discovered that there was a bird sitting on top of the pole – presumably one of the black ones he had glimpsed earlier that day. The bird was sitting completely still, and didn't seem the least bit bothered by his presence. It looked more like a big, skinny crow, but unlike its European cousins the bird's powerful beak was gently hooked – almost like a scimitar.

As HP approached the bird jerked its head and looked straight at him.

There was something about the look in those peppercorn eyes that made him feel uneasy, and he stopped just a metre or so from his target.

The bird went on staring at him in silence, and for

some reason HP couldn't tear his eyes away. He was holding his breath.

Suddenly the coarse beak opened a centimetre or so, and for a moment HP almost imagined that the bird was trying to tell him something.

He could feel the hairs on his arms stand up.

This was totally fucking . . .

'Ghourab Al-Bain!'

HP jumped.

It was Emir, their driver, who had appeared right behind him.

Fuck, he scared the shit out of him!

'W-what?'

'Ghourab Al-Bain.' The man pointed at the bird.

'A desert raven. They bring bad luck, bad things – you understand?'

And then the raven cried out – a low, rolling sound that vibrated off HP's chest.

Then it tilted its head and gave HP a last glance before setting off from its lookout post with a couple of heavy wing-beats.

Seconds later the bird had been swallowed up by the desert night.

'You shouldn't wander off like this, boss. It's easy to get lost out there. Easy to disappear, you understand?'

Oh yes, HP was pretty sure he understood.

'Bad things,' he mumbled, peering out into the darkness.

5

Bad things

Pillars of Society forum
Posted: 7 November, 21:28
By: **MayBey**

The worst thing a police officer can experience is not being able to trust his or her colleagues . . .

This post has 29 comments

When he came out of the toilets he almost ran straight into Anna Argos.

She had her back to him, and he guessed she was waiting for someone.

Presumably Frankie Frog-Eater . . .

Then he saw the shiny mobile against her ear and it was like an electric shock of recognition. The flames of resentment that had almost died down suddenly flared up again and he took a couple of angry steps forward.

'No, no-one followed me, everything's fine. I'm on the

other side of the world,' he heard her say quickly in English just before he grabbed her arm.

The look in her eyes was exactly as terrified as it had been in his imagination up in the hotel lounge, and, just like in his fantasy, all the fury drained away from him in an instant.

Whoever Anna Argos was, however fucking cool and savvy she pretended to be, there was still something – or more likely someone – who scared the shit out of her, even from the other side of the world. She ended the call.

It only took her a second or so to pull herself together and angrily shake herself free from his grasp – but he still had time to realize how intense her fear was.

'Let me go, you still smell disgusting!'

'Sorry,' he muttered, taking a couple of shaky steps back as he held his hands up in front of him.

'I think I've had a bit too much . . . Peace!'

She gave him an angry stare and then turned her back on him again, ignoring him.

'You know, my sister used to go out with one of those . . . wife-beaters,' he added.

She turned her head and looked at him suspiciously. When she opened her mouth to speak a couple of seconds later, her tone wasn't quite as unfriendly.

'So?'

'I killed the bastard,' he grinned, then walked away unsteadily into the camp.

They had hung up their radios and bulletproof vests, locked their weapons away in the gun-cabinet and changed into civilian clothing. Anderberg had booked a conference room for the obligatory debriefing, and now everyone was waiting impatiently to get going.

It would take at least an hour to go through the whole

chain of events, then another before they were allowed to go home to their families.

But even if she was at least as tired as the others, she wasn't in any rush to get home.

'We're waiting for Runeberg,' Anderberg said when he noticed how impatient they were.

'Ah, here he is.'

Runeberg walked into the room.

'Change of plan,' he said abruptly. 'Normén, you'll do your debriefing alone once the others are finished. You can write up your report of what happened in the meantime.'

She jerked and opened her mouth to protest. This wasn't usual procedure, and she had absolutely no desire to be forced from the room in front of her own team.

But before she had time to say anything, Runeberg cut her off.

'Off you go, Normén. The sooner we get this done, the sooner we can all go home . . .'

Seconds later the door of the conference room closed behind her.

At last!

He was lying among the silk cushions of the shisha pavilion, inhaling deep, relaxing mouthfuls of smoke. The water-pipe in front of him was bubbling nicely as the cool, damp smoke spread down his throat, curling down his airways and into his greedy lungs.

Sweet!

One of the Frenchmen – he couldn't remember which one – had sorted out the blend. A bit of grass at the bottom, just enough tobacco on top, before the foil and the charcoal. Whoever he was, he clearly knew what he was doing. The trip was almost perfectly balanced.

My compliments to the chef!

He felt calmer now, considerably more relaxed.

He couldn't help glancing down at his tourist t-shirt and suddenly burst out laughing.

Fuck, it looked ridiculous, and he must look ridiculous wearing it, as well as buying one of those bloody tablecloths to wrap round his head.

He was chuckling with laughter and his good mood seemed to spread out to the others in the pavilion.

'Hey, Thomas. What's so funny?'

'Nothing special, mate, nothing special,' he giggled, unable to stop. 'Just this whole fucking country, you know? So fucking fake, yeah?'

He took another deep drag of the bubbling smoke, held it in for a few seconds, then fell back among the cushions.

'Sure, we get it, Tommy,' another of the Frenchmen muttered. 'Everything's fake, nothing's real, *d'accord*?'

He said something in French and they all started laughing.

'Exactly . . .' HP mumbled at the ceiling as secret Stasi Agent 007 Sleep finally showed up, loosening the muscles around his eyelids and slowly rolling down the shutters.

'Nothing's real. It's all just . . .'

'*A Game?*'

He opened his eyes. The whisper came from the right of him, somewhere near the entrance, but in the weak light his clouded gaze could only make out dark silhouettes.

'What? W-who said something about . . .?'

No answer, just more giggling. Had he heard wrong, was it just the little lads' choir of the withdrawal section piping up again?

He blinked a few times and tried to clear his gaze, but the veils of marijuana memory loss in his head wouldn't ease up. Maybe that pipe-blend had been a bit too strong after all . . .

'Have you ever done anything real, Thomas?'

This time it was the Frenchman next to him.

'What do you mean?' HP slurred, scratching his neck.

'Something that made your whole being, your body and soul, feel absolutely present in the moment? As if the whole world had stopped just to look at you?'

More laughter, including from him, even if he wasn't entirely sure why he was laughing.

Part of his brain suspected that the Frenchmen might be laughing at him – that they were making fun of him, but he couldn't quite work out how.

'You've got no idea, mate,' he muttered, then suddenly realized that he was talking Swedish.

He repeated what he had just said in English. If these guys only knew who they were sharing a pipe with . . . A total fucking legend, that's what he was!

The thin white drapes at the entrance to the pavilion were swaying gently to and fro in the light desert breeze.

To . . .

. . . aaaand . . .

. . . fro.

'So what have you done, Tom? Tell us!'

One of the girls this time, maybe the pretty one he'd been dancing with?

He shook his head slowly and it took a while before he realized that none of them could see his movements in the gloom.

'Nope – I never talk to anyone about that. I stick to rule number . . .'

'*One!*'

This time it wasn't his imagination, he was certain of that. The same low whisper somewhere off to the right, and he sat up unsteadily. The world was swaying and he was having trouble focusing.

'How are you doing, Tommy, old friend? Aren't you feeling well?'

This voice was familiar – it was Vincent. But what the fuck was he doing in here? Why wasn't he outside by the cars, practicing his precision parking with Anna Argos?

The Frenchman landed on the cushions with a bounce, and put his arm round him.

'Look, my friend, have some more and it will all feel better.'

He passed the mouthpiece of the shisha-pipe to HP, who took it after a moment's hesitation.

The bubbling sound of the water-pipe helped calm him down, as he slowly let the smoke out through his nose.

He heard Vincent say something, followed by more laughter, but by the time the man's hands gently lowered him onto the cushions HP was already fast asleep.

The shadow was approaching quickly and she knew almost immediately who it was. She put her hand to her belt but in the dream she had no gun, and felt panic rising. Then the man burst through the cloud of dust.

His arm was outstretched and the shiny revolver was aimed straight at her.

The gun was even bigger than she remembered it – the barrel looked like a deep, pitch-black well.

She screwed her eyes shut, tensed her body and waited for the shot.

But nothing happened.

Why didn't he shoot?

When she opened her eyes again everything had changed.

It was as if the cloud of dust, the man and his gun had never existed.

A dream within a dream . . .

Instead she was standing in the middle of a desert.

No matter what direction she looked in, identical sand-dunes stretched out, all the way to the horizon.

In the distance some dark birds were slowly circling. Round and round above the same point in the desert sand.

When she woke up with the sheets sticking to her body, the image of those black birds was still ingrained on her retinas.

'Bad omens,' she muttered to herself, without really knowing why.

The pavilion was empty. He was lying alone among the cushions, and the water-pipe had gone out.

Outside the whole camp was bathed in white light.

The large floodlights had been lit and he could see people running about across the open space. The music had fallen silent, he could hear shouting in different languages, but he was too groggy to make out what was being said.

Then he heard the sound of an engine approaching – a muffled, pulsing noise. It sounded like a helicopter, possibly more than one? His head felt like a lump of concrete, his tongue was sticking to the roof of his mouth and when he tried to get up he found that his body did not want to obey him.

The engine sound got louder and louder and a sudden gust of wind made the drapes around him billow violently. He brushed the fabric aside and managed a couple of stumbling steps towards the entrance.

At that moment he discovered to his surprise that his tourist garb was gone and that he was once again wearing his silk shirt from Thailand – it was soaking wet.

For a few seconds he began to suspect that everything that had happened in the camp had all been in his imagination.

That the dance, the ominous bird, the whispering voice and everything else were just details from a hash dream that he had just woken up from.

It wasn't until he staggered out into the light and people started pointing at him that he realized that his shirt was drenched in blood.

6

Double dealing

Pillars of Society forum
Posted: 11 November, 09:13
By: **MayBey**

All good police officers end up facing an official investigation sooner or later . . .

This post has 32 comments

'Interview with Police Inspector Rebecca Normén concerning suspected misuse or gross misuse of office during an event that occurred in Darfur Province in western Sudan on 8 November.

'The purpose of this interview is primarily to gather information. Conducting the interview are Inspectors Walthers and Westergren from the National Police Complaints Commission. Also present is Normén's witness for the defence, Superintendent Ludvig Runeberg.'

Walthers was an overweight man in his fifties, who looked like a kindly uncle and had a twinkle in his eye as he sat back and adjusted the microphone on the table between them.

Misuse of office. She'd had to get out a copy of the criminal code when she received the summons, if only to check that some sort of absurd joke wasn't being played on her.

But no, the first paragraph of chapter twenty of the penal code was definitely no laughing matter:

> *A person who in the exercise of public authority by act or by omission, intentionally or through carelessness, disregards the duties of his office, shall be sentenced for misuse of office to a fine or imprisonment for at most two years.*

Then, a little further down the same page:

> *If a crime mentioned in the first paragraph has been committed intentionally and is regarded as gross, a sentence for gross misuse of office to imprisonment for at least six months and at most six years shall be imposed. In assessing whether the crime is gross, special attention shall be given to whether the offender seriously abused his position or whether the crime occasioned serious harm to an individual or the public sector or a substantial improper benefit.*

At first she wasn't even going to mention it to her boss, just get the interview out of the way and then forget about it. It ought to be a purely routine matter – after all, she had done her job and not done anything wrong. At least that was what she kept telling herself . . .

But Runeberg already seemed to know that she had been summoned to an internal investigation and suggested that he come along as a witness.

'It's only a fact-finding interview, though, I'm not actually under suspicion for anything, Ludvig,' she protested.

'That's what they want you to think, Normén. Almost

all internal investigations begin with fact-finding. That's to make you feel safe and encourage you to help them, one colleague to another. Then all of sudden you've said too much, a prosecutor appears and before you know it you're facing official charges. Remember that internal investigators aren't like the rest of us. They've got their own agenda!'

And now here they all were in the interview room . . .

The only question was: who was responsible for her ending up there?

There was hardly any shortage of suspects.

A small, tiled room that smelled of bleach, a bunk, a table and two chairs that were fixed to the floor – that was all.

Somewhere in the distance an air-conditioner rumbled into action and soon he felt a cold stream of air against his bare back.

They had removed all his clothes apart from his underpants, and it was only a matter of minutes before he started shivering.

His head was aching and even if he was presumably back in the city, his mouth still felt like it was full of desert sand.

The whole thing was shrouded in dense fog, interspersed with just a few random sequences of images. The cops' helicopter landing beside the camp, commando yells, people shouting all at the same time.

In the next clip his hands were cuffed behind his back and he had been tied to one of the seats.

He must have passed out again, because he couldn't remember much of the actual flight.

He was in pretty desperate need of some clothes, a cup of Java and a warm shower – but most of all an explanation for what the fuck was going on!

He was freezing his arse off in there, which was fucking ironic seeing as it was probably thirty degrees outside.

Two minutes after his teeth started chattering uncontrollably the door opened and a plump, moustached little man in a neatly-pressed beige uniform walked in.

The man put a grey folder on the table, then sat down on the chair opposite HP. He opened the folder, slowly took out a pair of reading glasses from his breast pocket and began to read.

'E-e-e-embassssssy,' HP stammered. 'N-need Embass-ssy, but you haven't got a cluuue what I'm s-s-saying, have y-y-you? I h-have rights, you know, r-r-rights!'

'Oh, I can understand what you're saying perfectly well,' the man replied, and his faultless English brought HP up with a start.

'The problem is that I don't know which embassy I should contact. Certainly not the Norwegian Embassy, seeing as your passport is fake.'

He looked at HP over his thin glasses.

'My name is Sergeant Aziz, I'm a detective with the Royal Dubai Police. So, who are you really?'

He looked curiously at HP.

'We haven't managed to find any information at all about your true identity, neither on you, nor among your belongings at the hotel. It's tempting to think that you don't actually exist. And a man who doesn't exist . . .'

The police officer leaned across the table.

'. . . can't have any rights – can he?'

'So, Normén, to sum up: you arrived at the scene and found the approach road blocked by a crowd. Instead of offloading and walking to the building with bodyguards and an escort of government soldiers, you decided to abort the operation. Am I right so far?'

'You're forgetting the attacker,' she interjected, getting more and more annoyed by the lead interviewer's sarcastic tone of voice.

Westergren turned and gave his colleague a long look.

'But he didn't show up until you were back in your vehicles?'

'No. I caught sight of him while we were standing there – before I took the decision to abort.'

'And was he armed then?' This from nice, bald, little Uncle Walthers, and she turned towards him.

'Not, not then. He was carrying a bag and I thought I could see a glimpse of a gun in it.'

'*Thought? A glimpse?* You weren't sure?'

Westergren again, still with the same irritating tone. She took a deep breath.

'Like I've already said, I thought it was a gun. Everything was happening very fast, it's impossible to say exactly what happened when . . .'

'We appreciate that, Rebecca,' Walthers nodded. 'But we'd still like you to try to break down the sequence of events as much as you can, down to the very smallest detail. That will help us understand everything better, because obviously neither Per nor I were there.'

He nodded towards his colleague and gave her another friendly smile that she couldn't help reciprocating.

'It happened exactly the way I keep telling you. We arrived, stopped, then, while I was trying to evaluate the situation, I caught sight of the assailant in the crowd. After watching him for a few seconds I concluded that the situation was so threatening that both our charge and my team itself were in danger, and as a result I took the decision to abort.'

She gave Walthers a relieved smile, then glanced at Runeberg. Her boss's face wasn't giving anything away. He was sitting there with his arms folded, watching the two men on the other side of the table.

'And then what happened, Rebecca?' Walthers went on gently.

'We began to move backwards and the crowd started to go mad. They got through the cordon and chaos broke out. I was almost knocked off my feet but managed to stay upright and draw my pistol. Then the firing started . . .'

'You were firing at live targets ?' Westergren snapped, quick as a cobra, but she didn't take the bait.

'No, I fired warning shots – three, to be precise, but because it wasn't possible to fire at the ground because of the risk of hitting third parties I was obliged to fire into the air. At about the same time someone else, probably the soldiers in amongst the crowd, opened fire.'

Walthers gestured to her to go on.

'I saw, or maybe heard, people being hit by gunfire, panic broke out and people started running in all directions. We carried on reversing. I was caught between the car and the door and that's when he came running up.'

'The assailant, you mean?'

'Exactly.'

'You wrote in your report that he was running in front of the car, and that you saw him reach for his gun and draw it. That you considered firing at him, but that your visibility and the movement of the car made that impossible . . .'

'Exactly,' she repeated, more impatiently this time. They had been through the whole sequence of events several times now, and it had all been recorded. What was it they didn't understand?

'Rebecca, could it have been like this – and I'm merely raising this as a possibility, one colleague to another . . .'

Walthers peered at her from over the top of his reading glasses.

'Considering that none of the other bodyguards or anyone else at the scene noticed any assailant – might it have been the case that the stressful situation and limited visibility were affecting your judgement? That you might have been mistaken with regard to the attacker?'

She opened her mouth to reply but he interrupted her.

'No-one here would think that strange. Quite the contrary.' He gestured towards the others in the room. 'We all know what it's like when the adrenalin kicks in. You get tunnel vision and focus on individual details that really need to be seen in a broader context. A mobile phone becomes a hand-grenade, a camera becomes a revolver . . . That sort of thing has happened before. Could that have been what happened in this case, Rebecca?'

She opened her mouth to reply, but Runeberg put his hand on her knee. Clearly she had underestimated the kindly uncle. Even if he wrapped things up nicely, he was still the one trying to trick her into making some kind of admission.

She took a deep breath.

'It really isn't my place to comment on what anyone else saw or didn't see. I can only speak for myself,' she said as calmly as she could, and noticed Walthers' friendly smile slowly fade away.

'I saw an attacker and a weapon, a clear danger to both our charge and my team, so I responded accordingly in line with my duty.'

She gave Runeberg a quick sideways glance and was rewarded with a nod of encouragement. Disappointed, Walthers looked down at his papers and Westergren took over.

'What's your response to the fact that people died at the scene, Normén? In all likelihood as a direct consequence of your dubious actions . . .'

Rebecca jerked. She had realized that people must have been hurt, possibly even killed when the soldiers opened fire – but having it thrown in her face like this was an entirely different matter. To judge from the expression on Westergren's face, he didn't care if he'd crossed a boundary.

'Once again . . .' she said, as calmly as she could even though her anger was bubbling closer and closer to the surface. 'I made my evaluation based upon the threat to my team and the person in my charge. I can't take responsibility for what anyone else did or didn't do.'

'So you're saying you don't care that people were being killed around you?'

'Of course I'm not!' she snapped, but before she could go on Runeberg interrupted her.

'Where are you trying to get with these questions, Westergren?'

The two men stared at each other.

'Interview witnesses must stay silent during interviews,' Walthers piped up from the side, but neither of them looked at him.

'I'm interested in whether or not Police Inspector Normén really understands that one of the consequences of her questionable actions was that people died. That she directly or indirectly caused their deaths by provoking the soldiers to open fire.'

'That's out of order, Per . . .'

'Am I really, *Ludvig*? Maybe you should pay a bit more attention to the sections of the penal code dealing with misuse of office instead of spending so much time in the gym?'

Runeberg slowly stood up, and Westergren did the same.

'Okay, let's all just calm down,' Walthers quacked. He stood up as well and, with some difficulty, placed himself between the two men.

'Interview suspended at 09.51 for a short break.'

He had spent something like three days in this cell. At least he thought he had. Sleeping on the wooden bunk, shitting in a bucket and trying to pass the time as best he could. And obviously he was so desperate for a cigarette he felt he was going to explode. But at least he had been given some clothes.

A white t-shirt and a pair of orange overalls that were at least two sizes too small.

During the first few hours he had quite literally shat himself in terror, but as he gradually came round and ate and drank something, the fog began to disperse and he started to piece a few things together.

He had been seriously doped-up when the cops arrested him, and now they had also worked out his passport was fake. But even if both crimes were pretty serious down here, they still didn't quite warrant this sort of treatment.

There was something that didn't make sense . . .

'What the hell was that all about?' She glowered at Runeberg as her boss fiddled absent-mindedly with the coffee-machine.

'Nothing special . . .'

'Oh, come on! You were about to start fighting in there, you and Westergren . . . "Per". So you know each other?'

Runeberg nodded reluctantly.

'Per and I were beat cops together, a long time ago, and he was a difficult bastard even then – not very collegial, if you get what I mean?'

She shrugged in reply.

'So?'

Runeberg sighed.

'He applied to join the Security Police a few years ago. When I was asked about it I advised against his appointment. Somehow he found out and ever since he's been waiting for a chance to get back at me. I had a feeling he'd jump on this case. I mean, how often does a bodyguard end up in Police Complaints?'

'So that was why you suggested coming along? To play at being my guardian?'

He muttered something in reply.

'I appreciate the thought, but it would have been better if you'd told me this at the start . . .'

He nodded.

'You're quite right – I should have. But everyone makes mistakes, don't they?'

He gave her a long look that she was still trying to interpret when they were called back into the interview room.

'We've outlined the case to the prosecutor . . .' Walthers began. 'The usual procedure in cases like this is that we inform your boss in writing of our decision . . .'

Westergren butted in.

'But now we're in the fortunate position of having your boss here with you as a witness to proceedings, so we can tell you both that as of now, Normén, you are officially under suspicion of misuse of office, possibly gross misuse.'

He nodded to Runeberg, smiling.

'Superintendent Runeberg will inform you about what is going to happen now, but in cases where an officer is suspected of misconduct during the course of their duties, the new rules are crystal clear. Maybe you'd like to take it from here, *Ludvig* . . .'

Runeberg's face had gone completely white. He opened his mouth as if to protest, but shut it again almost at once. He paused briefly and turned to Rebecca.

'You're relieved of duty from this moment, Rebecca. You'll be on full salary, but for the duration of the investigation I'm afraid I shall have to ask you to hand over your keys and passcard.'

They walked back to Police Headquarters together. The air was dry and cold and a few feeble snowflakes occasionally drifted down, only to disintegrate on the black tarmac. Neither of them said much.

Runeberg grunted a few short sentences about routine procedure in internal investigations, then some clichés about being sure everything would sort itself out. She could hardly be bothered to reply.

When they reached the department she had to hand over her passcard and her key to the weapons store.

She was allowed to keep her police ID.

In other words she was still a police officer – for a bit longer.

Small mercy.

Runeberg looked as if there was something else troubling him, but she didn't feel like listening. On the way out she bumped into Karolina Modin, but the other woman merely said hello quickly and avoided looking Rebecca in the eye.

The moment the gate closed behind her, the strange, dreamlike sensation returned.

As if nothing that was happening was . . .

. . . actually real.

He'd been locked up before, admittedly back home in Sweden, but the routines ought to be roughly the same.

To start with, they should have interviewed him at least a couple of times by now.

They should have told him exactly what crimes he was suspected of, and possibly also allowed him access to some sort of legal representation. You didn't waste precious hours letting your suspect shiver in a cell, you only had to watch a bit of CSI to know the basics of forensics and investigating the crime scene . . .

No-one had taken any blood samples or fingerprints, or even his photograph, at least not that he could recall. He'd had a nosebleed while he was asleep. He'd had grass-nose before, and it always looked worse than it was, so he must have scared the life out of the people in the camp. But if the cops hadn't taken a blood sample while he was unconscious, then his shirt was bound to contain all the samples they could possibly need.

But just like the whole of this fucking country, the scenario felt fake, almost contrived.

He could barely finish the thought without his heart starting to race, and he forced himself to be calm.

Several deep breaths later, the fact was that however he looked at it, however hard he examined all the details of the past few days, he couldn't quite shake the idea that it was all just some sort of . . .

More deep breaths.

Game . . .

7

Boardgames

Pillars of Society forum
Posted: 12 November, 23:18
By: **MayBey**

There are only three types of citizen – police, prisoners, and those who haven't been caught yet.

This post has 36 comments

The door banged open and suddenly they were inside the cell. Four sweaty guards and a huge officer with an acne-scarred face and a filthy shirt.

HP didn't even have time to get up before they were on him.

'Name! You tell me name now!' the pock-marked man screamed into HP's face.

Before he had a chance to reply the others had pulled his arms up behind his back, strapped his legs together, then carried him out like a parcel. It all happened so fast that he didn't even have time to feel scared.

The room they carried him into was slightly larger than his cell. There was a narrow table at its centre and he could see straps hanging down from the sides. The table slanted down at one end, but rather than put him down with his head at the higher end, they tied him down with his feet at the top. It was distinctly uncomfortable, lying head-down, and it only got worse when they strapped his arms and legs down.

He could feel his heart pounding hard in his chest.

'You tell me name!' Scarface hissed in his face, so close that he could smell the stale tobacco on the man's breath.

'T-Thomas Andersen,' HP replied, not sounding quite as cool as he would have liked. On the way in he had noticed the camera in one corner of the room, and now he was almost completely certain:

The Game had found him!

He had every reason to be afraid, terrified even.

Weirdly enough, though, it wasn't just fear that was making his pulse race.

Scarface nodded to one of the guard-orcs, who pulled a black hood over HP's face. Everything went dark. He heard the trolls talking to each other, but once again he couldn't understand a word. But he did think he'd picked up one thing.

If they really wanted to get rid of him, there was no reason to drag it out. But instead of burying him out in the desert they had put time and effort into staging this whole charade. That had to mean something.

Suddenly he could make out the sound of liquid dripping onto the stone floor.

What the fuck were they actually up to?

A moment later a wet cloth was pressed over his face.

The first two seconds weren't too bad – he could still

breathe even if he could feel the hood pulling tighter as he breathed in. There was a smell of wet towelling, which was more reassuring than frightening. Then he noticed a wet gurgling sound and suddenly water was seeping through the fabric and into his nose and mouth.

It wasn't much – but enough to make him gasp for breath, which merely meant he sucked more water through the cloth. Some of it caught in his throat, making him choke. He coughed, then took several quick breaths out of reflex, which immediately resulted in him breathing in more water.

More choking, breathing, coughing and water.

But no air . . .

Fucking hell – these bastards were drowning him!

His air supply was almost gone and panic set in.

He tried to twist his head to get the cloth off his face. But he couldn't move at all.

He coughed again, but his gag reflex merely sent down more water and his screaming turned into gurgling.

Suddenly the cloth was removed, then the hood. He coughed, bringing up little splashes of water, then finally managed to take a ragged, liberating breath.

Then another one.

His panic slowly subsided.

Then Scarface's voice in one ear.

'Who . . . are . . . you . . .?'

He tried to shake his head but was interrupted by another fit of coughing, so tried again.

'Take it easy, for fuck's sake . . .'

Several hands pushed him down, the hood was pulled over his head and the wet towel stifled his protests.

More water, more choking. He was jerking his body like mad, trying to kick, but he was held tight in an iron grip. He let out a roar – only to breathe in even more water.

His vision started to turn black. His panic was raging. These bastards really were about to kill him!

The bar over her shoulders, one yellow fifteen-kilo weight on either side, her feet wide apart. She took a deep breath, sank down until her knees were bent at a ninety-degree angle, then, as she pushed up, she blew the air from her lungs.

'Eight,' counted Nina Brandt, standing behind her. 'Two more, Becca!'

She could feel the lactic acid burning in her thighs, but not even a tough series of knee-thrusts could stop her thoughts.

Relieved of duty – or a bit of free holiday, if you were inclined to laugh it off. Unfortunately she wasn't.

So, who had filed the complaint?

The list of candidates ran to at least three names. Gladh was obviously number one. When they left him, Berglund and the interpreter at the dusty little airfield in Darfur, he had looked capable of murdering her. She had wrecked the whole of his lovely official visit, and presumably dealt a serious blow to his reputation and self-image.

She breathed in, bent her knees and then pushed once more. The lactic acid stepped up a couple of notches but she hardly noticed.

Number two on the list was her own deputy, David Malmén.

He definitely didn't seem to have accepted her as his new boss, and here he had a golden opportunity to get rid of her. The idea that neither he nor Karolina Modin had seen their attacker made no sense at all, to put it mildly. Like a story concocted to undermine their leader's credibility.

In the short term Malmén was actually the only person

who appeared to have benefited from her suspension; at least, she assumed he had been put in charge of the group again.

'T-ten.'

With some effort she completed the last lift, then got help putting the bar back on its support. She jogged quickly round the gym to shake off the acid and finish her thoughts.

Third place on the list was rather more dubious, but after some consideration she decided it might well be shared by Karolina Modin and her colleagues Esbjörnsson and Göransson. They would all want to keep in with Malmén, and even if she and Modin had got on fairly well to start with, neither she nor any of the others had backed her up when it mattered.

So what was she to do now?

The investigation was bound to take at least a month. Everyone involved would have to be questioned, and they would have to extract information from the Sudanese authorities.

She was only 'officially under suspicion', the lesser degree, so evidently the investigators didn't have sufficient evidence yet for the prosecutor to want to raise a case against her.

It was her word against theirs – the only question was how unanimous the other testimonies were. Maybe it was time to get hold of a lawyer after all, to show that she wasn't going to take any more shit? But she still felt reluctant.

She hated this type of . . .

Game!

A fake arrest, a mocked up interrogation and a load of actors playing *Midnight Express*, just like last time.

They had cracked him on that occasion, and even though he had made up his mind to stick it out, they were well on the way to doing so again.

Fear of dying had him in its iron grip, his heart was beating double-time and he was throwing up like a fountain across the stone floor.

They had torn the hood off again, loosened the straps and sat him up.

'You tell me name,' Scarface said, more as a statement than a request as he scratched his stubble.

HP could only nod between the fits of coughing. He was sobbing like a little kid. His tears burned on his cheeks – the vomit was burning in his throat and he was prepared to tell them everything. The Kennedy murder, the Lindbergh baby, who framed Roger fucking Rabbit – he was prepared to confess the whole lot as long as he could escape that bastard towel!

'Pettersson,' he sniffed. 'Henrik Pettersson, Player 128.'

'Tenk you!' Scarface nodded happily. 'Next question . . .'

HP stiffened. They'd cracked him, he had lost. So what more was there to say.

Then he got it . . .

Suddenly he started to cry again.

He'd been wrong – fucking wrong!

This wasn't a trial, it wasn't an evaluation or a second chance, the way his little brain, desperate for affirmation, had almost managed to convince him. No, this was all about money, nothing else. The Game wanted the money back, that was all.

Bank account number, user IDs, passwords – he'd give them the lot if it meant he could get down from this fucking table.

What then? After all this, he was pretty sure the Game Master wasn't just going to let him go . . .

'The money, yes?' he sniffed.

Scarface gave him a strange look and threw his hands out.

'No money, no no!'

For some reason the man looked almost insulted.

'Next question,' he repeated, glaring angrily at HP as he pulled a notebook out of one of the pockets of his grubby shirt.

'Did . . . you . . .' the police officer said, and HP nodded.

Time to put a stop to all this.

'Did you . . . kill her . . .?'

And suddenly he didn't understand anything.

'Do you feel like talking about it?'

'Not really,' Rebecca replied abruptly.

She was pulling a comb through her wet hair, then gathered it into a tight ponytail at the back of her neck.

'You know most of it already, so what else is there to say? I'm relieved of duty until the investigation is over, and until then all I can do is play *Guess Who Filed the Complaint Against Me*.'

She and Nina Brandt had met at Police Academy, then worked together for a couple of years. They were actually very different, not just in appearance. Too different to be properly close friends. But they still worked well together, at least superficially.

In contrast to her, Nina Brandt was blonde, short and curvy. The sort that men and women alike turned round to look at in the corridor, and the sort who knew how to make the most of that.

Nina enjoyed attention and was happiest among other people, preferably as many as possible, which was probably the reason why she worked in the licensed premises unit.

Rebecca couldn't imagine ever wanting to work there.

Pubs and bars and attention were things she felt very little desire for.

But the advantage of the licensed premises unit was that Nina knew the owner of every single bar and gym in the city, and it had been simple for her to sort out alternative exercise arrangements for Rebecca now that she was excluded from Police Headquarters.

And what a place . . .

She'd only heard about this gym before now. Which wasn't really that odd – ordinary mortals didn't come here. Evidently this was where celebrities hung out, proper ones, not the fifteen-minute variety . . .

According to rumour, this was where the kids from the royal family came, and that could very well be true. The place felt extremely exclusive – more like a spa than an exercise centre. The receptionist had given them both towels and dressing gowns before escorting them into the sandalwood-scented changing room and showing them to their lockers.

Rebecca had always thought the gym in Police Headquarters was one of the best she'd ever seen. But this was a *palace*, almost a thousand square metres, she guessed, all of it elaborately designed and in perfect condition. Bare brick walls, spot-lit steel beams, high arched windows. And naturally not so much as a single dustball anywhere on the vast hardwood floors.

She could only imagine what membership would really cost.

Considerably more that a police salary could cope with, at any rate . . .

But Nina had got them in free, so she could hardly complain.

'Did you kill her?' Scarface repeated.

HP still didn't understand anything.

'Kill who?' he squawked.

His head suddenly began spinning.

'Mrs Argos, did you kill Mrs Argos?' Scarface spelled his way angrily through the words in his notepad, then glared back at HP.

'What, er . . . No! Fuck, no!' he managed to say as the spin-cycle went up a gear. 'I didn't even know that she was . . . Okay, just listen!'

Scarface gave one of the orcs a curt nod and suddenly the hood was pulled back over HP's head and he was forced down onto the table. 'Noooo!' he roared, panicking and trying to pull free.

'Nooo, for fuck's sake, I'm innocent . . .'

The towel muffled his cries, then the water made him shut up.

The smell of bleach in the room merged with the smell of warm piss.

'It seems weird that Runeberg's got unfinished business with the head of the investigation – Westerberg, was that his name?'

Nina came and stood beside her in front of the mirror and fixed her hair. Even though the mirror was huge and the other woman a head shorter than Rebecca, it still felt as if she took up all the space.

'Westergren,' Rebecca said, unconsciously taking a step to the side. 'They were in uniform together in Norrmalm years ago. Seems like they fell out there, and then Ludvig killed off Westergren's application to join the Security Police.'

Nina looked up at the ceiling as she adjusted a couple of blonde locks that she didn't seem happy with. In spite of the exercise and sauna, she still looked smart enough to go straight out on the town.

'That sounds a bit too straightforward, don't you think?' she muttered, running a lip pencil round her mouth. 'I mean, you said they almost started fighting. You don't do that over a rejected job application and some bad memories from your time in uniform. All that must be, what, at least ten years ago?'

Rebecca shrugged, picked her trainers up off the limestone floor and began to pack her bag.

'Ludvig didn't go into much detail, and it definitely wasn't the time to ask.'

Brandt abandoned the mirror and turned to Rebecca.

'Listen, before you go, there's something I feel I ought to tell you . . .'

When the hood was pulled off for the third time he was done for.

He coughed a couple of times, threw up another load of watery slime all down his front, then gasped desperately for air.

'Wait!' he spluttered when Scarface nodded to the guards again. 'Wait a moment, for fuck's sake!'

Scarface gave a sign and he was helped to sit up.

'You kill her,' Scarface repeated in a tone that was almost friendly.

There was only one answer, one word that could save him from the table.

Red or blue?

'Y-y . . .' HP began.

At that moment the door to the cell was pulled open.

'What's going on here, Sergeant Moussad?'

'Do you know about the Pillars of Society?'

'What, the book, you mean?'

Nina Brandt shook her head.

'No, no. The online forum, of course.'

'Oh, you mean that gossip site? Well, I looked at it a couple of times when it first started and everyone was talking about it, but that was a while ago. Mostly a load of whining police officers and aspiring officers, I seem to remember. Not really my thing . . .'

She closed her gym bag and got ready to leave.

'Maybe you should take another look.'

There was something in the tone of Nina Brandt's voice that made her stop.

'What for?'

Nina pulled a face.

'Because I think they've started writing about you . . .'

'Sorry about this, Mr Pettersson,' Aziz said a few minutes later when they were back in HP's cell. 'Sergeant Moussad and I belong to different departments of the police force, as well as different schools of thought, you could say. He had no right to subject you to that sort of treatment.'

HP nodded apathetically as he tugged at his wet clothes to release them from his skin.

His brain was working in overdrive, but there was no avoiding the acrid smell of piss coming from his overalls, and he glanced at Aziz to see if the detective had noticed it.

'We're getting some dry clothes for you, and you can have a warm shower if you like?'

HP went on with his glassy nodding.

A shower!

A warm fucking shower and a few minutes to do a bit of thinking . . .

'But first we just need to sort out a few things,' Aziz said in a businesslike tone of voice, pushing a sheet of lined paper and a pen over to HP's side of the table.

'Please, write down how you know Mrs Argos and

everything that happened in the Bedouin camp. As soon as that's done you'll get the chance to have a wash and change clothes.'

HP was still nodding. His hand was shaking so much that the pen drew little squiggles on the paper before he managed to get it under control.

8

Redrum?

Pillars of Society forum
Posted: 13 November, 08:11
By: **MayBey**

Who can be imagined to have committed a crime? Everyone.
So everyone is a suspect.

This post has 41 comments

'We have a big problem, Mr Pettersson.'

No fucking kidding – talk about understatement of the year! During the past twenty-four hours, HP had been through all the stages of crisis, more than once.

Denial, despair, panic, shitting himself, apathy, and then straight to jail without passing go.

This simply couldn't be true!

No matter how his overheated thinking tried to handle it, he still couldn't get past a few hard facts.

Everything was real, fucking bloody real – quite literally.

Anna Argos was missing, swallowed up by the desert night. And, according to the cops, he was the prime suspect.

He still had little more than fragmentary memories of that evening. Which wasn't actually that surprising, the combo of beer, dope and car-sickness had presumably all been too much for his already exhausted system.

'Like I say, a big problem, Mr Pettersson,' Aziz repeated, interrupting his thoughts.

HP looked up and met the detective's worried gaze.

'We've matched the blood we found on your shirt with DNA we found in Mrs Argos's hotel room, and a couple of hours ago the helicopter found some remains about five kilometres from the camp. Mostly bloodstained clothing and fragments of skin. The birds and desert foxes have all done their worst, sadly. We've seen it happen many times before with people who've got lost out there, but the preliminary results match Mrs Argos's profile.'

He gestured vaguely to the world beyond the walls.

'For the time being we don't know if the body was driven there, or if these are just fragments moved there by animals. So we are continuing the search, both close to the camp as well as further away.'

He leaned over the table.

'Naturally, her death could have been a tragic accident. An argument in a secluded place, a few moments of rage with terrible consequences. Perhaps Mrs Argos was merely wounded, in spite of the amount of blood. Left there on the assumption that she would be able to get help? But instead, in her bewildered state, she went in the wrong direction – straight out into the desert . . .'

The detective gave HP a long look.

'If that was the case, I daresay the judge would show some sympathy.'

He paused, and seemed to be waiting for a response.

HP was trying in vain to control the maelstrom in his head.

There was an explanation to all this, he was sure of that. A perfectly natural explanation that would prove that he was innocent. Purely theoretically, he might very well have wandered about the camp – decided to get rid of that stupid t-shirt and rescue his expensive Thai silk shirt from the bin. A few vomit-stains were hardly the sort of thing that was going to bother you when you were stoned . . .

But then what?

The murderer had obviously gone into the toilets. Tried to wash off the blood as quickly as possible, and found his shirt in the bin.

It sounded pretty fucking unlikely, but stranger things had happened.

He fast-forwarded through this scenario one more time, just to be on the safe side. Flimsy – but not unthinkable.

Even so, he still couldn't stop one unpleasant thought from leaking out.

What if Aziz was right?!

For a while back there in the camp he really had felt like strangling Anna Argos – squeezing her neck tight and choking that arrogant fucking smirk from her face . . .

'B-but what about the others? Vincent and his gang?'

He could hear how shaky his voice sounded.

Almost as if he had already guessed what the detective was going to say.

'Ah yes, I had almost forgotten the mysterious Frenchman . . .'

Aziz put on his reading glasses and leafed through the folder in front of him.

'What we've managed to ascertain is that you and Mrs

Argos arrived at the camp together. You were seen eating dinner at the same table, and later during the evening a witness saw you arguing beside the opening in the fence, close to the toilets. The witness describes the argument as physical, and also claims that Mrs Argos looked terrified.'

He paused to turn the page and HP gulped a couple of times in an attempt to moisten his bone-dry throat.

'Your French travelling companions had unfortunately left the camp by the time we arrived, but we spoke to them the following day at their hotel. They all agree that you were angry about Mrs Argos making fun of your "accident" in the car, and that she later – possibly as a result of this – seemed to prefer other people's company to yours.'

He turned the page and went on.

'Admittedly, the Frenchmen confirm your story about having met them in India, but they claim that getting together in Dubai and going on the desert safari was your idea.'

The detective paused and glanced at HP over the frame of his glasses.

It took several seconds for HP to absorb the information.

'B-but, the ride into the desert was their idea. Vincent called me at the hotel, they picked us up. Ask the drivers, they'll know!'

'Unfortunately we haven't been able to reach the drivers, Emir and Bashid. According to their boss, this isn't unusual. They're paid by the hour and go home to their families in Yemen during the low season. According to him, the cars were booked from your hotel in the name of Sinclair, and one of the credit cards we found in your wallet was used to confirm the booking. A MasterCard in the name of a Jerome Sinclair.

'Jerome *Vincent* Sinclair . . .'

Welcome to the Pillars of Society
– we're the ones holding all the crap up!

In actual fact the idea was neither particularly remarkable, nor terribly new. A discussion forum open to all sorts of complaints, gossip and cocksure claims – with the possible distinction that this one seemed to be aimed at police officers, or at least to people in uniform. Which of course felt really original and ground-breaking . . .

But after reading a few of the posts she began to realize why this particular forum had got people talking. One of the most regular contributors, someone calling themselves MayBey, was good – very good, in fact. Unlike the other posters, he or she didn't moan about faulty equipment or the quality of the latest crop of recruits. The language MayBey chose to use was unusual, short sentences containing a lot of dark humour, instead of the bloated posts full of the officialese so beloved of most Swedish police officers.

'Caught three joy-riders tonight. Chase lasted almost twenty minutes.

Three yobs ditched the car at Junksta junction. Dog good for a change – picked up the trail at once. We got all three under a tree ten minutes later!

Big relief!

Then four hours at the station getting them booked in and interviewed. So far, so good. Duty Prosecutor Turnstile only needed a single minute. And then they were all free again.

All our work down the drain while he rolled over and went back to sleep.

Only wish I could sleep as soundly as that . . .'

Every police officer had experienced a car chase like that, and MayBey – whoever he or she was – had managed to capture the whole thing in just a few lines. The excitement of the chase, relief at the arrests, the drawn-out paperwork and then anger when the yobs were let go.

There were fifty-eight comments to the post, five times more than most other contributors got, and they all shared MayBey's frustration.

The other thing that made the post interesting was the recognition factor. The Junksta junction could very well be the Hjulsta junction, and she knew that there was a prosecutor in the district whose name meant roughly the same as turnstile.

Out of curiosity she went onto the Stockholm Police website, but couldn't find any report of anything matching the description on the forum. So what did that mean?

Nothing really.

MayBey could be from another district, or else he or she could be describing an old incident. But for some reason Rebecca was still fairly sure that the post referred to Stockholm.

She could certainly recognize the caricatures in MayBey's older posts. Police Chief Teflon, whose white shirt never picked up any stains. Superintendent Spineless who always managed to be unavailable when there were difficult decisions to be taken. Detective Inspector Birkenscholl who shuffled round the corridors fully occupied with trying to avoid doing any work.

She was sure she'd worked with all of them – but, on the other hand, she probably wasn't alone in that . . .

But it was the latest post from MayBey that really caught her interest . . .

The detective was looking at him as if he was expecting a reaction, but for once HP didn't know what to say. He tried desperately to conjure up a picture of Vincent in his mind, but for some reason the man's features seemed suddenly unclear – almost hazy.

He opened and closed his mouth but failed to get a single sensible word out.

'We've been very thorough, Mr Pettersson. Murders are rare here in Dubai, so for that reason we're looking under every stone. My men have checked all the fingerprints we've been able to find, both in the car and on the table you ate at, and we've found prints belonging to you, Mrs Argos and all the others in your party. We've even contacted the police authorities in your respective home countries, but everyone involved has a clean record. Everyone except you, Mr Pettersson . . .'

Aziz gave HP another long look over his bundle of papers.

'All the prints match up, there are none unaccounted for. In other words, there's no trace of this so-called Vincent . . .'

Another look to match his tone of voice, but HP hardly noticed.

Now that he came to think about it, he couldn't actually remember Vincent ever saying anything about himself.

One day when he had been sitting in a bar feeling pretty fucking depressed, the Frenchman had just appeared.

Offering him beer and a smoke, someone to talk to who made him feel a bit better.

So who was Jerome Sinclair? His wallet was full of different credit cards – different characters who had helped him manage his nomadic, sleep-walking life. He could only remember a few of them:

Jim Shooter
Will Parcher
Tyler Durdan

He had picked most of the names as a joke – at least that was what he told himself. A gang of made-up imaginary friends from film-history. People who had never existed outside of the minds of characters in films.

He seemed to have a vague memory of Jerome Sinclair as a series of embossed letters on a plastic card.

Were Jerome and Vincent one and the same person?

Someone who didn't exist outside his own head?

The detective put his papers down and leaned across the table.

'Let me summarize the situation, Mr Pettersson. You – with a previous conviction for murder – enter the country on a false passport. You meet Mrs Argos at the hotel, pick her up and then arrange a desert safari together with some fleeting acquaintances. She however scornfully rejects your advances, which quite understandably makes you angry. Because of course you were the one who arranged everything, possibly even for her sake, and now she rejects you. Sometime that evening Mrs Argos disappears, and you are found badly affected by drugs and with her blood all over your shirt.

'And your only defence is to blame a mysterious man whose existence nothing and no-one else can prove.'

He paused briefly to let his words sink in.

'Like I said, murder is extremely rare here in Dubai, possibly because all murderers are punished hard. Very hard, Mr Pettersson . . .'

Another pause, so that HP didn't miss what he was saying.

'But if the defendant cooperates, the judge is usually sympathetic. Your life is very much in your own hands, so I would ask you to think very carefully before you answer my next question.'

A third pause, entirely unnecessary this time.

'Did you kill Mrs Argos?'

HP's head was filled with flickering screendumps – all of them containing different information, all of it fucking alarming.

Had his tortured brain finally started making things up?

BLINK

Showing him things that didn't exist?

BLINK

Mixing up fantasy and reality?

BLINK

Yes?

BLINK

No?

FUCKING HELL!!!

He screwed his eyes shut and covered his face with his hands to stop the flashing in his head. But the images carried on flickering across his retinas.

Shooter

Parcher

Durdan

All work and no play makes Jack a dull boy!

Redrum, redrum, redrum . . .

Could he really have beaten up a bitchy bird?

Shit, he'd even fantasized about how it would feel . . .

Time to decide.

Red or blue?

* * *

The world's best Bodyguard, Regina Righteous, seems to be having a few problems. Looks like she got sunstroke down in Africa and saw something that wasn't there.
Or is there another reason why she was hallucinating? Maybe because she's been suspended? Does anyone out there know?

This post has 17 comments

Regina Righteous. Great name. Just as Nina had said, it wasn't exactly hard to work out who they were talking about . . .

And seventeen comments as well, pretty much all of them negative.

'What else do you expect from Internal Investigations?'
'That's what happens when you have quotas for women . . .'
'She was fucking difficult even at the Academy'
'Probably took too many tranquilizers. WBUP, for sure . . .'

She had to Google that last comment. WBUP – Will Break Under Pressure. So this was how the rest of the world saw her. Someone who couldn't handle pressure . . .

'N-no,' he croaked, and cleared his throat again.

'No, I didn't,' he went on, slightly steadier this time, almost as though he were trying to convince himself.

Aziz let out a deep sigh. He gathered his papers, stood up, then knocked twice on the steel door.

'I'm afraid I can't help you any more, Mr Pettersson,' Aziz said, almost sadly.

He stepped aside as Moussad and four sweaty guard-orcs squeezed into the room.

A moment later they were on him.

He was yelling, lashing out in panic, and actually managed to land a couple of decent punches before the orcs got him down on the floor.

He was going to die, he got that now. Either Scarface and his gang were going to drown him, or, more likely – he'd end up confessing everything. And would be sentenced to death by some shady judge and dragged out into the desert for a shot in the back of the neck, for which his sister would be sent the bill. Followed by eternal membership of the Association of Morons, along with Dag and Dad!

Hello, my name is Henrik, and I am a ladykiller!

He was finished – fucked – toast!

Suddenly a synapse in his terrified brain made a connection.

'W-wait!' he yelled at Aziz, just as they were about to carry him out.

'Wait, for fuck's sake, I know where to find evidence of Vincent. Just give me . . .'

Moussad whacked him in the side of the head to shut him up, but it didn't keep him quiet for long. He had his fingers on a life-raft and wasn't about to let go.

'One of my trouser pockets, a gold cigarette lighter. It's his. Vincent's. Check it for fingerprints, DNA, whatever you fucking like . . .'

Another blow, this time hard enough for him to taste blood in his mouth. He heard Aziz fire off some sentences in Arabic at the guards, then Moussad, who seemed to be giving contradictory orders.

The sweaty orcs around him shuffled uncomfortably and exchanged glances as if they were unsure of what to do. Both of their commanding officers rattled off new orders. Still no reaction. HP managed to twist his head and could see Moussad and Aziz facing off against each other – just a few centimetres apart.

Moussad's face was bright red, and he was clenching and unclenching his fists. He was a head taller than Aziz, and from HP's lowly perspective he looked even bigger and more unpleasant.

But Aziz wasn't letting himself be intimidated – instead he took another half-pace forward so that the shirts of the two men's uniforms were almost touching.

For a moment it looked as if the pair of them were about to start fighting.

HP and the guards held their breath.

Then Moussad slowly stepped back.

Aziz roared another order, louder this time, and a moment later HP found himself sitting on the interview chair while one of the guards reluctantly undid his cuffs.

'Tell me more,' Aziz said curtly once the cell door closed and they were alone.

9

Fata Morgana

'Hello?'

'Good evening, my friend. Has everything gone well?'

'Everything has gone excellently, entirely according to plan – but of course you already know that.'

'Any pain?'

'No more than necessary.'

'Good, and the retreat?'

'No problems there either. How have things been going with . . .'

'The Player? It's a little too early to say yet. I'll keep you informed.'

They came in the middle of the night. Four Guantanamo gorillas, and just like last time they dragged him off the bunk and cuffed his hands behind his back. This time he couldn't summon up the energy to put up a fight.

He was Nick Orton, Thomas Andersen, Charles Herman and so many other names that he could hardly even remember them.

Imaginary characters that he had made real, at least for as long as he needed them.

So why not Vincent Sinclair?

The hood was pulled on while they were still in his cell, but the guards seemed to notice how apathetic he was and didn't bother to tie his legs. They led him, stumbling, down one flight of steps, and then another.

His body felt as heavy as lead.

More steps – he tripped and the guards had to catch him to stop him falling. But they didn't stop to put him back on his feet. Instead they grabbed him under his arms and picked him up, so high that the tips of his toes just touched the ground. And then the steps came to an end.

The room they entered was larger, so large that the strained grunts from the guards echoed drily off the walls. Had they really come this way before?

A faint smell of petrol and exhaust fumes filtered in under the hood and all of a sudden he felt completely sure. They weren't on their way to the torture chamber!

A moment later he was put down in a seat and a heavy car door slammed on him.

A squeal of tyres, a sudden jolt and they were on their way.

HP was trying desperately to take in this new information. Someone was sitting to his left in the back seat, because he kept getting whiffs of aftershave. And the car had to have a driver as well.

So in other words there had to be at least two people apart from him in the vehicle – possibly as many as three – but none of them was saying a word.

Wherever it was they were going, the driver appeared to be in a hurry. The big engine was roaring and the vehicle's movements were so abrupt that he kept sliding around on the leather seat.

Then he noticed a change in the road surface as they switched from smooth tarmac to gravel. A few minutes later the noise disappeared almost entirely and the vehicle began to slip and slide in a very familiar way. HP's stomach got the message much quicker than his brain, and the panic-stricken lump down there was fast turning into nausea. More lurching, and the hiss as sprays of sand hit the windows.

They were on their way out into the desert!

'You'll see, Becca, it'll all be fine. I mean, it's not as if you've done anything wrong . . .'

Micke put his arm round her on the sofa and she fought a sudden urge to shove it off. And to grab hold of the nearest solid object and smash his head in.

It'll all be fine, you'll see . . . If she had twenty kronor for each time she'd heard that comment over the past week. Ludvig, Nina Brandt and a whole load of other well-meaning souls.

Was that really the best people could come up with whenever someone was in the shit?

'Of course I haven't done anything wrong,' she snapped, unable to stop herself. 'What, don't you believe we were being attacked either?'

'Of course I do,' he replied quickly, but she took her chance to straighten up and shake off his arm.

'I just mean this is bound to blow over soon . . .'

She interrupted him with a snort.

'I wouldn't bet on that. There are enough people who want to get at me, who don't actually have to do much more than keep their mouths shut and just watch the show. Gladh, Malmén, Modin and the others in the team . . .'

'Don't forget Gladh's assistant . . .'

'Berglund? No, not him!'

She bit her tongue but it was too late.

'Why not? I mean, it would make sense for Gladh to

ask his assistant to look after something unpleasant like this, wouldn't it?'

'Sure,' she muttered, shrugging her shoulders.

She slid back down in the sofa and locked her eyes quickly on the television.

'I was thinking of making some tea, do you want a cup?' she said in a far gentler voice a minute or so later.

'Mmm,' he replied.

On her way out into the kitchen she surreptitiously picked up her mobile from the hall table.

They had been rolling around for quarter of an hour or so, and finally the pieces of the puzzle had fallen into place.

There weren't going to be any more questions.

Just as Aziz had said, he had a previous conviction for murder, had entered the country on a false passport, and appeared to be closely connected to the crime. No-one believed he was innocent – not even him.

What with all the bling, he'd forgotten that the country was actually a dictatorship. A poor, helpless western woman – kidnapped and murdered out in the desert. That sort of thing could scare off tourists and big business alike. It would cost millions of dollars in bad PR and lost business deals. Much better to put a lid on it and pretend it never happened. All they had to do was get rid of the last remaining loose thread and literally bury the story where it started.

In the sand . . .

He could feel tears of panic bubbling in his chest and bit his bottom lip to stop them escaping.

Suddenly the car stopped and he heard the driver's door slam shut.

This train terminates here – all change, please!
Fuckfuckfuckfuckfuckfuck!!!

She really shouldn't let it bother her.

So what if someone was talking shit about her? It had probably happened plenty of times before, the only difference this time was that she had the chance to follow what was being said.

Most of them probably didn't even know her, had no idea who she was or what she'd done. But what if she was wrong?

What if they were fellow officers, colleagues she'd said hello to in the corridors, or even worked closely with?

Obviously she should just ignore it all, forget the website and leave the idiots to say whatever they wanted. But she still couldn't keep away.

She kept making little trips to the bedroom to wake the computer from stand-by mode and check if anything new had appeared.

Wallowing in the muck, picking at the scab and tormenting herself with every detail, every single comment until her stomach was a tightly clenched lump and she could hardly breathe the air inside the flat.

She clattered deliberately noisily with the teapot in an attempt to drown out her thoughts, but it didn't really work. She'd decided not to tell Micke about the forum. This rubbish was bad enough, but she was worried that other rumours would start to appear. Rumours that happened to be true . . . Everything looked so good on paper.

Promotion, her own bodyguard team and a considerate boyfriend. A villa, a dog and a Volvo waiting round the corner. All the stuff that had plagued her for years – that was like a tight band of barbed wire over her chest – was finally history. It hadn't been her fault, so she no longer had any reason to torment herself. Ignoring gossip ought to be child's play . . .

So why couldn't she do it?

Was it really so hard just being happy?

While the kettle boiled she glanced quickly into the living room.

Micke was still concentrating on the television.

She took out her mobile.

Wednesday at seven
Usual place

Then she pressed send.

'You're a fortunate man, Mr Pettersson,' said a clean-shaven Moussad from the seat beside him, in English that was almost as perfect as Anna Argos's.

HP's overwrought imagination crashed and while it was rebooting he missed the start of Moussad's story.

'A clean fingerprint on the lighter and enough traces of skin to check for mitochondrial DNA. We heard from Interpol this morning, they both match a Bruno Hamel, a French-Canadian citizen with an interesting reputation, to put it mildly . . .'

The police officer paused long enough for HP's synapses to make at least one functioning connection.

'W-what?'

'Evidently Monsieur Hamel has made a career for himself as a contract killer. There are at least four open cases that have been put down to him. Would you care to guess what his speciality is?'

Another smile.

HP nodded silently.

'Single women . . .'

HP suddenly felt his nausea rising.

All the blood rushed from his head and he was forced to lean forward so as not to pass out.

Even though Moussad was sitting right next to him, his voice seemed to be coming from far away.

'What Colonel Aziz didn't tell you during your conversations was that Mrs Argos had received death-threats. We got confirmation of that when we contacted the police in her home country.'

'C-colonel . . .?' HP stammered, confused.

Moussad chuckled.

'It's a little trick we sometimes use to get quick results. For some reason, unshaven Arabic men who don't speak English seem to prompt the majority of westerners to cooperate. Colonel Aziz is my boss, and he's actually in charge of the whole of the Royal Dubai Criminal Investigation Division.'

The police officer took a deep breath and held it for a couple of seconds while he waited for HP to straighten up.

'You understand, Mr Pettersson, everything seemed crystal clear. The blood, the witnesses, your relationship with Mrs Argos and so on . . . But there was one thing that didn't quite make sense . . .'

He waved a finger to underline what he was saying.

'No genuine witness statements fit together a hundred per cent, Mr Pettersson. People simply perceive things differently. But all five of the French citizens who gave statements against you told the same story – exactly the same story, down to the very smallest detail. Do you understand?'

He went on without waiting for an answer.

'We suspected something was wrong, and in the end you gave us the evidence we had been looking for,' Moussad continued. 'Imagine their faces when we showed the witnesses Interpol pictures of Hamel – a professional hitman wanted in several countries, and someone they had done all they could to protect . . .'

He smiled again, then paused as if he was waiting for some sort of reaction from HP.

When he didn't get any response Moussad went on, with almost exaggerated clarity, 'Someone had Mrs Argos murdered . . .'

Still no response.

'. . . and this someone also went to great lengths to frame you, Mr Pettersson.'

HP's world was lurching, and at last his nausea got the better of him. As if on a given signal, the car door was opened from outside.

A moment later he was on all fours and throwing up onto the desert sand.

Déjà vu!

The reply came within a minute or so.

Sure – thought you were going to back out ;)

She began to write a sarcastic reply but changed her mind. She heard Micke moving on the sofa and quickly deleted the received text.

The water had boiled and she put two mugs of tea and some biscuits on a small tray.

When she sat back down on the sofa he put his arm round her and pulled her to him.

'Good to have you home again,' he muttered.

She didn't answer.

'By the way . . .' she said after a short pause.

'Hmm?'

'I won't be home on Wednesday evening. I thought I

might go to the cinema with Nina. I need to clear my head a bit . . .'

'Okay.'

He didn't even look away from the television, which made the lie easier.

'We might go for a drink afterwards, so you don't have to wait up. I mean, you don't have to hang around here if you'd rather sleep at yours . . .'

He turned and gave her a quick sideways glance, and for a moment it looked like he was going to say something. Then he sank back onto the sofa and went on staring at the television.

'Okay, have fun . . .'

They shepherded him like a sheep between the indoor palms of the vast terminal building. Moussad on one side of him, the driver on the other. People on the moving walkway hurried to get out of the way, presumably thinking he was a mass murderer or something.

When he saw the familiar blue and white sign he almost burst into tears.

For a few terrified seconds he was scared they were going to carry on past it. That all this was yet another trick to break his fragile mental state. But they got off the walkway at the right place, went up to the desk and Moussad handed over a ticket and some documents to the woman behind the SAS counter.

He didn't understand a word that was said, but a minute or so later they were standing in the smoking booth by the gate and Moussad was offering him a cigarette from a little flat metal case. HP's hands were shaking so much he had trouble getting the cigarette lit.

Then wonderful, deep lungfuls of smoke . . .

None of them said anything for a while.

'W-what about the French blokes?' HP eventually muttered. 'What's going to happen to them?'

'We'll hold them for a few weeks while their rich daddies pull every string they can to get them home. In the end I'm sure we'll find a solution that works for everyone. After all, the ones we're really after are Monsieur Hamel and his employer . . .'

HP nodded. Perjury really didn't matter that much in the greater scheme of things.

Business is money.

God, he was so sick of this fucking place!

'Have they said anything about why . . .? I mean, why they agreed to try to frame me?' he clarified in a monotone.

Moussad nodded and took a drag on his cigarette.

'Apparently they met Monsieur Hamel in Goa just a few days before they met you.' He waved his cigarette, sending smoke rising towards the ceiling in little spirals.

'Just after you left them the Indian police made a raid and a number of the group were found in possession of various illegal substances. Hamel solved the situation there and then, without any of them having to call home to daddy and making a fool of themselves. My guess is that he actually staged the whole thing to make them feel indebted to him. These people have their own rules, Mr Pettersson . . .'

'So they paid the drivers to go home to Yemen . . . and maybe drop off Vin— I mean Hamel at the airport on the way back?'

'Something like that,' Moussad nodded. 'A name matching one of Hamel's aliases was used to leave the country shortly afterwards. We're not entirely sure it was him, the camera footage from the airport isn't good enough for a hundred percent identification, but it seems likely.'

* * *

Moussad accompanied him on board, even helping him to stash his luggage in the overhead locker before holding out his hand in farewell.

'Well, goodbye, Mr Pettersson.'

HP hesitated for a couple of seconds, then shook the man's hand. Strangely enough, the gesture seemed to make the police officer more relaxed.

'If you hear anything about Mrs Argos back home in Sweden, anything you think might be of use to the investigation, I'd appreciate it if you got in touch . . . Someone hired Hamel to murder Mrs Argos, and we're very keen to get hold of whoever that was.'

He pulled out a little white business card from the pocket of his neatly pressed shirt.

HP nodded mutely, and tucked the card away without bothering to look at it.

The police officer had got as far as the door before HP's addled brain finally caught up.

'Moussad . . .?'

The man turned round.

'What makes you think I might hear anything about Anna Argos back home?'

'So you didn't know?' Moussad smiled.

'What?'

'That Anna Argos was Swedish?'

10

Hide and seek

Pillars of Society forum
Posted: 14 November, 16:19
By: **MayBey**

Lying, misleading and manipulating are natural talents for a psychopath.
The rest of us have to practise to get good at it . . .

This post has 45 comments

Now, in hindsight, she seemed to recall having seen the man the first time she came to the gym. Just as they were about to leave Nina had bumped into one of the owners, someone she'd obviously dated for a while. It was while they were kissing each other on the cheek and exchanging small-talk – a discussion that had ended with Rebecca being given a month's free membership – that she thought she had seen him, on one of the running machines.

A man with cropped hair, not much taller than her. Fit, in the sinewy way she preferred over the gym-pumped version. But it wasn't primarily the man's appearance that made her notice him. It was the way he was running. Determined, focused, as if he were pushing for a place in the Olympics.

And now here he was again – on the same running machine over in one corner, running in exactly the same way.

His tempo was ridiculously high. The man's arms were pumping at his sides like muscular pistons, and his eyes were locked on his own reflection in the mirror. His suntanned body was pouring with sweat; his thin vest was already soaked. His feet were pounding on the machine. Bang-bang-bang-bang.

There was something about the whole scenario that drew your attention, and she realized that she had almost stopped concentrating on her own weight training.

Then – just for a second – Rebecca met the man's gaze in the mirror and found herself shuddering.

Obviously, it *could* all be an unfortunate coincidence.

That Hamel just happened to pick him as the scapegoat, so that he himself could vanish without trace. Just as Moussad had pointed out, he was pretty much typecast for the role of fall-guy.

Even if it obviously seemed way too much of a long shot, the theory couldn't be discounted altogether.

But whoever was behind all this hadn't bumped off Anna Argos just to get at him, he was sure of that. Game or no Game, she was the JFK character, whereas he had merely been given the role of Lee Harvey Oswald. A useless, no-good patsy.

Just like him, Anna had been on the run, and had tried to put half the planet between herself and those trying to find her.

In those first paranoid moments in the hotel lounge he had picked up Game vibes. And actually thought she was another Player who'd been sent out to track him down.

What if he'd been right, or at least half right?

That she really was a Player, but had chosen to get out, just like him?

In which case it was pretty fucking stupid of her not to dump her phone.

Maybe she thought it was enough just to change the SIM-card?

BIG mistake!

He pinched the bridge of his nose in an attempt to stop his imagination running away.

But instead a new image popped into his head. Of those desert ravens circling slowly above . . . Anna's lifeless body, closer and closer until the bravest of them dared to land beside her on the sand. A couple of ungainly steps, and then . . .

He took a deep breath, then gestured to an air-stewardess to have his drink topped up.

Anna may have been a fully fledged massive bitch, but no-one deserved that sort of end. Whoever had employed Hamel to get rid of Anna must have really hated her.

But Hamel and his employer had made a mistake.

They had left him down there with the Dubai cops in the belief that he was finished. Letting other people finish the job when they should have sent Jack Ruby.

Instead of a gunshot to the back of the head or lifetime in the Bangkok Hilton, he was sitting here – on a plane back home to Sweden. He had crawled through a world full of shit and come out on the other side, alive if not exactly clean.

'So, how did you get on at the gym?'

'Fine.'

'Are you hungry?'

She nodded and gave Micke a dutiful peck on the cheek. Really she would have preferred to be left alone, making the most of her physical exhaustion from the gym to get a decent night of dream-free sleep. But she had already lied her way to one free evening this week.

Besides, he'd made dinner.

'Oh, I almost forgot. Someone rang a little while ago. She said you were colleagues.'

'Nina Brandt?' Rebecca mumbled as she got the plates out.

'No, that wasn't it. Hang on, I wrote it down on the pad next to the phone. Karolina, that was the name,' he called from the hall a moment or so later.

'Karolina Modin. She said she'd tried your mobile, but it was switched off. She wanted to talk to you about something, but she didn't want to say what. It sounded like it was important . . .'

Apart from his hand luggage he only had two things. A plane ticket with no name and a sheet of paper Moussad had given him. LOC – Letter of Cessation. He was evidently supposed to hand it over at passport control at Arlanda. Even if the Game had nothing to do with his little adventure in the desert, they'd know where he was the moment his ID number was tapped into the police computer system.

It wasn't too difficult to work out what would happen next . . .

If he was going to stand any chance at all he had to find a way of getting into the country without being picked up by the Game's radar.

It was actually much simpler than it sounded.

Forget movie stunts like hiding in the toilet, creeping

out through the undercarriage and scampering off over the runway. All he needed was a passport – a little red booklet with a photograph that looked vaguely like him.

Like the one sticking out of the back pocket of the bloke three rows in front of him . . .

He flew out of his seat a few seconds before the plane stopped at the gate and the pilot switched off the seatbelt sign. He quickly grabbed his bag from the overhead locker and then positioned himself right next to his target, holding his bag at just the right height to conceal what he was doing. Just as he had hoped, the man was fully occupied with his mobile phone. Seven hours without social media was a long time for iMorons . . .

A neat shoulder-tackle in the middle of a status update, and suddenly @arlanda was suddenly @unknownplaceon-thefloorbetweentheseats . . .

As soon as the man leaned over to rescue his pride and joy, HP snatched his passport from his back pocket and headed towards the exit as quickly as he could.

A few moments later he was out in the connecting walkway and on his way into the arrivals terminal.

He was now Lars Tommy Gunke from Linköping, according to the passport. He tasted the name a couple of times as he walked quickly towards passport control.

'Lasse – Lasse Gunke here, hi!'

He glanced quickly at one of the clocks on the wall. He had three or four minutes, maybe five. That ought to be enough . . .

Two sturdy police officers in dark uniforms were standing over by the passport control desk. The men looked bored, but a little LOC form and someone without a passport would doubtless save their morning.

HP aimed at the shortest queue and tried to look innocent.

Another glance at the time.

Two minutes had already passed and as usual he had chosen the wrong queue. The line of people beside him was sailing through, but he wasn't moving at all.

And now it was too late to switch, he had metal railings on both sides and more passengers lined up behind him.

What the hell was taking so long?

It looked like the old bag at the front of the queue was having trouble with her passport, he could see her waving her arms at the woman behind the desk, as if she was trying to explain something.

He took a careful look over his shoulder. Loads of people behind him, but no sign of the real Lasse G. Yet.

'Hi Rebecca, sorry I'm a bit late. I'm just going to grab some coffee, do you want a refill?'

'Sure . . .'

Rebecca watched Karolina Modin as she filled the coffee cups over by the till.

Modin was the youngest member of the team at twenty-five, a whole decade younger than Rebecca herself.

Modin's boyish appearance and short, jagged fringe made her look even younger than she actually was, which definitely wasn't a good thing when you were trying to justify your position in the force. All too often, seniority still counted for more than ability.

So why had Modin really wanted to see her? She hadn't wanted to say much on the phone – just that she wanted to meet.

Rebecca really ought to have insisted that they do the whole thing over the phone, but it wasn't as if she had anything better to do.

Modin returned with their coffee and sat down opposite Rebecca. They each took a sip.

'Well, I was at another internal investigation interview yesterday, and there's something I wanted to tell you . . .'

Modin was clearly the sort of person who got straight to the point, which Rebecca appreciated. But this didn't sound good.

'Oh?'

'I've done a lot of thinking about what happened down there. In Darfur, I mean. Everything happened so quickly – the whole thing, the evacuation and so on. We hardly had any time to talk . . . And Ludvig split us up as soon as we got home.'

Modin looked anxiously at Rebecca, as though she were expecting some sort of agreement.

'Mmh?'

'Well, I wasn't sure to start with . . . I mean, I was concentrating on driving and hardly looked out of the front of the car at all. Then there was complete chaos when the crowd broke, then the shooting, all the dust and . . . well, all that.'

Modin glanced at her uncertainly again, but Rebecca kept her expression the same.

'Anyway, I've had time to think, and looking back now I think I did actually see someone running in front of the car, while you were hanging off the door . . . I'm pretty sure I did.'

Rebecca couldn't help twitching, and Modin seemed to notice.

'Well, I didn't see any details, no gun or anything, but for some reason the colour yellow is fixed in my mind. Was he wearing something yellow, a top, or a scarf or something else loose?'

'A plastic bag,' Rebecca muttered indistinctly. She cleared her throat and repeated herself, as her heart pounded faster and faster. 'The suspect had the gun in a bright yellow plastic bag that he was holding in his left hand.'

'Hmm . . . it could well have been a bag, and that's what I told the investigator when he asked. Per Westergren, you've probably already spoken to him . . .'

'Yes, we've met,' Rebecca nodded, unable to hold back a smile.

Karolina Modin smiled back.

'Right. He asked a lot of questions about you. What you were like as a boss, and so on. I said we hadn't worked together long, but that you were one of my role-models in the bodyguard unit . . . That you're always one hundred per cent professional . . .'

All of a sudden Rebecca had no idea what she was supposed to say.

'Thanks, Karolina. I mean . . . I really appreciate . . . well . . . your testimony and everything. I'm sure it'll mean a lot in the investigation.'

'Yes, that's exactly what David said too . . . He was the one who suggested I call and ask to be interviewed again.'

'David?'

'Yes, David . . . David Malmén,' Karolina Modin said, and smiled another one of her boyish grins.

The other queue was still moving smoothly.

He should have been through by now.

On safe ground.

Shit!

Even though he was trying to play it cool, he couldn't help squirming, and he got the impression that the cops had noticed.

Four minutes had passed and he still hadn't moved.

The cops had started glowering at him

For fuck's sake, just get moving, you old bag!

Another glance over his shoulder – still no Lasse.

Suddenly the cops began to move.

He leafed frenetically through his passport, pretending that its contents were really, really interesting.

The police officers strolled slowly along the queue. Five minutes had passed and he thought he could detect some sort of anxiety at the very back of the queue.

The cops exchanged a look and one of them said something into the radio microphone attached to his shoulder.

Fuckfuckfuckfuckfu . . .

'You there!'

One of the cops was pointing at him.

'Erm . . . what, me?'

HP was playing for time.

'Yes, you.'

The cop beckoned him over and HP moved slowly closer to the railing. But the policeman kept on beckoning and after a moment's hesitation HP ducked under the railing and took several more slow steps in their direction.

What the hell was he going to do?

'Passport, please!'

The cop with most stripes on his shoulder held out his hand.

'Erm . . .' HP glanced towards the exit behind the police officers.

If he really went for it, he might just . . .

'Passport!'

The policeman took the little red booklet that HP was still clutching hard in one hand, and for a moment they stood there like that – almost in a tug of war. Then HP let go.

The cops were standing shoulder to shoulder, there was no chance of sneaking between them. The railing was blocking his escape on the right and he probably wouldn't have time to skirt round to their left. He had to play it cool, wait for the right moment . . .

One of the cops looked through the passport. HP felt a drop of sweat on his forehead, then another. The handle of his bag felt sticky in his hand.

'LOC?'

HP was sure this was what the cop holding the passport muttered while the other grinned.

Fuck!

His cover was blown, the cops knew who he was!

Was he supposed to just hand over his deportation papers and go along nicely to the police station with them?

Hell, no!

Time to do what he was best at, run for his life!

He took a cautious step to the side, trying to find a gap.

The cops moved and the distance between them grew.

On your marks . . .!

The gap opened up a bit more.

Get set . . .!

The head cop looked up with a frown.

'Don't you like ice-hockey?'

'W-what?'

HP stopped, on tiptoe, his eyes still fixed on his escape route.

'LHC – Linköping Hockey Club . . .?'

The cops grinned and exchanged a look.

'Thomas and I support AIK – we're playing you in the Globe tonight. Top against bottom, you could say . . .'

'Sure, yeah . . .' HP muttered while his brain made an effort to catch up.

The policeman handed him the passport.

'Welcome home, Linköping, and good luck. You're going to need it . . .'

11

Homecoming

'We have a problem . . .'

'I see – that doesn't sound good. How big?'

'We're not quite sure yet – right now we're evaluating the situation. But we may need to use your services again . . .'

'That's okay – I almost expected that. I've actually made a number of preparations . . .'

She had been dreaming about him again.

The man on the running machine.

As she climbed the steps out of the underground she tried to remember what the dream had been about, but annoyingly the details were just out of reach. The look in his eyes was all she could remember. That penetrating black look that she had met in the mirror, almost making her lose her breath. She had seen it before, plenty of times. But back then it had belonged to a completely different man. A man she had loved – and hated . . .

But Dag was dead and gone, and she had carried on without him. Started a new, better life with someone who didn't treat her badly. So why was she doing this? What made a completely unknown man so interesting that she was dreaming about him?

Without the slightest warning, that feeling washed over her again and she stopped dead in the middle of the pavement. Just like in the car down in Darfur, when they had been rushing through the cloud of sand and away from the threat, the world seemed to slow down. Every detail, every little movement around her suddenly appeared crystal clear, and for just a fraction of a second she imagined she could see something out of the corner of her eye. An indistinct silhouette visible through all the passersby.

But the moment she started to turn her head, the world went back to its normal speed, her line of sight was obscured and the silhouette was gone.

She waited a few seconds, then slipped between two parked cars and quickly crossed the street. Nothing, not the slightest movement.

There was no-one following her. Anyway, who on earth would be?

She went round the corner and turned into a little side street, and stopped in front of a doorway.

For a brief second she hesitated, then tapped in the code, and looked over her shoulder just to make sure before going in.

Two floors up she took out her bunch of keys and unlocked the door to the flat.

After someone tried to burn down Henke's flat the insurance company had not only paid for the hall to be restored, but also a reinforced door, so if your average burglar wanted to break in they'd have their work cut out for them. Which made it all the more annoying that the flat was uninhabited.

Henke's belongings were still in storage with Shureguard, so the whole flat, with the exception of the mattress on the floor, was pretty much empty of furniture.

She fetched a glass of water from the kitchen, and had just finished it when there was a knock at the door. Three cautious little knocks.

She didn't bother looking through the peep-hole, and just opened the door.

'Please, no talking – can't we just fuck?' she said to the person outside.

He really shouldn't. There were so many reasons not to that he had already lost count.

But he still felt obliged to.

The toilets looked just the same as they had before he left.

He found the right cubicle, locked the door and stood on the toilet seat. He looked anxiously around the top of the cubicle, then gently lifted one of the ceiling tiles.

He felt inside the enclosed space, his heart pounding faster and faster. For a few seconds he thought it was gone, that the security staff had found it. Or possibly someone else . . .

Someone coughed a couple of cubicles away from him, and the sudden noise made him start.

He looked around in panic, then caught sight of an electronic gadget in the ceiling and thought for a few moments that he'd been caught. That they were already on their way . . .

But then his fingertips touched something hard, and he breathed out.

How fucking paranoid could you get?

In purely logical terms, the toilets in the departure

hall were the perfect hiding place. Basically impossible to monitor. But logic was nowhere near enough to explain why he had decided to pick up the silvery little phone.

It took him almost five days to pull himself together. He stayed shut in his room, sleeping like a corpse and only getting up to go to the toilet or let room service in – which, at this elegant establishment meant paying the shagged-out-looking bloke in reception to close his hatch and go across the street to McDonald's.

But as the days drifted past even the receptionist began to give him funny looks through the crack in the door, and eventually HP realized he was going to have to get his shit together.

So at least now he had more or less cleaned himself up.

The washed-out dressing gown he had pulled on after his much-needed shower lay in a heap on the stained carpet. He had only had it on for a few seconds when the feeling and smell of wet towelling made him pull it off in panic.

The television was showing pretty much the same shit as ever.

Channel five proudly presents: semi-famous people allowing themselves to be humiliated in new ways.

Zap.

American sitcom on six – season ten, episode sixty-eight . . .

Zap.

Advert for Dressman.

Zap.

Award-winning Iranian women's drama – on the national broadcaster, SVT, where else . . .?

Double zap!

A crime series, featuring some sort of serial killer. Big surprise . . .

Zap again.

Big Brother, version 4.5.

Zap.

Ice hockey . . .

Zap.

Sitcom . . .

Zap.

A repeat of Swedish Idol.

Zap.

Advert for Dress . . .

Zap.

Zap.

ZAP!!

He was back home and nothing had changed except for him.

He thought about pressing the PayTV button and ordering a ridiculously overpriced porn film, but for some reason he wasn't in the mood.

He was acting like he was still in exile because he was, even in Stockholm.

Anger roused him. He had a sister here, but if the Game was after him he couldn't risk seeing Rebecca.

He got out of bed and dug out a notepad and pen from the battered little desk.

He opened the window the five centimetres permitted by the safety catch, clambered up onto the windowsill and lit a cigarette. There may have been no-smoking stickers here and there, but to judge by the smell and the nicotine-stained embossed wallpaper, he was hardly the first person to break that particular rule.

All his credit cards had been taken from him in Dubai – they told him they were fake, which in a way was true.

Fortunately they had missed the backup card he had had the foresight to stick between the layers of rubber on one of his flip-flops.

Twenty thousand in the account – enough to be able to book in anonymously here at the Hotel California, and buy the essentials. As soon he could get back online it would be simple enough to top up his account.

Laptop, he scrawled on the pad, then, after a brief hesitation:

Mobile.

He cast a long glance at the little wardrobe.

He'd taped the phone to the back of one of the drawers, and for a moment he was seized by an almost irresistible urge to get it out and look at it.

Just for a few minutes . . .

You have to put a stop to this, Normén!

It was way past one o'clock at night, but as usual she was wide awake. She glanced at the sleeping form beside her on the mattress, trying to identify what she felt for it, but didn't really succeed.

Sex – that was all this was about, at least for her. An undemanding fuck – enough to fend off the angst for a few hours.

She wasn't entirely sure if it was the purely technical aspects that made the sex good, or if it was because what they were doing was forbidden.

Probably a mixture of the two.

Either way, she couldn't carry on like this. She was starting to get paranoid, imagining that people were staring at her when she was on her way to another of their sordid little meetings. She had to put a stop to this, once and for all. Preferably today, or at the very latest by the end of the week, she thought, letting her hand slide over the pale back beside her. The touch made the back's owner turn towards her and pull her closer. A hand roamed over her breast, then warm breath on her skin.

By Friday at the latest, she thought.

The list – he had to focus on the list and get his shit together.

He added clothes, toiletries and some other useful stuff before he stopped again. Through the television, the radio was playing a Neil Young song that he recognized, and he sat still in the window and listened aimlessly until the obligatory ad break made him start thinking again.

So, what exactly were his plans?

Questions were still buzzing round inside his head like a swarm of angry hornets, but he had no answers. Or rather: he had far too many, and his five days of R&R had unfortunately left him none the wiser.

Obviously he ought to get out of the city. That was practically a no-brainer.

But he was fed up of running – completely fucking done with it.

Wasn't it actually pretty smart to hide right here, right under their noses? Surely this would be the last place anyone would ever think of looking?

The problem was that no matter how much of a stroke of genius this Million Dollar Hotel was, he couldn't stay up here pulling his Anne Frank routine for the rest of his life. He was a social creature, he'd already tried living as a hermit and had almost gone mad as a result. If he carried on along that path it would end with 'Brooks was here' and a length of Venetian blind cord from a lamp hook, he was pretty sure of that. And his sister would have to identify his body.

He finished his cigarette, flicked the butt out of the

window, two storeys down into the courtyard. The fall through the air made it glow until it suddenly went out as it hit the damp little patch of grass below his window.

Whatever had actually happened out there in the desert, it had something to do with his mysterious compatriot Anna Argos, and if he was the least bit interested in making any sense of this whole crazy story, he had to start with her. The only question was how.

He glanced at the wardrobe again as he felt in the packet for another cigarette, then realized at the same moment that he'd just smoked his last one.

Fucking bollocks!

Cigs, he wrote on the list, then began, without any great expectation, to search through the pile of used clothes in the hope of finding a forgotten little fag-end.

Instead he found himself holding a business card in his hand. The little white rectangle contained a long sequence of hand-written numbers that started with +971, and he was just about to toss Moussad's contact details in the bin when he realized there was something on the other side.

ArgosEye.com

Knowledge · Security · Control

And suddenly he had an idea.

A crazy, fucked-up, stupid idea that he turned over in his mind for several minutes before making the decision. It was hardly going to be easy – possibly actually life-threatening.

But just the thought of what he was considering made him feel insanely excited!

Better to burn out than fade away!

12

Roleplay

From: customerservice@uscreening.com
To: goodboy.821@hotmail.com

Subject: business details as per order number 2352/11

Company name: ArgosEye.com
Type of company: Limited
Address: Sergels torg 12, 111 57 Stockholm
OMX abbreviation: N/A – company not listed on stock market
Authorized signatories: Argos, Anna; Argos, Philip J.
Results and accounts: See appendix A

History

The company was originally founded in 1998 by Anna Argos and several of her fellow students at the Stockholm School of Economics (see appendix C).

According to the company's business

description, it offered IT consultancy services. Like many other businesses in the same field, it profited from the IT boom of the late nineties, and at its height had one hundred employees in ten countries, with a turnover of approximately one hundred million kronor. A stock market launch was planned but never carried out as a result of the general decline in the market during the early 2000s.

In 2001 the company suffered a serious decline in profitability, and all its offices except Stockholm were closed, and almost all staff made redundant.

In 2002 Anna Argos bought out the other partners and took over management of the company.

Between 2002 and 2005 the company began to focus more on various IT-related communications strategies and slowly began to grow once more.

In 2006 Anna Argos married Philip John Martinsson, who adopted her surname.

He became a partner in the company at the same time.

Martinsson has a background in military intelligence and the security service, where he worked on risk and crisis management in communications. He also worked for the American PR agency Burston-Marsteiner, leaving with excellent references to take up the post of MD of ArgosEye.

Current activities

Under Philip Argos's leadership, ArgosEye has

chosen to focus primarily on questions of internet-related communications risk and crisis management, popularly known as 'Buzz control' – an area in which, in spite of the company's relatively limited size, it has quickly become a significant player. Buzz control is regarded as highly sensitive and is therefore surrounded by a great deal of secrecy. It is therefore unclear precisely how many companies have employed ArgosEye's offices. However, according to unconfirmed sources, a number of Swedish and foreign multinationals already use ArgosEye's services, most likely indirectly through other consultancy agencies rather than as direct clients.

Internet searches for ArgosEye generate keywords such as 'internet strategies', 'communication', 'risk management', 'Buzz control', 'toplist optimization', 'social media strategies' and 'crisis management'.

The company's turnover and number of employees have increased rapidly in recent years, which has meant that the company has occasionally had difficulties with short-term liquidity. In order to continue to expand, the company will probably have to depend upon an injection of external capital, suggesting that stock market flotation is likely.

Ownership

Anna Argos is registered with the Swedish Patent and Registration Office as owning 40% of the shares in ArgosEye Ltd.

The remainder of the shares are owned by

a number of minority shareholders of whom Philip Argos, with 20%, has the largest holding (see complete list in appendix B).

Other information

The Argoses first filed for divorce early in 2008, but this was withdrawn before the trial period elapsed. A second application was made during the latter half of 2009, and Roslagen District Court authorized the divorce in April 2010. Shortly after that the villa they shared in Täby was sold.

Both parties have until recently been registered as living at separate addresses in central Stockholm.

Anna Argos applied to the Tax Office to be removed from their register as recently as one month ago.

According to this application, she is currently living in London, England. The extent to which she is still involved in the daily activity of the company is unclear.

'Central Investigation Office, Westergren.'

'Hello, this is Rebecca Normén from the Bodyguard Unit.'

She was making an effort to keep her voice neutral. There were a few moments' silence on the line.

'I see. And how can I help you?'

Westergren's tone of voice was curt but not directly unpleasant. Not much, anyway . . .

'I was just wondering how far you'd got with my case? If anything new has emerged?'

More silence.

'And what might that be, Normén?'

Nice move – turning the question back on her. Pretending nothing had happened and making her lay her own cards on the table.

But she had already noted the faint hint of annoyance in his voice and side-stepped the trap.

'I was hoping you might be able to tell me, Westergren,' she replied.

Several more seconds of silence.

'I know exactly why you're calling, Normén,' he suddenly snarled. 'You, Runeberg and your other colleagues have had plenty of time to work something out, which is exactly what I told the prosecutor a short while ago. You can tell Ludvig that we haven't got anything new to say and that the case is still very much open!'

The line went dead.

Rebecca slowly put the receiver down.

So what did this mean?

Well, in the unlikely event that it was Modin who filed the complaint against her, then her altered testimony ought to have punctured the entire investigation. The prosecutor was usually quick to write off shaky cases like this, and simultaneously improve the statistics, seeing as 'case abandoned' was, oddly enough, a result . . .

But Modin had never been the prime suspect, so this whole line of reasoning was probably largely theoretical. For instance, why would Modin report her for misuse of office only to change her mind a few days later . . .?

Considerably more interesting were the circumstances surrounding her altered testimony. Rebecca could actually understand why Westergren was so annoyed. Even if Modin had done her best to make her story sound believable when they spoke, it still didn't sound quite right, more like something she'd come up with later on. But on paper the story worked perfectly. No precise details that could be checked, no absolute contradictions that would sound odd after her original statement. Taken as a whole, Modin's version of events did actually strengthen her own. So she should really just be grateful for it . . .

If David Malmén really was the person who, one way or another, had 'helped' Modin to remember, then Rebecca had seriously misjudged him, clearly. Although of course it was also possible that her deputy was acting on orders from above . . .

No matter, she could remove him and Modin from the list of suspects, and with them probably the other two members of the team. Which left just the embassy counsellor, Gladh. Not really much of a surprise.

She was back to square one again – but at least she no longer had to watch her back.

At least she hoped not . . .

Everything was laid out on the stained bedspread. Every item neatly arranged so he could tick it off his list. He felt like some secret agent getting ready for a dangerous mission. Which might well turn out to be the case . . .

The paranoia that had followed him halfway round the world had grown stronger, which probably wasn't that strange really. Somewhere out there people were looking for him, people who wanted nothing more than to get their hands on Player 128 and hand him over to the Game Master.

But he had to try to shake it off. There was no proof that they had found him, none at all. He was still one step ahead, and as long as he trod carefully and didn't wake up any guard dogs then that would remain the case.

What he really needed to do was focus on his new mission.

He opened his laptop and started to type out a message, but stopped after just a couple of sentences.

Shit, in the bitter glare of hindsight he could see that picking up the phone hadn't exactly been his smartest move. Okay, so it was switched off and drained of power. Not even the best batteries in the world would last fourteen months, so he wasn't worried about being traced.

His problem went rather deeper than that.

Even though the phone was physically stone-dead, it was as if it was still sending out signals.

Inaudible little enticements to the part of his brain that still longed for everything the Game could offer him.

And that was presumably why he hadn't been able to leave it where it was out at Arlanda.

Just holding it felt undeniably good. Feeling the cool metal against the palm of his hand, his fingertips sliding over the touch-screen.

And for a few seconds, a few wonderful seconds, the feeling was back.

Introducing Player 128, first runner-up, the public's favourite – the hottest guy in the Game. Heeeeenrik Petteeerssooon!

Almost all phones could be charged up the same way these days. A little cable to one of the computer's USB ports was all it would take . . .

But obviously he wasn't going to switch it on, he wasn't completely thick, for fuck's sake!

There were plenty of other things to be getting on with, ways to keep his mind occupied and at a safe distance from that lethal track. It was just like that mental exercise.

Whenever you think about the Game, you lose!

'Hi Rebecca, this is Håkan! Håkan Berglund,' he clarified when she didn't say anything.

'Oh, hi . . .'

She was holding the phone between her cheek and shoulder so she could pour a cup of coffee.

'I'm back in Stockholm and was wondering if you felt like having that meal we talked about. How about this Friday?'

She took a deep breath.

'I'm not sure that's such a great idea . . .' she began.

'Oh, come on!' he interrupted. 'I got the feeling we clicked pretty well, and I'd like to see you again. I can pick you up around seven . . .'

She sighed.

Evidently she'd got Håkan Berglund all wrong.

The fact that he dared to call at all was pretty surprising in itself, considering how little he'd done to support her down in Darfur. And now he didn't seem to be the sort who could take a hint.

She really didn't like pushy people.

'Sorry, Håkan, but I've actually already got a boyfriend,' she said bluntly.

There was silence on the line.

'Hello?' she said.

But he had already hung up.

'Magnus Sandström?'

'That's me.'

He got up from the sofa in the waiting area and followed the receptionist to a small meeting room.

'Welcome, Magnus, take a seat and Eliza will be with you shortly. We're running slightly late with the interviews, but she shouldn't be too long.'

'No problem!'

'Great. Can I get you anything while you're waiting? Coffee, tea . . .?'

'Thanks, I'm good,' he smiled.

She gave him a little wave as she went out, closing the door carefully behind her.

He made himself comfortable on one of the six metal-tubed chairs around the table. One wall was made entirely of glass and through it he could see straight down onto Sergels torg. The sound of traffic was only just audible as faint background noise. The skyscrapers of Hötorget had to be one of the best office addresses in the city.

The door opened and a solidly built woman walked in.

'Magnus?'

He nodded and she marched quickly across the room.

Her handshake was limp and slightly damp.

'Eliza Poole, head of personnel. Welcome!'

She gestured at the chair he had just stood up from.

'Sit yourself down and tell me why you're interested in working for us here at ArgosEye . . .'

He sat down, crossed his legs and leaned back.

'Well, I've worked for a long time in the computer business, and questions of risk and crisis management in communications have long been a subject close to my heart . . .'

HP smiled his smoothest smile, nudged his glasses into place and brushed an invisible speck of dust from the sleeve of his jacket.

'By the way, call me Manga. Everyone does!'

13

Raising the stakes

Pillars of Society forum
Posted: 21 November, 06:53
By: **MayBey**

If you want something to change, sometimes you have to take matters into your own hands.

This post has 56 comments

Shit, it still felt weird not recognizing yourself . . . Short, cropped hair, clean-shaven, Buddy Holly glasses with clear lenses perched on his nose.

When they were little some people used to think he and Manga were brothers.

Sometimes they actually pretended that they were.

That was where he got the idea from.

Obviously it had been a total shot in the dark, emailing his CV, but ArgosEye had taken the bait at once. Manga's CV was pretty solid, and with a bit of tinkering and a basic course in Photoshop you could knock the world dead. Throw in his own winning personality and the outcome was a foregone conclusion.

Bearing in mind what the company did, he had coolly calculated that they would Google him, so he had opened accounts on Facebook, MySpace, Spotify and LinkedIn.

Each profile was adorned with a slightly distorted picture of his face, so that no-one could tag his photograph.

The real Manga Sandström was far too paranoid to appear anywhere out there with his actual name and picture. And besides, as luck would have it Mangalito just happened to be out of the office – according to the spotty youth in his computer shop, the little convert was on a pilgrimage in Saudi Arabia with his father-in-law.

He didn't actually have the faintest idea what he was hoping to achieve with this little charade. The only thing he knew with anything approaching certainty was that Anna Argos's death was connected to her company – why else would Moussad have given him the business card and asked him to keep his eyes open?

Her ex-husband was obviously top of the list of suspects. But things weren't always the way they seemed. There were no simple truths – you couldn't take anything for granted.

Especially not if the Game was involved . . .

Half an hour on Google had so far left her none the wiser. MayBey seemed to be a play on the English word *maybe*, and she was fairly sure the misspelling was intentional, which seemed to suggest that the name had some sort of significance.

Sadly Google hadn't been much help. The first few hits on the search list were people who had simply got their spelling wrong, followed by a removals company in Albany, New York, then a few people on Facebook whose surname really was MayBey. None of them was Swedish, as far as she was able to tell.

She switched to Wiktionary and looked up the word *maybe.*

> **Maybe** [meibi]
> Perhaps – something which might be true (adv.)
> Indicating a lack of certainty (adv.)
> Synonymous with words such as perhaps, mayhaps, possibly

You could also rearrange the letters to make three other words:

> *beamy* – meaning radiant
> *embay* – meaning to enclose, shut in or trap
> *abyme* – apparently an obsolete word for chasm, abyss

So she really wasn't any the wiser . . .

'Say hello to Manga here – he's our new troll.'

Three heads looked up from the around the coffee table and nodded in greeting as his new boss introduced him.

'Dejan is in charge of the Filter – that's the gang with all the screens and the wall-projector over in the glass room.'

HP's boss gestured over his shoulder with his thumb towards the right-hand end of the office.

'Hi, good to meet you,' Dejan said. He was a short bloke with thinning hair, around thirty.

'Rilke's in charge of the Blogs, and Beens looks after the Laundry.'

HP shook hands with them both. His mouth felt incredibly dry and his heart was still pounding with both fear and excitement, but he did his best to appear cool and relaxed. The gang sitting round the table in front of him were hardly anything to be frightened of.

Beens both looked and behaved like a chubby little computer nerd. A greasy parting, military issue glasses and a coffee mug with a Blade Runner quote on it. But oddly enough, he was wearing neither a washed-out t-shirt nor jeans that were too short for him. In this place everyone seemed to wear the standard business uniform. Suit, tie, neatly ironed shirt for the gentlemen, something along the same lines for the ladies. There was a bit of a Jehovah's Witness feel to the whole thing.

HP would have much rather had Rilke as his boss instead of the grinning pretty-boy who had met him at reception. Olive-coloured skin, dark eyes and matching hair.

Her handshake was soft and her voice slightly teasing.

'I hope Frank hasn't put you off too much already . . .' She smiled, nodding towards HP's boss. 'Life as king of the trolls sometimes seems to go to his head . . .'

They all grinned, and HP did his best to look as though he got the joke.

'Okay – the short version of how it all works,' Frank said as they headed off down the glass corridor towards the part of the hyper-modern office that was evidently known as the Troll Mine.

'Our clients employ us to protect their trademarks – but of course you know that. We make sure that they know everything that's being said about them out there, and help deal with any problems . . .'

He gestured over his shoulder with his thumb again.

'Dejan and his team over in the glass bubble work with a program we call the Filter. The program sweeps all known search engines looking for hits that contain our clients' names, as well as various combinations of negative buzz.'

'Like Nestlé and monkeys' fingers, or BP and environmental disasters . . .?'

'More or less,' Frank smiled. 'But of course the Filter is much more sophisticated . . . You'd have to check with Dejan, but I'm pretty sure that the program now contains several thousand different combinations of negatively loaded comments, and his team update it on a daily basis as new expressions crop up.'

They reached a door and Frank tapped his passcard against a reader.

'This is the Strategy Department. Stoffe's usually in charge of this lot, but he's on holiday at the moment so Milla over there is covering for him.'

Frank waved at a deathly pale Goth girl who was so deeply absorbed in her screen that she hardly seemed to have noticed them.

'We call her Lisbeth,' he whispered. 'But only when she can't hear us . . .'

HP nodded, trying at the same time to keep his head down.

Even if the risk was small, he couldn't shake the feeling that he was about to be unmasked at any moment.

'Whenever the Filter comes across any sort of buzz that could be damaging to our clients, it's the Strats' job to work out what we should do to handle the problem, so to speak,' Frank went on.

HP nodded mechanically.

'Everything gets fed into the risk management model that Philip designed. Depending on the outcome of the modelling, information is passed on to us in the operational sections . . .'

'Right, yes, of course . . . what were they again . . .?' HP muttered.

Frank gave him a disgruntled look.

'The Trolls, the Laundry and the Blogs . . . By the way, Manga, the way you're dressed . . .' He glanced at HP's badly fitting suit and brightly patterned tie.

'What?'

'Remind me to give you the address of our tailor before Philip catches sight of you . . .'

They left the room and carried on along the steel-grey carpet of the corridor towards another locked door. Just like the last one, Frank touched his passcard against a discreet reader and then opened the door.

'Well, we're home. Welcome to the Troll Mine, Manga!'

The alarm on her mobile started to bleep and she sat up with a start.

It was one o'clock at night, and high time to make her way home.

She glanced at his solid body, listened to his heavy breathing for a few seconds, and tried to summon up some sort of feeling for him. But all she felt was distaste. For him, for herself, for the whole situation.

She got up from the mattress and gathered her clothes together.

A quick wash in the bathroom to get as much of his smell off her before she made her way home.

Just as she was pulling her jacket on she heard a noise from the front door. At first she thought it was the paper being delivered, then she remembered where she was. Obviously no papers got delivered to Henke's empty flat.

She listened again.

There was a faint metallic clicking sound from the door, almost as if someone were messing about with the lock. The lights inside the flat were all off, so she ought to have been able to see a point of light from the peephole in the door. But it was completely dark.

She took a few steps out into the hall.

One of the new floorboards creaked beneath her foot and she stood still.

The clicking had stopped.

She padded carefully over to the door and tried to look out of the peephole.

But the stairwell was completely dark.

Then she suddenly heard quick footsteps on the stairs, and a moment or so later the front door of the building opening. She ran over to the window, peered down into the alley and managed to catch a glimpse of a dark figure disappearing round the corner.

'Wossup?' he muttered sleepily from the mattress.

'Burglar,' she replied without taking her eyes off the street.

But for some reason she didn't feel entirely sure about that . . .

14

Death by Powerpoint

He'd sat through thirty different slides about the company's 'core values', 'mission statement' and 'code of conduct', and he and the two other new employees had been obliged to sign a hefty bundle of papers covering all manner of confidentiality regulations.

The worst of his nerves had settled but the feeling of joining a sect had definitely not subsided.

But at least the personnel manager's evangelical presentation seemed to be almost over now.

'Well, if no-one's got any more questions, that's it from me. Now for a few words from our MD . . . As I said earlier, he would have spoken first, but Philip's just got in from the airport so we're having to work around his schedule.'

Eliza Poole opened the door and muttered something to the girl out in reception.

The other two new employees instantly pulled out their smartphones, but HP used the pause to fill his water glass instead. His mouth was dry and his head was throbbing with a tension headache.

He had zoned out a couple of minutes into the

presentation and was gradually starting to wonder if this project was really such a good idea. Maybe he should have thought it through a bit better, come up with some sort of plan instead of just jumping at the first thing that popped into his head, as usual?

What did he actually think he was going to be able to achieve, anyway?

The door opened and a sinewy man with cropped hair, probably somewhere in his early fifties, stepped into the room. His pin-striped suit looked like it was glued to his extremely trim body, his shirt was silky smooth and his tie impeccably knotted. A precisely measured and no doubt genuine suntan made him look healthy and relaxed.

'Almost as if he'd just got home from a long holiday,' HP thought, and felt his heartbeat speed up.

Energetic Eliza, who was actually about the same height as mister pin-stripe, and definitely a couple of weight-classes above him, suddenly seemed rather submissive.

'Allow me to introduce our managing director – Philip Argos,' she said, a little too loudly.

She tried to instigate a round of applause, but stopped instantly after a quick sideways glance from her boss.

'Thank you, Eliza.'

He nodded at the personnel manager, who blushed bright red and backed away quickly.

'Welcome to ArgosEye,' Philip Argos began, in a surprisingly soft voice. HP leaned forward so as not to miss anything. He suddenly realized there was something familiar about the man, but he couldn't quite work out what.

MayBey was obviously the website's big star.

No-one else's threads had anything like the same number of comments, and his or her readership appeared to be constantly growing.

The last post was pretty good.

Picked up a lowlife dealer today. Found him at the top of a stairwell. During the search my partner stabbed himself on a syringe in one of the fucker's jacket pockets. The dealer got it straight away. Went completely white and started to cry. He'd broken the rules. Whether he meant to or not. The punishment was still the same . . .

The post had thirty-six different comments; another four had appeared since she last checked half an hour ago. Practically all of them knew exactly what had happened.

It was an unspoken rule that addicts always told the police if they had needles on them before they were searched. A tiny scratch from a dirty needle meant a whole load of blood tests followed by weeks of uncertainty. Weeks when you hardly dared to be in the same room as your family, going through every possible diagnosis over and over again . . .

Hepatitis A, B or C? Or worse . . .

The rule was unconditional, which in all likelihood meant that MayBey and his unfortunate partner had given the dealer a severe beating. She would have done the same if she'd been in their shoes. Reluctantly, maybe, but still . . .

'Hope you castrated the fucker!'
'Hit him till your baton bends.'
'Semper Fi – do or die!'

And a whole load of other moronic comments in the same vein.

Hardly surprising. Half the comments probably weren't even from cops, but idiots with a fetish for uniforms who'd failed to get into Police Academy and were now stuck in their mum's basement watching *Cops*.

But on the net they could all play whatever role they wanted to.

@Applelover 672
Your well wrong there, mate. Everyone knows Android's way better. Why spend a shitload more money on a phone that every fucker will have in six months?
@lost – get an Android, fella! You won't regret it!

HP clicked the send button and moments later his contribution appeared on the technology forum. He pressed Alt+tab and switched to the *Dagens Nyheter* discussion page as he glanced at the printout next to the keyboard.

It hasn't been proven that GMO products are in any way harmful to people. On the contrary, a number of tests show that the human body actually finds it easier to absorb nutrition from this type of product . . .

The send button again, posting the contribution under the right article, then Alt+tab again. *Expressen* this time, and the comment section under a film review:

Can't understand what the reviewer means. Saw the film yesterday and it's way better than the first one!!

Shit, only three days into the job and he was already good at this troll business! Fucking good, even! His contributions usually got loads of feedback – mostly from people agreeing with him. He couldn't help wondering what sort of people had the time to devote so much energy to commenting on things. Some of them seemed to live the whole of their pathetic little lives in the piss-filled gutters of the newspapers . . .

A quick glance at the time told him he was well on schedule and that it would soon be time for a well deserved coffee break. But first he was going to surf through one of the big travel websites and let a few different aliases tell the world what a fantastic time they'd had in a hotel he'd never heard of.

He had about fifty different trolls in his stable, and his job was to keep them all going. Maintaining their hotmail addresses and keeping their Facebook pages active, posting opinions that were in line with their predetermined attitudes on one of the many hundreds of forums out there. A few of his trolls were angry and shouty, others more reserved and sarcastic. Each one had its own little folder with a character description:

'Male, 50 years old, self-employed, votes to the right and reads thrillers. Likes Swedish sitcoms, boxed red wine, and spending Friday evenings on the sofa. Dislikes: the leftwing in general, environmental cars, traffic restrictions and taxes on wealth and property. Angry, loud and often spells things wrong. Usually supports category A3 clients.'

Or:

'Female, 25 years old, student, votes to the left, reads Nobel prize-winners, likes world music, Apple, fair-trade products

and Iranian films. Dislikes: rightwing politics, 4x4s, meat, designer clothes and the USA in general. Expresses herself in a controlled, articulate way. Mostly supports category A6 clients.'

On a chart he carefully jotted down which trolls had had an outing, and on which forums. Which ones had been engaged in heated discussions in defence of which clients, and which ones were currently inactive. He couldn't help being impressed by the whole set-up. If a client's trademark was getting a hammering somewhere, you just had to choose a suitable troll and deploy it.

Clicking to like something, or writing a few positive contributions. More or less as he was about to do on the travel site. Evidently the hotel's average score had fallen below an acceptable level, and needed some positive feedback to get the average up again.

Simple!

Frank had told him about a consultancy firm that got into trouble a few years ago and had been stupid enough to get its employees to write comments in defence of the company under entirely new usernames. It only took a couple of days for the blogosphere to yank the idiots' trousers down and wreck the trademark to the extent that the company had had to change name.

It was different with tame trolls. Because they were already established out in cyberspace, no-one could call into question where they had appeared from. So they could be used to clients' advantage without risking the indignant fury of the internet. Smart. Really smart, actually!

But if he could choose, he would probably rather work at the other end. Causing trouble and trying to get undesirable discussions to spin so far out of control that the moderator had to shut them down. Unfortunately he hadn't been allocated an attack troll yet, they were managed by his colleagues at the bank of desks to his right.

Not that he'd had that many jobs, but this was one of the best of them, if not *the* best.

His workmates were okay, the money was more than decent and he got on pretty well with Frank. As he found his feet his fear of being uncovered gradually subsided. The only person who still gave him bad vibes was Philip Argos. He was an imposing figure, no doubt about that, and he seemed sharp as a razor. Everyone who had spent any time working with Philip had something like admiration on their faces when they talked about him. Maybe that wasn't so odd – Philip Argos was clearly a charismatic leader. But not just that, he was also really . . .

Unnerving! That was the best word she could think of to describe him.

Even though she had basically only seen his back and met his gaze in the mirror, he radiated something that both scared and appealed to her.

Control.

That was it.

This man had complete control – both over himself and over the world around him. He was usually already on the running machine by the time she arrived at the gym just after seven, which meant he was an early-riser. Her exercise sessions usually lasted just under an hour, and on most occasions the man was still there when she left. At least one and half hours on the machine, in other words, which at the speed he went must mean something like thirty kilometres of concentrated running.

Only once had she seen him interrupt his session. She had been warming up on one of the cross-trainers, and when she glanced over at him as she usually did, he suddenly stepped off the machine. For a moment she thought he'd seen her looking and was on his way over to her. But before she had time to analyse what she felt about this impending contact, he had turned away to answer a mobile phone that had been in front of him.

It must have been an important call to make him interrupt his session, and she couldn't help switching off her iPod and trying to listen to what he was saying. But to her disappointment he was talking quietly, almost whispering, and in a language she didn't understand either.

It sounded like French . . .

15

Bee handlers

Pillars of Society forum
Posted: 27 November, 17:44
By: **MayBey**

. . . yanked open the driver's door and emptied the pepper-spray in his face. Then dragged him onto the road. Baton out. Almost bent it. Then we let the dog loose.
The bastard shat himself. God, what a stink.
Had to wrap him in the vomit-sheet.
And drive in with the windows down.
Instant justice, you could say.

This post has 69 comments

'Sure – no problem, Frank, I'll find it . . . See you there!'

He ended the call, tossed his mobile on the bed and dashed for the little wardrobe. Beige chinos and a neatly ironed shirt – that was the sort of thing his Manga character would wear for a bonding session with his workmates.

It was Friday evening and he'd been starting to wonder

if he ought to get in touch with Becca. He missed her more than he was prepared to admit. But last time he got her mixed up in the Game he almost managed to kill her – quite literally, in fact.

Talking of the Game . . .

That morning when he woke up the phone was on the little writing desk.

After a few moments of blind panic he suddenly remembered that he'd taken it out when he'd got up for a pee during the night. But he couldn't quite remember why . . .

Bloody lucky that there was no charge left in it, anyway . . .

He was suddenly interrupted by a cautious knock at the door.

Strange: he hadn't ordered any grub, and the cleaner only came once a week.

He put the safety-chain on and carefully opened the door. A skinny little man in oversized pilot's glasses, Brylcreamed grey hair and a Hep Stars t-shirt nodded at him.

'Hi. I'm out of fags and got no money. Wondered if I could cadge a couple . . .?'

HP looked at the man in amusement. Who the hell was this? Rock-granddad?

The bloke seemed distinctly unthreatening, and for some reason it just didn't feel right to slam the door shut in his face.

'Sure, come in . . .'

He took the safety chain off and opened the door wide.

'Cheers!' the man nodded when HP, in a sudden attack of generosity handed him an unopened packet of Marlboros.

'I'm Nox. You're new here, aren't you?'

HP opened his mouth to reply, but after a couple of seconds' reflection he shut it again without saying anything but an indistinct mumble. However much he might have liked to chat to this funny little gnome, he realized that this wasn't the time. If this whole undercover routine was going to work, he had to avoid making up any more lies than was strictly necessary. It was hard enough to keep track of the ones he was juggling at work, and now all of a sudden he regretted opening the door. He seemed to have a serious problem with his impulse control . . .

'Okay, cool, man. You're not the type of guy who wants to say much, I respect that.'

Nox, as rock-granddad evidently wanted to be called, put his hand to his chest.

'But if there's anything you need, just knock on my door, down at number twenty-four.'

He gestured along the narrow corridor.

'I'm one of the regulars, yeah . . .'

HP nodded thoughtfully.

Maybe he could squeeze something useful out of this little Nescafé visit.

'I suppose you have a pretty good idea of who lives here . . .?' he began. '. . . who comes and goes, I mean?'

'Of course! You, for instance, have been here almost three weeks, and social services came past with a couple of new arrivals the day before yesterday . . .'

'Great, look, maybe you can do me a favour and keep an eye out for me? If anything unusual happens, I mean. People who don't seem to fit it, and so on . . .'

'Only people who don't fit in live in a place like this . . .' Nox grinned. 'But I get what you mean.'

HP tossed him another packet of fags and the funny little man caught it midair. On his way out he tapped his nose with one finger.

'Just say if you need anything, man, Nox is at your service!'

'Okay,' HP said hesitantly. 'Well, maybe I could ask another favour . . .?'

Nox stopped in the doorway.

'It might be worth a couple of cartons.'

'Sure, you name it! . . .'

'You see, I need help to store something. There's something I need to get out of the house, if you get what I mean . . .'

'Aren't you Rebecca? Rebecca Pettersson? Erland's daughter?'

He was standing on the pavement right in front of her and she had no choice but to stop. An older gentleman in a dark overcoat and hat.

'Normén,' she mumbled as she tried to work out who the man was.

'Of course, yes, how silly of me. You changed your name after your mother . . . You don't recognize me, do you?'

She looked at him carefully. He was slightly taller than her, around 1.80 metres, and at a guess somewhere round sixty.

There was undeniably something familiar about the man's posture and stiff features, but she couldn't quite place him. He was probably one of her father's colleagues from the reserve unit.

'Tage, Tage Sammer, but you and your brother used to call me Uncle Tage. You came to stay at my summer cottage up in Rättvik years ago, if you remember?'

He smiled and something in his look made her do the same.

'Of course, yes,' she said through her smile. 'Uncle Tage, how are you?'

'Very well, thanks. I was just going to ask you the same thing?'

‘Fine, thanks,’ she lied.

‘Are you still working for the Security Police?’

She was taken aback, and he seemed to notice.

‘Your father had a lot of friends, Rebecca, and we’ve done our best to keep an eye on you both. As a last favour to Erland. He would have been so proud of you, you were always his favourite.’

He smiled again and suddenly she felt a little lump starting to form in her throat.

She swallowed to get rid of it.

‘By the way, I’m sorry I couldn’t come to your mother’s funeral,’ he went on. ‘We sent a wreath, I hope it arrived?’

She nodded, she could remember the wreath clearly.

A last farewell from your old friends.

‘I was on service abroad in Africa. Unfortunately I was injured and was unable to travel . . .’

He nodded at his leg, and only now did she notice the stick in his right hand.

‘A very sad story, both your dad and your mum,’ he went on. ‘Erland didn’t deserve to be taken from us so early. And certainly not under those circumstances . . .’

She frowned and opened her mouth to say something, but he interrupted her.

‘Well, it was very nice to bump into you like this, Rebecca.’

He put his hand in his inside pocket and took out a neat little business card.

‘Feel free to get in touch, it would make an old man very happy.’

‘I promise, Uncle Tage.’

They shook hands, then, acting on impulse, she took a step forward and gave him a quick peck on the cheek. He smelled of cigars and aftershave, almost exactly the same smell as her dad, and for a few seconds the lump was back again.

'By the way,' he said just before they parted. 'Your brother, Henrik, do you ever hear from him?'

'So, Manga, Frank says you're our new hotshot down in the Mine . . .'

Their party had been put in a separate room some way from the entrance, which suited HP perfectly.

His role as Manga may have been good enough to fool strangers, but he wasn't sure if people who knew him would be as easily deceived. But on the other hand neither his nor Manga's friends tended to hang out at posh places like this.

They had finished eating, and had already got through several beers. All the departmental bosses apart from the Goth Queen were there. Unfortunately HP had arrived too late to be able to sit next to Rilke. Instead he had to make do with Beens, who seemed to have loosened up already with a few pints.

But it didn't matter much. The guy obviously liked talking almost as much as he liked drinking beer.

'Yep, it's going pretty well. Interesting company, ArgosEye!' HP gave Beens a crooked smile and tried to sound humble.

'Mmm, the company's quite an unusual workplace, but I'm sure you've already worked that out. Hardly anyone ever leaves – at least not voluntarily. All of us here have been there from the start.'

Beens pointed at the others round the table.

'Dejan and Rilke have worked with Anna for almost ten years, and Stoffe, who'll be back in a couple of weeks, came over with Philip from Burston. Frank and I worked together for another company but Anna recruited us at roughly the same time. Our little gang has more or less built ArgosEye from the ground up. We're actually all partners – Philip's idea.'

Beens's garlic breath was no trifling matter, and to make matters worse he was the sort who liked to lean a bit *too* close when he talked, but HP grinned and bore it.

'I don't think I got the chance to meet Anna . . .?' he attempted, then held his breath.

Dejan shook his head and took a couple of gulps from his glass of beer.

This was the first time anyone had even mentioned Anna's name, and HP hadn't been able to resist the temptation. Damn, this clearly wasn't the right moment to start talking about the dead . . .

Beens put his glass down and wiped his mouth with the back of his hand.

'No, we don't see much of her since she and Philip got divorced . . .'

HP jerked involuntarily, and shuffled on his chair in an attempt to disguise the fact.

'Ouch. The bad sort of divorce?' he went on, trying to project just the right level of interest.

'You could say that. Neither of them is really the compromising type . . .'

The waitress walked past and HP gestured to her to bring another round.

Did Beens really not know that Anna was dead, or was he just putting it on?

It was impossible to tell.

'So did things get better once Anna pulled out?' he went on, as neutrally as he could.

Beens shrugged his shoulders.

'I'm not sure that she *pulled out*, exactly, but with her gone Philip can run the company the way he wants.

'The way we all want,' he added, draining his glass. 'The only problem is that Anna still owns a share of the company. As long as that's the case, we can't . . .'

Beens stopped abruptly and HP noticed Rilke giving him a quick look. The others round the table also seemed to have heard the comment – conversation around them suddenly died away. But instead of staying quiet Beens tried to make good his mistake.

'Look . . . don't get me wrong. Anna's been bloody important for the company. But, I mean, really . . .'

He held his hands out in front of him, as though hoping the others would agree with him.

'. . . in purely business terms, everyone stands to gain if she vanished for good.'

16

Whispers, rumours and reports

Pillars of Society forum
Posted: 30 November, 10:53
By: **MayBey**

Little Regina Righteous has really messed things up for herself.
Rumour suggests her boss had an affair with the wife of a certain Internal Investigator. If I were Regina, I'd have a lot of trouble sleeping these days . . .

This post has 23 comments

Rebecca read the post several times before the words actually sank in.

She pushed her chair back half a metre, then sat there rocking on it as she made up her mind.

What a fucking mess she'd got caught up in. Okay, so she only had herself to blame for most of it. Instead of simply showing up quietly at the interview, she ought to have taken along the union and a sharp lawyer. And put a bit of pressure on those Internal Investigation vultures right from the start, not played along with their little game. Then she'd most likely have escaped this whole disaster.

And she should have stood her ground much more firmly within the department, particularly after they returned from Darfur. She should have insisted on them doing the debriefing together as a team, whether or not she was suspected of any wrongdoing. But, just like when Runeberg persuaded her to take the job as head of the unit, she had been too busy proving what a good girl she was. Nodding and not saying anything and sticking to her role as over-achieving Rebecca, the way everyone expected her to, while the rest of the world evidently did whatever they felt like.

God, she was so sick of herself!

'Can you stay on this evening, Manga? There's a big job on the way and we need to start by rolling out a bit of artificial grass.'

HP had no idea what his boss was talking about, but nodded anyway. But Frank picked up on his hesitation.

'Artificial grass, Astroturf, yeah? We roll out a carpet of opinion via a number of different channels, and try to get other people to play along, as part of the plan, on our turf, so to speak . . .'

'Cool!' HP said, even though he still wasn't quite sure what this was all about. 'So what's the message?'

'Lower VAT leads to more jobs. You can probably guess who the client is,' Frank grinned.

'No problem, I'm up for it, I can go all night if necessary!'

'Great! Philip usually comes down to check, so tonight we really need to be on top of our game.'

'So you lied to me about Westergren . . .!?'

He flew up from his chair behind the desk, rushed past her and closed the door to his office.

'Calm down, for God's sake, Rebecca, people can hear you!' he hissed, taking hold of her arm.

She shook his hand off.

'I've got no intention of calming down until you tell me what the hell you're up to. You lied to me about Westergren. You and his wife . . .'

His eyes suddenly turned black and she stopped. For a couple of seconds they stood facing each other, exchanging angry glares.

'Sit down,' he ordered, pointing at a chair.

Rebecca folded her arms.

'Sit down!' he repeated, louder this time, but she still didn't move from the spot.

Her boss let out a deep sigh.

'Please, sit down, Becca,' he said in a considerably friendlier voice, and this time she did as he asked. She sat down exaggeratedly slowly on the chair.

Runeberg returned to his side of the desk.

'You look tired. Do you want anything, coffee, tea . . .?'

She shook her head.

'Okay . . .' he said. 'What have you heard, and who from?'

'Three, two, one. GO, GO, GO!!'

Ten keyboards began to clatter at almost exactly the same moment. The tame trolls were set loose and gradually began to roll out the artificial turf over the pitch. Twenty different discussion forums were the targets. Eight newspapers, five political websites and seven general discussion boards. All the trolls were supposed to post short comments that either supported lowering the rate of tax, or attacked their opponents' arguments.

HP was in his element. He'd worked out that a special program bounced their comments off a load of different servers out in cyberspace, spreading their posts among a mass of different IP addresses so that they all looked genuine. As if the grassroots really had risen up to push this particular issue. The blog gang would join in over the next few days, and probably a couple of the newspaper columnists that had been bought and paid for. Then they just needed the radio and television news to pick up on it, and the game would become reality and their artificial turf would be transformed into a real grass pitch.

'This is the nine o'clock news. In the past few days an increasing number of voices have been raised calling for the VAT rate to be lowered. Now the government has responded with a proposal . . .'

He hadn't had this much fun since . . . Well, he didn't actually know how long it had been.

What he and the others in the office were engaged in was nothing more than a massive scam, a manipulation of public opinion on a huge scale that he was absolutely delighted to be part of. That feeling of having the upper hand, not just over your average Svensson, but the whole media elite. Being part of something bigger, something smarter, that only a few select individuals were aware of.

Such a familiar feeling, but still so fucking sweet!

He let his fingers dance over the keyboard, sending out troll after troll to grab their part of the turf. Making comments and contributions according to the script Frank had handed out.

'If VAT on restaurants was lower, more people could afford to eat out . . .'

Enter, bang, switch windows and onto the next troll.

'I'd be able to employ at least three more people if we had lower tax . . .'

Send, then Alt+tab.

'My employer couldn't afford to take me on fulltime after my probationary period . . .'

'Calm down, Manga,' his boss called from his desk.

But HP wasn't listening. He opened new cages, letting more tame trolls loose, and sending them out into the fray at once.

'Erik Hagström', 'Millan S', '50cParty', 'L Berntsen' and 'Benjyboy' all made their cyber voices heard before he quickly rushed to the next cellblock.

'Hatta42', 'Stefan Johnsson', 'TronGuy' and 'VAO'.

Setting them all free.

'Manga, slow down, the rest us can't keep up . . .'

Beads of sweat began to form on his brow but HP didn't notice. His fingers were flying over the keyboard. Another set, even more voices added to the crowd. He'd long since given up following the script.

'Down with VAT on bars!'

Send!

'It's the small businesses that keep our economy afloat . . .'

Post!

'Completely agree with the previous post . . .'

Comment!

'Nurture, not neuter!'

Add!

'Time to fight the tax monster . . .'

Enter!

Then back to the stable for reinforcements. New recruits he had created himself specifically for an occasion like this.

'Knotty', 'Lisel8' and 'DPtr0t'.

Their voices melded together in his head, becoming a single carpet of noise. Sweat was pouring off him, tickling his eyebrows, but instead of stopping typing he leaned his head forward and wiped his brow on his shirtsleeve.

There, done!

New window – new voices. Fuck, this was cool! He was the Lord of Astroturf. The buzziest bee in the hive. Troll-handler with a capital T. Per fucking Gynt, that was who he was . . .

'MANGA!!'

HP looked up from his screen reluctantly. The room was completely silent and Philip Argos was standing in the doorway.

'My office in ten minutes,' he said abruptly, pointing at HP.

'It really isn't as black and white as you seem to think,' Runeberg muttered. 'Therese and I had known each other since Police Academy, we used to flirt back then, I suppose you could say. But nothing ever came of it.'

He looked at her as if he was expecting some sort of reaction, but when he got none he went on.

'In the second term she got together with Per and we used to hang out together. Not that we were best friends or anything . . .' Another look that went unanswered.

'Either way,' he continued, 'after the Academy Per and I were allocated to the same law and order unit. I would bump into Therese every now and then, and the flirting never quite stopped even though we both got married eventually to other people. A couple of years later we ended up on the same UN mission, and . . . well . . .'

He shrugged.

'When you're a long way from home and experiencing a whole load of shit together, it's easy to get close to someone. A bit too close, maybe . . .'

He shifted uneasily on his chair, as if the seat were chafing against his massive body.

'When we got home Therese wanted us to carry on, she wanted us to leave our partners and move in together, but I didn't want to. My kids were small, and to be honest . . .'

He sighed.

'Therese was fairly brittle right from the start, and that UN mission hadn't made things any better. I suppose I'd . . .'

'. . . got bored,' she finished, in a surprisingly firm voice.

Philip's office was on the nineteenth floor.

Even though that was only one floor above theirs, the lift-journey seemed to take forever.

He and Frank were leaning against opposite walls, each of them doing his best not to meet the other's gaze.

This really was a mistake of biblical proportions. What in the name of holy hell had he been thinking?

Dressing up and applying for a job under a false name so that he could single-handedly try to solve some fucking murder mystery? Seriously, who the hell did he think he was? Nancy fucking Drew?

Didn't he have enough problems already without actively trying to add a few more?

And he didn't even have the sense to keep a low profile either . . .

Great work, HP!

The lift doors opened, they got out and Frank pointed at a glass door with the company logo, exactly the same as on their own floor.

There would usually have been a receptionist sitting there, but at this time of evening the door was locked and Frank had to knock.

'Our passcards don't work up here,' he hissed at HP. 'Only Philip, his secretary and the twin detectives have access.'

'The twin what?'

'Shh, for God's sake, not so loud! You'll see . . .'

The door was opened by a man with short red hair, also dressed in a suit that clung to his large body like a glove.

'Hi, Elroy. Philip asked us to come up.'

Frank took half a pace forward but was almost left with his foot in the air when the red-haired man made no sign of moving.

'Not you, just him,' he muttered, nodding at HP.

Frank opened his mouth to protest, but stopped himself.

'Well, good luck . . .' he said quietly from the corner of his mouth as HP walked past him.

The reception area looked the same as the one on the floor below. A small, stylish waiting area with a few leather and tubular steel chairs, plus the usual selection of lifestyle magazines. Then a reception desk made of sand-blasted glass and, behind that, a couple of small meeting rooms. But apart from that, this floor looked very different. Instead of an airy, open-plan office divided only by glass walls, here there was just a locked steel door with a card-reader at one side.

The discreet little spherical camera was similar to those on the floor below, but because the ceiling was lower here it was so prominent that HP almost imagined he could see its lens adjusting as it followed their movements.

He gulped hard a couple of times, but his mouth still felt horribly dry.

Instead of taking out a card, the red-haired man simply raised his right thumb to the reader. The little red lamp switched to green and HP heard the lock whirring. For some reason he couldn't suppress a shudder.

17

The hive

'The complaint then, what about that?'

'I don't quite understand what you mean, Becca . . .?'

'The official complaint about misuse of office, do you know who's responsible for that?'

He squirmed again.

'Of course I know.'

'So who was it, then? Sixten Gladh?'

'No, in purely formal terms it was actually me . . .'

She stood up from her chair.

'Fuck, that's low, Ludvig . . .!'

'Calm down, Becca, for God's sake!'

He held his hands out.

'It's nothing personal, if that's what you're thinking.'

She glared at him, without sitting back down.

'Okay, just think about it, Becca, and try to forget that we know each other. Paragraph nine of the Police Act, does that sound familiar? If a police officer becomes aware of a crime that is liable to prosecution, he or she is obliged to report it . . . Does that ring any bells? To be honest, I thought you already knew this, but you don't seem to be quite yourself . . .'

She carried on glaring at him.

'Okay, try this: after your incident in Darfur my phone was ringing constantly with people from the Foreign Ministry claiming that you were guilty of all sorts of things. So what do you think I should have done? Put a lid on it? Pretend nothing had happened? A couple of days later Gladh and the Foreign Ministry gang would have had us both swinging from the gallows . . .'

He looked at her, as though he were expecting her to say something.

'Go on!' she said curtly.

'The conclusion I came to, and I still believe it was the right one, by the way, was that if a police officer is suspected of a crime then a report has to be filed and the ensuing investigation will determine what happened. That's the normal procedure for incidents of this nature, and anything else would have looked very strange. So I asked Ann-Margret to raise a brief preliminary report, officially instigated by me.'

He gestured towards the area outside his office, where the department's civilian secretary had her desk.

'It wasn't until much later that I discovered that the case had ended up on Per Westergren's desk, and realized what a tricky situation I'd inadvertently landed you in. Having my name on the report was hardly going to help, and obviously it was stupid of me to suggest coming in as your witness, I realized that just a couple of minutes into the interview. But by then it was already too late . . .'

A large open-plan office with subdued lighting. But unlike the floor below, which was a hive of activity, this one had just two desks in the middle of the room. The contrast between the vast, darkened room and these two illuminated workplaces made everything look very odd, almost surreal.

At one of the desks a tall, broad-shouldered woman was bent over a computer screen. HP was taken aback and almost came to a stop. He didn't know if it was the way she sat, the suit or her sharp features that fooled him, but the woman at the desk actually looked like Rebecca.

The illusion lasted no more than a second. As he got closer he realized that the woman's hair was much fairer, actually it was red, and she was much more like the red-haired man walking ahead of him than Rebecca. He guessed that they were brother and sister, probably twins, if Frank's nickname meant anything.

As they walked past the woman looked up from her screen. HP gave her a short nod but she made no attempt to return the greeting, she just stared at him.

There was something about the way she looked at him that made him feel uneasy, and he took a couple of quicker steps to catch up with his guide.

The red-haired man whom Frank had called Elroy pressed his thumb against another reader beside a frosted glass door. He let HP through.

'Wait here,' he said tersely.

Surely you see that you can't treat me like this?!!

Oh yes, she certainly could, and right now she was finally angry enough to dump him once and for all.

Maybe it wasn't nice, but a quick end was best for both of them. Anyway, what was there to talk about? They were each being unfaithful, they each had a partner they were lying to. And what for?

Love?

Hardly – at least not from her side.

All they had shared were a few sweaty orgasms on the floor of an empty flat.

Secret meetings that made life more bearable but which neither of them was really prepared to pick up the tab for. And besides, she had started to get bored.

Recriminations, jealousy and wounded feelings were the last thing she needed . . .

Just stop it! We're both adults.
It's over – full stop!!

The two exterior walls were basically huge windows offering a fantastic view over Stockholm city centre. There was red lettering on Kulturhuset, blue from the Sergel arcade and the square far below him, and, high above to the left, the illuminated clock of the NK department store.

The hands said it was exactly seven o'clock, and for a moment HP's heart almost skipped a beat.

But it took him just a couple of seconds to regain control of his racing imagination.

The hands were showing seven o'clock – not because anyone had stopped the clock, but because it *was* actually seven o'clock in the evening.

He took a couple of steps into the room. Philip Argos's desk was almost entirely empty. Two linked computer screens, a keyboard and a wireless mouse – that was all. The same almost clinical state applied to the rest of the room. There wasn't any sign of habitation, not a single loose sheet of paper or post-it note or abandoned coffee-cup.

The left-hand wall was covered with framed certificates hung in laser-straight rows, and the white wall-to-wall carpet must have been washed regularly seeing as it showed no trace of having ever been walked on, let alone had coffee spilt on it.

In one corner was a set of white leather sofas. Five leadership magazines were laid out in a perfect, zen-like fan on the little coffee-table. The top one had Philip Argos himself on the cover. 'The Man in Control', declared the caption. The precision of the room made HP feel even more uncomfortable, and he couldn't resist the temptation to nudge at the magazines, just a bit, to make the room seem slightly more human.

As he was doing that, he noticed two small, framed photographs above the sofa. The first was black and white, and showed Philip Argos with the man whose name was evidently Elroy. They were both wearing berets and camouflage uniform, crouching down with their arms round each other's shoulders, smiling at the camera.

The other photograph was of a chalk-white beach, the outlines of a few dark palm trees, and a blood-red sunset which – apart from the magazines – appeared to provide the only splash of colour in the monochrome room.

The picture intrigued HP, and he walked round the coffee-table to take a closer look. The photograph actually looked like . . .

'Marmaris,' a dry voice said behind HP, making him jump.

'W-what?'

Philip Argos pointed at the picture.

'That's the view from my villa in Marmaris. In Turkey,' he clarified. 'I go there as often as I can to unwind. It's a good place to fill your soul with positive energy . . .'

'Aha, okay! I – I was just admiring the colours,' HP muttered.

'Sit yourself down, Magnus.' Philip gestured towards

the leather sofa. 'Would you like anything to drink? Water, tea?'

HP realized his mouth was bone-dry.

'Water, please.'

He glanced up at Philip, but the expression on his face gave no clue about what was to come.

Philip pulled out his mobile phone from a holster on his belt, but instead of dialling a number he just pressed a button on the side, then spoke into it as if it were a microphone.

'Sophie, would you mind bringing in some mineral water for me and Magnus.'

He let go of the button and waited a moment. The mobile let out two distinct bleeps.

Philip returned it to its holster and sat down in the armchair opposite HP. He adjusted the journals on the table, crossed one leg over the other and leaned back. Then he smiled, and for the second time that evening HP couldn't help shivering.

'Magnus . . . that is your name, isn't it?'

18

Oh what a tangled web we weave . . .

Fucking hell – his cover was blown!

'Er . . . what?!' he mumbled, trying to win a bit of time.

Philip Argos smiled again – an unsettling, reptilian leer that made the hair on the back of HP's neck stand up.

'I said, your real name isn't really Magnus Sandström, is it?'

'Er . . . N-no . . .' HP managed to say as he desperately ran through his options.

He'd been found out and he was stuck on the nineteenth floor. The door was closed and outside stood the society of red-heads. Both siblings looked like they would be capable of causing him a fair degree of physical harm – not to mention Philip Argos himself. The man looked like a rattlesnake working out how best to attack an unusually stupid desert rat . . .

'Did you really think we wouldn't check you out properly? I mean, a person with your sort of reputation and experience . . .?' Philip chuckled.

HP shrugged and adopted a resigned face to gain a few more seconds thinking time. In the harsh light of hindsight the whole of his undercover project looked more insane than ever.

What the hell had he been thinking? That he could just waltz in through the door in his cheap suit and even cheaper disguise and, hey presto, would suddenly get access to a whole load of secrets?

He glanced over at the door again. Through the frosted glass he thought he could make out the twins' threatening silhouettes. As if they were waiting out there, ready to jump him the moment their boss pressed the button . . .

'It didn't take a great deal of digging to unmask you,' Philip Argos went on. 'Like I said, you do have something of a reputation . . . We're very careful here at ArgosEye. Trust is good, but making certain is, as I'm sure you've already heard, always preferable . . .'

Philip Argos smiled another rattlesnake smile and HP made a brave attempt to return it.

All aboard! The next train to fucksville is about to depart from platform four!

'Farook Al-Hassan!'

'W-what?'

'Farook Al-Hassan, that's what you're called these days, isn't it?'

Philip gave him a encouraging nod.

'S-sure . . .' HP stammered after a couple of seconds of confused thought.

'Of course . . .' he added as his grin grew gradually wider. 'But you can carry on calling me Manga if you like. I'm not too fussy about that. When you apply for jobs Manga sounds a bit better, if you see what I mean . . .?'

Philip Argos nodded.

'It wouldn't have made any difference here. We go by people's abilities, not what their surnames happen to be, but obviously I respect your wishes. To tell you the truth, you impressed me the moment I saw your CV. On paper you were precisely the sort of person we needed here at the company, someone who knows what he's doing and is prepared to do whatever it takes to grow in line with the business. That's why I asked the others to take special care of you from day one . . .'

HP really was trying not to, but he still couldn't stop grinning. His disguise was still intact. His cover wasn't blown. In fact it even looked as if he might be heading for . . .

'. . . promotion,' Philip Argos went on. 'From what I saw down in the Mine this evening, it would be foolish of me not to give you the chance to develop further. My job as a boss is to seek out talented individuals and help them to reach their full potential. That's how you build up a successful enterprize . . .'

HP was nodding as if he knew exactly what Philip Argos meant. His grin was still glued to his face, but not only because he felt so relieved. There was something about Philip's style and way of talking that appealed to him.

'I'm going to let you move around a bit, find out how everything works, then when an opportunity arises you'll be in the front line to take the step up,' Philip went on, before being interrupted by a short knock.

The door opened and the strapping tall red-head whose name was evidently Sophie came in with a tray. As she put the glasses and bottles on the table she gave HP a quick but considerably less hostile look than before, and HP caught himself extending his vulpine grin in her direction.

'Thanks, Sophie,' Philip Argos said when she was almost finished.

He took hold of her elbow with one hand. An odd gesture that seemed simultaneously intimate and stern, and she turned her face towards her boss at once, almost like a dog waiting for orders from its master.

'You can tell Elroy to have the car ready in ten minutes. We'll be dropping off Fa . . . I mean Magnus here on the way home.'

Sophie nodded and gave HP another glance before she left the room. This time he could have sworn he caught a hint of a smile.

She undid all three locks on the door of the flat, taking the opportunity to inspect both the door and frame. But, just as before, there were no signs of any attempted break-in.

She locked the door behind her and peered into the living room. The mattress and bedclothes were still on the floor where they had left them. She rolled the whole lot up into a bundle and tied it up with a length of nylon rope.

She had no intention of ever using any of them again, so it would be just as well to dump the whole lot down in the garbage room in the basement. A fitting end to the affair. Fucking a colleague on a thin mattress in an empty flat, and – even worse – a notorious lady's man whom she had seduced at a staff party. Things really didn't get any more sordid than that.

She put the rolled-up mattress in the hall and took a last walk around the flat. The bedroom door was closed and when she opened it a waft of stagnant air hit her. She took a couple of steps towards the window to air the room, and was about halfway there when she realized that there was another sort of smell in there.

It reminded her of aftershave.

He had asked them to drop him off by a Seven-Eleven some way from the hotel, claiming he had to get some shopping. Elroy the gorilla was in the driver's seat, with his twin sister beside him. HP and Philip Argos were sitting next to each other on the capacious back seat.

'Thirty thousand terabytes, do you know how much that is? Of course you know, Farook, how stupid of me. I almost forgot who I'm talking to!' Philip chuckled. 'Thirty million, billion bytes, that's how much information flows through the internet every hour, at least according to some sources. Thirty million, billion letters, numbers and other signifiers, carrying all manner of information. Three thousand hours of new film clips on YouTube, over five thousand new blog-posts or tweets. Two hundred thousand new user profiles on all sorts of social forums. All in just one measly little hour. It's a dizzying thought, isn't it?'

HP nodded. Dizzying was one word for it . . .

He was feeling giddy, almost a bit high.

'Most people, including politicians and leaders, have no idea about how astonishingly comprehensive the torrent of information out there actually is,' Philip went on. 'But if anyone dares even breathe the word *surveillance* there are instant, massive protests. Of course people always think of the National Defence Radio Centre, the National Security Agency and other state organizations . . .'

He shook his head.

'But of course that's actually completely wrong, in democratic countries, at least. The state is usually only bothered about what a tiny little group have to say on a certain, extremely narrow subject area. But big business, on the other hand . . .'

He waved his hand towards the world outside the car.

'. . . is interested in what almost everyone has to say, especially if it's got anything to do with patterns of consumption or perception of their cherished trademarks.

That type of information is everywhere out there, the whole net is basically overflowing with it, and why? Because most people hand out that sort of information entirely voluntarily by clicking a little box at the bottom of a page, or, even better, by taking the initiative and posting their opinions and preferences on one of the plethora of forums available to them. In other words, modern, freedom-loving, integrity-cherishing human beings map out themselves down to the most private little detail. Not even George Orwell could have predicted a scenario like this . . .'

A short bleep from Philip's belt-holster signalled that he'd got a message, but he had warmed to his theme so much that he didn't even seem to notice.

'The internet is positively groaning with information that people are forcing on each other. Favourite television programmes, films and books, religious and political opinions, the kids' Christmas presents or what they made for dinner. And why? Well, all because the vast majority of us are longing for just one thing.'

'Affirmation,' HP muttered.

'Exactly! We're getting more and more dependent on having other people tell us how smart or attractive or clever we are. What a wonderful life we've built up, with our lovely partners and wonderful children, and how happy our lives are in comparison to other people's. People who have the wrong sense of humour, eat the wrong food, wear the wrong clothes, live in the wrong sort of house, raise their children wrong or simply have the wrong opinions in general . . .'

He leaned over to HP's side of the seat.

'Basically anything that's worth knowing is already out there, and all you need is a way of filtering the torrent for the type of information that could be of use to potential clients.'

HP was nodding with more and more interest.

'The advantage that the authorities and those in power have had for almost four hundred years when it comes to information has been demolished. Information no longer flows from the top down, but in every other direction as well.

'Thousands upon thousands of people can communicate directly with each other within a matter of seconds, without having to ask anyone for permission. None of the old truths apply any more, everything can be questioned, changed or rejected. The rules of the game have changed forever, and anyone who doesn't realize this is doomed to fall. Just look at north Africa.'

Philip paused briefly and glanced out of the window before going on.

'What we offer our clients is a way of handling and preventing crises by constantly monitoring everything that is said about them, and by whom. Giving them a way to stop any snowball before it turns into an avalanche, if you see what I mean?'

He gestured towards the snow outside, which seemed to be falling harder now.

Oh yes, HP understood all right, but Philip's pause was so brief that he didn't have time to say anything. Instead he went on listening with growing fascination.

'But,' Philip went on, 'once our clients have got detailed information about the mechanisms at work on the net, the daily mechanisms that have a direct effect on the bottom line of their accounts, it doesn't usually take long before they ask for the next step . . .'

'Control,' HP suggested.

'Exactly, my friend!' Philip Argos grinned another of his reptilian smiles. 'And that's where our unique services come into the picture. Because when you strip away all the fine words, the policy documents and elegant phrases, that's exactly what it all comes down to in the end . . .'

Control!

That was what she was lacking. Lacking – and longing for!

She had let the situation control her instead of the other way round. Clearly she should have behaved differently at her interview, that much was almost painfully obvious now . . . She hadn't done anything wrong, and had actually probably saved a whole lot of people's lives.

And how had the world thanked her?

By suspending her and accusing her of various offences – colleagues looking askance at her, and, last but by no means least, a boss who hadn't exactly put much effort into supporting her. On the contrary, he had actually contributed to making her position even worse. It was high time to take matters into her own hands, and try to work out how all the pieces fitted into the puzzle.

She had put off doing so for too long.

She thought of Henke suddenly. Should she start with Henke if she was going to get a grip on her present difficulty? But she hadn't heard from him in over a year. Not since he sent her that package. Six bolts. Six rusty bolts that turned her whole life upside down. And set her free. She had thought she killed Dag, but those bolts meant she hadn't after all.

She thought of Henke a lot.

None of the phone numbers he used to have seemed to work anymore.

The same thing applied to his email and messenger . . .

She stamped the snow from her boots and closed the door of the flat behind her. Right now Micke was the only good thing in her life, and seeing as Henke wasn't around she would have to start there if she was going to stand any chance of getting back on her feet. Even if she hadn't exactly been treating him well, he had at least always been there for her.

Maybe he would understand, she certainly hoped so. Either way, she owed him the truth. The whole truth, not just the crumbs she had been feeding him so far.

But the flat was empty and silent. No shoes and no jacket in the hall telling her that he was home.

On the kitchen table she found a note.

Think we need a break.
Call me when you're ready.
/M

She didn't know whether to laugh or cry . . .

Her mobile suddenly bleeped and she almost ran back into the hall to get it from her jacket pocket.

But the text wasn't from Micke.

Just got home?

She began to type a snotty reply but stopped herself. Without turning on the lights in the living room, she crept over to the window, pressed close to the curtain, then peered down at the narrow street. Parked cars lined up, just like every other evening. A thin layer of snow on their bonnets let on that they had been there for a while.

A tiny point of light among the shadows in the park on the other side of the street brought her up short.

The glow from a cigarette.

There was someone standing there.

Someone who was watching her flat.

19

Buzzy bees

Pillars of Society forum
Posted: 6 December, 08:48
By: **MayBey**

I've heard a rumour that everyone's favourite bodyguard, Regina Righteous, is at her most accomplished between the sheets. Apparently there's a little shag-pad on Söder.
Anyone know anything about that?

This post has 23 comments

'There, Mr Sandström, I think we're done.'

The little man with the tape-measure still had a couple of pins in the corner of his mouth, but this evidently didn't stop him from sounding just the right sort of servile for HP.

Mr Sandström – very nice!

He had just been measured for a suit, as well as a number of matching shirts. This wasn't the first time he'd done this, but this tailor spoke the rather posh, nasal Östermalm dialect of Swedish, not Thai English. Of course the bills wouldn't look very similar either, but money was actually the least of his problems right now.

He had transferred more than enough funds from the Cayman Islands, and his first wages were on their way as well.

'Ready in a week,' the man concluded, handing him a receipt. 'Mr Argos's acquaintances take priority,' he added when he saw the look of surprise on HP's face.

'But I'm afraid we can't do any better than a week.'

HP left the little shop and waved down a taxi.

He leaned back in the seat and took a deep breath. He could definitely get used to this life.

She was woken by the doorbell.

Long, persistent rings, and it took her a while to pull on her jogging trousers and a top.

A delivery of some sort, she thought as she opened the door after checking the peephole.

'Hi, are you Rebecca Normén?'

'Yes, what's this about?'

'Delivery from Interflora.'

The man handed her what looked like a well-wrapped bouquet of flowers. She took it and nudged the paper aside to get at the card.

Red roses, at least a dozen, if not more.

She read the card. Then she handed the bouquet back.

'You can take them away again,' she said.

'W-what?'

'The flowers, I don't want them, so you can take them back.'

'B-but, er . . .'

The man seemed confused.

‘They’ve been paid for and everything, I don’t know how . . .’

‘Not my problem,’ she said. ‘You’re welcome to return them to the sender. Then he might finally get the message . . .’

‘Nice of Frank to loan out his big star for a couple of days. You’re supposed to be Philip’s new golden boy.’

Rilke winked at him and HP found himself blushing against his wishes.

God, he was still such a fucking approval junkie! Even though he was a superhero it was enough to get the slightest little pat on the shoulder from someone he respected or had the hots for, and there he was, wagging his tail like a fucking cocker spaniel . . .

‘S-so, what exactly do you do over in your corner?’ he muttered, turning his face away.

‘Ah, so Frank hasn’t said anything. You guys down in the mine keep yourselves to yourselves!’

She gave him another teasing smile and HP could feel himself grinning like an idiot in response.

‘The girls and I look after the blogs. Well, I say girls even though we do actually have one bloke in the team – apart from you now, I mean.’

She smiled again but this time he managed to keep up his poker-face.

‘It works pretty much the same way as the trolls, but every handler has a slightly smaller stable. We each look after four to seven different blog personalities. Music, film, technology, fashion, books, food, and politics of course. We cover the whole lot, basically. Some of us work on long-term projects, planting ideas, while others do more short-term work, pushing specific opinions or products. You’ll be sitting with Halil here, she’s my number two.’

Rilke stopped at a desk where a young woman in a tight black outfit and beige headscarf was busy typing in a text.

'There, all done!' she said, spinning her chair to face HP and Rilke and holding out her hand.

'Halil's the name – blogging's my game . . .'

'Manga,' HP mumbled.

'Good to meet you!'

Rilke pulled over a chair for him, then left them to it.

'Okay,' Halil began. 'Hang onto your hat, Manga, because we don't hang around here.'

She snapped her fingers.

'I handle mostly fashion and music. Sandy over there looks after the technological blogs. Anders and Rilke deal with politics and the other three pretty much look after the rest. The design and technology team sitting over there make sure that all the sites work and that everything looks kosher. I've got seven bloggers in my stable – six girls and one bloke. Half of them have got fronts, the other three are anonymous, a bit like your trolls . . . Musiklover, Blingdarling, well, you get it . . .'

Yeah, he got it, even if not quite . . .

'Fronts? I mean . . . what?'

'Real people fronting the blogs.'

It took him a couple of seconds to catch on.

'What, so you look after the blog for someone else? Like a sort of ghost-writer?'

'Bingo! Basically I take care of all the serious writing. The fronts are usually busy talking crap about each other or discussing their shopping habits, which is fine. Their computers and smartphones have an app that links through to me, so I always have the last word before anything gets posted. Most of the time I let them get on with it, but if it's something important I take over.'

She opened a mini-fridge standing on the corner of her

desk, took out a couple of cans of Coke and offered one to HP, who shook his head.

Halil opened her can and took a couple of deep gulps.

'But . . . I mean . . .' HP said after a few seconds of confused thought. '. . . what do they get out of it, the fronts?'

'More like what don't they get out of it! Apart from a monthly salary from us: attention, free samples, previews, VIP events, you name it . . . A few of them are now so well known that they get to appear on television and go to gala premieres.'

'What, like her . . . what's her name?. . . the one who keeps arguing with that other one . . .?'

HP searched his memory for her name but failed to find it.

Halil drew a tick in the air – and then another one.

'Yes to her, and to her opponent as well! They're both ours, and the squabbling only gets them even more readers. Over a million hits per week per blog, and neither of the girls has any idea that they actually work for the same company . . .

'You've got to admit, that's pretty damn good!'

Forty-five minutes of interval training on the cross trainer and the sweat was running down her back. She could almost taste the lactic acid on her tongue, but she had no intention of stopping until she'd done an hour. She knew that if she was going to get any sleep at all that night, the only thing that really worked was getting completely exhausted.

It was only since Darfur that MayBey had started mentioning her. And now she was suddenly the number one topic of conversation.

There had been twenty-three comments the last time

she checked. Twenty-three 'colleagues' all declaring themselves to know with either total or reasonable certainty that she had slept her way through the force. That she was in the habit of jumping into bed with anyone as long as it benefited her career. No doubt considerably more people who had read it mistook it for the truth – with a grin at home in front of their computers.

How could people, presumably thinking and perfectly logical individuals, take the time to slander and write shit about her and her personal life?

Were they driven by hate, jealousy, envy or bitterness? That would at least have a hint of logic to it. But she suspected that the truth was actually much worse than that.

That what was driving most of the haters out there wasn't any sort of grand, strong feeling, but just mundane, low-level stuff.

Something they did just because they could. As a way of passing the time.

So why was MayBey suddenly interested in her?

The people he or she heckled usually only popped up once or twice, mostly as passing incidental characters to make a good story even better. MayBey was the storyteller, and although readers were allowed to comment, they were never asked to contribute any information. But it was different with Regina Righteous.

MayBey had first brought up the whole issue of her suspension, then asked others to add what they knew. And now this post, constructed in the same way. The more she thought about it, the more convinced she was that MayBey knew that she was reading every single word that was being written. And that it was precisely this that had made him or her change behaviour and get more personal. Something else that was deeply bloody unsettling was the talk of a 'shag-pad' on Södermalm. Of course MayBey could have just been making it all up and happened to get it right. But if that wasn't the case, that meant that someone had been talking. And if that was right, then there was only one candidate. Unless someone had been following her, of course . . .

A bleep from the cross trainer interrupted her thoughts. The interval session was over and she had a couple of minutes to wind down.

She lowered her chin to her chest, took a few deep breaths, and so didn't notice when the man came into the room.

'Listen, Manga, it's all about setting trends! There are thousands of bloggers out there, and most of them spend the whole time sneaking anxious glances at each other, especially the big names. I usually think of the internet as a huge school playground. Almost everyone wants to hang out with the cool kids, be seen in the right company. So we don't need to control all of them, just a suitable number of the hip ones with enough cred to be able to steer the buzz in a direction that suits our clients.'

She took another gulp of her Coke.

'We start with a fronted blog, add a couple of anonymous bloggers in support, and hope someone takes the bait. Obviously not all the bloggers join in, but we don't need them to either. It's like there's a critical mass, a point where so many people are all saying the same thing that their opinion sudden becomes the accepted truth. And somewhere out there, there are thousands upon thousands of people who are so desperate to live a different life to the one they've got that they're only too happy to soak up what the right people serve up to them. Fragments of someone else's life, which they unconsciously fit into their own. Products, food trends, trademarks, opinions – you name it! You see how it works, Manga?'

Oh yes, he saw all right, but for once HP was totally speechless. Philip Argos really hadn't been joking when he talked about control. The trolls were one thing, poking about in a few forums and supporting their clients' version of a story. Throw in a few made-up blogs that did more or less the same thing, just on a slightly firmer foundation. But this was way bigger than that, and at the same time a fuck of a lot cooler! Only now was he starting to appreciate the full extent of what Philip had been talking about.

Knowledge – Security – Control

That was what it was all about, and the best way to . . .

Wrong!

Unquestionably the best way to control the buzz, or whatever name you chose to give the torrent of information out there, wasn't to adapt to the rumours. It was to start them.

She was just wiping down the cross trainer when he came over to her. Because she had her back to him she didn't see him at first, and his voice made her jump.

'Hi, you're new here, aren't you?'

It was the man from the running machine.

'Yes,' she replied curtly, going back to what she was doing.

He waited a few seconds until she had finished and was obliged to turn and face him.

'I thought as much,' he said with a slight smile. 'I've been coming here for a couple of years now and usually recognize everyone else. I'd definitely have remembered a beautiful woman like you.'

The man's smile revealed a row of sparkling white teeth that suited his deep suntan perfectly. She searched her mind for a suitable comment to get rid of him, but for some reason nothing popped up. Instead she suddenly found herself returning his smile.

There was something about him that made her feel in a slightly better mood. Something he radiated. Something she had been missing for a long time.

'My name's Rebecca,' she said, and to her own surprise held out her hand.

His handshake was dry and firm.

'Good to meet you, Rebecca! I was wondering if I could be cheeky enough to ask if you'd like to have dinner with me? How about next Saturday?'

20

I now inform you that you are too far from reality

'Hello?'

'Hello, my friend.'

'Oh, it's you. Has the problem been solved?'

'Not quite, but we're working hard on it . . . Very hard . . .'

'Hi, how's it going for our golden boy? Is he behaving himself?'

'It's going brilliantly. Manga is a natural! Three days here and he already knows how to do everything.'

Halil slapped him on the shoulder and reluctantly he stopped what he was doing, pushed his chair away from the desk and turned towards Rilke.

'It's pretty good, actually,' he replied. 'Brilliant fun, but I've got a way to go before I reach the blog-queen's level.'

He winked at his supervisor and Halil gestured as if to wave off the compliment.

'Great!' Rilke replied. 'I thought we could have lunch, if you're hungry?'

'Sure,' he said, getting up from his chair. 'Where do you want to go?'

'Hötorget,' Rilke replied, glancing briefly at the other woman.

'I was thinking of getting a late lunch, but you go ahead,' Halil said quickly, then went back to her computer.

'Looks like it's just you and me, then, Manga,' Rilke smiled.

That same feeling again! For the umpteenth time in the past few days she stopped short and looked over her shoulder. But just as on every previous occasion there was no-one there.

Well, that wasn't exactly true . . .

There were loads of people there, she was in the city centre after all. People on their way to work, window-shopping, walking their dogs, talking on their mobiles.

Woolly hats, thick coats, gloves – plumes of steam rising from people's mouths as they trudged on through the December darkness. Each with their own agenda and not a single one of them who looked more suspicious than anyone else.

But she still felt like she was being watched. As if some stranger's gaze was boring into her back, making her feel . . . exposed.

Presumably that was because of the text:

I've got my eye on you – just so you know!

When he and Rilke got back from their long lunch something seemed to have happened. There was a feeling of anxiety in the air and the usually quiet office was humming with voices. Philip, Eliza Poole and a woman HP didn't know were standing and talking in the open area by the reception desk, and people from the various departments were slowly gathering around them.

For a few seconds HP wondered if this was something to do with him, if his cover really was blown this time and that he was about to be unmasked in front of the whole office. His pulse began to race and he was just glancing at the exit when Rilke gently touched his arm.

'That's Monika Gregerson, Anna's sister,' she whispered so close to his ear that his paranoia vanished instantly.

'She worked here for a while but left a year or so back.'

'Everyone, if you wouldn't mind coming over here, please. We've got something important to tell you . . .'

Eliza Poole's voice was so shrill it was almost cracking. The forty or so people in the office slowly formed a circle around the trio. Eliza Poole fished out a well-used handkerchief from her jacket pocket and blew her nose loudly. She looked upset, red-faced and puffy, as if she'd been crying.

Suddenly HP began to guess what was about to happen.

Philip Argos raised one hand and there was immediate silence.

'For those of you who haven't met Monika, this is Anna's sister, and she knows all about our activities here at ArgosEye . . .'

He gestured towards the woman beside him.

HP had no trouble seeing the family likeness. The fair hair, turned up nose and the alert look in her eyes were pretty much the same, but this woman was either the big sister or else her cosmetic surgeon wasn't as good as Anna's. The dark rings under her eyes added a few more years as well. And she was considerably more plainly dressed, in a black skirt and matching blouse, buttoned almost all the way up to the neck. Evidently she was the more restrained of the Argos sisters . . .

'I'm afraid we've got some bad news . . .'

Philip Argos paused, which was completely unnecessary seeing as he had everyone's full attention.

'As you know, Anna took a year off from work to travel round the world. Sadly it looks as though she's been the victim of a tragic accident.'

'Is she okay?'

This from Rilke, and as far as HP could tell she was genuinely worried.

Philip Argos waited a couple of seconds before answering, and when he did eventually open his mouth, everyone had already guessed what his answer would be.

'I'm afraid Anna's dead.'

By now she had been through all the posts on the Pillars of Society. The site had been up and running for about six months so it took her a fair while, but the Word document that she had been using to record her observations actually included quite a lot of useful information.

MayBey had been involved almost from the start. His or her first posts had been made just a week or so after the site had been set up, and the number of comments – and presumably readers – had steadily grown since then.

But MayBey only started threads – that was all. Then he or she sat back and let other people take over with their own comments. Then, when that post began to run out of steam, another one would appear and the whole process would start again.

There was no discernible pattern in the timing and dates of the posts. All days of the week, and most times of day, were represented – something which seemed to fit someone who worked shifts. The events and people described suggested that MayBey had experienced quite a bit, and had probably been in the police force for some time.

It seemed likely that MayBey worked on the front line, but even if Rebecca had been fairly sure of this to start with, it didn't necessarily have to mean in uniform. The events and arrests that were described certainly seemed to fit the world of the beat officer, but they could equally well have been carried out by other units in the front line – the surveillance, narcotics or licensing units, for instance. Typical police work, basically, although she still had an overwhelming sense that MayBey was anything but a typical police officer.

But she also had something else to think about.

The letter had been lying on the hall mat when she got home.

A long, white envelope, made of the slightly thicker sort of paper that she hadn't seen in a very long time.

Her address was written in elegant, old-fashioned handwriting that was so familiar that for a moment she felt her heart-rate speed up. Even the slightly clipped turn of phrase was the same.

But of course the letter wasn't from her dad.

Dear Rebecca,
I hope you will forgive my impudence in writing, but it has come to my attention that you are in some difficulty as a result of an occurrence in the Darfur region of western Sudan.
According to my sources you are currently suspended for the duration of the investigation, and this is why I am writing.
The Swedish police are presumably obliged to work through official channels, which is not always the best way to reach the truth.

Things are not always the way they seem, and sometimes it takes a different way of looking at them to bring clarity to matters which at first glance appear relatively straightforward.
I have had an extensive network of contacts in Africa for many years, and it would be a great pleasure to me if you would permit me to investigate the matter on your behalf, naturally with the very greatest discretion.
I shall write my email address at the bottom of this, and hope that you will give my proposal careful consideration.

Yours sincerely,
Tage Sammer

So now it was official.

He had actually been thinking how odd it was that no-one seemed to know about Anna's death.

Unless they had all been pretending, of course.

A few of the women, among them Eliza Poole and Rilke, appeared to have genuine tears in their eyes. Others were more composed. As for himself, he tried to adopt a sombre expression whilst trying to observe everyone else's reactions.

An accident, then – not murder. He wondered where that revised version of the story came from. Had the Dubai police set up yet another smoke-screen, or had Philip simply decided that it was better for both morale and business if he stuck to a more easily digested version of Anna's demise?

For a few moments HP had the image of those black scavengers circling over their little feast back in his head.

He looked down at the floor and swallowed a couple of times.

When he looked up again he saw Monika Gregerson looking at him. The expression on her face seemed almost one of disgust, as though she too could see the images flickering through his mind.

HP had to fight to suppress a shudder. He looked away and walked off quickly towards the staffroom. A cup of top-quality instant coffee was bound to get his paranoid brain to change track.

In the corridor he bumped into Dejan and Philip, who seemed to be in the middle of a discussion.

'. . . Anna's shares?' HP managed to catch.

'Monika will inherit them,' Philip replied tersely, then stopped and nodded quickly at HP as he passed them and reluctantly walked on.

'I don't see that that should be a problem,' he went on in a low voice just before HP was out of earshot.

Okay, so news of the death and Monika Gregerson's presence had both been fairly uncomfortable, but at least he had been able to provide Rilke with a shoulder to cry on. He had given her a hug and generously offered her his shoulder, which she had gratefully accepted, before everyone was sent home for the rest of the day.

He found himself sniffing his jacket for any residual scent from her hair. Rilke was without doubt something special. Attractive, smart and funny – fun to work with, and to hang out with. Shit, he'd have to watch it, and make sure he didn't end up suffering from some sort of inverted Stockholm syndrome.

She could actually be a suspect – theoretically, anyway . . .

Whatever, at least he had found out a few more things.

One: Anna's big sister had worked for the company but had left because she didn't see eye to eye with Philip. Okay, so no-one had actually said that, but the vibes had been pretty obvious.

Two: his suspicion that Anna's death had something to do with the business had grown even stronger. Why else would they choose to hide the truth about how she really died?

Three: it looked as if Monika would be inheriting Anna's shares in ArgosEye. If Philip had planned to get rid of Anna to get control of the company, then obviously he should have done so before the divorce went through, while he was still her principal heir.

Which meant that HP should be looking round for a new prime suspect.

Possibly even a woman . . .

21

The PR of E

Pillars of Society forum
Posted: 8 December, 21:56
By: **MayBey**

Innocent citizens only exist until the moment they're uncovered. Guilt or innocence is mostly a question of timing.

This post has 59 comments

'Micke.'

'Hi, it's me.'

'Hello.'

His voice sounded reserved, which was perfectly understandable.

'How are you?'

'Fine . . .'

There was a short silence on the line. Obviously he wasn't going to make this easy for her.

'Listen, I know I haven't been much fun lately . . .'

More silence.

'. . . not exactly very good company.'

Still not a sound from him. Had he hung up?

'Are you still there?'

'Yep.'

'Okay . . .'

She had prepared what she wanted to say, had even written down a few keywords, but she had lost her thread already.

She took a deep breath and skipped to the last line of her notes.

'I need help with something, it's to do with everything that's been going on over the past few weeks. Work, my behaviour – everything. I know it's asking a lot, but I wouldn't ask you if it wasn't important . . .'

More silence, as she held her breath and waited.

More evening work – but this time sadly nothing to do with any new special job. Instead his internet training was continuing with an evening in the Laundry.

It had taken him a week or so to realize that ArgosEye never blinked.

Nights, weekends, Christmas – there were always a few people working in each department, with at least one section head on duty in the office.

'But you don't have to be awake,' Beens grinned, opening a door that HP had only ever walked past before.

'Cool, eh?'

The room was actually a small lounge. A comfortable sofa and armchairs grouped in front of a large flatscreen television with surround sound. Towards the back of the room was a small pantry with an espresso machine, microwave and fridge, then, beyond that, a closed door.

'The bedroom,' Beens said with a grin. 'But don't worry, darling, it's got bunk-beds.'

HP smiled back, sticking his thumb up to show just how impressed he was.

Beens might have been a section head, but he definitely wasn't cool. Even if his suit had probably come from the same smart Östermalm tailor as HP's, it didn't quite seem to fit him. It almost looked like his pale, chubby body was trying to shrug it off.

'So what, do we spend all night hanging out in here, then?'

'Nah, we've got to do some work first. Or at least look like that's what we're doing . . .'

Beens winked at HP.

'New guys don't usually get to know more than they have to, but you seem to have taken over from Stoffe as Philip's new favourite. Either way, I've been told to show you how everything works, so we may as well start over in our section, then take a look at the Filter, and then cause a bit of trouble for the Strats before we settle down . . .?'

'Sounds good to me.'

'Great, stay close to me and I'll let you in. Your card won't work on all the doors, only the chosen few get that honour . . .'

Once they had made it into the Laundry, where the nightshift was already in full flow, Beens said:

'Okay, it's like this. Here in the Laundry we deal with a sort of reverse toplist optimization, if you see what I mean?'

HP did his best to look as if he did, but evidently Beens still felt that he had to offer an explanation.

'Our clients pay us to keep their search results neat and tidy. The Filter scans their trademarks and domains on the most common search engines – Google, Yahoo, Bing and so on – and if the hits throw up any crap, then we're the ones who get to wash it off.'

He walked over to his overflowing desk, pulled up an extra chair for HP, then sat down.

'Ninety percent of the people searching on Google never go beyond the first page, and another five percent fall away on the second page. By the time you get past the third page, there's only a hard core of people left.

'Our job is basically to make sure that the first two pages of results for our clients are kept clear of negative buzz. That might be blogs dissing them, competitors spreading cyber gossip, or even obsessives who start up whole sites to put people off using Volvo or Telia, for instance.'

He waved one hand in the direction of a projector screen at the far end of the room.

'So how do you go about cleaning things up?' HP asked.

'Oh, there are plenty of different ways, but I'll give you a couple of examples.'

He counted on his fingers.

'One: you fill the hit lists with your own information, often by splitting your main site into different links. If you try looking up Microsoft you'll see that almost all the hits in the first few pages are variations on microsoft.com. The basic principle is the same as filling up a notice-board with your own posters so that no-one else gets any space. Are you with me?'

HP nodded.

'Two: if that's not enough, Rilke's bloggers get to work and add a bit of positive buzz around the client, or one or more of their trademarks. Twitter's good, it generates loads of traffic, especially if it comes from people who are in at the moment. But the principle is exactly the same . . .'

'. . . piling on as much positive buzz as possible so that the negative hits slip beyond the second page,' HP concluded for him.

'Exactly, Manga, you've hit it right on the head! There are other variations on the same theme: YouTube clips and Wikipedia articles, for instance. The search engines almost always promote that sort of thing to the top ten.'

'What if that doesn't work? If you don't manage to suppress the negative buzz with your own message?' HP interrupted quickly. 'Suppose there's a persistent little nutter out there, beavering away to stop his hate-site ending up on the sidelines . . .?'

'Erm . . . that doesn't actually happen very often . . .'

Beens was already holding up a third finger, but seemed to have lost his thread.

'Well . . .' he muttered after a few seconds' pause, 'we hardly ever get it wrong, maybe once a month at most, something like that.'

He looked round in both directions, then leaned closer to HP.

'But seeing as you asked . . .' he said, almost in a whisper. 'The very few cases that we don't manage to fix get sent upstairs.'

He gestured with his head towards the ceiling.

'To the top floor,' he added when HP evidently didn't respond in the correct way.

'Ah – okay! To the twin detectives, you mean?' HP hazarded.

'Exactly! It works every time. A couple of days there and, hey presto, it's clean . . .'

Beens raised his eyebrows and nodded in a conspiratorial way. HP had no choice but to join in.

'So they're some sort of computer geniuses, then?'

'I doubt it,' Beens snorted. 'I can't imagine any of their desktops contain anything beyond the basic Office package, even if they do have unlimited access . . . But they've got contacts, fucking good contacts. The sort who seem to be able to fix anything!'

He glanced quickly over the edge of his screen at his section of the office, then leaned closer to HP again.

'We're talking code, Manga . . .'

'Code?'

Beens gave him an irritated look.

'The code, the spiral, the syntax, the PR of E? Does that ring any little bells?'

HP shook his head slowly.

'Shit, Manga, and you're supposed to be our new hotshot,' Beens sighed.

'PageRank, Google's search algorithm!'

'Sure, of course . . .' he replied after a few seconds. 'Just tell me what you need.'

His voice no longer sounded quite so hostile. She breathed out.

'I need help checking out a website. Someone's writing loads of stuff about me on there.

'Lies,' she added when he didn't respond. 'Whoever's writing them seems to be out to hurt me, and I'd like to try to find out who it is. I'm starting to think it must be someone I know . . .'

The leather sofa in the overnight lounge, 23.48.

Beens was already snoring away on his half, which wasn't really that surprising considering the turgid Monty Python film he had put on.

HP should have headed over to the bunk-beds and tried to get some sleep, but he already knew he wouldn't be able to sleep. Not after what he'd just heard . . .

Last year, when he was caught up in the Game, he had tried to dig out some more information about it. Searching with all manner of different parameters: Game, The Game, Alternate Reality Games and so on, but never found anything more exciting than Wikipedia articles about mind games, or various book and film sites.

During his long exile, on the rare occasions when he felt completely safe and didn't think anyone would be able to trace him, he had tried a few more times. But the end result had always been the same.

Not a single hit. Not the slightest buzz, rumour or even a whisper about everything he had been through. It was as if the Game had never existed.

But after listening to Beens's explanation, understanding was beginning to dawn and the whole of his undercover mission suddenly started to pay serious dividends.

The perfect hiding place.

Deep Internet!

He'd heard the phrase before but had always thought it sounded most like a myth: that part of the internet was hidden from the rest of the world, that you couldn't see it because all connections to the surface had either been cut or were so well hidden that search engines couldn't find them.

But now that he tried to make sense of his evening with Beens, everything appeared in a completely different light. Because what was the fundamental business idea of this company? Identifying and then burying things people didn't want anyone to see . . .

Beens actually seemed a bit too excited about the idea that the gang upstairs had once worked in military intelligence. He had gone on about them probably working for the National Defence Radio Centre, the National Security Agency and other similar organizations, and that they could get Google and co. to change their algorithms and make certain hits just disappear.

To begin with he hadn't really been listening – Beens just seemed to have watched too much television. But the more he thought about it, the more convinced he became that the whole idea of secret contacts probably did have some truth in it. But this wasn't a matter of a few old spy friends scratching each others' backs. That sort of thing was far too easy to uncover, and no way would Google and Yahoo with their armadas of lawyers ever buy a story about the NSA wanting to get rid of a stroppy blog-post from *Katla in Kungsängen* . . .

But if he took off his conspiracy-theory hat and tried to think about it sensibly, and then added it to everything he already knew, he soon ended up at a new and considerably more believable conclusion. The thought alone was enough to make the hair on the back of his neck stand up. He had already suspected that Anna Argos was involved in the Game in some way. There had been Game vibes there, he was pretty certain about that. And he was still having trouble swallowing the idea that his role as the scapegoat was just a complete coincidence.

And now the pieces of the puzzle were slowly falling into place.

The reason why he hadn't been able to find any information about the Game out on the net was because someone was filtering it out, cutting all the threads and making sure they could stay hidden way down there in the depths. Hidden beneath layer upon layer of more or less meaningless buzz . . .

And this someone would presumably be able to inform the Game Master about anyone out there in cyberspace breaking rule number one, trying to post confidential information or asking difficult questions.

What happened next wasn't too hard to work out. As soon as they had a name and address, a Player would be dispatched to pay a little home visit. Some attention-seeking little nobody who didn't have the faintest idea of the real reason behind their task, and who in actual fact didn't give a shit as long as they could go on getting their kicks.

Fuck, he'd even done a mission like that himself, out in Birkastan! Spraying a threatening message from the Game Master on someone's door, about the importance of keeping quiet.

Maybe some of his other tasks had actually been ways of plugging leaks? Getting people to shut up when they started blabbing about the wrong things?

He ran through them in his head: the lawyer whose car he had sabotaged, the television presenter he'd called and threatened . . . Fuck, this really could explain all that!

Piece by piece everything started to slot into place, as the lines joining the dots began to build up more of a picture. A fucking unsettling picture.

The air in the little lounge suddenly felt stagnant and difficult to breathe. HP flew up from the sofa, pulled his shoes on and dashed out through the door. He followed the corridor that ran the length of the office, not stopping until he reached the metal door over in the corner of the Troll Mine.

Emergency exit only, the luminous green sign said – but he really didn't care a flying fuck about that. A quick shove of the hip on the bar locking the door, and then he was out on a dimly lit landing in the stairwell, breathing in long, cool gulps of air.

He had guessed that everything fitted together somehow, but hadn't been able to put his finger on it before now.

ArgosEye was working for the Game!

22

In for a penny

Pillars of Society forum
Posted: 11 December, 20:03
By: **MayBey**

Big and strong always beats small and weak . . .

This post has 67 comments

She pulled on her running gear, headed through the grounds of the teacher training college, over towards Rålambshov Park, then followed the water back under the three bridges on the south side of the island. The circuit was probably five kilometres over uneven terrain, one that she had run plenty of times before.

Only a handful of people were defying the winter darkness and cold to get some exercise on the footpaths, which suited her fine. Just her and her thoughts – and her iPod, of course.

On the way back she headed up across the ridge of Atterbomsvägen, then set off towards her own little street.

The downhill slope made her legs move a bit faster than she really wanted.

She was so tired that she forgot to stop and look before crossing Rålambshovsvägen, but it didn't really matter. At this time of day there tended to be very little traffic, and the speed limit was so low that she'd have plenty of time to react.

But when she'd taken a couple of strides onto the carriageway she suddenly noticed a car out of the corner of her eye.

The vehicle was parked about twenty metres away, so she could just carry on across the road.

But just as she reached the opposite pavement her police brain suddenly kicked in.

There was something about the car that didn't make sense and she slowed down, switched off her iPod and jogged on the spot for a moment.

The car was parked on its own, presumably because it was in a no-parking zone. Now that she was looking properly, she saw that it was actually parked across the T-junction with her own street, and that most certainly wasn't permitted.

It was a Mazda, not the latest model at a guess, but it was hard to tell seeing as the grille and front bumper were missing, which was probably what had set her alarm bells ringing. A typical yob's car: rusty, no licence plate, probably not insured and not even roadworthy.

She looked around.

So where were its occupants?

Considering how cold it was, the most likely option was that they'd gone into one of the doorways.

She'd just made up her mind to go and check her own door when she noticed something else about the car. The windows were misted up. There was someone inside it.

* * *

'Hello?'

'Hi, Hollywood, Nox here!'

'Hi!'

HP stood up from his desk and walked to a quieter part of the office.

'You're not very easy to track down, man. I knocked on your door but you weren't home. I was out of credit so I couldn't call earlier. An away match?'

'Work,' HP replied curtly.

'Okay, yeah. Call in and see me, there's something I want to tell you, but I don't want to do it over the phone, if you get me?'

'Sure,' HP muttered.

'How are you, Hollywood? You sound a bit weird . . .'

'I'm fine, just been working a lot. Doing nights,' he added, but the call was already over.

What the hell was all that about, and what did the guy mean, calling him Hollywood?

Really she ought to just let it go. Head back home to a warm bath and let the uniforms deal with it. She had more than enough to think about, and it wasn't impossible that MayBey had posted something else while she'd been out.

But the idea of being a police officer again, if only to scare the crap out a couple of little hooligans, felt strangely cheering. A few seconds of complete control in the midst of the chaos surrounding her.

She felt in her pocket for her police ID, closed her hand around the rectangular leather holder and headed off across the grass towards the car. She was jogging lightly, trying not to let the loose grit on the road give her away.

She couldn't see any movement inside the car.

With a bit of luck the people inside were sharing a fix

and wouldn't see her approaching until she banged on the window.

She was mid-stride when the car's headlights suddenly went on.

He hadn't been in the downstairs corridor of the hotel before. It was, if possible, even narrower and darker than upstairs. Old bicycles, plastic bags and general clutter was piled against the peeling walls, like a corridor in some run-down student hostel.

A couple of the lights in the ceiling were out, and the remainder cast a feeble, low-energy glow that was so weak he had to screw his eyes up to read the numbers on the doors.

The rooms down here must have their own little kitchens, because the corridor smelled of food, ingrained cigarette smoke and some other musty smell that he couldn't quite place. Somewhere up ahead a radio was playing and as he got closer to the noise he realized that he recognized the song.

Nacka Skoglund, the football player, singing *We're All With You.*

Talk about a golden oldie! In fact this whole place felt pretty stone-age . . .

He pulled out the carton of cigarettes he had bought from the Seven-Eleven and headed to the far end of the corridor.

As he got closer to Nox's flat he saw that the door was ajar. The music seemed to be coming from inside, and a scratchy trumpet fanfare signalled that the song was starting up again.

> *Truu dutteduttduttedut dutteduttduttedutt tuutt!*
> *A few other players, and little old me . . .*

HP knocked on the door and it slid open until the safety chain caught it from inside. The room was dark and all he could make out were a couple of little green diodes further in the room that must belong to the stereo.

He looked around in the corridor but there was no-one in sight. For a few seconds he contemplated going back upstairs to his own room.

But Nox had sounded pretty keen on the phone. One last try, then he'd give up . . .

He tucked the carton of cigarettes under his arm, squeezed his head through the gap and peered into the room. It really did smell musty – a sweet, nauseous smell that reminded him of a festering bin.

A little of the weak light from the corridor crept in through the crack and as his eyes got used to the gloom inside more details emerged. A full bag of rubbish, a broken chair on its side, and something large and square that had to be the end of the bed.

'Nox?' he hissed.

Nacka replied:

We're all with you – we're all with you . . .
I don't know why, but we're all with you . . .

Suddenly HP realized someone was lying in the bed. A pair of waxen, pale, inert feet were sticking out from under the covers. His stomach was first to understand, and had time to lurch before his brain worked out what he was staring at.

What the . . .?

The phone!

The stupid fucker must have tried to get it going. Breaking his instructions and sticking a charger into it.

Which meant . . .?

Truu dutteduttduttedut dutteduttduttedutt tuutt!

They'd found him!

The hairs on HP's neck stood up. He took a step backwards and dropped the carton of cigarettes. Suddenly he felt a pair of hands grab him by the shoulders.

She stopped dead, fighting against the law of gravity as her shoes slid on the grit on the road. The car's engine revved hard and for a fraction of a second she was caught in the light from the headlamps – blinded, paralysed like a rabbit on a country road while the car came roaring straight at her.

Then instinct took over, her feet finally got a grip and she threw herself at the pavement. In midair something struck the bottom of her leg, making her body change direction, and she hit the frozen ground with her face and shoulder.

Battered and bruised, she got to her knees and watched as the car's rear lights disappeared in the direction of the *Dagens Nyheter* skyscraper. The driver didn't appear to have slowed down at all.

'For fuck's sake, don't wake the Chief!' a voice hissed.

HP span round, only just managing to suppress the urge to swing his arms wildly.

It was Nox.

'What? W-who?'

Fuck me, Amadeus, he was so shocked he'd practically shat himself!

'The Chief . . .'

Nox nodded towards his flat, where Nacka Skoglund had just started up again.

'I usually let him stay at mine for a while when things

get a bit rough for him. He's nice enough, but his top floor isn't properly furnished, if you get me? Can't sleep if he isn't listening to that fucking song. Says it reminds him of when he was little. Happy street and all that . . .'

'For fuck's sake, it smells like something crawled in there and died!'

'What? Oh that, nah . . .'

Nox grinned.

'He's got some weird illness that makes him smell a bit funny. It's got some Latin name, but don't ask him about it, for God's sake, or he'll get seriously fucking angry. The Chief's actually pretty hygienic, which isn't something you can say about most people in his position.'

He shrugged his shoulders. He didn't seem to mind the smell. He didn't even seem to mind being stuck in the dingy corridor with his own door chained from the inside.

'Whatever, he ends up in a bloody bad mood if he gets woken up. Totally fucking loopy, you could say, and the Chief doesn't always remember how fucking enormous he actually is. One time he threw Eskil – you know, the bloke in reception – against the wall so hard that the plasterboard cracked. The poor sod fainted and broke three ribs.'

Nox scratched his neck.

'I had to keep the Chief away from here for six months until things had calmed down. Is that for me, by the way?'

He pointed at the carton of cigarettes that was still on the floor.

'Sure, here you go.'

HP picked up the box of Marlboros and handed it to Nox, who immediately tore off the plastic and fished out a packet.

'Want one?'

HP took a cigarette and pulled out his trusty Zippo to light them both.

His hands were still shaking and he pressed his elbows to his sides to steady them.

'That thing I asked you to look after . . .?' he began.

'The phone? Don't worry, man. It's in a safe place, just like you told me . . .'

'Good, but I'm going to have to ask for it back . . .'

She had a serious black-eye, she could hardly raise her left arm above her shoulder, and she had a rectangular bruise in a nasty shade of reddish blue on her right shin. One of the car's wing-mirrors had probably caught her in midair. She might have a tiny hairline fracture, but nothing serious, according to the weary duty doctor.

All in all, a whole night wasted in various waiting rooms just to get a couple of painkillers and a 'come back if it doesn't get any better'.

She kept replaying the incident in her mind, without finding any more details.

But she was getting more and more convinced that she hadn't almost been run down by a couple of yobs high on amphetamines.

When she got home from seeing the doctor she even limped back up to Rålambshovsvägen. Just as she thought, the place where the car had been parked was ideal if you wanted to keep an eye on her flat but still be able to make a quick getaway.

If you put together everything that had happened over the past few weeks, it all seemed pretty obvious.

The car had been there because of her.

23

Trust is good

From: Holmblad, Eva
Subject: Lunch
Date/time: Today, 13.00
Place: Eriks Bakficka, Fredrikshovsgatan 4
Participants: Sandström, Magnus; Argos, Philip

Accept?
Decline?

For a couple of seconds his panic at the idea of being unmasked flared up, but he quickly got it back under control. Eriks was a smart restaurant in Östermalm and Philip would hardly have chosen it if he wanted to discuss anything unpleasant. Besides, he thought they connected pretty well the last time they met.

So what was this about, then?

There was only one way to find out.

She had parked her aching body in front of the computer so she could go through all the posts again.

The first few times she had read through them she hadn't really noticed anything special.

But as she kept digging away at it, she became more and more convinced that there was actually some sort of pattern.

Well, pattern was probably the wrong word . . .

It had all started fairly gently. MayBey's first seven or eight posts were fairly jokey. Black humour, certainly, but still very funny. They were about a Superintendent Superstud, someone female colleagues ought to watch out for if they found themselves paired up with him. Then there was Police Commission Chairman Completely-Stuffed, who on more than one occasion had been pulled in for drunkenness and had had to spend the night in the cells, and County Police Commissioner Teflon, to whom no shit ever stuck, and plenty more in the same vein . . .

But as the number of readers grew, MayBey's posts slowly began to change character. The humour had been gradually replaced by cynicism, and the tales of various types of arrests had become darker.

The readers didn't seem to have noticed anything, though, or else they simply liked MayBey's new style, because the number of comments kept growing with each new post – and there actually seemed to be more of them whenever MayBey did or described something that was right on the boundary of acceptable behaviour . . .

. . . a cocky little teenage joy-rider in a shellsuit trying to play tough. Refused to say what his partner in crime's name was – spat at my partner.

Al Pacino in an oversized tracksuit . . .

So we cuffed him and put him in the car. Then the dog-handler let go of his dog in there and I shut the door. A couple of minutes screaming and crying, then little baby Al sang like a bird about anyone and everything.

And he was polite too – didn't say a word, even though we made him scrub the piss off the seat himself back at the station. You'd probably have liked our instant justice, Regina?

That post had attracted more than fifty comments, all of them positive.

'ROFL – you're the man, MayBey!'
'Ought to be more like you in the force.'
'Have been grinning about this all day.'

The strange thing was that for some reason – she didn't really know why – she had got the impression that MayBey wasn't writing about these incidents to make other people laugh. Just like the other posts, she got a feeling that MayBey wanted to say something, but that the message had got lost, drowned under all the comment and cheering. She also got the feeling that she recognized the incident, that she might even be able to remember who had talked about it.

She had spent an hour thinking about it. Looked at purely objectively, obviously the whole thing was completely ridiculous!

She had plenty of things to sort out, considerably more important than some internet phantom.

But still she couldn't shake the intuition that it was all somehow connected.

MayBey, Darfur, her suspension, Ludvig Runeberg and

Westergren, the yobs in the car, and not least the uncomfortable sense of being watched the whole time, a sense that was only getting worse. Either MayBey was part of it, or he or she was trying to say something – tell *her* something. She had to work out what it was MayBey was trying to say and go from there.

He was five minutes early but Philip Argos was already there.

'Take a seat, Magnus. I took the liberty of ordering for us both. What would you like to drink with the meal? I'm having a South African red.'

'Then I'll have the same,' HP replied, then suddenly noticed a subtle change in the other man's face.

Shit, of course, he was supposed to be a devout Muslim!

'Do you have any non-alcoholic wine?' he quickly asked the waiter who had appeared the moment HP sat down.

A minute later he was sipping the unfamiliar drink, smiling at Philip Argos and trying to look relaxed.

'So, Magnus,' Philip began, 'how have you been getting on over the past few days?'

'Fine, thanks!' HP replied, as he tried to swallow the grape juice.

'You're being rather too modest, aren't you . . .?' Philip smiled. 'I've heard that you've gone from strength to strength. Your section head is already letting you handle attack trolls, and that's usually a job reserved for people who've been with us for a while.'

HP nodded and tried to adopt a humble expression.

'Like I said at our last meeting, you're exactly the sort of person we need at ArgosEye. Someone who is prepared to do whatever it takes to be successful . . .'

HP extended his humble nodding. He noticed that his

heart was beating faster for some reason. As far as he could remember, this was the first time he had ever been praised for his work. It certainly wasn't an unpleasant sensation.

The waiter arrived with their main courses, some sort of fish dish with wheat germ and fresh vegetables. It tasted superb, even for a carnivore like him. He was bloody lucky that he hadn't been able to order for himself, seeing as he would almost certainly have ordered that day's meat dish, pork fillet, and thereby fucked up severely . . .

But after a couple of minutes of pleasure the silence began to feel oppressive. His boss was focusing entirely on the meal, as if eating demanded all his concentration, and still hadn't given any clue as to what this meeting was actually about.

'Sooo, how did you get the idea for all this, Philip?' he managed to say after a few moments' thought. 'For ArgosEye, I mean,' he added, just to be clear.

Philip Argos slowly finished his mouthful, then put his knife and fork down.

'An excellent start, Magnus. I'm sure you have many more pressing questions, but it's always best to take things from the beginning. *He who controls the past controls the future.* George Orwell, one of my favourite quotations, actually.'

He dabbed at his mouth with his linen napkin.

'I daresay I've had the idea within me ever since my time in the Military Intelligence and Security Service, but it wasn't until I started at Burston that it started to firm up. We worked in a way which at least in part prefigured what we do today at ArgosEye, with the difference that Burston's clients only came to us once the crisis was a fact. A company in an acute crisis is a grateful client in many respects, not least when it comes to being able to charge liberally for your services . . .'

He took a sip of his wine and HP took the chance to take another mouthful of grape juice.

'Among other things, we handled the situation that arose with Dole when that documentary was released claiming that they were poisoning their employees in South America. They were using a banned insecticide on their bananas – maybe you remember it?'

HP nodded.

'Dole had tried threatening to sue the director of the film, which is basically the very worst thing you could do. You've probably heard of the Streisand Effect, where your efforts to conceal information only serve to increase the attention being paid to it? That was the situation when we got involved. Obviously the film couldn't be stopped, but we found another solution which at least enabled us to bring some balance to the debate. We paid for sponsored links alongside any keywords that had anything to do with the film. The title, the film-maker's name, the chemical compound of the poison – you name it.'

He gestured towards the ceiling.

'If anyone searched for any of those words, they always got Dole's corrected version of the story three centimetres to the right of their search results. The links only cost a few hundred dollars, but the invoice we presented Dole with was at least a thousand times that amount . . .'

He smiled and paused long enough for them both to take another mouthful of food.

'The actual idea was brilliant. Using the mechanics of the internet to defend the interests of a client . . .'

He finished his mouthful before going on.

'. . . but as time went on I started to get tired of having to put out fires that were already blazing. Instead I started to think of a way to discover and deal with likely fires before they had time to flare up, pretty much the way we did in military intelligence. We used to have a tool that was managed by the National Defence Radio Centre, a sort of search matrix for monitoring communications, looking for certain loaded terms, like bomb, terrorist, explosion and so on . . .'

'The famous National Defence Radio Centre filter, the one that caused all those protests? Reading people's emails?' HP interjected.

'That's the one,' Philip nodded. 'Which was actually all rather ridiculous seeing as the National Defence Radio Centre neither could nor would ever want to read everyone's emails. Their filter merely picks up things that might be worth checking, maybe one email in a million, if someone used the right combination of terms. In terms of integrity, it's no more invasive that using a supermarket loyalty card . . .'

'Exactly!' HP agreed. 'So that was where you got the idea? A National Defence Radio Centre, but for businesses?'

He regretted his comment at once, and cursed his inability to keep his mouth shut.

Philip gave him a long look.

'Well, that's probably taking the comparison a bit far, Magnus . . .'

HP gulped.

'. . . at least that's what I usually say to the few journalists who are intelligent enough to ask the same question . . .'

Philip paused to take another sip of his wine.

'But, just between the two of us, you're thinking along exactly the right lines . . .' he concluded and gave HP a wink.

Everything was connected, she was more and more certain of that now, especially once she'd spoken to Micke.

'The IP address was concealed by one of the anonymizing sites,' he explained. 'But we managed to get past that. The problem was that we just got stuck in another similar server somewhere else, and my guess is that it would go on like that for quite a while. Whoever set this up knows what he's doing, and definitely doesn't want to be traced.'

'Okay,' she said, trying to write down what he had just told her so she could refer back to it later.

'So we're stuffed, in other words?'

'Well,' he said, and his tone of voice made her feel suddenly more cheerful. 'We're not exactly novices at this sort of thing, we've seen stuff like this before. Give us another week or so and we can probably get to the bottom of it.'

'Thanks,' she said. 'I really appreciate your help with this!'

'That goes without saying. And just so you know, I don't believe a word of the shit that's been written about you.'

A few seconds of silence followed, before he went on. 'One more thing – I was going to ask what you're doing on Saturday?'

'Nothing special, why?'

As soon as she answered she realized that it wasn't actually true. In a moment of weakness she'd agreed to have dinner with John, the man on the running machine. But of course she could always cancel that . . .

'This is going to sound a bit odd, but I've got to go to a funeral and I was wondering if you'd like to come. It's to do with work, and if you're still considering the job offer, it would be a good opportunity for me to introduce you. Besides, I'd like to show off my beautiful girlfriend . . .'

The question caught her by surprise.

She'd been hoping for a meal and the cinema, a chance to patch things up. But this?

Networking at a funeral? What on earth was he thinking?

Besides, she'd already made it clear that she wasn't interested in changing jobs.

The last funeral she'd been to had been Dag's, when she'd rushed out after just a few minutes. She'd fought so hard to leave all that behind – make a new life for herself, far away from the person she used to be. And she had almost succeeded as well . . .

But the thought of standing in a church with a load of people dressed in black made her skin crawl.

'No thanks!'

Her abrupt answer seemed to take him by surprise almost as much as her.

'Er, what? But you said you could . . .'

'Yes, I could . . .' she went on. 'But I don't want to.'

'So what have you managed to learn so far, Magnus?'

HP thought fast.

'That everything is about perception . . .' He glanced at Philip.

'Good. Go on.'

'That monopoly control of the flow of information is a thing of the past, and the only way to limit damage is to try to steer the flood of information in the right direction. Filling the notice-board with your own posters, so to speak.'

Philip opened his mouth to say something, but HP was warming to his theme.

'Going full-throttle on loads of different channels at the same time to drown out your opponent, and if that doesn't work, shifting the focus and getting people to look at something else until it's all blown over. The media's memory has always been short, and on the internet it's even shorter.' He stopped himself and took a deep breath.

'People can only deal with one story at a time,' he concluded, glancing at Philip once more.

'Good, Magnus. Excellent, in fact. You've learned more than I had dared to hope, which makes it even easier to get to my point today,' Philip said with a smile.

He wiped his mouth again, then leaned across the table as he adopted a more serious expression. HP suddenly realized he was holding his breath.

'Kristoffer will be coming back from abroad next week and in conjunction with his return I'm thinking of changing things around a bit in the management team. I would have liked to have done so before now, but for various reasons it hasn't happened . . .'

He made a face that HP had trouble interpreting.

'Over the next few weeks the company is going to be facing some serious challenges. I'm afraid I can't share all the details with you, but one thing that's very clear is that the demands on each and every one of us are going to increase considerably. It's a whole new ballgame, as the Americans would say . . . As you might have noticed already, there are certain people who haven't quite kept up with developments. Who no longer match our profile, if you understand what I mean . . .?'

HP nodded. His heart was suddenly racing with expectation.

'Obviously this is just between the two of us, but as soon as we've got past Anna's funeral, there's going to be a reorganization. I'm thinking of moving Frank to the Laundry, which will mean that we need a new team leader in the Troll Mine. I don't suppose you can think of anyone who might be suitable for the job . . .?'

'I can probably think of at least one candidate,' HP replied with a broad grin.

24

MUD

To: t.sammer@gmail.com
From: becca.normen@hotmail.com

Dear Uncle Tage,
Thanks for your kind letter.
I would be happy to accept your offer, right now I could do with all the help I can get.

Best wishes,
Rebecca Normén

She realized she was clutching at straws, but in her situation she hardly had anything to lose. If nothing happened soon, she'd be both out of a job and a convicted criminal.

Besides, there was something about the old man that appealed to her, something she couldn't quite put her finger on. But that was probably mostly just rubbish . . . Tage Sammer reminded her of her dad, that was obviously it, and that was probably why she'd decided to email him.

* * *

'Well, like I said. This flat is practically unique. The view, the location and not least the original features . . .'

The blonde estate agent gestured towards the brick wall in one corner of the room, then at the exposed beams in the ceiling as if she were a museum guide in the middle of a tour.

The flat was undeniably impressive. An old loft, renovated to make a spacious three-room apartment at the top of Stigberget on Södermalm, with a magnificent view of Djurgården and the entrance to Stockholm harbour. The previous owner must have been an architect, because it looked like it came straight out of one of the design magazines HP usually found at the barber's. From his point of view, he couldn't really understand how people could get so excited about Danish design from the fifties, Teppanyaki grills or imported Italian limestone. But design was the fetish of the twenty-first century. You only had to compare the feeble little shelf of shame reserved for porn mags with the massive display of interior design magazines in any petrol station to realize that. Everyone who was anyone evidently fucked on colourful Carl Malmsten sofas instead of a sturdy old Klippan covered in sweaty fake leather from Ikea . . . And speaking of the F-word: Rilke seemed completely blown away by interior design porn. She soaked up every cliché that fell from the estate agent's mouth, giggled in a false way at the right places, and at one point he got the impression that the two women were flirting with each other. Ordinarily he would have found the whole scenario a bit sexy. But for some reason the adult-film director who usually lived inside his head seemed to have gone to lunch, because the giggling and the little intimate touches were actually making him more annoyed than excited. He glanced at the time. It was almost an hour since they left the office, and they hadn't even had lunch yet.

He didn't have time for this sort of nonsense – he actually had a job to do, and so did Rilke, especially if she was going to be able to afford a place like this . . .

Rilke seemed to pick up on his irritation, because she concluded her discussion with the estate agent, exchanged air-kisses, and then came over to him with a key-ring dangling teasingly from her finger.

'Mette's letting us have a look on our own for a while,' she said as the front door closed. 'What do you say about starting in the bedroom?'

To: becca.normen@hotmail.com
From: t.sammer@gmail.com

Dear Rebecca,
You've made an old man very happy.
I'll write again as soon as I have any relevant information to give you, probably within the next few days. Try not to worry, my dear, this will all work out, you'll see.

Best wishes,
Uncle Tage

She read through the email more times that she needed to, and for some reason she couldn't help smiling. She liked his tone, and even if the message was short, it still felt strangely reassuring.

A dream.

That was what it felt like.

For the first time in his life he had an exciting job with a good salary, and he seemed to be the boss's favourite. As well as that, he had met a girl, a real ten-pointer who was as attractive as she was smart.

Money, career and love. This was what life was supposed to be like!

There was just one problem. It wasn't his dream.

It belonged to Magnus Sandström; the fake one, though, not the original.

But ever since that lunch with Philip, he found himself toying more and more with a rather pleasant thought. Dumping the phone in the nearest drain, moving into that flat with Rilke, forgetting all about Anna Argos and the Game, and making a normal life for himself.

Difficult – of course! But not impossible.

Most of it seemed to be going brilliantly – if it weren't for what Nox had told him the other evening.

It wasn't really that dramatic. But Nox had taken his surveillance duties very seriously, and had seen two lads, eighteen to twenty or so, hanging around for several hours in a doorway on the other side of the street from the hotel. Nox recognized everyone who lived in the whole block, and these two definitely didn't fit in. They were well-dressed and polished, and had seemed nervous.

Nox hadn't seen any mobiles or cameras, he was definite on that point, but HP still found himself increasingly uneasy about the two men.

If the Game, against all expectation, had found out that he'd come back home to Stockholm, he couldn't see any way that he could be traced to the Hotel Hopeless. It would have been far more likely for them to send their spies to his old flat in Maria Trappgränd, or to Becca's place out in Fredhäll, but he'd been careful to steer well clear of both of those. Okay, so he'd popped into Manga's shop briefly, and in hindsight that could be seen as an unnecessary risk. But he hadn't been able to resist the temptation to see a friendly face, and the shop was only a few blocks from the hotel, and he had disguised himself well. Unfortunately his visit had been in vain, seeing as Manga hadn't even been there, just his pimply stand-in.

Could they have been watching the shop and followed him back to the hotel?

He didn't think so, but on the other hand you could never be entirely certain . . .

25

RAT

Pillars of Society forum
Posted: 18 December, 11:38
By: **MayBey**

If you work undercover long enough, sooner or later you start to wonder who you're looking at in the bathroom mirror . . .

This post has 59 comments

One good thing about his impending promotion was that his passcard suddenly worked on all the doors. That meant he could move about unhindered between the Filter at one end of the office and the Laundry at the other.

Beens didn't appear to have noticed that his days were probably numbered, because he was still making just as little effort as before. He loitered in the staffroom, hovered around other people's desks and kept coming up with 'jokey' little pranks.

It was hardly surprising that Philip wanted to replace him with Frank. The other night Beens and his mates had come up with the idea of reprogramming the speed-dial buttons of the phones in the Troll Mine. HP had nothing against practical jokes, quite the opposite, in fact. But this was all a bit nerdy and studenty, to put it mildly. Twenty minutes of his valuable time wasted deleting the speaking clock, Horny Veronica and the Samaritans from his phone, and then reinstalling the numbers he needed in order to be able to do his job.

As if that weren't bad enough, HP had managed to press the wrong option on one of the menus and inadvertently deleted one of the universal speed-dial numbers shared by all the phones in the office . . .

In the end he had been forced to grasp the nettle and ask Åsa in reception for her help sorting everything out. Her silence had cost him a round of takeaway lattes, but there was no way he was going to let the rest of the office get hold of that little titbit. He had his reputation to think of, after all.

Unlike certain others . . .

When the day of departure finally arrived, Frank was going to have a hell of a job tidying up after Beens. But that was hardly HP's problem. Even if he couldn't help getting wound up by the retarded idiot who didn't seem to have realized that things had changed.

During their cosy night together Beens, aside from his high-school pranks, had also managed to demonstrate the tools they used in the Laundry. In principle it was nothing more than a list of negative search terms and where they stood in relation to the terms they were trying to keep clean. The hits came from the Filter, passed through the Strategy department and finally ended up on the projection wall in the Laundry.

The list on the wall contained only posts that needed to be cleaned away, and they dropped off whenever the

Laundry's elves managed to deal with them, to be replaced by new ones. The whole thing basically happened in real time, and it was practically impossible for an outsider like him to pick up anything that might be of any use.

But as luck would have it, Beens had been quick to show him the little Access database he'd put together himself to keep tabs on everything, whilst simultaneously helping him keep his own workload to a minimum. The lazy sod even sat there boasting about how he had designed the program a long time ago, when no-one had a complete grasp of the system, and that the application wouldn't be regarded as kosher by Philip.

If HP's suspicions were justified, and if ArgosEye really was what kept the Game secret, cleaning up and cutting off enough information threads for the Game Master and his followers to be able to stay hidden way down in the darkness, then the evidence ought to be there in Beens's unauthorized little database. All he had to do was get hold of it.

But really he ought to think about it, lie low for a while until things had calmed down. There was a lot going on, and this definitely wasn't the right time to take any risks.

The only problem was that the fat lady was already waiting in the wings . . . The funeral was on Saturday, and the much-vaunted Stoffe was coming back on Monday. Considering how tightly Philip ran this ship, Beens's database would be history the moment his scuffed size tens made their last exit on Friday afternoon, and with that his hottest lead would be lost. In other words, he didn't have a lot of choice.

He might as well drop the whole undercover act at once if he wasn't going to try to get hold of that database.

It was now Wednesday, it was almost half past eleven,

and he could practically hear Beens's stomach rumbling on the other side of the office door.

He tapped his passcard against the reader and was instantly granted access to the Laundry. A few heads looked up, but a moment later their hands were once again flying over their keyboards in their respective cubicles.

'All right, Manga?'

'Hello, you lot!' he said loudly in response to the mumbled greetings, as he swung round the corner into Beens's larger cubicle, set slightly apart from the others.

'Hi Beens, time for lunch? Carbonara down at the corner, my treat!'

'Great, okay! I'm up for that.'

'Good, but you need to shift your arse.'

HP pretended to look at his watch.

'I've got a meeting at quarter past twelve, so we need to be quick.'

Beens quickly stood up and grabbed his padded coat from the hanger dangling from the side-wall of his cubicle.

'Okay, I'm all done,' he panted as he struggled with the sleeves.

'You sure are,' HP grinned, slapping him on the back.

The computer screen was still showing a YouTube window, and HP hurriedly positioned himself in the way. He put one hand on Beens's shoulder and steered him swiftly out of the cubicle without giving him a chance to lock his computer.

He still hadn't quite made up his mind . . .

'You're not upset about that thing with the phones, are you . . .?' Beens grinned as they headed off towards reception.

'God, no, that was a good laugh . . .' HP said, doing his best to sound like he meant it. 'Fuck you if you can't take a joke, as I always say . . .'

'Quite right! Sometimes this place gets a bit too uptight with Philip and his control mania. I mean, for fuck's sake, the phones have even got 112 on speed-dial. Check number one for yourself if you don't believe me!' Beens grinned again, and once more HP felt obliged to smile back.

Oh yes, he knew perfectly well what speed-dial number one was, seeing as he had managed to erase it when he was trying to clean up the mess caused by the prank.

One one two is hard to do . . .

He had to make up his mind, take a decision.

Safe or all in?

As they passed reception Åsa waved at him.

'Thanks for the coffee, Manga!'

'My pleasure,' he muttered, giving the back of Beens's head the evil eye.

Okay, he'd made his decision. No matter what happened afterwards, he couldn't pass up the chance of getting hold of the joker's little homemade database.

'Shit, I forgot to finish an email I promised to send before twelve!' he groaned, slapping his forehead in true drama school fashion.

'It'll only take five minutes, max. You go on ahead and get a table . . .'

He herded Beens out through the door, watched him long enough to see him get in the lift, then jogged back towards the Laundry.

A quick glance at the time. Only a minute left before the screensaver automatically locked Beens's computer. This was going to be fucking tight . . .

In spite of the rumbling aches in her body she decided to take a walk.

She looked around carefully as she stepped out into the street, and stopped a couple more times to check.

But she couldn't see anyone following her, and after twenty minutes or so out in the cold she went back home.

On the stairs on the way up to her flat she saw that something was different.

There was something hanging from her door, and as she got closer she saw what it was. A bouquet of dry, dead roses.

No-one reacted as he carefully slid back into the Laundry. Beens's screen was just fading as he slipped into the cubicle. He quickly pressed the space bar and the YouTube window reappeared. Five seconds later and the computer would have locked him out.

He moved the mouse to an icon of two angry, staring, predatory eyes.

The computer whirred.

Wake up – time to die!

A quick double-click and suddenly the database was open.

He felt in one of his jacket pockets and pulled out his new USB memory stick. Ten gigabytes – that ought to be more than enough for Beens's little extracurricular project. He put the stick next to one of the USB ports, but suddenly hesitated. Was he absolutely certain this was a good idea?

Maybe not, but he was sure he'd never get another chance like it.

He really didn't have any choice at all.

He pressed the memory stick into the slot and waited a few seconds.

Once the computer had finished thinking, he opened Explorer, then clicked and dragged the pair of eyes towards the symbol for the external memory.

No response.

He tried again. Still nothing.

Shit!

He tried a different way, going back to the database and selecting 'export to', with the external memory as the destination.

Suddenly there was a warning bleep, and then a dialogue box appeared in the middle of the screen.

Unauthorized external memory found.
Continue?

He clicked the icon for yes.

Nothing happened.

Shit! He only had a few minutes before Beens the carbonara king would start to get impatient. He tried once more, but got the error message again.

Evidently there was some sort of program that blocked anyone from saving files to an external memory.

Bollocks – he should have guessed!

Lex Wikileaks, for fuck's sake! It was obvious that Philip would have done his homework.

Okay, time for a different plan, and PDQ!

He couldn't copy the database and look through it at home in peace and quiet as he had hoped. He'd just have to check it there and then, fast as fuck!

So how did it work?

After a bit of random clicking he brought up a search box and quickly typed in *Game*.

The database responded instantly, and HP's pulse shifted up a gear.

Six hundred and twelve results!

He checked the first, only to realize that it had nothing to do with what he was looking for. Same thing with the second and third.

He glanced at the time. He only had another minute, two at the most, before he had to go.

He tried searching for *game + game master*.

One hundred and nineteen results – much better.

Just as he was moving the cursor onto the first result he heard the office door open quickly.

'Hi Elroy,' he heard someone call out, then some indistinct chatter that he couldn't make out.

Shit!

No matter what the reason for Elroy's visit down there was, he mustn't find him at Beens's computer, that much was fucking obvious.

But this was his last chance to get a look at the database.

He cautiously raised his head above the screen and the sight of the back of Elroy's closely-cropped head made him duck down again at once.

'External memory? No, for God's sake, see for yourself. That's against company policy,' he heard one of the Laundry guys say.

Damn!

The bastard memory stick must have triggered some sort of alarm. He ought to have realized that a company like ArgosEye would have cast-iron procedures to stop people downloading and taking any information home with them. Suddenly he remembered that one of the many pieces of paper he had signed on his first day at work had dealt with that very issue.

Christ, how stupid!

He had something like fifteen or twenty seconds before Elroy blocked him off inside the cubicle and he was toast.

He yanked out the USB stick and took a last look at the screen.

What exactly is the Game?

was the heading of the first search result, and it took every last bit of his self-control not to click on it.

Fuckingbastardbollocks!

The voices were getting closer. With excruciating reluctance he hammered at the escape key and then quickly pressed Ctrl+Alt+Del. Just as the screen locked he threw himself under the desk.

He could see movement through the cracks in the cubicle walls.

Hurry up, hurry up!

He snaked into the narrow cable run that led between the panels, pressed down against the floor and pulled the desk chair in behind him. A moment later a pair of well polished size tens appeared in his field of vision, so close that he thought he could smell the polish.

There were a few seconds of silence.

Then he heard Elroy's voice.

'I'm in position, but there's nothing here. Whoever it was, he must have been smart enough to give up – over!'

'Understood,' Philip's voice said over the radio. 'We need to keep our eyes open. It looks like we've got a rat . . .'

26

Ashes to ashes . . .

Pillars of Society forum
Posted: 20 December, 16:56
By: **MayBey**

An eye for an eye – is that really such a bad idea?

This post has 76 comments

It was Micke who emailed the link to the Facebook page. Regina Righteous evidently had her own profile on there. The date of birth, education and workplace all matched hers, but the rest was a complete fabrication. The two companies listed under *activities and interests* turned out to be sites for people wanting affairs, and her status was given as *in an open relationship*. That, and the fact that she had turned him down, presumably explained why his email had been so short and to the point.

But worst of all was the photograph.

A picture of her in her running gear, and it took her a

matter of moments to work out where and when it had been taken.

Right outside her door, the evening she had been run down.

Coincidence?

Hardly.

The floral arrangements in the little cemetery were so imposing that they made the urn look tiny. The whole thing resembled a mafia funeral. Loads of people in dark overcoats and raincoats, with black umbrellas swaying above them to fend off the worst of the sleety snow.

All that was missing were a bunch of feds writing down car licence numbers over in the carpark.

HP had always hated funerals.

Well, always was pushing it . . .

He'd actually only been to two. He hardly remembered his dad's, mainly because he had been seriously stoned. One last farewell *fuck you* for the old man to take with him on the express train south, that was how he had reasoned.

He had vague memories of Wagner on the church organ, and a load of faces that smelled of drink and old-fashioned aftershave, all staring at him. One old man in uniform who must have been one of Dad's colleagues from the reserve unit had even tried to straighten him out at the reception after the funeral.

'Your father was a great man, Henrik. A true patriot. You should be proud of him.'

Yeah, right . . .

As if draping the coffin with the Swedish flag and singing the national anthem in three-part harmony was suddenly going to get him to see the old bastard in a new light . . .

Mum's funeral had been considerably calmer.

Just him, Becca, Dag and Aunt Britt.

Becca and Dag close together, his heavy paw around her shoulders. But his arm wasn't there to comfort her, any idiot could see that. It looked more like Dag was keeping hold of Becca – hard, almost as if he were afraid she might try to escape if he let go. As if his sister would have dared. The sunglasses she was wearing were almost certainly not there to hide her tears or protect her from the weak spring sunshine.

That was actually when he made up his mind. The moment the sick fucker had given him one of his usual supercilious grins over his sister's head, HP had realized what he had to do. Mum had been Becca's last lifeline, the only thing stopping Dag from taking complete control.

Apart from him . . .

'Come on, it's our turn.'

Rilke tugged gently at his arm and they went up to Philip and Monika.

He still hadn't really worked out what sort of relationship they had, him and Rilke. He had spent the past few nights at hers. Cuddled up on the sofa in front of the television, having breakfast together.

So were they a couple now?

The jury was still out on that point. But he was hoping for a yes . . .

After the incident in the Laundry he had kept a low profile, doing his job impeccably and trying as hard as he could to avoid suspicion. It seemed to have worked.

'Sorry for your loss,' he muttered to Anna Argos's sister.

She kept hold of his hand for a few seconds and gave him a long look.

'You must be Magnus?'

'Mmm,' he nodded.

'Did you know my sister?'

'No . . . er, I've only been with the firm for a month or so,' he mumbled, trying to avoid eye contact. He didn't usually have any trouble lying, but for some reason it felt as though she could see right through him. He wondered how she'd react if he told her the truth?

I don't know if I really knew her, that depends on how you look at it. Your little sister shagged the crap out of me in a hotel suite in Dubai, then just after that I was arrested on suspicion of killing her. So I suppose you could say that we were acquainted . . .

Monika suddenly let go of his hand, almost as if it were burning her. She gave him an odd look as he hurried off to catch up with Rilke.

'Magnus.'

Philip held out his hand.

'It's good of you to come, thanks for the beautiful wreath.'

HP nodded in reply as he tried to rediscover the funeral expression that Monika had almost made him forget.

'My . . . *our* pleasure!' he corrected himself, giving Rilke a short sideways glance.

Philip still hadn't let go of his hand, and had actually raised the stakes by taking a firm grasp of HP's elbow.

'Yes, I've noticed that you seem to enjoy each other's company . . .' he smiled. 'Friendship is important, almost as important as loyalty. Wouldn't you say, Magnus?'

She didn't really understand why she'd said yes. Dinner with a stranger? As if she didn't have enough to think about already. But there was something appealing about

John, something that made her forget her troubles, for a short while at least.

She should really have called the whole thing off. That would have been the sensible thing to do. But she was tired of being sensible. Tired of always being Regina Righteous . . .

'Manga, Manga Sandström? It is you, isn't it?'

The tall, suntanned man had appeared out of nowhere while everyone was still mingling about with their first drink.

The restaurant was close to Strandvägen and, according to Rilke, Philip lived at the top of the same building. He couldn't work out if it was the slight hint of admiration in her voice when she talked about their boss, or the fact that she had dropped him like a stone to network among Philip's business contacts that annoyed him most.

Matters weren't made any better by the fact that he was forced to stick to orange juice while everyone else was making the most of the free bar . . .

'Hellooo . . .'

He shook the man's hand and tried to look as if he was searching for the right name.

'Stoffe. Kristoffer Stensson,' the man said helpfully. 'You were two years below me at the Royal Institute of Technology, but I think you'd have been in most of the same classes as us . . .?'

'That's right,' HP mumbled. 'Stoffe, of course. Good to see you again!'

So this was the famous Stoffe. The bloke actually looked like a mini-me version of the boss. Tailor-made pin-striped suit, impeccable white shirt, his blue tie knotted in a perfectly centred double Windsor. Even his glasses and cropped hair were identical, but Stoffe was at least one metre eighty-five tall, a whole ten centimetres taller than his idol.

'I didn't actually believe Philip when he said Manga Sandström had started working for us. I thought it must be someone else with the same name, but I recognize you now. I mean, don't get me wrong . . .'

He held his hands up in front of him.

'. . . no disrespect to ArgosEye, but you were a bit of a prodigy at RIT. You must have got loads of interesting offers, so I couldn't understand why you'd want to start from scratch with us . . .? I mean, someone like you . . . in the Troll Mine, of all places?'

Stoffe was looking at HP as if he was expecting a damn good answer. The problem was just that he didn't have one.

'Well . . . er,' he began, as he searched his head desperately for a suitable opening. 'You see . . .'

'Have you heard? Fuck, this is so mental! In Sweden, of all places . . .'

Dejan stumbled in from the left holding his iPhone aloft. HP breathed out. Saved by the bell . . .

'What the hell are you talking about?'

'The bomb! The bombs! Don't tell me you haven't heard?'

HP and Stoffe shook their heads in unison.

'Some crazy fucker blew himself up on Drottninggatan half an hour ago. The media have gone completely mad . . .'

He held out his phone to show them what he meant.

NEWSFLASH
SUICIDE BOMBER
IN CENTRAL STOCKHOLM

She took a long shower. Slowly increased the temperature a little at a time, gradually rotating to spread the delicious feeling of warmth over her whole body. Round and round until her skin was burning and she couldn't take any more.

Then she shaved her legs and took the opportunity to trim a couple of other strategic places.

She dug out her best underwear, pulled on a white blouse and the jeans she kept at the back of the wardrobe because they were a bit too tight for her liking.

Then she blow-dried her hair, quickly put her face on in front of the hall mirror, then took a step back to inspect the result.

She hardly recognized herself

Philip merely had to stand up for the noise in the private dining room to subside at once. There were about a hundred people there if HP had counted right, most of them apparently business acquaintances.

Neither party in the Argos marriage seemed the type to spend time making real friends.

Business comes first.

'As you've no doubt already heard, there have been dramatic events in the city this evening,' Philip began. 'It looks as if there are still roadblocks in place, and public transport isn't running, so getting home might prove difficult. But my good friend Baris here . . .'

He raised his hand towards the restaurant-owner who was standing over by the wall.

'. . . has promised to keep the bar open as long as we need it.'

There was a burst of cheerful chatter, and Philip waited a few moments before going on.

'But for those of you who work for me, I'd just like to say that I want to see section-heads tomorrow morning at ten o'clock. I'm aware that it's Sunday and that you've earned a day off, but unfortunately this evening's events have rather changed things . . .'

He raised his glass.

'Now that's out of the way, Monika and I would like to thank you all for coming here this evening to honour our beloved Anna. Anna was, as you all know, a very special person. ArgosEye was her dream, her life's work, and I'm convinced that she would want nothing more than for us to continue to develop the company in the direction that she had staked out. A toast, to Anna!'

'To Anna!'

Instead of calling for a taxi she had pulled her jacket on and trudged up to the hotdog kiosk. They stayed open late and gave a discount to police officers and taxi drivers, which meant that one way or the other she was bound to get a lift. But that evening, unusually enough, there was only one taxi parked outside. The driver was actually on his way home, but after a bit of feminine persuasion he agreed to drive her. Fixed price with the meter switched off, the sort of thing that usually made her pull out her police ID.

He was the one who told her about the bombs. A suicide bomber, albeit something of a failure as such. But still . . .

In Stockholm, of all places.

Completely crazy!

According to the taxi driver, the whole of the city centre was pretty much cordoned off, and the underground wasn't working. The entire city was a blur of flashing blue lights and police, and they had to take a long detour to get to where she was going. Two bombs, and the only fatality so far was the bomber himself, but until further attacks could be ruled out every single police officer would be on duty.

For a moment she wondered if she should ask him to drive her to Police Headquarters instead of Östermalm. But she was still suspended, and however much she might want to help they probably wouldn't let her through the door.

The bombs weren't her problem, and this evening she was going to do her best to forget the mess that her life had become. Hand over control to someone else.

He got back from the toilet to see Monika Gregerson on her way out of the main door, and found himself sighing with relief. He had noticed the way she had looked at him a couple of times during dinner, and there was something in her eyes that made him feel uneasy. As if they could bore right through his expensive Manga disguise and see him as he really was.

If he was still trying to find out what had happened to Anna, obviously he ought to have tried to talk to her. But somehow the restaurant seemed to have organized a whole fleet of taxis and before HP could push his way through to the door she was already gone.

Maybe that was just as well . . .

How smart would it have been to pump Monika for information right under Philip's nose? And how would he actually have opened the conversation?

So who do you think killed your sister? or *Did Anna ever mention someone called the Game Master?*

Maybe not . . .

Besides, he had pretty much made up his mind to put his investigation on ice for a while, at least until things had calmed down. And maybe even longer than that . . .

He caught sight of Rilke in the bar and headed in that direction. Most of the outsiders seemed to have left already, or were on their way, so the bar was almost entirely populated by people he knew.

'Hey, Manga, want a beer?'

He shook his head at the offers that rained down on him as he elbowed his way through various conversations towards Rilke.

'Don't you get it . . .? If it all works out we'll soon be able to fix anything. Googlebomber, whistleblowers – you name it. It won't matter how many channels they use, we'll still have enough muscle to hold them down on the mat . . .'

HP jerked his head quickly. Beens, of course. Who the hell else? In the middle of a flock of his closest disciples from the Laundry, but HP also saw a couple of faces he didn't recognize.

Fucking idiot, what the hell did he think he was doing?

Without really knowing why he forced his way into the circle and grabbed the top of Beens's arm.

'What the hell are you up to, Beens? We don't talk about company business with outsiders, you know that perfectly fucking well,' he hissed in the other man's ear.

'What?!' Beens took a step back, giving HP a lungful of brewery-sponsored breath. 'None of your fucking business, and anyway, what the fuck do you know about company business? You only started the day before yesterday. Read the fucking manual before you open your mouth, newbie!'

He turned back to his supporters with a grin, and clearly found the hesitant laughter he got in return enough to make him go on:

'You're only so damn cocky because you're fucking Rilke, but here's a newsflash for you.'

He moved his red-flushed face closer to HP's.

'Little Rilke's a success junkie. As long as you're Philip's golden boy, she'll let you stick your hand in the sweet-jar, but as soon as you start to lose speed she'll move on to someone else.'

He finished his sentence by poking HP in the chest with one of his sausage fingers.

'Ask Stoffe if you don't believe me . . .'

Beens turned his head and grinned stupidly towards his fan-club, but this time only a couple of the bravest dared to follow his example.

'She's aiming for the top. Her wet dream is to snap up Philip and take over Anna's place at the helm, and if you don't get tha . . . *aaiyyee* . . .!'

The last words slid into a groan while the colour of Beens's face went from beery-pink to stroke-red. His eyes bulged like ping-pong balls and he gurgled something unintelligible as his hands tried desperately to loosen the cast-iron one-handed grip HP had taken of his testicles.

'Now listen very fucking carefully, you sack of shit,' HP hissed in the other man's ear. 'If I ever hear you blabbing about the company again, or dissing the people you work with, you'll end up eating your bollocks for breakfast. Got that?'

HP gave a little extra squeeze to underline his point, felt Beens sway and for a moment was worried the man was going to faint.

He quickly let go.

'Good! Well, off you go home, take a couple of paracetamol and put a box of ice-lollies round your crown jewels, and everything will feel much better in the morning, you'll see,' he said in as friendly a tone as he could muster.

Beens gasped for air a few times, and his face went back to something approaching its normal colour. He sniffed and nodded jerkily, then stumbled straight off towards the door.

HP already regretted what he'd done. What in the name of holy shit had got into him? Okay, so Beens was a blabbermouthed idiot, but still. Since when had he become a corporate crony?

Suddenly HP felt someone pulling at his arm. He spun round in a flash.

'Easy, Tiger!' Elroy grinned, holding his hands up in front of him. 'There are some people who'd like you to join them at the bar.'

'Who?'

'See for yourself, Champ!'

Elroy nodded towards the bar.

When HP turned to look at the bar a few metres away, he saw Rilke and Sophie waving at him. Both women were smiling.

The taxi let her out on the other side of the road, but just as she was about to cross three police cars raced past, all blue lights and sirens. She quickly retreated to the pavement again and waited until they had gone before braving the slush on the street again.

There was a restaurant in the ground floor of the building, and judging by the number of smartly dressed people both inside and outside, it looked like some sort of private party was going on in there. She quickly cruised between the hardy little groups of smokers huddled under the gas heaters, reached the door and pressed the button for the loft apartment. After a couple of seconds the lock on the door whirred.

'We saw most of it, but you've got to tell us exactly what happened,' Rilke panted excitedly in his ear.

'Okay . . .'

He wasn't entirely sure what to say. He didn't really

know why he'd got so furious with Beens. Okay, so the guy had been a bit gobby, but even so . . .

'He needed to be taught how to behave . . .' he began.

'Go on.'

Rilke's eyes sparkled. She was comfortably drunk, that much was clear, but that didn't explain the change in her.

The way she was looking at him. Almost . . . admiringly?

Suddenly he noticed that even Sophie the She-woman seemed to be looking at him differently as well.

'Well . . . Beens needed to learn to keep his mouth shut about company business . . .' he went on, more confidently, leaning back against the bar.

'. . . to stick to rule number one!'

27

Three can play that game

She really shouldn't be here.

There were probably a hundred good reasons why – such as, for instance, the fact that she had a boyfriend, or that her life was quite complicated enough without any need to start dating strangers . . .

But there was something about him she couldn't resist.

Ever since he opened the door and gave her an assured kiss on the cheek, he had been in complete control. No uncertain eyes, no anxious questions about what she thought, wanted or liked. No decisions to take – everything was already decided.

All she had to do was lie back and enjoy it. The wonderful food must have come from the restaurant downstairs, but she assumed that the wine was from his own cellar. First a properly dry Martini, a drink she'd actually never tasted before, and which only added to the whole James Bond vibe that he radiated.

Sean Connery, definitely not Roger Moore, she giggled to herself.

A light white wine with the starter, followed by a

considerably more robust red with the main course. Then port with the cheese, and finally a smooth cognac to go with the pitch-black little espresso. Neither she nor Micke were that big on wine, most of the bottles they bought or had been given were standing unopened in various cupboards.

She hadn't drunk this much since . . . when, exactly?

She couldn't actually remember. The room swayed slightly when she got up to go to the bathroom, but for once she really didn't care.

The bathroom was just as restrained as the rest of the loft apartment. Limestone floor, tiny inset spotlights and Japanese rice-paper paintings on the walls. Subtle little details everywhere. Three different types of soap arranged in a pyramid next to the washbasin, none of them looked as if they'd ever been used. A stack of perfectly folded little flannels instead of towels to dry your hands on, and beside them a discreet little basket to leave them in, obviously covered by a lid so you didn't have to see the disorderly mess of flannels.

It actually all reminded her of the gym they both went to. It couldn't have been an accident that he chose that one in particular.

And he was handsome too, she found herself thinking. She'd noticed his body the first time she saw him. Fit, in that slim, sinewy way, not like gym-pumped hundred kilo heavyweights like Dag or Ludvig, who almost couldn't move for all their bulging muscles.

He was about the same height as her, and probably no more than ten kilos heavier. He was probably something like the same number of years older than her too, not that that mattered.

His chiselled cheekbones were accentuated by his extremely narrow glasses, and then there was that look in his eyes that had made her almost lose her breath the first time she noticed him.

She had seen it before, plenty of times . . . Well, she hadn't, actually, the wine was making her mind wander. But okay, maybe this man did remind her a tiny bit of Dag.

The way he'd managed to make her feel safe and cared for in just a few seconds was undeniably familiar. But John was a completely different person, considerably more intelligent and worldly.

He didn't exude any of the uncertainty that sometimes used to slip out of Dag, which had probably been the fundamental reason why he . . . well . . .

Oh, this was ridiculous, she had to stop this wine-fuelled pseudo-psychology! John was a gentleman and his only offence so far was that he had had to leave her a few times to answer his shiny little mobile phone.

But obviously she was prepared to overlook that tiny breach of the rules, especially as he apologized and took the opportunity to refill her glass each time.

She got up from the wall-mounted toilet, pulled up her underwear and trousers before flushing, then took the chance to adjust her hair in front of the mirror. Her cheeks were rosy, her eyes glossy with alcohol, and she couldn't help smiling at her own reflection. She hadn't felt as lively as this in a very long time.

There was something between them, that much was abundantly obvious. The only question was what was going to happen now?

Three little pills. Yellow in colour and with a little smiley face stamped in the middle of them. He didn't actually know who had conjured them up, but suddenly Rilke had popped two of them in her mouth. Then she pulled him to her, opened her mouth, and as their tongues met she pushed one of the pills across into his mouth.

It was all quite unnecessary, he'd been popping acid since Dacke died, and he didn't need any instruction. But he had to maintain his cover and carry on playing the role of the devout Muslim who didn't drink or take drugs – at least not without a bit of feminine persuasion. But by this point he could probably get away with pretty much anything. The atmosphere in the bar was peculiar. Fucking peculiar, in fact.

By now everyone knew what had happened in the city centre, and maybe it was the funeral, combined with the sudden realization that life was fragile, that had led to them all suddenly deciding to party like it was their last day on earth. Matters weren't helped by the fact that the DJ kept playing REM's *End of the world as we know it.*

If he was honest, he hated quasi-intellectual environmental muppets like REM and their soppy message of love and peace. So fucking what if some idiot blew himself to pieces on Drottninggatan?

What the fuck did that have to do with him?

He felt the tingle as the acid kick spread through his body. He closed his eyes to enjoy the moment when his eyelids transformed into cascades of colour.

Suddenly he realized that he had the wrong attitude. Totally fucking wrong, in fact! He was a lover, not a hater. Now he came to think about it, he loved almost the whole world. Environmental muppets, suicide bombers, REM, even fucking lard-arse Beens.

If the guy was – against all expectation – still there on Monday, he'd buy a family-size pizza for the cuddly little Barbapappa, to make up for it.

He leaned over the bar.

'A double Stoli, please . . . actually, better make that a triple!'

Just as he turned round Rilke was repeating her pill trick with Sophie. For a moment he just stood there grinning as the two women kissed.

The kiss was practically inevitable. The tension she felt when his lips first touched her cheek when he opened the door had carried on building throughout the meal. She could hardly remember what they had talked about.

It certainly hadn't been work, or at any rate not hers, she was sure of that.

Travel, that was it . . .

Different places around the world that ought to be visited.

Turkey was his favourite. With the Arabian peninsula in second place. She'd come up with Australia, even though she'd never even been. Apart from places she'd had to go to for work, she hadn't really been anywhere. But that didn't matter, she was happy to let him do the talking. His soft, low voice only increased the tension between them.

Then he had almost imperceptibly managed to manoeuvre her onto the sofa, and in that position they both knew what was going to happen.

His thin lips were surprisingly soft, she could smell his aftershave and taste the cognac on his tongue. He pulled her to him, holding her tight as if he already knew what she liked, and she let out a gasp of both surprise and pleasure.

This really was crazy! But for once she was thinking of letting herself go.

Falling free . . .

His mouth moved down to her neck and she squirmed

with pleasure and began to fiddle with the buttons of his shirt.

He wasn't really sure how they'd ended up here, or where they were going, but suddenly they were wrapped around each other in the lift. Him, Rilke and Sophie. He had one hand round Rilke's waist, and the other on Sophie's impressive posterior.

One of the women – he didn't actually know which – was doing a considerably more pleasant version of his Beens grip on his crotch, his shirt was unbuttoned halfway down to his navel, and Rilke was busy licking off the tequila she'd just splashed on his chest, while Sophie chewed rather too hard on one of his earlobes.

The third floor sailed past, then the fourth. He made a silent prayer that the building had ten floors.

She felt his mobile vibrate against her hip and felt him tense.

'I'm really sorry,' he said curtly as he sat up. 'This is the last time, I promise . . . Things aren't quite the same as usual this evening . . .'

She just nodded and leaned back against the cushions on the sofa. Above her head the ceiling gently span anticlockwise, and she couldn't help smiling.

No, things certainly weren't the same as usual this evening . . .

He stood up from the sofa and took a couple of steps away from her as he pulled his mobile from its holster on his belt. The conversation was short, no more than a couple of sentences.

'. . . so you're on your way. Good!' she managed to catch before he hung up.

Then he switched the phone off and put it on the coffee-table.

'How about moving into the bedroom?' he said, in a way that left no room for protest.

Not that she felt like protesting . . .

Fifth floor, lift door, wandering hands. The rattle of keys, the click of a lock.

And then they were inside a flat.

The bed he threw her down on was enormous. Big enough for four or five people, she thought, and once again she couldn't help giggling. She was definitely drunk, no doubt about it.

He practically tore off her clothes. Her blouse was already off, her trousers well on the way. She had lost all control of the situation, but she really didn't care in the slightest.

Somewhere she thought she heard a door slamming shut.

Most of their clothes came off in the hall, then the rest as they pulled him further inside the darkened flat.

The girls took care of the whole show, they seemed to work together so well that he actually began to suspect that they'd done this before.

He'd had a vague idea that Rilke played on both sides of the pitch that time when she was chatting to the estate agent, and he should probably have been jealous about the fact that his almost-girlfriend was letting herself be seduced by Sophie.

But right now he really didn't care! His cock was hard enough to drill through concrete, and tonight all of stiff one-eye's dreams were finally going to come true!

He felt the back of his knee hit something, and a

moment later he tumbled backwards onto what had to be a large double-bed.

She caught sight of something from the corner of her eye and couldn't help glancing in that direction. A large flatscreen on one wall had suddenly come to life, and she had a bird's eye view of a dimly lit room where several people were rolling around on a large bed.

For a couple of confused moments she thought she was watching herself, that John had a camera hidden somewhere in the ceiling.

The she realized that there were three people on the screen, and that even if the taller of the women actually looked a bit like her, what she was busy doing wasn't really her thing . . .

'Do you like the performance?' John whispered in her ear.

She honestly didn't know how to reply.

He was back in the saddle! That whole experience with Anna Argos had in some weird way almost made him doubt his abilities. But now everything was back to normal!

Although . . .

Obviously, there was nothing normal about what they were doing. Normal stuff was for average Swedes! His body was shiny with sweat, probably due as much to the acid as the fact that he was taking Sophie from behind like there was no tomorrow. Rilke was lying on the bed a short distance in front of him, with Sophie's head between her legs, and to judge from the noises she was making, She-woman knew what she was doing.

He closed his eyes for a few seconds to enjoy the lightshow of the pill he had popped just a minute or so ago, but quickly opened them again. To be honest, he didn't want to miss a second of the scenario unfolding in front of him. His overloaded brain was on the point of exploding from all the information it was absorbing.

Not to mention his cock . . .

There was undeniably something titillating about watching other people have sex at the same time as her, even if the trio on the screen were still some way ahead of them. She suddenly got the feeling that the man on screen was vaguely familiar. There was something about the way he held his head, the way he moved . . .

John's mouth was on its way from her breasts down over her stomach and she shut her eyes for a couple of seconds. When she opened them again the gang on the screen seemed to have changed angles, and she found herself mainly looking at the man's back.

He had short hair, was fairly slim, and didn't look like a regular gym-goer. Not really the ideal porn star. But, on the other hand, this film didn't seem to be a terribly professional production.

He was pretty suntanned, though, even below his waist.

When the man moved into the light a jagged pattern of long white scars suddenly came into view at the base of his spine.

Suddenly she froze!

She sat up and pushed John's head away.

She snaked backwards across the bed to get a bit closer to the screen. He grabbed hold of her legs and pulled her back.

'Stop it,' she muttered, kicking free.

The similarity became more and more striking the closer she looked.

He pulled her back again, harder this time, and tried to spread her legs.

'Stop it, for fuck's sake,' she snapped, and shook herself free again.

She rolled over onto her stomach and made another attempt to crawl closer to the screen. Could that really be . . .?

No, it was impossible!

Suddenly he was on top of her, landing so hard that she almost lost her breath.

He put one hand round her neck and pulled her head up.

'I give the orders round here,' he hissed in her ear, and suddenly his voice didn't sound anywhere near as gentle as before. She opened her mouth to protest, but he just squeezed her neck tighter and she couldn't get a sound out.

Her eyes began to flicker. She could feel his weight on top of her, pressing her down onto the bed. Could feel him fumbling with his free hand.

What the hell was going on?

This couldn't be happening! Brewer's droop – now – of all fucking occasions! In the middle of a fucking porn film fantasy, and the tool of the trade was letting him down!!!!

How the hell could he be stupid enough to mix drink with acid like some fucking rookie?! He looked down at his deflating pride and joy, and suddenly felt close to tears . . .

Fucking bastard bloody . . .

The girls hardly seemed to notice him.

Sophie was lying on top of Rilke, and they were exchanging increasingly animated oral services, but neither the sight nor the noises they were making did anything to ease his predicament. All he could do was watch.

Completely fucking . . .

. . . paralysed.

Unable to move – hardly able to breathe – while the man on top of her did his best to penetrate her from behind.

The hand round her neck, the body pressing her down. His panting grunts in her ear. All so familiar, so . . . so . . .

Reassuring . . .?

And wasn't this, in spite of everything, what she had really wanted? What she had been looking for the whole time?

What she deserved . . .

She caught sight of the television screen out of the corner of her eye. All of a sudden he was just sitting there watching as the two women carried on without him. His shoulders slumped, his head hanging.

He looked so small and helpless. Almost sad.

She could see her own reflection in the screen. Her own helpless face superimposed on his. And for a second she could have sworn he was looking at her. That he turned his face towards the camera and looked her right in the eye . . .

'You're my little whore now, aren't you,' John hissed in her ear.

Or was it actually Dag?

'No,' she replied drily.

And a moment later she broke his nose . . .

'Here.'

Rilke seemed to have noticed his condition. She rolled away from Sophie and managed to grab hold of her handbag.

A little blue pill, and another white one.

It took him a couple of seconds to realize.

Then he downed them both, swallowing them with the last dribble in the bottle of tequila.

The effect was almost instantaneous.

He was back!

Back in the fucking Game!

Her swivelling elbow caught him right across the nose. There was a crunching sound of bone and gristle breaking, then she was free. She kicked out with her knees and rolled off the bed. Then both feet firmly on the floor, fists clenched ready to fight.

But this man wasn't Dag. His counterattack was half-hearted, almost as if he didn't know what he was hoping to achieve. Trying to slap her from a kneeling position with the back of the hand that wasn't clutching his shattered nose. He probably wasn't used to anyone putting up any resistance – at least not properly . . .

She parried the blow easily and as he tried to get up from the bed she kicked his legs out from under him. He fell flat on the floor and she quickly kneed him in the back as she dragged one of his arms back in a rock-solid shoulder-lock.

Her head was still spinning slightly, but the adrenalin shock seemed to have taken the edge off her drunkenness.

'Okay, this is what we're going to do,' she said, as calmly as she could. 'In a little while I'm going to let you up from the floor, and then I'm going to get dressed and leave. I suggest that we simply pretend that this never happened. I never actually told you what my job is – I'm a police officer, so if you're considering attacking me again, I can assure you that you'll end the evening in the cells of Norrmalm Police Station on suspicion of attempted rape and assault. Nod if you understood what I just said!'

His head raised and lowered mechanically.

A trickle of blood from his nose was dripping onto the white carpet, but he didn't say a word.

'Good! I'll let you up in a minute so you can sort yourself out . . .'

She glanced over at the screen, where the three-way seemed to have got going again with renewed energy.

'But first you're going to tell me what my little brother's doing on your television . . .'

28

Joe Blown

Pillars of Society forum
Posted: 21 December, 06:51
By: **MayBey**

Sometimes people actually get what they deserve.
But not often enough . . .

This post has 2 comments

He woke up slowly.

His mouth felt parched, his tongue was stuck to his palate, and the Met Office had just issued a warning about an impending headache. He was also naked. Not that that was much of a surprise . . .

What was probably more unexpected was the fact that his hands and feet had been tied to the ends of the bed with velvet straps. He twisted to get loose, and felt the patches of candle-wax on his chest peel off. What a fucking night!

The little flat belonged to the company, he had worked

that much out. It was next door to Philip's own attic apartment, and was evidently used as an emergency crash-pad, probably most often by Sophie, seeing as she had been the one with the key.

He grinned and made a fresh attempt to get free.

He certainly had no cause for complaint when it came to ArgosEye's personnel policies. Even if in hindsight it felt a bit odd to have shared Rilke with someone else.

So where had the two women gone?

The room was still in darkness, even though it ought to be morning. There was no clock in the room, and his own ridiculously expensive watch was probably on the floor somewhere between the door of the flat and the little bedroom, along with the rest of his clothes.

He was just about to jokily call for help, when he suddenly realized that he wasn't alone.

There was someone sitting in the armchair over in the darkest corner of the room.

Someone he recognized . . .

'Good morning, Magnus . . .' Philip Argos said slowly. 'But perhaps you'd rather I call you by your real name?'

HP started, then tried to stay calm. It was mostly all rather embarrassing, something they could laugh about later over a few beers. But for some reason his heart was still galloping. There was something about Philip Argos's tone of voice, something creepy. Fucking creepy, in fact . . .

He twisted to break free, but the ties round his hands were knotted tight.

Philip got up slowly from the armchair and took a couple of steps towards the bed. To his surprise HP saw that his boss had a large bandage over his nose. What in the name of holy fuck was going on?

'Henrik . . . Henrik Pettersson. That is your name, isn't it?'

Obviously she ought to go straight home, get in the shower and try to wash off the whole of this terrible evening as best she could. Just the thought of it was enough to make her stomach churn.

John, or whatever his name was – for some reason she felt certain that wasn't his real name – may not have been a Dag. Not when it came down to the actual violence. But somehow they still belonged in the same league, the only difference was in the tools they used.

It was all about power, being able to control another person down to the smallest detail.

John was considerably more sophisticated in his approach than Dag ever was. In John's little world, violence was just a spice, something you used because you could. When you no longer anticipated any resistance. That was probably what she found most disturbing.

They had only met a few times, had talked on the phone and eaten one meal together.

But he had still managed to get such a grip on her that he had dared to do what he did.

As if she had unconsciously been transmitting helplessness signals? Actually, how unconsciously . . .?

On some level or other she had worked out what type he was the very first time she saw him in the gym, she could hardly deny that. Yet she still hadn't given him the brush-off. Quite the contrary . . . she had flirted with him, got all dressed up and gone round to his flat the moment he called. Got drunk and let him take control, and had even wanted him to. But once again Henke had come to her rescue. Saving her from herself.

* * *

Fucking hell!

For a moment he thought he was going to shit himself. Then he had to fight a sudden urge to burst into tears.

'I . . . I . . . er . . .' he quacked, but Philip interrupted him.

'Shhhh!' He put a finger to his lips. 'From now on, you speak only when I say you can. We've got a few little things to sort out, you and I . . .'

He leaned over HP, showing him his two black eyes.

'To begin with, I thought you might like to tell me who employed you to infiltrate us.'

He raised his eyebrows to indicate that he was expecting an answer.

'Er . . . hmm . . . What?' HP mumbled as he desperately tried to snap himself out of the urge to start crying and kick-start his aching brain. 'I mean . . . well . . . No-one did . . .'

Philip nodded.

'I would have been disappointed if you'd given up that easily . . . Henrik.'

He gestured towards the door.

'As luck would have it, we're quite good at persuasion . . .'

Elroy came into the room. In one hand he was carrying two jump-leads. In the other was a car battery.

She was sitting in a rental car a block from the doorway. John hadn't been particularly talkative, even with his arm in a half-nelson. But she had worked some of it out in retrospect. There had been no DVD to pop out, no hard drive to take away with her. And the reason for that was simple: what she had seen on the screen hadn't been a recording, but live images.

The trio were only there for one reason. Because John had arranged it. A helpless little doll on the bed, and three marionettes on the screen. She really did manage to attract some great guys . . .

In theory the three-way could have been taking place anywhere, and been broadcast via a webcam. But she was convinced that wasn't the case.

She had made a mistake, albeit perhaps an understandable one given the circumstances.

Instead of just asking general questions about the people on the screen and trying to winkle out a few details, she had immediately blurted out both Henke's name, and the fact he was her younger brother. John hadn't said anything, the expression on his face had hardly changed from the moment she dragged him up off the floor until the door slammed shut behind her. But for a split second she still imagined she had seen something when she said Henke's name. A tiny, involuntary micro-expression that his brain couldn't stop. Surprise, anger and something else, something even less benign.

The expression had only been there for a fraction of a second, but still she saw it.

Half an hour or so ago a dark Mercedes had pulled up outside the door and a well-built man had got out. He got some things out of the boot, but before she could get a closer look at him he disappeared in through the door.

There was something about the man's posture, the decisiveness of his movements, that finally convinced her.

Henke was inside that building, and not only that. He was in danger.

And it was probably her fault . . .

The first shock wasn't actually quite as terrible as he'd expected. A sudden shooting pain that made his thigh muscles cramp for a couple of seconds. Then it was over. Elroy had started just above his knees. Giving him a warning shock so he realized how serious the situation was, which wasn't really necessary. He got it. The next shock would be rather higher up . . .

How the fuck had they cracked his cover? Who had talked?

'So, Henrik. Both Elroy and I would very much like to know what someone like you is doing in our company, and right now, of all possible occasions . . .?'

HP opened his mouth before he realized that Philip wasn't finished.

'I'm very disappointed in you, I have to confess . . . We had such great hopes of you, Henrik.'

For some reason the tone of Philip's voice hurt almost as much as the electric shock he had just got in his thighs, and once again he felt close to tears.

'Well, it wasn't . . .'

BANG!

Another shock, halfway up his thighs this time. The muscles in his stomach and groin contracted into a little ball of pain and he groaned loudly.

Fuuck!!

When he opened his eyes Elroy's grinning face came into view. These guys were deadly serious. But weirdly enough, fear was no longer the strongest thing he felt, more like . . .

Sorrow?

As if he were sad about disappointing Philip?

Fucked up!

'I obviously didn't make myself clear enough, Henrik. You speak when I give you permission, understood?'

HP nodded.

'Good! As I'm sure you realize, we know all about you now. You've got something of a reputation, to put it mildly.'

Philip gave him a long look, and HP had to bite his

tongue to stifle the urge to reply. But he certainly wasn't going to give Elroy that satisfaction again. The guy looked almost disappointed as he stood there bent over his legs with a jump-lead in each hand.

'As you probably know, our company is going through a particularly sensitive time,' Philip went on. 'Things are going on in the world around us, things that have great significance for our future. There are forces out there that are trying to stop us, Henrik, and the best way to do that would be to send someone like you. A sharp, unscrupulous individual who is prepared to do practically anything as long as it serves his own interests, if you understand what I mean?'

HP nodded again.

'Good, it looks as if we understand one another . . .'

Philip sounded pleased, and oddly enough this made HP feel a tiny bit glad.

'So, let's get back to my original question: who sent you to infiltrate us, and what were your exact instructions?'

So what the hell was Henke doing here?

How long had he been in Sweden, and why hadn't he got in touch?

And who was this mysterious John, and what was his connection to her hapless little brother?

A bleep from her phone interrupted the spiral of thoughts going round her head.

Fuck, you were seriously tarted up last night.
New boyfriend, or what?
Does the old one know about him?

Her heart began to beat faster and she couldn't help looking round, then checking carefully in all the rear-view mirrors. But it was still early Sunday morning, and not a car or even a bleary-eyed dog-walker was visible on the street.

She scrolled up to the sender's number, and spent a few seconds wondering what to do. More angry texts in reply would hardly help, she'd already tried that. But on the other hand the tactic of simply ignoring him didn't seem to work either. She had to do something about it, something that would make sure he got the message, once and for all.

She tapped menu on her phone and, after a few unfamiliar clicks, she managed to get the web-browser going. It took her almost ten minutes to find the information she was looking for.

BANG!

This time the shocks came towards the top of his thighs. All the air flew out of him, the muscles in his abdomen cramped and for a moment he thought he was going to piss himself. Tears were streaming from his eyes as the cramps slowly faded to a rumbling ache. Fuck, that hurt! A couple more shocks like that and he'd been ready for a care home.

Elroy had his sights set on an even higher target.

'Next time it'll be your balls,' he grinned.

There's a surprise, you pervy moron . . .

Oddly enough, he still wasn't anywhere near as terrified as he should have been. Scared, yes, no question about that . . . But not totally panic-stricken and petrified he was going to die, like down in Dubai.

Okay, so a twelve-volt battery could cause a fuck of a lot of pain, and getting his bollocks jump-started wasn't exactly something he was looking forward to, but at least it was unlikely to kill him.

Well, he didn't think it would . . .

He tugged tentatively at the straps. One advantage of his wild convulsions was that the ties had loosened slightly. As he gradually regained control of his limbs, he did his best to loosen them further without anyone noticing.

'So, Henrik, you seriously expect us to believe that you infiltrated us entirely of your own volition? That you assumed a false identity simply because you were seized with an irresistible desire to get a job . . .?'

The two men at the end of the bed smirked at each other, and HP took the chance to stretch the loops a little more.

His cover was blown, they knew his name, but the real question was what else they had managed to find out during the night? Did they know he was Player 128, the man they had framed for Anna's death, or were they happy simply to have identified him as Henrik Pettersson?

He needed to keep a cool head, get them to play all their cards whilst simultaneously keeping his own story close enough to the truth to seem credible.

'It's true. Honestly! Why would I lie? I needed a job, I'd heard good things about you but there was no way you'd employ me given my criminal record . . .' He paused but there was no electric shock. 'Manga, the real Manga, I mean, is away, and I just borrowed him . . . People doctor their CVs every day. The net's full of fabricated identities. No big deal . . .'

Still no shock. HP had stopped pulling at the straps. Philip actually seemed to be listening to what he was saying. And why not? For once he was actually telling the truth . . .

'Everything I've done while I've been with you has been real. I've done my best. I like the job, the whole deal with the company and . . . well, everything . . .' he concluded, aiming a long look at Elroy.

A few seconds of silence followed.

HP didn't move a muscle.

'You certainly seem quite genuine, Henrik . . .' Philip said thoughtfully.

HP nodded. It was actually all true, totally fucking true, in fact! For the first time in his life he had a job he liked, regular female company and something resembling a future.

The twelve-volt kick had woken him from the dream, dumped him back in reality, which in a way was actually a hell of a relief! Now at least he wouldn't have to start each day with a reality check to keep fact and fantasy separate. The only question was: what happened now?

Could he be forgiven . . .?

Philip seemed to have softened slightly. In spite of everything, he was bloody good at what he did, a fucking self-made guy . . . ArgosEye's very own golden boy.

'Let me vocalize a thought which has been growing stronger and stronger as you've been talking, Henrik . . .'

HP was nodding furiously.

Vocalize, thought, stronger . . .

That sounded promising!

'When I worked in the Military Intelligence and Security Service, we had to deal with infiltrators, or spies as they're sometimes known . . .'

HP's head was still moving up and down, but the movement was gradually slowing down.

'The very best of them, the ones who are hardest to crack, don't even know that they're spies. They believe that what they're doing is in a good cause, and they don't understand that everything is just a game. That they're actually being manipulated by outside forces . . .'

HP's nodding died away completely. His mouth suddenly felt as if it were full of sand.

'Could that be the case, Henrik? That you seriously believe that your intentions are good, but that someone else is actually pulling the strings? Someone who's manipulating you into doing things?

'Someone who's making you see things that might not actually be real?'

She quickly jotted down the information on the screen of her mobile onto the rental-firm label that was dangling from the rear-view mirror.

SALK tennis hall, tomorrow evening, 18.30.

That was earlier than she had imagined. But it was just as well to get it over and done with as soon as possible. She folded the note and put it in the pocket of her jeans, then went back to her surveillance.

It was almost half past nine. The red-haired man had been in there for more than an hour but she still hadn't seen any sign of either Henke or John. The whole district seemed just as sleepy as Östermalm ought to be at that time on a Sunday morning, but she still couldn't shake the feeling that Henke was in some sort of trouble.

Elroy leaned over him, and for a second he let the jump-leads touch each other right in front of his nose. A flash of blue lightning sparked between them and HP twisted his body to move his head away from them.

Philip hadn't bought his story, which probably wasn't all that strange. He hardly knew himself why he had taken the job at ArgosEye.

Where had he actually got the idea from?

'So, how do you want it?' Elroy muttered, repeating the trick with the jump-leads in front of his nose.

Another blue flash, larger this time. Then another.

BLINK.

Hallucinations . . .

BLINK.

Things that didn't exist . . .

BLINK.

A

BLINK.

dream?

Elroy attached one of the jump-leads to one of HP's nostrils, putting an abrupt stop to the screen-dumps in his head. The metal was ice-cold and almost numbed the pain in his skin. Then, with exaggerated slowness, he moved the second lead towards the first.

HP was writhing his body, twisting his head desperately, but all he could manage was to win himself a couple of seconds' reprieve.

Fuck, fuck, FUCK!!

Elroy put one knee on his chest, locking him to the bed as he waved the loose jump-lead in the direction of his face.

Red.

Which meant that the blue one was already in position.

This time he didn't get to make the decision.

Both pills at the same time.

Open up and swallow . . .

The lead was approaching his face. He didn't exactly have any choice. Double or quits?

Red or blue?

The lead was almost there.

5

4

3

2 . . .

'Ghourab Al-Bain!' he roared just before the leads touched and everything went black.

29

I'm out!

Voices.

Agitated voices.

'. . . did you hear what he said?'

'Rourab Al-Bain . . .?'

'. . . group we've never heard of . . .'

'. . . international connections . . .'

'This could jeopardize the whole operation . . .'

'We'll postpone the meeting for a few hours until we know more. I'll be back in a couple of minutes . . .'

He kept his eyes closed on purpose, but ran a quick function check. Sight, hearing, arms and legs all seemed more or less okay. His crotch ought to be throbbing with pain, but somewhere along the way his brain seemed simply to have decided to shut down its connection to his groin, because he could hardly feel anything.

He heard the door of the flat slam, then steps returning to the bedroom. But this time the sound seemed to come from just one person and he opened one eye a crack to see if he was right.

True enough, Elroy had been left on guard while his boss went to check this worrying new information. A minute or so of his best dying swan seemed to do the trick, because he heard steps in the hall, then a tap running in the kitchen.

He carefully opened his eyes.

The room was empty.

The straps around his wrists, which had already shown signs of giving way, hadn't withstood his convulsions, and it took him just a few seconds to get one hand free. Whichever one of the girl-guides had been responsible for his arms should have her knot badge withdrawn, because he dealt with the second one even quicker. The straps around his ankles were tied rather more tightly, however.

Elroy was clattering about in the kitchen, it sounded like he was busy with the coffee-machine.

With some difficulty, HP managed to untie the third knot. Only one leg left, the only question was would he be able to slip out through the hall and out of the door without the red-haired gorilla catching him?

Two hours' surveillance without any result whatsoever. But at least she had worked out what to do about her meeting tomorrow. She'd only get one chance, if she hesitated or seemed even slightly uncertain he'd just carry on, assuming that she'd change her mind, the way she had before. But the difference this time was that she really did want to get rid of him.

For good!

Her mobile bleeped.

> We think we've found his broadband supplier.
> MayBey seems to be based to the east of
> the city.
> Hugs
> Micke

* * *

He tugged at the strap but the last knot refused to budge. But as luck would have it, the girls had only used one long length of fabric at each end, looping it around the frame of the bed to tie both limbs. Even if the knot was tied too tightly round his ankle to undo, at least he was free from the bed.

He wound the strap round his leg a few times, then knotted it loosely to stop him from tripping over it.

Then he stood up laboriously from the bed and took a couple of unsteady steps across the bedroom floor. The connection between his brain and his groin was gradually kicking in again, and he had to bite his lip not to groan out loud from the pain.

He poked his head out into the little hallway, but quickly pulled back. The flat was considerably smaller than he had thought, and Elroy's back was just a couple of metres away. There was no chance of making it to the front door, certainly not in his current state.

He retreated into the bedroom, went round the double bed and struggled over to the curtained window.

He carefully nudged the curtain aside, and instead of windows there was a glass door leading to a small terrace. He tried the handle gently.

Locked.

Fuck!

But then he discovered the child safety-catch at the top of the handle. He pressed the little button in and tried again.

YES!

The handle went down and he opened the door as carefully as he could. One centimetre at a time, until the gap was wide enough for him to squeeze through.

Fuck, it was cold!

He had almost managed to suppress the fact that he

was still naked. It had to be five, maybe ten degrees below freezing, and there was a stiff wind. He glanced quickly over his shoulder, but so far his escape seemed to have gone unnoticed. He peered over the railing of the terrace.

Shit! That was a serious drop! Five floors down to street level, and no sign of life below. Fucking Östermalm! The majority of its inhabitants already had one foot in the grave, and the rest were probably away 'in the country' for Christmas, which presumably meant some small castle in Södermanland or an old merchant's villa out in the archipelago . . .

And where were the cops when you actually needed one for once?

With a sudden crash the terrace door flew open behind him.

The news from Micke sounded promising, but right now she had matters of a more practical nature to think about. She had been desperate for a pee for a while now, and her bladder was so uncomfortable that she could no longer sit still. There were no shops open nearby, and the thought of squatting down in the gutter when it was minus six degrees outside wasn't particularly appealing.

So she would have to leave her post, at least for fifteen minutes or so. Not ideal, but she didn't have much choice.

She started the car, put it in gear and rolled slowly away from the edge of the pavement. She drove past the red-haired man's illegally parked Mercedes, and was just about to turn right, down towards Strandvägen, when she suddenly changed her mind.

She did a u-turn and stopped right behind the big Merc. Call it police instinct or whatever, but something was telling her it would be a good idea to take a closer look at the car before she left.

She pulled on the handbrake and took out her mobile.

Elroy raced through the terrace door, heading straight for him.

Without even thinking, HP climbed over the railing. There was a balcony a couple of metres below him, slightly to one side of him, and if he dangled from the railings he might be able to lower himself down.

He turned to face the building, struggled to lock his hands around the railings, then, as Elroy lunged at him, he did a little jump and let his body fall.

But he had misjudged his speed. His cold fingers couldn't quite take the strain and instead of dangling from his arms from the bottom of the railing, he found himself falling helplessly.

He landed on a small pile of snow, but the force was still enough to knock the air from him. It took him to a few moments to catch his breath, and when he looked up at the roof terrace there was no longer anyone in sight.

Quick, time to move!

The balcony was long, stretching most of the way along the front of the building. He ran past several windows until he reached a door. The cold was making his skin sting, his body ached both from the hard landing and the electric shocks earlier as he threw himself at the glass and banged on it with both fists.

A scared old lady's face appeared on the inside.

'Open up!' he screamed. 'Open up!' For fuck's sake, you old bag!

The old lady didn't move.

Would he have opened the door to a completely naked man who had suddenly landed on his balcony?

'Please, let me in . . .' he tried.

Suddenly the woman was gone. He took a couple of steps back and peered over the edge.

A similar balcony two floors below. Could he . . .?

He returned to the door, pressed his face against the glass and raised his hand to bang on it again. But instead he jerked back towards the balcony railing. Philip Argos was suddenly staring at him through the glass.

'Don't do anything stupid, now, Henrik,' Philip said, trying the door handle.

The old lady's face appeared, she seemed to be showing Philip how to release the safety-catch. Another dark figure came into view behind her. Presumably Elroy.

HP laboriously swung one leg over the wrought-iron railing, His body was getting stiffer and stiffer, and he could feel that he was losing the sensation in his fingers.

'Stop and think about this, Henrik . . .' Philip's muffled voice cajoled from the other side of the door.

He was right, this was never going to work. It had to be six or seven metres down, and even if – against all reasonable expectation – he managed to dangle from his arms this time, there was a still a long way to drop.

Philip and the old lady seemed to be almost fighting over the door handle. He had just a matter of seconds to make up his mind.

Suddenly he caught sight of the length of velvet wound round his ankle. He leaned over to get it off. Weirdly it slipped off his foot almost with ease. Must have been the cold.

He looped the strap around the railing and then wound the ends around his wrists. Then he clambered over the railing and squatted down.

The door flew open with a crash.

Bodies tumbling out into the cold. Feet slipping, swearing, hands reaching out for him.

He jumped . . .

A rattling sound made her look up, but the view through the windscreen was limited and all she could see was falling snow.

She had just spoken to central command. A check on the car number-plate hadn't produced much. A company car registered to ArgosEye Ltd, with an address in one of the skyscrapers at Hötorget. Maybe there'd be something more interesting inside the car. She opened the door and got out of the driver's seat.

A clump of snow landed on the pavement a few metres away, but she paid no attention to it.

The jolt was hard, and made the narrow velvet strap cut into his frozen wrists. He could feel someone pulling at it, and looked up to see Elroy hanging over the railing a couple of metres above him. For a few seconds he dangled in front of the building like some naked fucking puppet as they tried to pull him back up.

Then he managed to get his hands free, and fell the last few metres onto the balcony below. The landing was considerably softer this time, but by now his feet were numb with cold and he barely noticed the difference. He didn't waste any time banging on windows. His pursuers weren't stupid, and in the unlikely event of him being let into the apartment, he'd still have to deal with them in the stairwell.

The street was still at least six metres below him, but the balcony he was on now was the lowest one. He stumbled along the building trying in vain to find a way out.

Then he noticed the awning of the restaurant on the ground floor.

She tried to look in at the back seat through the tinted windows, but even though she had her hands cupped round her eyes it was all but impossible. The front seats were no problem, but sadly there was nothing interesting there. A couple of paper cups and the previous day's evening paper, and that was all.

The cold was making her want to pee more than ever and she made up her mind to leave.

A moment later a naked body landed on the roof of the car.

30

Homecoming

Pillars of Society forum
Posted: 22 December, 17:26
By: **MayBey**

Sometimes I fantasize about killing someone. Finding some worthless little shit. A parasite on the body of society who's just begging to be removed.
All of you out there can decide. Should I do it? Thumbs up, or down?

I already know what the answer will be.
It would never occur to you to try to stop me.
Could I even be stopped?
Can you actually protect yourself against someone who might not even exist?

This post has 107 comments

He dreamed about a bird.

A black desert crow with enormous wings that threw itself at him as he stood on the roof. He saw it coming, raised his arm to his eyes instinctively, and took a couple of steps back.

And a moment later he fell over the edge. He fell in slow motion between the buildings, whose windows had been replaced by giant, flickering screens. Messages washed over him, filling his head. Almost making him forget the ground, which was getting closer and closer.

'. . . as a Friend Of Law and Order, I have to say . . .'
'Congratulations, Skövde, now we're rolling . . .'
'. . . legislation that can't come soon . . .'
'Recently it has become more and . . .'
'The writer doesn't actually realize . . .'
'Hello to Vanderlay Industries . . .'
'What Sweden needs is a new . . .'
'Suicide bomber!'
'. . . ready to take responsibility . . .'
'The Six O'clock News . . .'
'. . . meaningless . . .'
'Dressman . . .'
'*You Are* . . .'
'Terrorist'
'. . . *Always* . . .'
'bomber!'
'*Playing*'
'voices'
'buzz'
'*The*'

And then finally, just before his brain realized what was about to happen. The moment before his dream body smashed onto the tarmac . . .

Game
Game
Game

He drifted in and out of sleep and it took him a long time to make any sense of things. The bed was familiar, as was the room he was in. Extremely familiar, and for a moment he thought he was still dreaming. But then the pain caught up with him. Okay, so you could feel pain in dreams, but this was the mother of all pains . . .

His head, stomach, crotch, arms, legs, feet and hands. Basically there wasn't a single part of him that didn't hurt. So he must be awake. So – how in holy hell had he ended up here?

The door opened slowly and a familiar face looked in.

'Hi, Henke,' she said quietly.

Obviously she should have taken him to Accident & Emergency straight away. But he had begged and pleaded with her not to.

'Not hospital, please . . . I'm fucked if I end up on a database. FUCKED, get it?'

So she had taken him home, helped him to stagger up to her flat, and then given him several of her strongest knockout pills before tucking him up in bed.

His sleep had been unsettled, and he had woken several times babbling about desert birds, Dressman and a whole load of other incoherent nonsense.

She really ought to be beside herself with worry. But at the same time it was so incredibly good to see him, to have him here in the flat. Safe . . .

It was more than likely that the state Henke was in had some connection with her own disastrous evening with John. You didn't have to be Einstein to work out that he must have been furious with her, and had in all likelihood taken out his anger on Henke.

Of course she should never have let on that he was her little brother . . .

Nice work, Normén!

Things could have been better . . .

His cover was blown, he had been tortured and chased, and had almost killed himself playing Spiderman in Östermalm. But he couldn't deny that it was good to see her . . .

So, how much did he actually dare tell her?

He had already tried telling her some things the day before, but the combination of the pain and the pills had fogged his thoughts.

Now he had to make an effort, at least. She definitely deserved that.

She had basically saved his life.

What astonishing luck that she just happened to be there.

But this wasn't the first time that he had been surprised by karma, so he just had to sit back and be grateful.

He got up out of bed and took a couple of unsteady steps across the floor. It actually went better than he had expected.

He opened the door and limped out towards the living room. She met him in the hall with her jacket on.

'Hello, are you up and about?'

'Hmm, feeling a bit better. I thought we could talk . . .'

'I'd love to, I really would! But there's something I've got to deal with first, something I should have taken care of a long time ago. It'll only take a couple of hours, okay . . .?'

'Okay,' he mumbled.

He followed her to the door like a tired dog. She picked up on his disappointment.

'I'll be back soon,' she said as she pulled on her woolly hat and gloves. 'Make yourself at home in the meantime. You know where everything is.'

She slipped out of the door but stopped halfway down the stairs.

'Don't worry, little brother. What was it you used to say . . .? *I will clean it up!*'

'*Them* . . .' he muttered. 'I will clean *them* all up . . .'

But she had already gone.

He was sitting in the far stand, just a few rows from the courts and with his sturdy back towards her. Two boys in their upper teens were playing a match, but she had no idea which one was winning.

Tennis had never interested her.

She walked slowly down the steps, then slipped into the row of seats behind him, quietly folded down one of the blue seats and sat down. He was still completely focused on the match and didn't seem to have noticed her.

'Oh, shit!'

One of the teenagers missed what looked like an easy ball and she heard him swear. His voice made her heart beat a bit faster.

Calm, now . . .

She took a deep breath to compose herself.

'Hello, Tobias!' she said.

He span round and for a moment he looked almost scared. No police officer liked being taken by surprise.

'Becca! What the hell are you doing here?!'

She didn't answer.

He looked around the seats, then glanced anxiously at the court.

'I mean, shit, Becca . . . You can't just show up like this. That's my boy out there!'

She shrugged her shoulders.

'What's so odd about two former colleagues sitting here having a chat about work? Even if it's been a while since you left the personal protection unit, my boss is still your neighbour, and your best mate, isn't he . . .? BFF or whatever it is kids say these days.'

She gestured towards the court.

He squirmed again, as if the seat was chafing his considerable frame.

'But, I mean, surely you can see . . . I mean, we . . .'

'Had an affair?'

'Y-yes . . . exactly!' he nodded, then glanced at the court where one of the boys was about to serve.

'Then we're in complete agreement, Tobbe. We *had* an affair, but now it's over, so I want you to stop driving past my flat in the van, and to stop sending texts to my mobile. Got that?'

He stared at her without replying, but his stern police glare had no effect. Instead she turned towards the tennis court where the match had resumed.

'Looks like a good match. I ought to learn a bit more about tennis. There's a big under-18s tournament at the Royal Tennis Club in a couple of weeks, isn't there? Maybe I should look in, introduce myself to your wife, maybe call round at your house out in Näsby Park? *Hi, my name's Rebecca, until fairly recently I was having an affair with your husband, but he seems to be having trouble accepting that it's over . . .*'

He clenched his jaw and narrowed his lips to a thin white line.

'Okay.'

'Sorry? I didn't quite hear what you said, Tobbe . . .?'

'Okay, I get it!' he hissed.

He glanced at the court again, then ran his hand through his short fair hair.

'You won't hear from me again, I swear, so just go, for fuck's sake! Jonathan's really sensitive about this sort of thing, Jenny and I have only just managed to patch things up . . . For God's sake, we're having therapy as a family, Becca!'

'Yes, you really seem to be taking that seriously . . .' she interrupted. 'I'm about to go, but before I do there's one question I want answered. I know you've talked to the guys in the team about me, because police are police, after all . . .'

He was avoiding her gaze, but she went on.

'What I want to know is if any of your colleagues in the rapid response unit happen to be particularly keen on computers? Good enough to know how to set up an advanced anonymity cloak, for instance? Someone who's also pretty articulate when it comes to writing?'

'What?' He stared at her.

'You heard, and don't pretend you haven't read the shit that's been written about me,' she snarled. 'Is anyone in your immediate circle unusually good with computers, and if so, who?'

'Dad . . .' one of the boys called.

They both turned to look at the court. The match seemed to be over, and one of the boys was standing just below them. The family resemblance wasn't exactly striking. Unlike his father, Jonathan was skinny with long, greasy hair and a fair scattering of teenage acne.

'We're finished . . .' Jonathan said sullenly.

'Okay, great . . . Erm . . .'

'Wiped out, three love. Can we go home now?'

The boy gave Rebecca a long look.

'Sure, no problem. Go and grab a shower, Jon, and I'll get the car.'

He stood up, and Rebecca followed suit.

Jonathan drifted slowly towards the entrance to the changing room, glancing back over his shoulder a few times.

'Well?' she said, trying to keep up with him as he climbed the steps.

As soon as they were out of sight he stopped and appeared to think.

'Peter,' he finally said abruptly. 'Peter Gladh.'

How long had they known? One day, two? Maybe a whole week, or even longer?

He tried to think back through all the conversations he'd had at ArgosEye, breaking down every comment into its constituent parts in the hope of finding some sort of clue. Had they actually know all along, from the very first day?

He was fairly sure that wasn't the case. But no matter how closely he examined the past few weeks, the only conclusion he found himself coming to was that his cover had been blown on the day of the funeral.

Stoffe was obviously the strongest candidate. After all, he'd actually met the real Manga and had been suspicious as soon as he heard that ArgosEye had given him a job. But he couldn't rule out other alternatives . . .

Could Rilke have been involved, for instance?

Had he said anything to her, had something slipped out when they were curled up watching television on her sofa?

He didn't think so, but on the other hand his double life in recent weeks had taken its toll on his psyche. One single slip, that was all it would have taken. A name, or some tiny detail that didn't make sense. Rilke was more than smart enough to pick up on something like that.

Like the fact that he had suddenly started drinking vodka in the bar, even though he was supposed to be teetotal . . .

Maybe Rilke hadn't liked the attention he had paid to Sophie, and got jealous the next day and told Philip? He couldn't rule it out, unfortunately.

But there was something else.

He was in Becca's flat, a place that the Game must be keeping under regular surveillance.

As long as he was here, he was in danger.

And so was Becca . . .

When she got home she found him in front of the computer. His head was resting on his arms and he was fast asleep. She helped him back to bed and tucked him in, then sat down on the chair he had been sitting in.

The Pillars of Society website was open.

Nightshift.
Whores, pimps, drunks, dealers and ordinary citizens with all their fucking rights. The full moon seems to make people even more crazy than usual. I'm sick of it. Somewhere round three o'clock it started to rain, thank God, and the rabble crawled back to their holes. One day we're going to have some proper rain, to wash the trash off the sidewalk. One day, very soon . . .

Do you understand what I mean?

Do you understand, Regina?

31

. . . control is better

'Hello?'

'Good evening, my friend, I just thought I'd call, as arranged.'

'So how is it going?'

'At the moment I would say that everything is in the balance. The next few days will be decisive . . .'

Things were finally starting to go her way. The union had been brought in on her case, and she had got hold of a lawyer who had already started to work on both the prosecutor and the internal investigators.

Her affair with Tobbe was finally over, once and for all, and she also had a good idea who MayBey was. Peter Gladh, Tobbe's deputy, and the nephew of that infuriating bastard diplomat, Sixten Gladh, in Sudan. His home address was on Lidingö, east of the city, just as Micke had said.

She could have kicked herself for not checking that angle to start with. The old duffer had gone on about his nephew, saying that he knew from him how immoral the force had become . . . Now, in hindsight, it all seemed obvious, of course.

Peter Gladh had heard stories, both from Uncle Sixten and his rejected little boss, about what a terrible person Rebecca Normén was, and had taken the chance to exploit the situation to build up a bit of interest around his posts. And it had obviously worked. The latest post from MayBey had over a hundred comments, and presumably at least a hundred times more readers. But unlike the people he had caricatured before, Peter Gladh seemed to have got hung up on her, to put it mildly.

According to reliable sources, he was something of an odd fish. No girlfriend, spent all his time in the station, either working or training for the next TCA contest, Toughest Cop Alive – a sort of decathlon for police officers. Bench-presses, obstacle course, swimming and cross country running. It certainly took a certain sort of mentality to do something like that. But was he 'unusual' enough to hang around in a car outside her door? And almost run her down?

She still had no answer to that question.

Now she was standing in the middle of a Christmas crowd in a shop that felt cramped and sweaty, in spite of its size.

The day-before-Christmas-Eve desperation was all too evident in the customers in their far too bulky coats. The shop assistants were racing through their work, almost as if the running tracks painted on the floor were real and not just a gimmick.

As soon as Henke said he needed clothes, she had hurried out into the city. She knew that sooner or later she was going to have to tell him about John, the television screen and the consequences of her catastrophic date, but for some reason she felt like putting it off a bit longer. And Henke didn't seem too keen to tell his own story. A short summary of his holiday in Asia was all he had offered so far. Not a word about how he had ended up naked in Östermalm, and for understandable reasons she hadn't pressed him too hard. It would take no more than one counter-question about why she had been there, and she would have to tell him everything. And explain that she was probably the cause of him getting beaten up and coming close to killing himself.

But she couldn't deny that she was extremely interested to hear his story: when, where and how he had come home, and how he came to know John, and how the hell their two worlds had so suddenly and violently collided.

It took her an hour and a half to get everything, and when she finally squeezed into the jam-packed bus she had her hands full of carrier-bags. She had to shift the whole lot into her right hand so she could hang on to the roof-strap with her left.

Well, at least Henke wouldn't freeze.

Five thousand kronor in total, but he could have it as a combined Christmas and birthday present.

'Bit cramped, this,' the man beside her said in brisk voice.

'Yes, hot too . . .'

She let go of the strap to loosen her clothing, but almost fell when the bus lurched unexpectedly.

'I could hold your bags for you if you like?' the man said.

She hesitated for a moment. Letting a stranger hold her things . . . But the bus's heating system was going full-blast and she could feel the sweat trickling down between her shoulders. They were some way from the next stop, and besides, it was so crowded that he wouldn't get far with her bags before she caught him. And there were actually people who offered to help without having an ulterior motive . . . Where was her Christmas spirit?

Besides, the man didn't look like the sort who'd steal things on a bus, he looked more like a fellow officer. There was something about his frame and posture that made him seem familiar.

She didn't recognize him, but that didn't necessarily mean anything. There were more than 1,500 police in Stockholm, and many of them had started after her, and since she moved to the Security Police she had gradually lost touch with the uniformed branch.

For a moment she contemplated asking him straight out, then decided against it.

'Thanks,' she said instead, smiling as she handed over her bags.

He returned her smile and quickly shifted his own bag before taking hers.

She loosened her scarf, then opened her jacket, then breathed out.

Lovely!

It was all about control – not just control of the buzz out there, but of the very company itself. The shares, that had to be it.

Anna Argos had owned the biggest stake in the company, and would thus have always had the last word. No matter what fantastic plans Philip might have had as MD, he would always have had to ask the board for permission, which meant that one way or another, he would still have been in his ex-wife's hands.

The report he had paid for before starting work had mentioned rumours of a stock-market flotation. What if Philip had wanted to go public, but Anna had objected? He'd considered this theory before, before he got a bit too involved . . .

After all, ArgosEye had been Anna's life's work, Philip

himself had said that at the funeral, and maybe she wasn't prepared to give up control? Just as allergic to outside share-holders as old Ingvar Kamprad at Ikea, no matter how much it might swell the coffers? But what if Anna fell off her perch and Monika inherited the whole lot?

Something told him that the older sister would be considerably more amenable.

Beneath her disapproving façade he was fairly sure that Monika was scared of Philip.

Hardly surprising, really . . .

There had been something in the air the other evening. He had thought that everyone was partying like crazy because they thought the world was about to end. But in fact that might only have been part of the truth. Because if one world ends, doesn't that also mean that another one is born?

Philip had dropped little hints that something big was about to happen, calling all the section heads in for a meeting even though it was Sunday.

The section heads weren't just in charge of their own little fiefdoms, they were also share-owners, Beens had blurted that out that night they had pizza together, so whatever happened to the company over the next few weeks would have a direct impact on their wallets.

The more he thought about it, the more details started to pop up. Rilke looking at a loft apartment. Dejan sitting there looking through Maserati brochures. Beens with all his boasting, and now the famous Stoffe, back with a suntan from a long trip abroad . . .

Could he possibly have been to an obscure little Gulf state to hand over a case full of money? To thank Bruno Hamel, a.k.a. Vincent the Ladykiller, for his efforts?

He could understand that they were pissed off with

him, they had every right to be. He had betrayed their trust, after all. But to go from that to electric shocks?

No, something was obviously going on, something big, and the only way to find out more was to pay a home visit to big sister Argos. Besides, he felt he needed to get away from the flat. Draw their eyes away from Becca . . .

She had hardly made it through the door before he set about the bags, pulling off the tracksuit and t-shirt he'd borrowed, tearing off the labels and putting the clothes on.

'Are you going out now, right away? I thought we could have coffee together, we've got loads to catch up on . . .'

She sounded disappointed, but he didn't actually have any choice.

'Sorry, but like you said yesterday, there's something I've got to take care of. It can't wait . . .'

'But are you sure you're okay? Do you want me to come with . . .'

'No,' he interrupted, a bit too sharply. 'This is something I have to do on my own, Becca,' he added, rather more gently.

She gave him a long look.

'Okay, but you can at least take my mobile so I can call you.'

'Sure,' he said, taking it. He put it in one of the many pockets of the padded jacket. But just before he left the flat he took it out again and poked it between a couple of woolly hats on the shelf by the door.

When he reached the ground floor he carefully opened the front door and looked up and down the street before slipping out and rushing quickly into the park opposite. His battered body protested after just a twenty-metre run. Not a good sign.

All of a sudden he thought he could hear footsteps behind him. He stopped abruptly and nipped in behind a tree.

But it was just a woman out walking her dog.

He let her pass, then carried on cautiously along the path towards Fridhemsplan.

By the time he got out of the underground at Ropsten it was already getting dark.

There were only three or four people on the platform, all of them harmless. No-one was after him, he had run through all his best secret-agent tricks at Fridhemsplan, then again at the Central Station. He leaped onto a train, went one station, then doubled back on himself, then jumped on a train only to dash out again just before the doors closed.

In other words, everything ought to be okay. But he still took a detour down to the taxi rank at street-level. He hung about in the kiosk until he heard the little train come rattling over the Lidingö bridge, and waited until the last second before racing up the stairs again.

Well, maybe he didn't race. His body still felt incredibly sore, so he didn't have quite the usual spring in his step. The infrared sensor in the waiting room seemed to be broken, because he came close to being guillotined by the sliding doors as he stumbled out onto the platform.

Fucking local transport!

It must be at least five years since he last travelled on the Lidingö line, he hadn't been back since the time Klasse had a sublet single-room flat up in Larsberg and they would sometimes go back there to carry on partying after a night out.

Everything still looked the same, pretty much like some old film set. Tiny burgundy velvet seats, polished hardwood, and tin warning signs under every window with anachronistic messages, such as '*Kindly refrain from leaning out of the window*'. It looked and smelled like a movie from the fifties.

He jumped off the train one stop before his destination, lit a fag and walked the rest of the way. Silent roads lined with villas, where the snow muffled all sound.

Candlesticks, fairy lights on Christmas trees and television screens spilled their light out onto the road.

Her house was at the end of a cul-de-sac, and to be on the safe side he checked out the parked cars lining the road. Only two of them weren't covered with snow, which had to mean that they had been parked within the last half hour. They were both empty. The other cars were so covered in snow that if anyone was trying to keep watch from inside any of them, they'd be both frozen solid and unable to see a thing.

Just to be sure, he took the long route, going up the next road and then plodding up the poorly cleared cycle path linking the far ends of the two roads, and then he finally approached her house.

He could see candle flames flickering in a couple of the windows, so she was definitely home. He took a last look back at the road. Everything seemed quiet.

So he rang the doorbell. He heard footsteps approaching in the hall, then saw a dark shadow against the frosted glass. Then the rattle of the lock.

'I've been waiting for you to show up,' she said with a smile.

32

Do not feed the Troll!

Pillars of Society forum
Posted: 23 December, 19:11
By: **MayBey**

I have found the person I have been looking for.
A worthless little shit, a parasite on the body of society without whom we would definitely be better off.
Let's call him Henrik . . .

This post has 116 comments

So the bastard wasn't going to give up?

Either Tobbe hadn't said anything about their meeting, or Peter Gladh was the type who didn't take warnings seriously. But maybe that depended on where the warning came from?

She spent a couple of minutes setting up an online alias, then wrote a short message, double-checked it for spelling mistakes, and then clicked send.

Surely that ought to make the idiot realize?

Back the fuck off, MayBey – I know who you are and if you don't stop I'll come out and pay you a visit!
Sincerely, Regina Righteous

Weirdly, she had just let him in without asking any questions at all. Offered to make some tea and parked him on the sofa.

The house was a perfectly ordinary 1970s construction, but the furnishings were a bit odd. White gloss and egg tempera, with colourful abstract paintings on the walls and leaning against the skirting boards.

And hanging over all of it a vague smell of linseed oil and incense. The whole place felt a bit 'instant mindfulness', complete with uplights and strange mobiles spinning from the ceiling. The only thing missing was a whale-song CD. Helmut Lotti sings Moby Dick – Absolute Shamu, something along those lines . . .

'You're wondering why I'm not more surprised . . .' Monika Gregerson said when she returned with a little wooden tray holding two cups of tea and a plate of biscuits.

'Mmm.'

He blew on his tea, but had to put the cup down so as not to burn his fingers. Cups without handles, no doubt very feng shui but not really very practical if you weren't a bit of a masochist.

'There was something special about you, I noticed it the first time I saw you up in the office. Your aura was different, stronger. As if you were there for a particular reason . . .'

She waved her hand at him.

'It's all right, you don't have to be polite and pretend

you don't think I'm crazy. Everything around us consists of energy, and that's from Einstein, not me. Yet we in the West still have terrible difficulty accepting the fact that our energies affect us. And how we ourselves affect the people around us. I'm pretty used to it by now, so how about we skip the small talk and get straight to the point? If you like, you can just pretend that I was charmed by your smile and decided to trust you . . .'

She took a slurp of her tea and gave him a few seconds to compose himself.

'Now, I'd like to know why you're here . . . Magnus.'

He took a deep breath. Just as he'd suspected, the woman was a bit on the soft-boiled side.

Energies and feng shui, okay . . . Hell, she didn't even know what his real name was!

But straight to the point suited him fine.

'I want to know what's behind your beef . . . I mean, your dislike of Philip. What happened between him and Anna. And what's this big deal the company's got going on?'

She pulled on her hat and gloves, then yanked at her jacket so hard that the hanger fell to the floor.

So the little fucker wanted war, did he? Okay, he could have it!

A quick call to the personnel department and she had both an address and telephone number for Police Sergeant Peter Gladh, alias internet bully and shit of the first order MayBey.

It's not about what you know, Regina. It's about what you can prove!

She tied her boots, then stopped in the doorway for a few moments. Then she went back in and, from the bottom drawer of the hall cupboard, took out a long, cylindrical object that she put in her jacket pocket. Gladh seemed to be a fairly unusual character, to say the least, so a bit of insurance wouldn't hurt . . .

* * *

'You've heard of the expression, a love/hate relationship?'

He nodded, and sipped the bitter tea.

'That's exactly how it was between Philip and Anna. They knew how to press each other's buttons, playing all sorts of weird games . . .'

She shook her head slowly.

'Anna was always very unusual. She loved anything competitive, even when we were little she loved to challenge me any way she could, even at things where she couldn't possibly win. It was as if the actual competitive element, the contest itself, was what appealed to her rather than winning.'

She took another careful sip from her cup.

'No matter whether Anna won or lost, she always seemed just as disappointed when it was all over. She played all sorts of different sports, got brilliant grades at high school and the School of Economics. But she still didn't really seem satisfied. When she met Philip, it was as if she'd found a worthy opponent. Someone who could constantly challenge her, if you see what I mean?'

He nodded.

'The only problem was that their constant battle for control, which was doubtless very inspiring to start with, gradually turned into something far more unpleasant . . .'

'He used to hit her?'

Monika pulled a face.

'Well . . . it wasn't quite as simple as that . . .'

She took a deep breath.

'Their power struggle took place on so many different levels, not just physical. As time went on it escalated until eventually neither of them was prepared to back down, not an inch, and not about anything. Never! And it got worse, especially when things started to go well for the company. I worked there for a year or so, but in the end their tug of war got too painful to watch. Whichever one of them was most determined to win had to use whatever tactics they could, no holds barred, you know?'

She gave him a long look and he nodded once more.

'But they ended up getting divorced. Didn't that improve things?'

'Yes and no . . . They carried on working together, and Anna sometimes used to stay in the company flat. It's right next door to Philip's, and I think she sometimes used to take other men back there . . .'

'Ah . . .'

HP had a sudden flashback to the double bed in Östermalm.

'In the end I think she simply went too far. Something happened between them, something terrible, because all of a sudden she was terrified of him, and Anna wasn't the sort who scared easily. I'm not sure, but I think the others were involved somehow. Kristoffer, Rilke, Dejan . . .'

'Sophie and Elroy . . .?' he asked.

'No, those two have always been Philip's faithful henchmen. He brought them with him from the military, but you probably know that. Maybe you even know what they get up to up on the top floor?'

He shook his head.

'They've got some sort of register of anyone who might in any way be regarded as an opponent of the company's clients. Mapping them down to the smallest detail. Photos, opinions, social circle, everything you can think of.

'Most of it comes from Facebook and other social forums, but they also use all sorts of official databases to find information . . .'

She put her teacup down slightly too hard.

'I trained as a lawyer, and the idea was that I would take care of legal matters for the company. But when I confronted Philip, told him their register was illegal and asked him to explain what it was for, he became almost threatening. Said that what Sophie and Elroy were doing was way outside my area of responsibility and that I should mind my own business. A couple of days later I resigned, there was no way I could possibly be involved in that sort of thing . . .'

HP nodded slowly.

His conflict-detector had evidently been correct.

'You said the section heads were involved somehow . . .?'

'Sorry, I got a bit sidetracked, didn't I?'

She poured them more tea.

'All the section heads apart from Kristoffer were chosen by Anna, before Philip came into the picture. You could say they were her protégées, and she was very attached to them. But somehow Philip managed to turn them against her.'

'The shares . . .? Philip and Anna owned half each, but gave some to the section heads . . .'

She gave him a long look, without either confirming or denying what he had just said.

'But Anna still had the majority holding?'

'Well, that depends a bit on how you count . . . The redistribution was Philip's idea, but Anna actually supported it. She saw it as a way to tie the section heads more closely to the company, a way of retaining their experience and skills. After the allocation Anna kept forty percent of the shares, Philip twenty, and the four section heads ten percent each. That was no doubt why she agreed to it. Seeing as Philip was the one who was giving up most, she probably saw it as a victory. Because to vote her down, he'd need to have all the section heads on his side, and she couldn't imagine that they would ever let her down, at least not all of them . . .'

'But that's what happened . . .?'

She nodded.

'Somehow he managed to get them all on his side, don't ask me how, then at the last shareholder meeting they all voted in favour of Philip's proposal . . .'

'Stock-market flotation . . .?'

'No, no, absolutely not!' she laughed. 'Stock-market flotation would have meant having to account for their activities, telling a load of strangers who the company was actually doing business with, and that's the last thing Philip would have wanted. No, what they actually forced through was a sell-off . . .'

She hung about at the back of the building for a while. Waiting for the worst of her anger to subside, and to give her a chance to consider if this was really such a great idea.

But now she had been waiting out in the cold for a good while, and she was still just as furious as she had been when she stormed out of her flat almost an hour before. Peter Gladh lived on the second floor of a building containing four separate apartments, but he probably had a sublet seeing as his name wasn't on the list by the entry-phone.

The house was set high up, with its back facing a small patch of woodland, and she had had to abandon the hire-car and scramble up through the trees to find a decent vantage point.

There were lights in a couple of the windows, and at one point she thought she saw a silhouette pass by. So he was home. Now she just needed to get in, because that was her plan, wasn't it? Ring on his door and confront him?

She didn't really know. She might just as well find a nice big stone and chuck it through his window. An eye for an eye, so to speak . . . After all, that was the sort of thing he liked . . .

She had just started looking round for a suitable projectile when suddenly a little dog came sniffing through the snow between the trees. The wind must have been in the wrong direction, because the animal didn't notice her until it was almost upon her. Then it suddenly lurched backwards and started barking madly.

'Tarzan? Tarzan!' she heard someone should from the illuminated path some hundred metres away to her right. Then she saw two silhouettes approaching quickly through the trees.

Shit, she had no inclination to explain what she was doing hiding in the woods to a couple of dog-walkers.

The figures were approaching fast, two men, she guessed. The larger of them was carrying a torch, and a much smaller one was running ahead. She waited for them to reach her while Tarzan went on barking hysterically.

'Shhhh,' she tried. 'Nice doggy, good Tarzan.'

She took a couple of steps towards the little dog, squatting down in an attempt to calm it down a bit. But the dog just launched itself furiously at her legs and she stood up rapidly.

Little bastard!

'There you are, Tarzan . . .!'

The shorter of the men grabbed the little dog and picked

it up, almost like a child. The dog fell silent at once and started to lick the man's face.

'Sorry,' he said. 'Tarzan's not used to bumping into anyone when he runs around here in the evening. I'm sorry if he startled you . . .'

'No problem,' she muttered. 'I think he was probably more scared.'

The other man caught up with them. His torch was pointing down at the snow-covered ground. But the light was still strong enough for her to recognize him from the police station gym. It was Peter Gladh.

33

Mirage

'Have you ever heard about the PayTag Group?'

The name sounded vaguely familiar, but he couldn't quite place it.

'It's a global consultancy firm that specializes in internet security, among other things. Somehow Philip managed to negotiate a huge bid from PayTag for a majority stake in ArgosEye. Philip and the others will all become rich, while the company acquires considerably more muscle, in purely business terms . . .'

HP leaned back on the sofa. So that's what Beens's little performance in the bar had been about? With a global company behind them and millions of fresh dollars in the kitty, they'd be able to expand, develop even better tools. Get even more control . . .

But apparently Anna hadn't agreed with the proposal. Just like Monika, she had found herself increasingly disapproving of the direction the company was going in.

She herself was one of the first IT entrepreneurs, and had literally built her career out of the development of the internet. And now she was going to help to limit it, muzzling people and hiding uncomfortable truths through the exploitation of the internet's own mechanisms.

Yep, he could understand perfectly why Anna had opposed the deal. And according to Monika she had had one last trump card. Even if the tribal council voted her out, she had evidently come up with a new way to stick a spanner in the works. Fucking up the whole deal right in front of the greedy little bastards' noses . . .

'Somehow Philip must have found out about it and confronted her . . .' Monika said as she came back from the kitchen with a fresh pot of tea.

'I've got no idea what happened, all I know is that Anna was scared, utterly bloody terrified, if you'll excuse my language . . .'

She took a sip of her tea.

'Was that why she left the country?'

Monika nodded.

'Anna called me from London, and just said she was going to be gone a few weeks, without giving me any explanation. But I could tell from the tone of her voice . . . Sometime later she called from Dubai and told me a bit more. Afterwards I worked it out – that was the evening when she . . .'

Monika fell silent.

'So that story Philip told everyone, about her year off . . .'

'Completely made up, just like the whole thing about her death being an accident. The police down there are sure Anna was murdered. They've even released an arrest warrant for their main suspect.'

He wriggled uncomfortably, but she didn't seem to notice.

'But Philip was very firm on that point. Nothing was allowed to get out that could jeopardize the deal, not under any circumstances. After what had happened to Anna, I didn't dare disagree. Anyway, I'm dependent upon his goodwill . . .'

'In what way?'

HP leaned forward keenly.

'I'm Anna's closest relative, our parents are dead, which means that I inherit her shares in the company.'

He frowned.

'How can that be a problem? I mean, you'll get a lot of money for them once the deal goes through.'

She snorted.

'Anna didn't want to take their money. No matter what happened, she was planning to keep hold of her shares and stop PayTag from swallowing up her life's work, at least as long as she could . . .'

Monika got up from the sofa and started to clear their still half-full cups. Then she suddenly stopped and turned to him.

'Would you have anything against coming out onto the terrace with me? I feel I need a cigarette . . .'

'But you're bleeding!' the man holding the dog said.

Gladh shone the torch at her leg. A small red stain was starting to show through her jeans on one of her calves, just above the top of her boot. She lifted her leg, pulled off her glove and touched it with her finger.

The man was right.

'Naughty Tarzan!' the man with the dog said. 'I really am very sorry . . .'

Gladh moved the beam of the torch slightly higher.

When it reached her face she noticed him tense up.

'My name's Pierre, and this is Peter,' the man with the dog said. 'We live over there.'

He pointed towards the house behind them.

'Come back with us and we can patch you up, and obviously we'll pay for new jeans . . .'

'There's really no need . . .' she began, but the man interrupted her.

'No, no, I insist, it really is the least we can do, isn't it, Peter?'

'Well, if she doesn't want to . . .' Gladh muttered.

'Nonsense!' said the man whose name was apparently Pierre. 'Come along!'

He took hold of her arm, not remotely unpleasantly, more like they were old friends, and started to steer her back towards the path. Tarzan protested mildly at her presence, but Pierre hushed him.

'Naughty Tarzan, you mustn't growl at our new friend! What did you say your name was?'

'Rebecca,' she mumbled. 'Rebecca Normén.'

She cast a quick glance over her shoulder at Gladh, but the darkness made it impossible to see the expression on his face.

She smoked blue Blend cigarettes, menthol, which didn't really surprise him. He pulled a Marlboro out of the packet he had bought in the kiosk at the underground station, then felt in his pocket for his new disposable lighter. He missed his trusty old Zippo.

'You said you were dependent on Philip's goodwill. What do you mean by that?' he said as he lit their cigarettes.

She took a deep drag before replying.

'I don't want any blood money from PayTag, there's no question of that. It would feel like a betrayal of Anna. But at the same time I don't want to hold onto the shares, because then I'd end up owning part of the monster my sister wanted to destroy, so I'm in a difficult position.'

She took a couple of quick, angry drags, then put the cigarette out in an upturned flowerpot on the plastic table beside them.

'Philip has offered to buy the shares from me himself, and, even if I realize that just means that he'll sell them on to PayTag, it seems the least worst option . . .'

'Hang on, couldn't you sell the shares to someone else? Someone on the outside?'

She made a resigned gesture.

'Like who? The company isn't listed on the stock market, and I haven't exactly got a lot of speculators lined up . . . I mean, ArgosEye doesn't even make a profit . . .'

HP took a deep drag, then flicked the butt out onto the snow-covered lawn. There was a little shower of sparks followed by a short hiss.

'I might have a suggestion,' he said with a smile.

The whole thing was pretty surreal.

Pierre the dog man pulled her inside his flat, parked her on a sofa and then quickly brewed up what had to be the most perfect cappuccino she had ever tasted in her life.

And now she was sitting there with Gladh on the divan opposite, while Pierre poked about for the first-aid kit out in the kitchen. For a few moments they just glared at each other.

He looked pretty tough, she couldn't deny that. A square face, dark eyes and a posture that suggested he was more than capable of looking after himself in a fight. She briefly regretted leaving the extendable baton in her jacket pocket. But surely he wouldn't have a go at her here, in front of a witness?

'You know who I am, don't you?' she began.

He nodded.

'Yep, we've bumped into each other a few times down in the station gym. But this is all rather . . .'

'Unexpected,' she interrupted. 'I don't suppose you expected me to show up here?'

'No . . .' he said, giving her a long look.

'Well, here I am, so now the question is what we do next.'

He squirmed, and cast a long look towards the kitchen, where it sounded like Pierre was still rummaging about.

'Well, I'd appreciate it if we could keep this between us . . .'

He leaned towards her.

'I don't want this coming out at work . . .'

'No, I can quite understand that,' she snarled, and she saw him flinch.

'Peter, have you seen the box of plasters. I'm sure it was in the bathroom?' Pierre called.

'No, I haven't,' Gladh called, without taking his eyes from her. 'But I don't think we need it, Rebecca's just leaving . . .'

'No, I'm not,' she hissed.

The train rattled on through the winter darkness on its way into the city. He had just managed to catch the last train that evening, and apart from the driver and a guy wearing headphones a couple of seats in front of him, the carriages were empty.

He really could understand why Philip had reacted the way he had. There was some seriously heavy stuff going on, and not only financially.

The PayTag Group. He was sure he'd heard the name before, and he was trying desperately to remember where. But the more he thought about it, the further he seemed to get from the answer.

But one thing was clear at least. He was finally starting to understand why Anna Argos had been murdered. Just as he had thought, she was caught up in the Game, but not as a simple little Player. She, and above all her company, played a considerably more significant role than that.

ArgosEye protected the Game, while at the same time presumably benefiting from its unique services. If the company was bought and gained access to seriously large amounts of money, they would be able to use the Game on a more regular basis, and exploit its full potential. Getting them to dig out secrets, misjudgements and general fuck-ups that people were desperate to keep hidden.

Then when the Game had done its thing, the victims could choose – become a client of ArgosEye, and we'll make sure your secrets are safe. A good old protection racket – Cosa Nostra goes cyberspace, basically. Their business would grow exponentially, and PayTag would be crying tears of joy over their profitable new acquisition.

An increase in revenue would mean the Game could continue to grow, recruiting more Ants and Players, and thus increasing both its power and its client-base. And a growing Game would require more effort to keep itself hidden, which would all be handled by the bigger, stronger ArgosEye, and then everyone was back at Go again.

The circle was closed, the pieces of the puzzle fell into place and the chain of logic held.

But as with all conspiracy theories, you had to ask: who benefited?

And in this case the answer was simple:

Everyone!

But then Anna Argos decided to be difficult.

A way to stop them, Monika had said.

Anna was a competitive person, and she would surely

rather have destroyed her life's work than look on as Philip and the treacherous section heads took it over.

Maybe she had even tried and failed?

Was that why she had fled the country?

But there was far too much at stake for them to just let her get away. As long as Anna was out there somewhere she would constitute a serious risk.

And risks had to be eliminated, as far as possible.

So: enter Vincent the Ladykiller.

Fuck, what a story!

Only one piece of the puzzle was missing . . .

Henrik HP Pettersson.

How did he fit into the picture?

Her fury was back, all of a sudden. For several weeks she had imagined what MayBey looked like, sitting there in front of his screen. She had almost come to think of him as some sort of monster in a black cape and with a deformed face. Instead MayBey was an over-tanned gym-junkie with a neat little goatee, sitting on a Turkish divan in a room that looked like something out of *A Thousand and One Nights* . . .

His pretence of being surprised wasn't going to work on her . . .

'You're a cheeky bastard, Peter! Storing up a load of rubbish that Uncle Sixten and your poor, spurned boss have unloaded onto you. Then you make me your target and spend weeks throwing all sorts of shit at me, just to get a bit of attention for your nasty little gossip site. And now you want us to act like nothing's happened, so that nothing comes out at work . . .? Clearly you're not as brave IRL as you are in front of your keyboard, are you, MayBey?'

Gladh stared at her hard for several seconds. Then he took a deep breath and opened his mouth.

At that moment Pierre came back into the room. He waved a little white box with a red cross on it.

'Here it is. Sorry, Rebecca, *someone* put it back in the bathroom cupboard instead of in the right place.'

He sat down on the sofa next to Rebecca and started to take out what he needed with a practiced hand.

'Sorry, I interrupted. What were you talking about?'

Gladh leaned forward slowly towards her.

'Yes, I was just wondering that . . . What the hell are you talking about, Normén?'

34

Cut, clip and remove

He had a fleeting sense that someone was watching him.

He looked anxiously around the carriage, but apart from the man with headphones in front of him, the train was empty.

Nothing to worry about.

He shut his eyes, took a deep breath through his nose, then let the air out slowly through his mouth. The whirlwind of thoughts in his head was gradually slowing down.

Anna, Vincent, Philip, Monika, Rilke and all the others. And, finally, him. What a fucking story . . .

The train stopped at AGA, but no passengers got on as far as he could tell.

His cover had held up to the evening after Anna's funeral, so everything he had found out up to that point had to be true. Then something had happened. Some external event which had changed the game. Stoffe. It couldn't really be anyone else. Now that he'd had time to calm down a bit, the idea that Rilke had blown his cover, or that he'd slipped up somehow, no longer seemed terribly likely.

No, Stoffe was the only new factor that had been added

to the equation, the only difference from the earlier scenario. With the possible exception of his sister . . . But that thought worried him more than he was prepared to admit.

'Good evening, Henrik!' a soft voice suddenly said behind his shoulder, and HP froze to ice.

Philip Argos.

'Peter, a phantom blogger? You're joking . . .'

Pierre burst into chuckling laughter which under normal circumstances was probably very contagious. But she definitely wasn't in the mood for laughing. And Gladh didn't seem as amused as his partner.

'That's actually true, at most I can send emails and check the news websites.'

'But . . .' she said. 'Tobbe said that . . .'

She paused, trying to think of a way in.

'Okay, I think I'm starting to get it now. So, Tobbe Lundh put you onto me . . .?'

He looked at Pierre, who stopped laughing at once.

'Okay, it's like this, Normén,' Gladh sighed. 'I've always kept quiet about my sexuality. The force might have got a lot better officially, but if you're in the rapid response unit and compete in the TCA, it doesn't really fit the image if you also happen to be . . .'

'A poof!' Pierre said, quick as a flash. 'Peter and I don't entirely agree on this, but even if I think he's wrong, I respect his decision . . .'

Gladh gave Pierre a grateful look.

'Up until a couple of months ago everything worked pretty well,' he continued. 'A number of other officers must have known, or at least suspected, but no-one really seemed bothered.'

'But then something happened . . .?' Rebecca was still

trying to sort out her thoughts, and added, 'Something to do with Tobbe Lundh?'

Gladh nodded.

'He bumped into me and Pierre at a private party. His daughter was working as a waitress, and, being a bit of an overprotective dad, he picked her up just before the end . . .'

'A gay party,' Pierre said. 'A perfectly ordinary party, no drag or feather boas, no Eurovision theme, but it was still pretty obvious. You can imagine the rest . . .'

She could. Tobbe was rabidly homophobic, which was just one of the many characteristics which had really started to annoy her once the physical attraction had begun to wear off.

'So he started spreading shit about you . . .?'

'Well,' Gladh muttered, 'he's probably a bit too smart for that, I mean, he is in charge, and we did used to be mates. Some of the shit would have landed on him if he'd started spreading it, so he steered clear of that . . . But he treated me differently at work, which pretty much amounted to the same thing. In a close-knit group like ours, everyone notices at once if there's something wrong, and all of a sudden he was taking any chance he could to get me out of the van. Keeping me at arm's length, sending me on secondment to other units that were short-staffed. It didn't take long for the rest of them to join in. I got the hint and immediately applied for a transfer, before the gossip had time to really build up. For the past three weeks I've been working with the Youth Unit out in Roslagen.'

'And your uncle, Sixten . . .?'

She had pretty much worked out the answer for herself. Those comments about the lack of morals in the force had suddenly taken on a whole new meaning.

'Uncle Sixten? He's as homophobic as Tobbe Lundh, if not worse. We haven't spoken for years . . . What's he got to do with anything?'

His first instinct was to run, run for his life. But as he attempted to stand up he felt a heavy arm on his shoulders.

'Take it easy now, lad,' Elroy muttered in his ear as he pushed him back down onto his seat.

'You've certainly been busy tonight, Henrik.'

Philip sat down opposite him. Their knees were so close they were almost touching.

'So, what exciting stories did my former sister-in-law have to tell you? Let me guess! I tormented her little sister, forced her out of her own company, and now I'm planning to sell the whole lot to the devil. Right so far?'

HP nodded mutely. All of a sudden he felt nauseous. He was sure he hadn't been followed. He'd even left the house by the terrace door, cutting through the hedge into the woods.

So how the hell had they found him?

Someone must have blabbed.

But who?

He glanced quickly towards the front of the carriage. The man with the headphones was still there. As long as there was an outsider in the carriage with them, they probably wouldn't dare to harm him.

At least he hoped not . . .

Philip smiled amiably.

'Our last meeting was rather unfortunate, Henrik, and I take full responsibility for that.'

He felt in his coat pocket and HP stiffened.

'Throat pastille?'

Philip held out a little red box and for some reason HP obediently took one.

'*Makes people talk*,' Philip said with a chuckle, mimicking the advert. HP heard Elroy join in behind his neck. He couldn't help grinning nervously. His stomach lurched again and he swallowed a couple of times to get it under control.

'As you might have noticed, my sister-in-law is a rather unusual person,' Philip went on. 'Monika's focus is more on the supernatural plane, which means that she sometimes has difficulty accepting reality the way that it actually is. Anna's tragic death seems to have done nothing to help that . . .'

He pulled a sad face.

'As in every broken relationship, the fault is shared by both parties . . . But as far as ArgosEye is concerned, everything I have done has been strictly by the book, I can assure you of that. Well, enough of that . . .'

He flashed a glance at Elroy, then looked over his shoulder towards the man a few seats further forward.

'I thought we might continue our discussion in a more private setting, Henrik. We're still very interested in who sent you to us, and what instructions you were given. Besides, we have plenty more to discuss . . .' He held his hand up to stop HP from saying anything.

'No, no. No need to say anything now. We'll deal with all that when we can speak without fear of being disturbed . . . Sophie's waiting with the car in Ropsten, so my advice to you would be to take the chance to consider which direction you would like our impending conversation to take.'

'Easy or difficult, little Henke, you decide,' Elroy whispered in his ear. 'It's all the same to me!'

* * *

The train made one last stop before the bridge, but before HP had a chance to think about trying to run, Elroy had once again laid a hand on his shoulder. The young man with the headphones stood up and walked past them. HP tried to catch his eye, but the guy wasn't even looking in his direction. Then the train creaked into motion again and started the long sweep up towards the Lidingö bridge.

Philip took his mobile from the holster on his belt and put it to his ear.

'Hello?'

HP hadn't even heard it ringing.

'Yes, hello. The situation's under control . . . We go ahead as planned.'

HP looked out of the window. They were up on the bridge now, dark water far below on either side of them.

'Good,' Philip said into the phone. 'You have permission to proceed. We'll start phase three at midnight . . .'

Maybe he could make it. If he leaped to his feet, jumped on Philip and clambered over him . . .

No, even in the unlikely event of him getting his battered body away from both Philip and Elroy, he had no inclination at all to dive twenty metres into ice-cold water. It was a long way to shore, far too far, and there was no way he would survive a swim like that, certainly not in his current state . . .

Philip seemed to have ended the call. He sat with the phone in his hand for several seconds and then pressed a button on one side of it before raising it to his mouth.

'Sophie?' He released the button.

'I'm here!' her voice crackled over the little speaker.

'We're on the bridge, will be there in a couple of minutes. You can drive up now, over.'

'Understood!'

The other end of the bridge was getting closer and closer, and HP felt the train start to slow down.

'Well, Henrik, we seemed to have reached the end of the line . . .'

Her head was still spinning as she walked slowly back towards where she had left the hire-car.

Peter Gladh wasn't MayBey, unless he and his partner were extremely good actors. But she doubted that. They had both seemed genuine, and that whole story about Tobbe seemed to come from the heart.

Tobbe . . .

It was quite obvious that he'd tried to mislead her.

He probably didn't have a clue about MayBey, and had just given her Gladh's name to get her out of the tennis hall before little Jonathan could pick up the vibes.

But she couldn't quite shake the feeling that Tobbe was involved, one way or another.

Not just because MayBey seemed to know about them using Henke's flat, or that several of the events that had been described matched the sort of thing Tobbe had told her. The whole situation had also escalated at about the same time that she finished with him. But Tobbe wasn't MayBey, she'd worked that out early on. He simply wasn't good enough at expressing himself, not by a long shot. Besides, he didn't have the IT skills needed to keep MayBey anonymous.

But there was still something about the tone of the posts. It seemed so personal. As if MayBey knew exactly who she was, and genuinely didn't like – hated her, even.

He was terrified.

They had been watching him somehow, letting him off the leash for a while to see what he'd do. Anyone smarter than him would obviously have taken off. Packed his bag and got the hell out of Dodge, making them believe he was out of the Game and no longer any threat to them.

But not him. Oh, no . . . Instead he had merely demonstrated that he had no intention of giving up. That he was still a threat. The question he had asked himself in the flat was still waiting for an answer. Had they managed to see past Henrik Pettersson and realize that he was also Player 128? Did they even know that it was him that Vincent had framed for Anna's death?

The train pulled into the platform with a good deal of creaking, jolted a few times and then stopped abruptly.

'Time to get out,' Elroy muttered in HP's ear as he grabbed him by the arm. 'And just so you know . . .'

With his free hand he nudged his jacket open to reveal a black metallic object at his hip.

'Model 88, 9 millimetre, 19 bullets in the cartridge,' he grinned.

HP gulped a couple of times, then nodded slowly. His pulse was pounding in his ears.

They walked along the almost empty platform towards the ticket hall. Philip walked a couple of steps ahead, followed by HP, with Elroy glued to his left arm. He already knew where they were heading.

The same steep flight of steps down to street level, the one he had tried to run up just a few hours before. They were going to drive him out to some secluded place, a gravel pit or some forest clearing. This time he was far more scared. Just like Anna, he was a threat, a risk factor that needed to be dealt with. If he got inside that car he wouldn't return until some Thai berry-picker found his fox-gnawed skull in thirty or forty years time, he was sure of that.

He had to do something!

* * *

As she headed out across the Lidingö bridge she tried to sort out the radio. A bit of music, that was what she needed. Something to drown out the maelstrom in her head.

But instead she got the news.

'The Security Police are still declining to comment on the failed bomb attack in the centre of Stockholm. The 28-year-old perpetrator had no previous convictions, and was not known to the police, but the message the man left on Facebook suggests that his actions are linked to international terrorism . . .'

She changed channel, zapped about for a bit until she found a Babyshambles song she liked.

In the morning there's a buzz of flies
Between the pillows and the skies
That beg into your eyes
Through the looking glass
And between your thighs
And it's written no small surprise
Let's straight down the rabbit hole
There we go . . .

Only ten metres left before the ticket hall, then a few more to the flight of steps. Elroy's hand was holding him like a vice and he could feel the man's eyes boring into the back of his neck.

But he had had an idea. He slowed down slightly, just enough for his former boss to get another metre or so ahead of them.

The sliding doors opened to let Philip into the hall, and at that moment HP stopped.

'Don't stop . . .' Elroy muttered.

HP obeyed and took a step forward, so that they were in the middle of the doorway. Elroy squeezed his arm tighter and muttered irritably.

'Come on, come on, come on!!!'

The doors closed without warning.

The left-hand door hit Elroy on the arm, forcing him instinctively to take half a step back. At the same time HP took a quick step into the hall and twisted sideways. The right-hand door missed his back and a fraction of a second later crashed onto Elroy's already caught arm.

He heard Elroy yelp, felt his grip loosen and jerked his body quickly.

He was free!

Time to do what he did best: run for his life!

Philip had evidently heard the cry. He spun round, and reached out with his arms. But HP had already built up speed. He feinted left, then swerved round Philip's right side.

He set off for the escalator leading up to the underground platform, taking the steps two at a time the way he usually did, but he could feel his body protesting. When he reached the top he glanced quickly over his shoulder, only to discover that both Philip and Elroy were already hot on his heels.

Fuck!

He flew out onto the platform, choosing the right-hand side which was completely deserted.

His body felt weak and he was having to make a huge effort not to trip over his own feet.

A handful of passengers were waiting on the left-hand side of the platform, but obviously none of them was going to help him. Instead he took aim at the far end of the platform, and the long tunnel that led up to Hjorthagen.

Another glance over his shoulder made his heart-rate change gear into panic mode. His pursuers were gaining on him, already close enough for him to see the clenched expressions on their faces. Plumes of breath were puffing from their mouths and noses.

Fucking hell!

He could usually outrun pretty much anyone, but he was still injured, and these guys seemed to be pretty phenomenal runners.

He could forget the tunnel, they'd have caught up with him before he even reached the entrance, and even if by some miracle he did make it, a two hundred metre uphill slope was the last thing he needed right now.

For a second he thought about crossing the empty track and jumping the fence down towards Värtavägen, but the viaduct the platform was built on must be a good fifteen metres up, and there was no way he'd survive a fall like that.

He needed a new plan, fast as fuck!

Another glance over his shoulder, they were even closer now.

His muscles were aching, his lungs and throat burning and he could clearly feel his movements getting slower. They were going to catch him, he realized. Then he saw the sign announcing an approaching train light up on the left-hand side of the platform, and felt the familiar gust of air.

A chance . . .

A tiny, fucking dangerous little chance. But he didn't exactly have much choice . . .

He swerved sharply to the left, changing platform and cruising between a couple of lethargic passengers.

He heard their angry cries as his pursuers knocked them flying.

He veered right and carried on down this new platform. Then he saw the lights of the train emerging from the tunnel, heading straight towards him. His pursuers had almost caught him. He could feel their hands grabbing for his jacket and staked his last reserves of energy on a final, violent burst of speed. The train's brakes were squealing as he saw it getting closer. Hands brushed his back again.

His lungs felt like they were about to burst, his legs were on the point of giving out, but he forced them out over the edge of the platform. He felt a millisecond of weightlessness as he hung in the air in front of the train.

Then he heard someone scream, a long, drawn out scream that merged with the shrieking of the brakes.

Then ground, tarmac, metal and, finally: darkness . . .

35

The rabbit hole

Pillars of Society forum
Posted: 23 December, 22:49
By: **MayBey**

Maybe you're right, Regina . . .
Maybe I am just a ghost?
But dare you all ignore me?
Dare you*?*

This post has 96 comments

The pocket under the platform wasn't particularly big. Not quite seventy centimetres across, and maybe half as deep. Just enough for an average-sized person to be able to take cover there.

The wheels of the train were still rolling just a few centimetres away, and the shriek of the brakes made it almost impossible to think.

He did a quick check. His body ached, both from the run, the landing and his dive into the cubby-hole, and his heart was pounding like the bass at a death metal concert.

But to his immense relief he couldn't find any amputated stumps spurting cascades of blood. All his limbs seemed to be intact, even if they were badly battered. He tucked his arms under his body and tried to snake his way forward.

Not very easy . . .

His mate Vesa had once pointed out the protective pocket to him a long time ago. The guy clearly had a serious train fetish, but you didn't know about that sort of thing when you were fifteen. He'd eventually met a tragic fate, ending up as charcoal down in Älvsjö. He'd been riding on top of a carriage but hadn't realized that the power cables sometimes hung lower in the depot than they did out on along the tracks . . .

But they'd had fun back then.

They started hitching rides between the carriages, and other low-level stuff. They went on a tunnel safari at the abandoned station at Kymlinge. That was where HP tried out the safety pocket for the first time. One of the trains on the blue line had thundered past at almost eighty kilometres an hour, and for a few seconds the pressure wave and the ear-splitting noise almost made him crap himself. After that they tried the same stunt in other places, seeing as every station has the same little safety pocket. It was really more of a groove than a pocket, seeing as it ran the entire length of the platform. So he ought to be able to snake his way to the opening of the tunnel while the train stopped anyone seeing what he was doing from above. At least that was the theory . . .

The train had stopped and he could hear a buzz of agitated voices from the platform.

'No, no, for God's sake, you can't go down onto the track . . .' an authoritative male voice was saying. He guessed that was the train driver.

'The current has to be switched off before you can do that . . . We've got set routines for this sort of thing, we get almost one jumper each week . . . The police and fire brigade are on their way, so can everyone please take a step back?!'

The voices grew fainter as he snaked away from them.

He was making slower progress than he had hoped.

The rough stones beneath him were scraping his knees and elbows, and his thick jacket was making it harder to move. In the distance he could hear sirens approaching. He needed to be a fair way inside the tunnel before the fire brigade shut off the current and got down onto the track.

He paused for a few seconds, then laboriously wriggled out of his jacket. It would be cold without it, but he didn't have a lot of choice.

A quick double check of the pockets to make sure he didn't forget anything.

Wallet, keys and cigarettes.

All present and correct, and he stuffed them all into the pockets of his jeans. Only the lighter left, and he ran his hands over the jacket until he found it in one of the many little side pockets.

It was ridiculously difficult to pull out, it seemed like it had slipped inside the lining and for a moment he considered abandoning it. But then he realized that the walk through the tunnel to the next station at Gärdet would be fucking long without a fag, so he tried again.

This time he tore the lining open with his fingers.

That was more like it!

But the little rectangular object he fished out wasn't a lighter . . .

Elite GPS 311 it said in tiny letters on one side of the flat little rectangle. Well, that explained a whole lot. They had tagged him with a transmitter, tracking him like some fucking harbour seal! So that was why they had been able to locate him without him spotting them . . .

It was a smart place to put it, the jacket was thick and had enough zips and velcro fasteners for him not to notice even a hard little gizmo like that.

But there was one thing he couldn't make sense of. How the hell had they managed to plant it?

The jacket was brand new, he'd grabbed it from Becca's shopping bag just before he set out. Which in turn meant . . . well, what, Einstein?

A new factor in the equation . . .

Fuck.

Fuck.

FUCK!

He needed to get hold of her, find out who she'd been in contact with recently. Try to stop her getting even more involved than she already was.

But first he had to get out of here . . .

Tobias Lundh had obviously been a mistake, an error of judgement on her part, and one for which she was paying the price in more ways than one. Even though she never dated colleagues, unlike a lot of female police officers, she had suddenly thrown herself into an affair with a notorious ladies' man like Tobbe. Who just happened to be best friends with her boss, as well as his neighbour . . .

What the hell had she been thinking?

But of course that was the whole problem. Just like with John, she hadn't been thinking at all, just following the first impulse that popped into her head. After everything that had happened last year with Henke, and the attack she had managed to avert at the last minute, and not least the parcel containing those bolts, she had promised herself that she would try to relax a bit more. Lower her standards and give herself a chance to be more human . . .

Well, that had turned out really well.

Clearly she should have rectified the Tobbe Lundh mistake a long time ago, then she would have escaped his pathetic jealousy and constant text messages. She already had a boyfriend. A nice, considerate one, who maybe wasn't all that exciting, but at least he'd never cause this sort of mess. So why had she deceived Micke, betraying him for a bit of meaningless sex with a man she didn't even like? She had no good answer to that question. Or rather, she had far too many . . .

36

Out of the hole and down the slope

Location: Hotel Hopeless
Date and time: Christmas Day, 13.48
Clothing: In-room casual, which meant underpants and vest
Status: Bruised and hacked off

Droning.

That was what the phenomenon was called, he'd seen it on Discovery. Sleeping while you were walking. Well, sleeping? That definitely wasn't the right word for it. He'd been in a sort of trance, awake enough for his legs to carry on moving forward, but with his brain still way off in fucking lala-land.

The tunnel itself hadn't actually been all that long, maybe a kilometre or so. But seeing as it formed a broad curve under Hjorthagen it hadn't taken more than about ten metres before the light from the end of the tunnel at Ropsten had disappeared. The impenetrable darkness had certainly contributed to the experience.

He had seen things, terrible fucking H P Lovecraft things that had made the hair stand up on his arms and the back of his neck. Rats, bats and even bigger shapeless creatures tucked away in corners and side tunnels. Things that had hissed at him as he staggered past, scratching at his back with shitty, claw-like, down-and-out hands.

And the voices. Dad, Dag, that poor incinerated bastard, Erman. They had all whispered to him out of the darkness. Demanding answers from him.

Do you want to play a game, Henrik Pettersson?
Do you want to?
Are you completely sure?
Yes or No?

His lunch had just been delivered, a Royale with Cheese that cost him double the usual rate seeing as Burger King was a couple more blocks for the receptionist to walk. But it was worth it. The dressing dribbled out between his fingers and he greedily slurped up every last, greasy drop.

He had staggered out of the ghost tunnel at Gärdet, actually carrying on almost another hundred metres before realizing that the lights and fresh air were real and not just more hallucinations.

Then he had managed to get a taxi outside the TV4 building, and even if the driver had given him a funny look he had still agreed to drive his dirty and battered body home to Södermalm.

He had slept for almost twenty-four hours, then dragged himself up to shower and shave. After a bit of food he had logged on to the computer.

He had to find a way to contact Becca. Explain why he hadn't come back. She was bound to have been both pissed off and worried. But he didn't dare call her at home or try her mobile. If they could plant a GPS in his clothes, then they could certainly bug her phones. His adversaries weren't just anyone.

The whole thing was much bigger than he had thought, he realized that now, and a bit of good old googling had quickly reinforced the idea that he had started to develop out on Lidingö.

He had to find a different way to contact her. To keep her safe.

Christmas made everything twice as depressing.

She was almost as angry with herself as she was with Henke. First he quite literally drops from the sky, naked and battered, with some ridiculous story. Then a couple of days recovering while his nice big sister brings him food and looks after him, then he suddenly vanishes again without a word of explanation.

And she'd got Christmas food sorted, had even dragged some decorations out of storage in the attic, and he never showed up. Naturally she had called her mobile, only to find it tucked away on the hat-rack.

So fucking typical of Henke, and so fucking typical of her not to know better.

So she'd ended up spending Christmas on her own.

Micke had called a couple of times, but she hadn't felt comfortable talking to him. She blamed the fact that she was spending Christmas with her brother, and kept the conversations as short as she could. She was pretty sure that he must know about her affair with Tobbe by now. Not least from reading all the gossip on the Pillars of Society forum. Her lawyer hadn't helped to lighten the mood. Apparently the prosecutor was thinking of bringing charges against her early in January. Gross misuse of office, which meant she'd be fired if she was found guilty. *Fucking fantastic*, as Henke would have said . . .

She carefully packed her gym gear and left the flat. One of the big chains had a gym at Fridhemsplan, and she was thinking of getting a ten-session ticket there for the time being.

As she emerged onto the street she looked round carefully before walking off towards the bus stop. One block away an old car started up, but the sound of the engine was almost swallowed by the snowdrifts and she didn't notice it.

It was the photograph of the failed suicide bomber that put him on the scent. A terrible picture that the evening tabloids were making the most of, obviously.

The picture was taken from directly above – someone must have leaned right out of a window to look down. The lifeless body, the dark stains on the snow, debris and broken plate-glass windows, it was all clearly visible.

But what caught HP's attention was a small detail at the edge of the chaos. At the very top of the picture, on its own in the snow, was a little rectangular object that stopped him dead. The hair on the back of his neck stood up just like it had in the H P Lovecraft tunnel. He didn't even need to zoom in to work out what it was.

A mobile phone! A shiny one that looks very fucking similar to the one in his wardrobe.

Once his brain had made the connection it wasn't that hard to carry on with the rest of the puzzle. First a bit of googling among the traditional media.

'The second terrorist attack in Sweden in the last two years . . .'

'It's clear that international terrorism is here to stay.'

'Experts in terrorism agree that there are at least three hundred potential terrorists in Sweden . . .'

'The opposition parties, which had previously opposed increased surveillance, have now decided to back the measures . . .'

'A poll of our readers indicates that an overwhelming majority of the Swedish people support a strengthening of . . .'

It was that last sentence that made him change his focus and head out into his old hunting grounds. It didn't take him many minutes to find the right place. Some of the trolls seemed to have changed their names, but he could still recognize them by the way they expressed themselves.

'M00reon', 'M1crosrf' and 'JabRue' were his own creations. But there were also old favourites like 'VAO', 'Bosse Baldersson', 'Ljugo Juli' and 'Lasse Danielsson'. He tested every troll name he could remember, and the results exceeded all his expectations.

From the day after the bombing, all of them – the whole lot, *tutti* – without one single fucking exception, had posted comments that one way or another dealt with the terrorist attack. When he switched to the blogs the results were basically the same. Even the most superficial bloggers had something to say on the subject, even if it was just clichés like '*Fucking awful*' or '*My sisters best friend was like a minute from being blone up . . .*'

The conclusion was crystal clear!!

ArgosEye was fanning the flames as much as it possibly could, and the whole opinion-shaping machinery had cranked into action precisely twelve hours after the failed suicide bombing.

Coincidence?

Well, of course it could be.

But considering what he already knew . . .

NFW!

No Fucking Way!!!!!

She had a heavy bag of groceries in each hand and her gym bag on her back. She was only ten metres from the bus when the doors closed and it pulled away from the pavement with a hiss.

She swore loudly to herself, thought about waiting for the next one, then decided to walk the two kilometres or so home from Fridhemsplan.

By the time she was about halfway she had already regretted her decision several times.

In spite of her gloves, the bags were cutting into her hands and making her stop more and more often to let the blood back into her fingers. And the pavements hadn't been properly gritted and she came close to slipping over several times.

She had just passed the park beside the teacher training college when the dark car glided up next to her. To the right of her, on the other side of the high fence, cars were streaming out of the Fredhäll tunnel, and the noise and movement of the traffic down on the E4 was probably why she didn't react until the car had stopped and the thickset man was standing in her path.

'Get in,' he said abruptly and opened the back door.

'What?'

On the other side of the car the driver's door opened and a red-haired woman, about the same age as her, got out and walked round the car.

'Get in!' the man repeated. 'There's someone who wants to talk to you . . .'

She leaned over and peered inside the car, which she thought was a Mercedes.

John was sitting inside.

‘Please get in, Rebecca,’ he said softly.

She glanced quickly to her left. The woman was on the pavement behind her.

Like the man on the other side of her, the woman had her jacket undone in a way that Rebecca recognized, with one hand on her belt inside the opening of the jacket.

She took a step back towards the fence.

Suddenly she realized that she recognized the man beside her.

‘You were on my bus,’ she stated drily. ‘But you were much nicer then . . .’

‘Are you going to get in, or what . . .?’ he replied.

‘What happens if I say no?’

The man took half a pace forward, and the woman did the same on the other side.

‘Let’s all take this nice and calmly,’ John said from the rear seat of the car. ‘I’m sorry about our little misunderstanding the other day, I really am, Rebecca . . . I was tired and had had too much to drink, and as a result I misjudged the whole situation. I hope you can accept my apology, and I can assure you that I have no intention of seeking revenge in any way at all.’

He pointed to the plaster on his nose.

‘If you’d be so kind as to get in, we’ll drive you home. It’s only a few hundred metres, but those bags look heavy . . .’

As he finished his sentence the big man held out one hand to take her bags, repeating his gesture from the bus. She hesitated. The man and woman were almost imperceptibly closing in on her. Slowly she put the bags down on the ground and took a step backwards.

It had taken several days for the penny to drop. ACME Telecom Services Ltd – that was the company listed at the office bunker he and Rehyman the Boy Wonder had stealth-raided, the place they discovered that the Game was being steered from. Until he had blown the whole place sky high, that is . . .

So, ACME Telecom Services.

A proud member of the PayTag Group, it had said on their website.

If he had been even the slightest bit doubtful about his mission before, then all considerations were now totally Scarlett O'Hara'ed.

PayTag owned ACME, and ACME hosted the Game.

And your conclusion, Sherlock?

PayTag *was* the Game!

Suddenly the pavement was lit up by the lights of another car, very bright, albeit the car was a considerably scruffier one.

It stopped in the middle of the road for a few seconds, then backed sharply to park behind the Mercedes. A scrawny little man in a leather jacket, cowboy boots and pilot's sunglasses jumped out of the passenger side.

'What's all this then?' he said, taking several authoritative steps towards them.

The man and woman on either side of Rebecca exchanged glances.

'What do you mean?' the man replied, lowering the hand he had been holding out towards Rebecca.

'Renko, surveillance,' said the man in sunglasses, waving a little black wallet. 'No stopping here, and that applies to Mercs as well, yeah . . .?'

'We were just offering to give this lady a lift . . .'

'Off you go, now, my partner and I can drive Normén home.'

The man in sunglasses gestured over his shoulder with

his thumb towards the ramshackle car. The driver's door was open now. A man in a green army jacket got out with some difficulty and straightened up to his full height. Rebecca saw the woman to her left unconsciously take half a step back, and was close to doing the same herself.

The man was huge, at least 2.10 metres tall, and almost a metre across the shoulders.

His long hair hung down on both sides of his head, and what with that and a large fur hat, most of his face was hidden. Not that you really felt you wanted to see it.

'Okay, off you go, unless you want an A-penalty . . .' the man in sunglasses chattered, waving with one hand. 'Normén, you hop in the back, the rescue patrol is ready to depart.'

He pulled his sunglasses down onto the tip of his nose and winked at her.

Rebecca took a step towards the car. The woman was still standing in her way.

For a few seconds they just stared at each other.

Then the red-haired woman slowly stepped aside.

A few moments later Rebecca was sitting in the surveillance car. It was full of rubbish and smelled odd, almost as if something had died in there. The driver's seat was pushed so far back that the huge man at the wheel might as well have been sitting beside her on the back seat. The car radio was playing some old song she vaguely recognized.

The Mercedes performed an angry u-turn and drove off quickly in the direction of the Western Bridge.

'Okay!' she said, taking a deep breath. 'First: if you two clowns are going to play at being police officers again, it's an O-penalty, not A . . . And second: where's my idiot of a brother, and what the hell is he up to?'

37

Blamegames

Pillars of Society forum
Posted: 28 December, 18:06
By: **MayBey**

So what's it to be?
Do you want me to get him?
Thumbs up, or down?
Time to cast your vote . . .

This post has 231 comments

The more he thought about it, the more sense it all made. The takeover of the company and Anna's murder had been just the preamble. The real match had only started with the failed bombing.

The guy had been loaded with various explosives and other horrors, and had been just fifty metres from one of the busiest parts of Stockholm. Yet somehow he had still managed to fuck the whole thing up.

Even though he must have run the entire length of Drottninggatan, and presumably passed hundreds of

Christmas shoppers tipsy from mulled wine, the bomb had gone off in a place where basically no-one but him had been hurt.

Obviously it could be a miracle, or the poor sod might have panicked. Changed his mind or simply been a bit too heavy-handed with his home-brewed internet explosives.

But there was also another possibility.

That someone had detonated the bomb remotely so that it got maximum attention but did minimum damage. Pretty much like Player 128's little adventure with the Horse-Guards in Kista. He had thought long and hard about why the Game had made the call that would detonate the explosives so long before the cortege containing the US Secretary of State was due to get there. If he hadn't been smart enough to see through the Game Master's bullshit, he'd probably have been the only victim of the blast, just like the bomber in the city centre.

But it was all about shifting people's focus. Creating an event that was both spectacular and simultaneously raised enough questions for the media and all the so-called experts to be able to argue about on every news channel available.

And in the meantime other things vanished under the radar. In actual fact, the whole thing was just a variation of what the gang at ArgosEye did. Filling the notice-board with their own posters so there was no room for anything else.

Over the next few weeks absolutely everything would be about the explosion and all the question marks surrounding it, and ArgosEye would make sure that the shift in focus lasted long enough.

The only question was: what were they trying to hide?

It had to be something big, that much at least was obvious.

So what the fuck was he going to do now?

Obviously he could go to the press, but what evidence did he have? He, a convicted criminal who had just been deported from an Arab country, directing various unspecified accusations at a well-established Swedish businessman. Not only that, but a wonderful little combo of accusations involving global conspiracy theories, various intelligence agencies and secret societies. God, he might as well make himself a hand-painted sign and join the other nutters protesting outside parliament.

No, he really only had two options.

One: pack his bags and head off into the sunset like a poor lonesome cowboy.

Or two: so much easier! He'd find out what they were planning and put a stop to the whole thing!

Yippikayee, mothafuckers!

The guy in the pilot's sunglasses and his weird friend double-parked outside her door and went with her all the way up to her flat. They even carried her bags, and then politely declined her offer of a cup of coffee as thanks for their help.

'Here,' sunglasses said, rooting through his jacket pockets. During the drive he had introduced himself as Nox. 'Your brother wanted you to have this.'

He handed her a mobile phone and charger.

'Pay as you go. Keep it switched on, he'll call soon.'

He made an odd drumming gesture against the side of his nose.

'Don't you worry, little lady, Nox will look out for you!'

* * *

He watched the work-experience kid show up on his scooter, parking it right outside the door. It looked like the same guy he'd met several weeks ago, but all these kids looked the same. Long, greasy hair, his entire face covered in spots. Throw in a pair of washed-out jeans, red, Counterstrike eyes and a creased t-shirt and you'd pretty much covered all of Manga's little disciples.

A bit of rattling with the key in the lock, then a few minutes wait to let the guy switch off the alarm and start things up before he crossed the street.

He opened the door, but to his surprise he wasn't welcomed by the usual tune from the doorbell.

Maybe Wally Work-Experience had got fed up of it, or else he simply didn't share Manga's fascination with *Star Wars*?

Nor was the guy hanging over the counter with a cup of bitter coffee and a crumpled copy of *Metro* the way his master usually did. Instead HP found him towards the back of the shop, in front of one of the larger computers.

He was probably surfing for porn, playing pocket billiards, checking out the internet's latest accomplishments. 'Naughty Annie stuffs her Fanny', 'Donkey-Hung IV', or other cinematic masterpieces proudly presented by the world wide web . . .

'Does your boss know what you're doing?' HP shouted, making the young man almost fall off his chair.

'What!?'

The guy was staring at him in shock.

'Calm down, lad, I'm not that dangerous.'

HP grinned and pointed to his own chest.

'I come in peace. Take me to your leader!'

He nodded benevolently at the kid, who still looked completely blank.

'Ah, what the hell . . .' HP chuckled when the joke

seemed to pass him by. 'I need to get hold of Manga or Farook or whatever the fuck he's calling himself this week. Is he still away? His old email and Messenger don't seem to be working.'

'Er . . .?!'

Finally, something resembling a sign of life . . .

'Well . . . the boss is in Saudi or somewhere like that . . . He's got a new Hotmail. Do you want it . . .?'

'Bingo!'

The young man grinned with relief and a minute or so later he'd managed to dig out a scrap of paper and a pen.

'You're HP, yeah?' he went on in a slightly less shaky voice.

'Mmh,' HP muttered from the corner of his mouth while he was jotting down Manga's contact details.

'Manga has said a lot about you . . . You sound like a pretty cool dude. Seen a lot of stuff, I mean.'

'Really, you reckon?' HP said, looking up. 'Obviously, I can neither confirm or deny any rumours . . .' he added with a smile.

After all, you had to give kids a chance . . .

To: becca.normen@hotmail.com
From: t.sammer@gmail.com

Dear Rebecca,
I have encouraging news from Darfur.

It looks as if there is a sequence of film showing the incident.

Someone who was at the scene is said to have recorded the whole thing using the camera on his mobile, and we are currently doing our best to get hold of the recording.

Hopefully we will have it within a couple of days.

While I am writing, I wonder if I might ask for your help?

I should very much like to contact your brother.

For a long time now I have been hoping for an opportunity to talk to him in person, to tell him a little more about your father. I might perhaps even be able to rehabilitate Erland a little in Henrik's eyes. Unfortunately Henrik is not a very easy person to get hold of, and as I myself am often away travelling I haven't yet managed to arrange a meeting.

I shall be setting off again shortly, probably for a rather long trip, and I would very much appreciate it if you could tell me by return where I might be able to reach him.

With very best wishes,
Tage Sammer

She had just read the email when the phone rang.

'Hello?'

'Hi, it's me!'

'Yes, so I can hear . . .'

'We probably need to talk . . .'

'You reckon . . .?'

'Come on, Becca, this isn't the time to get all grumpy. Do you know Philip Argos, Nox said it looked like you did?'

'Who?'

'Philip Argos, previously known as Philip John

Martinsson. My former boss and a seriously fucking nasty piece of work . . .'

She sighed.

'It's complicated . . .'

Okay, so the situation was actually even worse that he had imagined.

Nox had done his job impeccably, which wasn't really that strange. After all, he had stumped up the rent on a flat for the Chief for the next six months, and thrown another ten cartons of cigarettes into the bargain, so now the two nutters were neighbours down on the ground floor.

But what he had found out over the past few days was considerably more troubling.

She'd lied to him!

She had never explained what she had been doing in Östermalm that morning, and as usual he had been a bit too focused on himself to ask.

What annoyed him most was that he had actually believed that the whole thing was a huge fucking coincidence. That karma had put her there like some angel of salvation . . .

Whereas in fact she was more like a tart who'd just tumbled out of Philip's bed after a night of passion . . .

His life had pretty much always been basically fucked up, but he had always been able to rely on Becca. She was the one who helped him keep his head above water. But now she'd let him down, several times over. First she'd jumped into bed with his worst enemy, and then lied about it, or at the very least neglected to tell the truth.

It wasn't Stoffe who'd blabbed about him – it was his own sister.

Fuck!

Fuck!

FUCK!!!

He had to take a break from the computer, go for a little four-metre walk to the door and back, until he calmed down a bit.

The whole thing was like some evil bastard flashback to the days when Dag had her under his thumb . . .

To begin with he had admired Dag, seeing him as a big brother. When Dag and Becca were dating, he hadn't really wanted to see the signs, because Dag was a cool guy, the sort you wanted to hang out with, get a pat on the back from. It had been Manga who woke him up from his admiring sleep and made him realize what Dag was really like, what was actually happening. Then he started to hate Dag almost as much as he hated his dad.

Up to now he hadn't actually hated Philip Argos. On some level HP had still been able to understand why his boss was acting the way he was. Because after all, he had betrayed Philip's trust, put his whole plan at risk. Cause and effect, so to speak. But now that had all changed.

Now it was fucking personal!

The situation was actually even worse than she had imagined.

Last time it had been the sinking of the Estonia and Palme's murder, but this . . .

When she had finally got him to start talking, he didn't stop. The words had tumbled out of him like a torrent, especially once she herself had been honest and at least tried to explain about her disastrous date with John, a.k.a. Philip Argos.

She had done her best to believe him, really, really tried hard. But it just wouldn't go in. Companies cleaning up the internet, directing blogs and discussion forums while simultaneously collaborating with forces that carried out fake terrorist attacks in order to shift the media's focus away from things they wanted to hide . . .

Seriously?

And as if that wasn't enough, he had thrown in a bit more – hired assassins, secret Google algorithms and clairvoyant Lidingö ladies, only to end up back where it had all started.

That bloody Game . . .

38

Online games

Pillars of Society forum
Posted: 29 December, 18:41
By: **MayBey**

Little Henrik's holed up in a shabby little hostel for single men on Södermalm. He probably thinks he's safe.
But we know better, don't we?

This post has 29 comments

Goodboy.821 says: Are you there?

Farook says: Good to hear from you brother. Long time no c . . . ;)

Goodboy.821 says: Far too long old friend – my bad . . .

Farook says: Did u miss me?? ☺

Goodboy.821 says: Fuck off Manga!1!1 ☺

Goodboy.821 says: Did you get my email?

Farook says: Yep but it took a while to decrypt. You're more paranoid about the net than me these days.

Goodboy.821 says: With good reason as you can see . . .

Farook says: Yeah I get it. I've read the whole thing.

Goodboy.821 says: And?

Farook says: I completely agree with you brother. What Argos is doing is wrong on more levels than I can think of. It goes against the whole point of the internet. I know loads of people who'd love to drag those trolls into the light. The trojan's no problem, I can put one of those together in a couple of days, even from here . . . The only question is how to get it into the system . . .

Farook says: But it must be possible to hack in. I know a few people who could probably manage it, but it might take a couple of months. And you never know how effective that's going to be, there's a pretty good chance the attack would be discovered and then the effect would be limited. Same thing if you try to email the trojan in as a hidden file . . .

Goodboy.821 says: Ok, not really the answer I was hoping for . . . ☹

Farook says: I can imagine . . .

Goodboy.821 says: Other ideas?

Farook says: Well, if you can't send it in from outside, the only other option is to introduce it manually.

Goodboy.821 says: Go on!

Farook says: Ok, thinking out loud here, but if you go down that road you need a computer with full access. An ordinary workstation won't do. You said yourself that they'd disabled the USB ports on the ordinary rigs so you need to find the right machine, you copy?

Goodboy.821 says: Copy!

Farook says: But obviously that's a lot more dangerous, you get that too?

Goodboy.821 says: Just sort the trojan and leave the rest with me . . .

She wound the clip backwards and forwards.

Grainy pictures, presumably taken with the camera of a mobile, but it wasn't hard to see what they showed. The red ground, people in ragged clothes, and in the middle of them the black cars. Then you heard shots, the camera lurched wildly between ground and sky. The whole scenario felt unreal. As if she had dreamed the same thing over and over again, but this time the dream was being projected on a screen instead of inside her head.

Then the vehicle reversing came so close that the cameraman had to jump out of the way. A short glimpse of a dark-haired woman hanging off the door. Then suddenly he was there.

Right in front of the car, and even if the camera only picked him up for a second, that was more than enough. If you paused the clip you could see plenty of detail. His clothes, far too neat and clean for him to blend in properly, then a glimpse of something like a well-polished, black army boot below one trouser leg. The yellow plastic bag dangling from his free hand.

Then, finally, the enormous black revolver pointing straight at the car.

'Sent in an anonymous email to the prosecutor yesterday,' her lawyer had told her.

The clip had been sent for analysis, but if it was genuine she could count on being back on duty after the New Year holiday.

In other words, Uncle Tage had kept his promise.

The least she could do in return was to do as he asked.

She pulled out the pay-as-you-go mobile and pressed the call button.

'Yes.' His voice sounded cold when he answered.

The sound of traffic in the background told her he was outside.

'Monument,' she said curtly.

'What?!'

'The Monument Hotel, that's where you're staying, isn't it?'

There was silence on the line.

'Are you still there?'

'Sure. So who told you?'

He was trying to sound relaxed, but she had no trouble hearing how worried he was.

'Have you ever heard of anyone calling themselves MayBey?'

'MayBey, you mean that pretend cop?'

'What do you mean, pretend . . .? You know him?'

'Sort of, I checked your computer the other night while you were out. Saw you'd pasted together a document with quotes, then took a look at the forum. That's the sort of thing I did when I was working for Philip . . .'

Then a car horn, and the sound cut out for a moment, and for a few seconds she thought the call had been broken.

Then she heard his footsteps. It sounded a bit like he was running.

'Did what, Henke?' she said irritably. 'Look, I don't feel like playing your silly games right now . . .'

'Trolling.'

'Like I . . .'

'Going into different forums anonymously and fucking up the debate, or trying to steer it in the *right* direction, so to speak. Weren't you listening when I told you all this the last time we spoke?'

She sighed.

'You said loads of stuff, Henke, and most of it wasn't very nice . . .'

'Fuck that,' he interrupted. 'Whatever, this MayBey shows all the symptoms of troll disease.'

'Which are . . .?'

'He picks up words and jargon from others on the forum. Manages to get accepted. Then he starts tossing in little fire-crackers, and soon enough everyone's attention is focused on him.

'He doesn't seem to be an attack troll, because he'd be swearing all the time and causing loads of trouble, so at a guess he's got some sort of agenda.'

'But how can you be so sure he's not a police officer?'

'Okay, so the police jargon sounds right. But a real cop would hardly need to throw in a load of film quotes.'

'What?!'

She could almost hear him grinning.

'So you hadn't noticed? Well, I didn't check that thoroughly, but there were quotes from De Niro and Clint, I'm sure of that. That line about *rain to wash the trash off the sidewalk*, that's from *Taxi Driver* . . .'

He paused, but she could still hear his quick footsteps.

'Besides, there's his name,' he went on. 'In the world of forums, names always mean something, even the trolls' . . . To show how fucking smart they are, dangling bait in front of people's noses without anyone noticing.'

'So, MayBey?'

'Well, to start with there's the obvious connection to Maybe. And that's the name of Judge Dredd's arch-enemy. A serial killer who loves playing all sorts of games with the police . . . But if that wasn't enough, there's the whole anagram thing. Internet jockeys love anagrams. MayBey – Abyme?'

He left a dramatic pause and she had no choice but to spring the trap.

'And?'

'*Mise en Abyme* is a film term for looking into an abyss. I learned that at Adult Education . . .'

For a moment his voice sounded strained and he cleared his throat.

'Like when you put two mirrors opposite each other,

kind of. A copy of a copy, ad infinitum. Doubly unreal, yeah? Like a dream within a . . .'

'Dream . . .' she concluded.

Shit, they were on his trail!

He ought to just forget about the hotel, forget about his stuff and find another hiding place at once. But he couldn't leave the phone there. It was his only link to the Game, and as long as he had that, he had at least some sort of physical proof that they actually existed.

He cautiously poked his head above the wall behind the hotel.

No obvious danger.

The little bit of wood he had poked into the catch of the emergency exit at the top of the fire escape was still there so he had no trouble getting to the right floor. The corridor was empty, but to be on the safe side he waited a minute or so before creeping up to his door.

He put his ear to it and listened.

Not a sound.

He didn't have much time.

If Becca was right and someone was posting information on the internet about where he was, it wouldn't be long before they showed up here. But why would that police troll have posted anything about him? And how had he found him?

He'd have to deal with all that once he'd found himself a more secure place to hide.

He put the key-card in the lock and opened the door. The room was dark. He took a cautious step inside but refrained from turning the light on. His eyes quickly adjusted. The room was empty, as was the bathroom. He grabbed his bag and hurriedly gathered together his things.

The phone went in first. He hadn't touched it since he'd

got it back from Nox. To be honest, he'd had so much to think about that he'd almost forgotten about it.

But now it felt like his life depended on it.

There – done!

He closed the bag and took a couple of steps towards the door. But instead of opening it and taking off towards the fire escape at the end of the corridor he stopped. He wasn't sure where the feeling came from, but something wasn't right. He leaned closer to the door and peered carefully through the peephole. At first he could only see part of the corridor. Then he saw movement over by the lift. Two figures in balaclavas and dark clothing, heading straight towards him.

In a flash he put the safety chain on, then grabbed the little chair by the desk and wedged it under the door handle.

Then he opened the window as far as the safety catch would allow and clambered up onto the windowsill.

Just as there was a rattle from the lock behind him he gave the window-frame a good kick, breaking the catch.

He tossed his bag down, then took aim at the snowdrift a few metres below.

The chair slid to the floor and the door opened a few centimetres before the security chain caught it.

'There!' a voice roared.

Then he jumped.

39

Battle for control

Pillars of Society forum
Posted: 30 December, 16:37
By: **MayBey**

The votes have been counted – you have decided.
Now Henrik must face the consequences of your decision.

This post has 149 comments

It looked like MayBey had lost his grip, but weirdly enough Rebecca seemed to be the only person reacting to it. Most of his readers appeared to think the whole thing was just kinda cool, writing encouraging comments, goading him to carry on with his plan to murder her brother. As if it was all some sort of game.

Like that poor girl who announced her suicide on Facebook, as a last cry for help, only to get scornful comments from her so-called friends.

'You haven't got the bottle'
'Go on – go for it!'

This whole thing was sick!

He had built himself a little den behind the empty boxes so that even if anyone opened the storeroom door, they wouldn't be able to see his little nest. A sleeping bag and cut-off cola bottle for pressing emergencies. The laptop, so he could stay in touch with the outside world. It was fine, the only problem was that he had to get up every ten minutes to press the timed red button if he wanted more light.

Okay, he could have tried to find another hotel, but he didn't actually have the time. Besides, the Game would be bound to check every place in the city now that they knew he was back.

The basement storeroom under the computer shop would have to do. But at least he'd got his very own little slave into the bargain. Well, two, actually, Wedge and Marky, but to be honest he was still having trouble telling the difference between Manga's little acolytes.

He had received the things he had ordered over the net faster than he had dared to hope. The list was more or less complete, there was just one thing missing . . .

He had just 'borrowed' the building's shower and sauna, and had put on the new clothes that Wedge and Marky had been kind enough to get for him. Just to be sure, he had gone with the whole hat and sunglasses routine all the way to her building.

He composed himself as he stood in front of the door, checked his breath and tugged as his collar to stop it sticking to his neck. He had to admit it, he felt nervous.

He had thought about her a fair bit over the past few

days. She had every right to be angry with him, disappointed even. After all, he had lied straight to her face. But without her help he wouldn't be able to do it. Besides, he missed her . . .

Shit, this was all so fucked up!

He took a deep breath, then rang the doorbell. Then he cupped his hand over the peephole in the door and saw the light from inside flicker as she approached the door.

He took a quick step to the side, to stay as far out of reach of the peephole as possible.

What if she didn't open the door?

She had to, his entire plan depended on it.

His mouth felt dry as dust and he swallowed a couple of times in an attempt to moisten it.

A drop of sweat ran down his spine, then another one.

Come on!

The lock rattled, then the door opened a crack. She had the chain on. Smart girl.

He opened with:

'Hi baby,' then added his very best smile as he held out the flowers he'd picked up down at the Seven-Eleven.

'What the fuck do you want?!' Rilke snapped, and for a moment he thought she was going to slam the door in his face.

'Calm down, I came to apologize. Here!'

He waved the flowers but she made no move to open the door and take them.

'You've got a fucking nerve, Magnus or Farook or whatever your real name is . . .'

'Henrik,' he interrupted. 'My name's Henrik Pettersson, but my friends call me HP.'

'Like I care,' she snarled. 'Philip's told me all about you. A traitor and a spy, sent to . . .'

'You're absolutely right,' he said. 'I'm all that, and quite a bit more . . .'

She opened her mouth but he quickly went on:

'But I've got a proposal for you, a very lucrative one. It's about the company . . .'

He fired off his best Valentino smile and crossed his fingers. She stood there without saying anything for a few seconds.

'Give me one good reason why I should let you in!' she said eventually.

'I'll give you forty! Since the day before yesterday, that's the percentage of ArgosEye that I own . . .'

There were eight people on her list. Five officers in Tobbe's rapid response unit, Nina Brandt, and another two names that she had reluctantly added after her conversation with Henke.

MayBey had some connection to Tobbe, the problem was that she didn't know what the connection was. Out of his five colleagues she thought she recognized two of the names. One who'd been in the same class as her at Police Academy, and another she'd worked with back when she was in uniform five or six years ago. But she honestly couldn't think of any reason why they should want to get at her.

Nina Brandt and Tobbe went out with each other for a while when they were at the academy, and she knew they were still good friends. It sounded pretty far-fetched, but she couldn't get away from the fact that Nina was the person who had first tipped her off about the Pillars of Society website.

Then there was Håkan Berglund, the guy she'd so rudely given the brush off.

That business with the faded flowers had undeniably

been a bit weird, so Håkan could probably be a suspect, especially as Henke seemed to think MayBey wasn't actually in the police.

The last name on the list made her feel a bit sick.

Micke . . .

Unlike the others on the list, he had both the skill and the right contacts to be able to take care of the technical side of MayBey, and he had plenty of reasons for wanting to cause her grief. But, as with Nina Brandt, she was having trouble thinking of Micke as a genuine suspect. He might have had every right to be angry with her, more than anyone else on the list, in fact. But still . . .

Anyway, he'd helped her to track down MayBey.

He had helped her, hadn't he?

She didn't believe him at first, not until he showed her his contract with Monika and the printout from the Patent and Registration Office. After that her tone got a bit more conciliatory. Not that she asked him right into the flat, but at least she agreed to go and get him a glass of water.

There were removal boxes in the hall, so presumably she had actually bought the apartment they had looked round. Maybe the plotters had already received an advance from PayTag?

There were several jackets hanging from the coat rack, and a couple of designer handbags, and beneath them a long row of shoes.

He ran his fingers over the leather of one of the handbags. Soft and pale brown, almost cream-coloured. Just like her skin. For a moment he felt a pang in his chest, and when she reappeared with his glass of water shortly afterwards he was surprised by an impulse to touch her. But he resisted.

'So, what's your proposal . . . Henrik?'

Her tone was cautious but considerably less hostile.

'It's very simple . . .'

He took a few sips of water as he kept his eye on her. God, she was pretty, even in jogging pants and a t-shirt she was still a clear ten-pointer. Funny to think that he'd been in a relationship with her, properly.

Well, almost . . .

He lowered the glass and looked at her.

'I've got forty percent, you've got ten. Together we control half the company. If you can think of anyone else who could be persuaded to support us . . .'

He took a deep breath.

'. . . then we could take over ArgosEye. Get rid of Philip as MD, and run the business however we want.'

He fell silent and stared at her. For a few seconds everything was almost back to normal, and once again he had to fight the urge to put his hand out and touch her.

'You're crazy,' she said, slowly shaking her head.

'Maybe. Prising Philip away from the helm wouldn't be easy, but we could manage it together. You and me, baby! What do you say?'

He tried to muster up an enthusiastic smile.

'That wasn't what I meant . . .' she said in a low voice.

'Oh?'

'What I meant is that you must be crazy if you think I'd betray Philip. After all he's done for the company, for us, for me personally. Do you really think I'd risk that for someone . . . like you?'

Her anger was back again, but there was something else in her voice, something he didn't like.

'Congratulations, Henrik, if that is your real name. You managed to trick Monika into selling you her shares, so now you own forty percent of a company where one hundred percent of the employees hate you!'

She took a step closer to him.

'My advice to you is to call Philip and sell your shares to him. If you're lucky you'll make a profit and can crawl back under whatever stone you came from, with a bit of extra money in your pocket. Because you're absolutely right about one thing . . .'

She poked him in the chest with her index finger, and even though HP was a head taller than her he still took a step back.

'. . . Philip would never let anyone else take over control of ArgosEye, not a chance. He'd kill anyone who even dared to try!'

She realized something was wrong when she heard the letterbox rattle. The post ought to have come a long while ago, and the bloke who delivered advertizements to her block didn't usually ignore the 'No adverts' sticker on the door.

She walked quickly out into the hall to see the little brown envelope land on the doormat. She picked it up and felt a hard little object through the paper.

A key, the sort that usually fitted a padlock. But which lock? And who had put it though her letterbox?

She pulled her shoes on and raced down the stairs. She heard the front door slam two floors below, but by the time she reached the darkened street there was no-one in sight.

Okay, now he was officially heartbroken.

It was probably the first time since primary school.

Rilke despised him, to her he was nothing but a bottom feeder, a disgusting insect that deserved to be trodden underfoot. It actually hurt more than he could have imagined.

Usually he didn't give a flying fuck what anyone thought

about him. But with her it was different. Even if he had worked out that the odds weren't on his side, on some level he still hadn't been able to stop himself hoping that she might be willing to support his little palace coup.

Change sides for his sake – the way women usually did in Bond films.

Instead she had probably leapt at the phone the moment the door slammed on his heartbroken sorry arse. And by now Philip must be aware that ArgosEye had a new partner, which only meant that the hunt for him would be stepped up another notch . . .

But he could take comfort in the fact that his plan could still work.

Tomorrow was New Year's Eve, and the office would be running at minimum strength. And thanks to the passcard he had pinched from Rilke's bag in her hall, he wouldn't have any problem getting in.

'Listen, HP, there's something I've been thinking.' Disciple number one, the one called Wedge.

The guys had closed the shop and pulled down the shutters the moment he crept in through the door.

'Fire away.'

HP took a deep toke on the joint, then passed it to his right while he carried on staring at the little patch of damp on the ceiling that had been absorbing their attention over the past few minutes.

'That whole story about ArgosEye, the bomb and everything . . .'

'Mmm.'

Marky, who was lying on the floor next to him, took a drag and then coughed violently.

'You're still rushing it too much, M. You need to dare to hold onto the smoke, feel the taste of Morocco, yeah?'

Marky half sat up and tried to nod between coughs. Wedge waited until the noise had stopped and Marky had lain back down before going on.

'Well . . . Marky and I have been thinking about what you said. That they set the bomb off to try to hide something else. We've been doing a bit of a project, looking at the flow of information on the net, so we gave it a try. Wait till you see what we found.'

He got up and stumbled across to one of the computers through the semi-darkness. Then the screen flickered into life.

'Okay, check this out. We looked at all the main news sites and listed the subjects that were most read or linked to during the days after the bombing. Like this, for instance . . .'

He moved the mouse onto a heading and clicked on it. A timeline popped up, with a red line showing the traffic on the subject.

'This is the debate about Swedish troops in Afghanistan cooperating with an American assassination unit. Hot as hell for two days or so, and top of almost every forum until the bomb went off, and then . . .'

The line that had been heading straight up suddenly dive-bombed down towards the bottom of the screen.

'Shit,' HP muttered.

'And look at this,' Wedge went on.

He went back to the list of news subjects, picked another heading, and a blue timeline showed up.

'Looks like someone high up in Volvo is going to be charged about the illegal export of weapons to Iraq. The newspapers picked up the story and it was red hot for about a day, then GONE . . .'

The line had hardly got going before it dived towards the bottom of the screen.

'You can choose pretty much whatever subject you like. Over the past ten days debate and speculation about the bomb has completely dominated all the media. Every other story is basically stone-dead, especially anything that's a bit complicated. Your theory fits perfectly so far.'

HP nodded.

'But have you managed to work out what the massive story is that they're trying to hide? The big Kahuna?'

'Not exactly,' Wedge said. 'But we did come up with another idea.'

He glanced at Marky, then leaned closer to HP.

'What if there isn't a massive story?' he whispered.

'What?'

HP sat up.

'Okay, try this,' Marky said. 'What if they weren't just trying to shift the focus . . .'

'. . . but?'

'. . . because *that* was actually the debate they really wanted.'

HP shook his head.

'But who would stand to gain from that? I mean, what vested interests would be willing to pay to promote tougher anti-terrorism laws in a miniscule country like Sweden?'

Mackan and Kilen exchanged satisfied glances.

'That depends what the law is about. Have you ever heard about the Data Retention Directive, HP?'

40

Let the games begin

Pillars of Society forum
Posted: 31 December, 22:03
By: **MayBey**

To be really sure, you have to know everything . . .

This post has 221 comments

Okay, time to go through the list.

Passcard – check.

USB memory stick – check.

Plans – check.

Flask of ballistic jelly – check.

Two dopey accomplices – check there as well, unfortunately.

He was sitting in the car in one of the narrow streets round the corner from the office. The exhausted air freshener dangling from the rear-view mirror stood no chance against the Chief's BO – but right now body odour was the least of HP's problems.

If this whole thing was going to work, he'd have to do a Clooney in more senses than one, but unlike both him and Francis Albert, he didn't have ten razor-sharp accomplices to help him. Instead his team consisted of an exiled technical guru and Islamic convert, a petty criminal Elvis impersonator, and, last but not least, the swamp monster from the stinking lagoon . . .

He had about as much chance of surviving intact as a girl with big tits in a horror movie, but he still had to give it his best shot. Because those fuckers couldn't be allowed to get away with this.

NFW!

Who'd have thought it would take two media-fixated schoolkids to work the whole thing out. The Data Retention Directive – of course!

Big brother EU wanted to force all internet providers to save all traffic from every user. Every single page you visited, every link you clicked, ever forum you posted on. Everything would be saved and stored for at least a year, even if there was no suspicion at all of any wrongdoing.

Up to now Sweden had objected, but now the subject was up for debate in parliament again.

'*In the event that crime-fighting authorities need the information*' was apparently the justification, and in the past few days they had added '*in the fight against terrorism*'.

In the aftermath of the blast on Drottninggatan the amount of opposition was bound to shrink. But storing all data traffic from all users wasn't an effective way of preventing terrorism, Philip Argos himself had explained that to him. But it was the perfect way to map patterns of consumption, internet behaviour and user networks, down to the very smallest detail, and over a lengthy period of time. The Stasi's wet dream, just twenty years too late!

Big business would drool over that type of information,

and would be prepared to do almost anything to get hold of it. Only the future would show which side of the law they would stick to.

The first step was getting the directive passed. And with the help of ArgosEye and a failed suicide bomber, they were well on the way.

Unless someone stopped them . . .

He cruised through the narrow streets, checking over his shoulder every so often. Everything seemed okay, there were a few hours left before midnight and the majority of ordinary Swedes were busy having their New Year's Eve dinner.

He reached the main entrance and looked round one last time before opening his shoulder-bag and taking out the passcard.

Shit, even on a photograph the size of a postage stamp Rilke still looked like a million dollars. On the subject of money, Monika Gregerson had been over the moon about his proposal, and thank God for that. Now she had loads of cash and a chance to deal out a bit of farewell payback to Philip. But forty percent wasn't enough to stop Philip's plans to join the PayTag Group. Anna had worked that out, and had tried to find another way instead.

And in all likelihood it had cost her her life.

But now it was his turn to try . . .

He slowly raised the passcard to the reader, and noticed that he was holding his breath. What if Rilke had noticed, what if she'd checked her bag and seen that the card was missing? What if she'd made a call and got the twins to block it . . .?

In that case he was . . .

The reader bleeped and flashed green, then the lock began to whirr.

* * *

Something was going on, she was sure of that. That key was hardly a coincidence. MayBey had put his or her plan into action, but all she could do was wait. In time she was bound to find out what was expected of her. Until then, she could work on her own plans.

She had managed to check out a theory that had started to bubble in her head, and so far she hadn't found anything that contradicted it. Quite the opposite, in fact.

Facebook was undeniably a fantastic tool for making yourself visible.

But including every last detail of your life also had its risks . . .

She switched windows and clicked the icon to update the page, but it didn't change.

No new messages from MayBey.

Not yet. But she was sure it wouldn't be long.

She went out into the kitchen and poured herself a glass of water.

He took the lift up.

The eighteenth floor of a possible nineteen. The reception area was of course closed, but Rilke's card worked perfectly.

He crept carefully past the meeting room, pulled his cap down over his face and kept close to the wall in an attempt to avoid the camera in the ceiling as best he could. But like so many other surveillance systems he had come across, he doubted anyone was actually sitting and watching the pictures live, and especially not on New Year's Eve. Tomorrow morning they would check the recordings and realize that they had had an unauthorized intruder, but by then it would be too late.

He stopped at the reception desk and leaned over for the telephone. He picked up the receiver and opened the phone's menu of options. He tapped in a number, then clicked save.

Then he tried the speed dial number.

'Hello?'

'It's me, Nox. I'm in – everything's okay.'

'Okay boss, understood. Be careful!'

By the time she got back to the computer the new post was already a minute old.

I have your brother, Regina. Come and get him if you dare!

She had been right. The opening move had been made. The game had begun.

Time for her response. She picked up her mobile and pressed the speed dial option.

'It's me,' she said when the person at the other end answered.

So far, so good!

He popped his head into the open area behind the reception desk. It was completely deserted, but the light from a few computer screens flickered from over in the glassed off part of the office. The nightshift in the Filter, maybe two or three people, but he wasn't too worried about them.

Even if he did bump into any of them, they probably wouldn't recognize him and would just say hello or possibly glance at the passcard he had fixed to his belt. There was no way they'd be able to see that the picture didn't match the person wearing it.

But the team leader was a different matter. Rilke wasn't working over New Year, he remembered that from when they were still together, which meant that one of Beens, Dejan, Stoffe and Frank was working that night. He had no great desire to run into any of them.

He turned left, into the darkened corridor that led towards the other three departments. Just as he was approaching the Troll Mine he saw the door open. Quick as a flash he darted behind one of the cupboards lining one side of the corridor.

'. . . okay, see you in a bit, I'm just going to grab something to eat,' he heard Frank say to someone inside.

Shit!

He had just passed the door to the overnight lounge, which meant that Frank would have to walk right past him.

HP slid down onto the floor and pressed up against the side of the cupboard. He heard steps coming towards him and tried to make himself as small as possible. Suddenly the lights came on and someone let out a whistle.

'Okay, let's say that, then.'

She ended the call and put the mobile down on the kitchen table.

Then she went out into the hall and began to put her outdoor clothes on.

This time she left her extending baton in its holster, and fixed the whole thing to her belt at the small of her back. She was ready for MayBey's next move.

If her suspicions were correct, and if he was the man she thought he was, it wouldn't be long coming.

'Frank!'

'Yeah, what is it?' he heard Frank say, probably no more than a metre away from him.

'The database just chucked me out, can you unlock it . . .?'

'Sure,' he heard Frank sigh.

Then footsteps moving away.

The door to the Troll Mine clicked, then everything was quiet.

HP carefully poked his head out into the corridor. Empty. He let out a sigh of relief.

That was close, fucking close, even . . .

But now he had a problem.

He had counted on being able to get out to the fire escape through the emergency exit in the Troll Mine, but now that way was blocked. Those stairs were his best hope of getting up to Philip's office and the server room, but now he'd have to find another way to get to them.

He jogged back to reception, ducked down behind the desk and pulled out the plan he had stolen from the fire cupboard on the ground floor.

The fire escape was the emergency exit for all nineteen floors, and ran all the way down to the basement. That was a hell of a lot of stairs to clamber up, but he didn't have much choice.

He would have to try the route through the basement.

Her mobile phone rang. Number withheld, and for some reason she hesitated for a couple of seconds before answering.

'Hello, Rebecca Normén,' she said as calmly as she could.

There was a man's voice at the other end.

It was fucking creepy down there.

The garage started right outside the lifts, and because it was a holiday, and night as well, only something like one in every four lights was lit. It was bound to be some stupid green scheme to save energy. But at least the weak lighting was enough for him to see where he was going.

He slipped between the few cars parked down there and double checked on the plan than he was going the right way.

A sudden noise made him jump. He took a couple of quick steps and dodged down between two cars, then put his head up slowly and tried to see through the car windows. Nothing, not the smallest movement out there in the gloom. Maybe a fan, or some other bit of service machinery coming on? Just to be sure, he waited another minute or so.

But everything was quiet.

He stood up and carried on to the corner where the staircase ought to be, but couldn't help glancing back over his shoulder a few times.

He found the door almost exactly where he expected it to be. Unfortunately it was locked. It could probably only be opened from the other side, which was perfectly logical considering that it was only supposed to be used by people going in one direction. But there was a card reader beside the door. A silver-coloured box with a keypad, like the one on the main door upstairs. He tried Rilke's card, and got a double bleep in response. The little light flickered between green and red, and it took him a couple of seconds to realize. The passcard was fine, but the reader was waiting for him to tap in some sort of code.

Shit!

The main door had never asked for any sort of fucking code, a card alone was enough.

He tried four zeros but got a firm red light in reply.

Come on – think!

It was Rilke's card, and presumably they all picked their own individual pin number. Four digits, most likely. So what would she have chosen?

Her birthday, the battle of Lützen, the French Revolution?

He tried all three, without success.

But what if that wasn't how the reader worked? Maybe there was just one code for this particular box, and you could get in as long as you had a card for the building and the shared code?

In which case there was a chance that . . .

Suddenly everything went pitch black.

For a few panic-stricken moments he had to fight the urge to drop everything and run back to the lifts. But instead he felt in his bag for his torch.

He heard a faint rustling sound somewhere off to his right and the noise made the hair on the back of his neck stand up. It could have been a rat . . .

Unless it was something else, a dark, shapeless figure creeping up on him, reaching out its clawed hands and . . .

His fingers touched something cylindrical and he yanked the torch out so hard that several other things flew out with it. His sweaty fingers felt for the switch, then . . .

The beam of light put a stop to his racing imagination and he moved it round in every direction just to be sure.

There was nothing there, nothing but parked cars and the things he'd just dropped on the floor.

He crouched down and put everything except a little spray-can back in his bag. There was the flask containing the ballistic gel, which he planned to use to fool the fingerprint reader, just like Rainman Rehyman had taught him out in Kista; the little crowbar for breaking open the door to the server room; and the earmuffs that would make it possible to put up with the noise from the intruder alarm.

He took a quick look at the time.

Almost an hour left until midnight, when the streets would be full of drunks watching fireworks who'd make life bloody difficult for any security guards and cops trying to make their way to a tricky central address like this.

Plenty of time, in other words . . .

He gave the keypad on the card reader a quick spray with the aerosol, waited a moment, then pressed the button on the torch. The light switched from white to violet and when he shone it at the keypad big white stains showed up on four of the buttons. 1350.

He held the card up again, then pressed the keys in numerical order.

Red light.

He stopped to think for a moment. Then he tried the more symmetrical 0135. A green lamp came on and he head the lock whirr.

YES!

The moment he touched the handle a burst of pain flashed through his body and for a few seconds his limbs shook uncontrollably. Then everything went black.

41

Capture the flag

'Yes, hello, can you tell me, whose number is this?' the man at the other end of the line said.

'Rebecca Normén's . . .'

'In Palace admin, or . . .?' The man sounded hesitant.

'Sorry . . . I don't understand. Who am I talking to?'

'My name's Sandberg, Captain Sandberg of the Life-Guards. I'm in charge of the guard up at the Palace tonight and we're standing in front of a door we suddenly find we can't open. If you change the locks, normal procedure requires that you inform . . .'

'Hang on a minute,' she interrupted. 'Where did you get my mobile number?'

'There's a sticker on the lock. What . . . don't you work in Palace admin? I thought . . .'

'Wait there, Captain, I'm on my way!'

She jogged down the stairs with the phone still pressed to her ear.

'Where does the door lead?'

'What?'

'The locked door . . .' she clarified as she pulled her boots on. 'Where does it lead?'

Someone was carrying him.

Or more than one, surely? One under each arm, his hands tied behind his back and a hood over his head.

Déjà vu!

He wondered briefly if this was all just a dream. That he was still in the garage in Dubai and the orcs were dragging him off to some Guantanamo pit.

His legs were moving, more or less, but the rest of his body still felt numb. The last few minutes were chopped into little fragments of memory. He had a feeling he had been taken somewhere, in some sort of vehicle. But that was more a feeling than a fact. As if the world around him had moved while he himself had been lying still.

They were dragging him up some sort of staircase. He heard a door squeak. Dry, cold air, but still not outdoors. Like some sort of huge attic . . .

She braked hard in the outer courtyard of the Palace and the car slid another metre or so on the slippery cobbles.

'Halt,' the downy teenager in the sentry box said, holding up one hand.

'The officer in charge of the guard,' she said quickly as she showed him her police ID. 'Captain Sandberg, where can I find him?'

Up another narrow staircase, and the person in front practically had to drag him.

Cold night air, voices, city noises in the distance revealed that they were definitely outside now. Stumbling steps across a slippery, slushy surface. Then hands pushing him down into a sitting position, pushing his legs over some sort of ledge. His feet were suddenly dangling freely and a gust of cold air blew up the legs of his trousers.

Like so many times before, his stomach was quicker than his brain. A roof! He was on some sort of roof.

Three guns in total, two automatic rifles and the officer's holstered pistol. For some reason they made her feel uneasy. The Guard may be largely ceremonial, but she couldn't help wondering.

Not dangerous, dangerous?

She guessed at the latter . . .

They were jogging up what seemed, strangely enough, to be a perfectly ordinary stairwell. Captain Sandberg in front of her, and two soldiers in camouflage uniforms just behind her. There were apartment doors on the landings, and a faint smell of cooking. She would never have imagined that people actually lived in the Palace, behind ordinary brown doors with letterboxes and nameplates, just like any other address in the city.

But on the other hand this was the western wing, a fair way from the royal apartments, the Palace church, the museums and all the other bits.

They stopped in front of a metal door at the very top of the stairwell.

'There,' Sandberg said, pointing at a bar across the door with a padlock hanging from it. 'We only realized something was wrong when our key wouldn't fit.'

On the lock was a small sticker with a phone number. It took her a fraction of a second to see that it was hers.

'Are you sure we shouldn't call the police . . . I mean, the uniformed police,' he corrected himself.

'Not yet . . .' she replied curtly.

She pulled the key from her jeans pocket and saw at once that it was the right size.

She put it in the lock and tried turning it. The lock clicked open straightaway, and one of the soldiers removed the bar and opened the door. She was hit by a cold smell of old wood and dust.

'Where does this lead . . .?'

She pointed into the darkness.

'The attic? It runs the whole length of the Palace, we use it to get to the flag . . .'

'The flag?'

'Yes, the three-tailed flag, the one that flies from the roof of the Palace when the King is in the country.'

What the hell had actually happened?

His brain was slowly catching up with reality.

He had grabbed the handle, and was just about to open the door to the stairwell when he had been . . . well, attacked, somehow?

Could the handle have been booby-trapped?

But if that were the case, his hand ought to be badly barbequed now. But apart from the plastic cord cutting into his wrists, his hands felt fine.

He moved his body gently and after a few moments thought he had identified a point at the base of his spine from where a burning pain seemed to be radiating.

He could hear whispering voices a short distance away from him.

Then a familiar voice that made him start.

A narrow path of double planks led them through the darkness. The smell of tarred wood got stronger and stronger the further in they went.

The roof was several metres above their heads, and in

the glow of the torches she occasionally caught glimpses of green-glinting copper plate.

'Careful,' Sandberg said, once again shining his torch at one of the thick cross beams that interrupted their path.

Then the path turned sharp right, into the next section of the Palace, and she realized that they must be in the north side now, the side facing the Parliament building. Ahead of them in the darkness a door slammed. Sandberg stopped and pointed the torch ahead of him. Twenty metres in front of them the outline of another staircase appeared.

'This is a site of national importance,' Sandberg said quietly. 'No-one's supposed to be here, and certainly not up there.'

They reached the stairs and aimed their torches towards its top. Another metal door, this time barred horizontally.

There was a bleeping sound from her pocket. She pulled out her mobile and read the message.

It was from Micke.

MayBey lives along the E18, most of his traffic passes through an exchange in Näsby Park.

She had been right!

MayBey wasn't the person he was pretending to be.

Unless that was precisely what he was . . .

An imitation, a copy of someone else entirely.

She turned to Sandberg.

'Wait here!' she said sharply.

Then she started to head up the steps on her own.

42

Head to head

'Welcome, Rebecca,' the man in the balaclava said.

The platform they were standing on was small, perhaps no more than seven or eight square metres. To her left was an ornate stone balustrade, and beyond that the drop to Lejonbacken, and on her right was a low wall, and then the gently sloping copper roof tilting down towards the inner courtyard.

She checked the time: 23:51.

In the distance was the sound of fireworks.

'We've been expecting you.'

He gestured with his head and she saw there was a person sitting curled up on the balustrade with his back towards her. For a moment she turned completely cold. His arms were tied behind his back, and he had a black hood pulled down over his head.

Beneath his feet the building dropped away, some twenty metres or more straight down to Lejonbacken.

She looked back at the man in the balaclava. Even if his black jacket and mask made him seem big, he was actually smaller than she had thought.

'Obviously, you see the poetic justice here . . .' he said.

She nodded briefly as she followed his movements with her eyes. His voice sounded strange, as if he were doing his best to disguise it.

'Your brother murdered your boyfriend by pushing him off a building . . .'

Her eyes darted to the hunched figure, then back across the little platform.

There was a black bag on the low stone wall about a metre away. She nodded again.

'Yes, I get it. Your law applies here, an eye for an eye . . .'

'Exactly . . .' he said, but something in his voice revealed that she hadn't reacted quite as he had expected.

The sound of New Year rockets began to grow, and through them blaring sirens approaching the Palace. Sandberg's patience had evidently run out.

The balaclava turned and its eyes glanced quickly towards the edge.

'They're on their way,' she said drily.

'Good, then you can go back down again . . .'

She took half a step towards the trapdoor again, then stopped.

'You know what, MayBey . . .? I think I'd rather stay here, actually . . .'

He started, and it looked like he was about to say something. But instead he took a step towards the seated figure.

'You obviously don't get it . . .' he purred.

'Oh, I get it.' She glanced at the bag.

The sirens were close now, at least three or four different vehicles.

The sound of rockets was still growing.

'I get the whole thing, actually. You're planning to push my brother there . . .'

She pointed at the seated figure.

'. . . off the roof, just as you've promised all your fans.

If it's okay with you, I thought I might stand here and watch while you do it.'

'W-what?'

His voice cracked, and for a moment it sounded almost shrill.

'I said you might as well get going and push Henke over the edge. You've been talking about it for weeks now, so you might as well get on with it.'

He appeared to consider this for a moment, then took another half step towards the balustrade. She saw the seated figure squirm anxiously.

The sirens had stopped, which probably meant that the police were already on their way up through the stairwell. Another minute to get through the attic and they'd have reached the last flight of steps.

She slowly slid her hand under her jacket.

'You don't seem to understand, Rebecca . . .' he said, raising one foot ready to kick out with it.

'No,' she said calmly as she closed her fingers round the object attached to her belt at the small of her back. 'You're the one who doesn't understand . . .'

She shot across the platform in two quick strides, snatching her hand out. The baton extended to its full length and hit MayBey on the back of the thigh.

The blow was so hard that she felt the bone crack through the metal.

He fell backwards but she didn't jump on him. Instead she planted her own foot against the back of the seated figure.

He could hear voices, two, to be precise. A man and a woman. They both sounded familiar, he knew that much, but his head was still far too groggy for him to be able to identify them.

Then he heard what sounded like rapid movements behind him.

Then someone put their foot against his back. HP HP HP?

'Here you go, MayBey, let me help you,' she yelled over the screaming rockets.

She pushed with her foot.

'Noooo!!'

The two panicked cries merged together to form one single brittle sound.

Having scared the shit out of whoever it was, she grabbed hold of the seated man, pulled him down from the balustrade and dragged him back onto the platform next to MayBey. Then she pulled her handcuffs from her back pocket.

Under his thick gloves and the heavy padded jacket, MayBey's wrists were slender and she had no trouble at all putting the cuffs on him.

'Time for a bit of unmasking, gentlemen.'

She pulled MayBey's balaclava off and looked coldly at the face.

Then she removed the other man's hood.

'Jonathan Lundh and I have already met . . .'

She nodded towards MayBey, who was still grimacing with pain.

'But who are you?'

'M-Marky,' the young man who was supposed to be her brother sniffed. 'Marcus Lillhage.'

'And how do you know Lundh junior here? Is your dad a policeman as well, by any chance?'

'N-no . . .' he sobbed. 'Wedge and I go to the same school . . .'

She nodded slowly and then turned towards the black bag.

'There's a camera in there, isn't there?'

The young man called Marky nodded.

She aimed her baton at Jonathan Lundh's chest.

'So, do you want to tell me, or should Marcus?'

He was clutching his injured thigh with both hands and trying not to look at her.

'Okay, Marcus, off you go.'

She rested the baton on her shoulder.

'It was a project . . . for school.'

'Go on.'

'Well, we had to do a project in media studies on the flow of information. We wanted to see if it was possible to get away with creating a fictitious character on a site. Wedge's dad used to look at that cops' site, that's where we got the idea.'

She glanced at Jonathan Lundh, who still wasn't talking.

'Then one night his dad sat on his mobile and accidentally called home. Wedge heard the way they talked in the van . . .'

'. . . about me,' she filled in, and saw Jonathan look up.

'You were fucking my dad . . .' he snarled. 'Even though you knew he had a family . . .' She nodded slowly.

'You're quite right, Jonathan,' she said. 'And it's not exactly something I'm proud of, if that's any consolation. So that was why you chose me?'

'Th-the project wasn't really supposed to be that big. We thought about pretending to be a cop who'd gone off the rails, who'd end up blogging about wanting to commit suicide. We wanted to see if his colleagues would try to help him,' Marcus went on.

'I mean, the whole thing was about creating a profile, becoming a name. Like that girl at art school who pretended to be psychotic and ended up really famous . . .'

'Marky, shut the fuck up!' Jonathan snapped. 'We

haven't got anything else to say to you, you fucking whore . . .'

She kicked him in the knee and he curled up into a ball.

'You should think a bit about what you're saying, Jonathan. Think about what they say about my state of mind on that site . . . A smart lad like you might be able to tell me what would happen if I broke your camera and then claimed I was forced to throw you both over the edge in self-defence?'

She saw his eyes open wide, as he tried to see any sign that she was joking. Instead she grabbed hold of his jacket and dragged him towards the edge.

Below a crowd had formed.

'You've been terrorizing me for weeks . . .' she went on, with her mouth close to his ear. 'You've encouraged people to throw all sorts of shit at me, you almost ran me over, and you've threatened my brother's life . . .'

She pulled him a bit closer to the edge. In spite of the whine and roar of the New Year fireworks, she could hear him gasp for breath.

'Isn't that right? The car outside my house, that was you, wasn't it?'

'Yes! Y-yes, for fuck's sake!' he yelled. 'We just wanted to check you out. Then when you came running over . . .'

'. . . you panicked?'

He nodded desperately, unable to tear his eyes from the cobblestones far below.

'What about my brother, how does he fit into the picture?'

'Coincidence. One day he just walked into the shop . . . Then everything just sort of fell into place . . .'

She pulled Jonathan Lundh back onto the platform and let go of him next to his friend.

'What about all this?' She nodded towards the roof of the Palace. 'Whose idea was this?'

'My brother's an officer in the Guard,' Marcus muttered. 'He brought me up here last summer when they were lowering the flag.'

'So the idea was that I'd think it was Henke sitting there on the edge? And I'd beg and plead for his life while you filmed it – okay, I get that. But how did you think you were going to get away?'

The two young men looked at each other, but neither of them answered. Rebecca thought for a few moments.

'I see,' she finally said. 'Being led down in handcuffs and getting on television and in the papers would be the perfect climax to your little project.' She nodded. 'And because you didn't actually have a hostage up here, you'd probably end up just getting a fine or a suspended sentence for some pissy minor offence. And I'd be hung out to dry while you got famous. Oh well, it's not too late yet!'

She dragged them to their feet, untied the flag cord, and before they had time to work out what she was doing, she threaded it through the cuffs behind their backs. Then she tied the cord to the pole with reef knots and then shoved the two young men towards the balustrade so hard that they both ended up leaning over it.

A double, terrified scream – and the flag cord snapped tight with a jolt, leaving them hanging in the air with their knees still on the balustrade.

She could see the flashes from the mobile phones down among the crowd.

'Smile and wave nicely, boys,' she said. 'You're going to be famous.'

She went over to the bag, fished out the camera and, after a bit of fiddling about, pulled out the memory card.

On the staircase on the way down she found a hostage

negotiator, and below him a heavily armed squad in black uniforms.

'Everything's fine,' she said, waving her police ID.

She pointed at the phone in one of the man's hands.

'But you can call Tobbe Lundh in the rapid response unit and tell him to come and get his son down. And tell him to bring two pairs of clean trousers . . .'

43

All Your Bases Belong To Us

The moment the hood was pulled off him, the world exploded into colours, whistles and explosions. It took him a moment to realize that it was midnight and then another to realize where he was.

Seventy metres above the city centre, with Sveavägen's salt-wet carriageways far below between his dangling feet, and just the narrow strip of the concrete ledge under his buttocks to stop him from falling.

The foot at his back pushed, shrinking the width of the strip by half and twisting his stomach into a panic-stricken lump.

He tried to push back and keep his centre of balance the right side of the edge. But the foot was stopping him, nudging him inexorably forward.

'Are you enjoying the view, loverboy?' Sophie whispered in his ear as the Stockholm sky exploded all round his head.

'Right-hand pocket of my trousers, a USB stick!' he roared, trying to make himself heard above the fireworks. 'Don't let me fall, for fuck's sake!'

His buttocks were slowly slipping across the ledge as Elroy continued to push him.

Nineteen floors below the street was full of New Year revellers.

'And what were you going to do with it, dear little Henrik?' Sophie again, right next to his ear.

'Plug it into the server, upload a trojan,' he sniffed. 'Please, please, don't let . . .'

Suddenly his backside lost contact with the concrete and he slid over the edge.

But just as he started to scream in terror Elroy caught him and dragged him back up onto the roof. They left him lying there while they searched him.

The USB stick was the first thing they took.

She had been right about most of it.

MayBey and Tobbe were connected.

But instead of a muscular cop in a dark uniform, her internet nemesis turned out to be two spotty little eighteen-year-olds who had watched too much television. It was the film quotes that had put her on the right track.

Judge Dredd, Clint, Taxi Driver. The whole thing felt like some teenage boy's bedroom fantasy. Once Jonathan Lundh's name occurred to her, she only had to look up his profile on Facebook, and sure enough all the films were there, neatly listed on his personal details page, along with the fact that he was attending a high school that specialized in IT. On the internet you might be able to pretend to be whoever you like, she thought. But the truth is also out there, if you know where to look for it.

Talking about looking . . .

She pulled out her mobile and dialled a number.

'Where are you?' she asked when the man at the other end answered.

* * *

They were herding him between them like a sheep.

Elroy was holding his upper arm, but there was no need for that at all. Even though they had cut the plastic binder-strap from his wrists, he was finished. He could still feel the after-effects from the taser they'd zapped him with, making his movements sluggish, and the whole nightmare scenario up on the roof had basically broken him.

He rubbed his nose with the bottom of one arm to get rid of the tears that persisted in leaking out.

When they reached the large, open room they could hear voices from Philip's office. He could make out silhouettes through the frosted glass walls. The clink of glasses, then the bubbling laughter that he recognized so well . . .

Without warning his legs suddenly gave out and he collapsed. His head hit the edge of Sophie's desk and he felt the skin on his forehead break.

They made no attempt to pick him up, and just left him crawling around on the floor for a few moments.

Grinning while he fumbled with his hands under the desk.

Then he got hold of the office chair and used it to clamber laboriously to his feet. He could feel a warm trickle of blood seeping slowly through his eyebrow.

'Here,' Elroy muttered, pressing a tissue into HP's hand as he shoved him forward.

A moment later the door opened and they were inside.

Six people in the room, all the section heads, all holding glasses of champagne.

'Welcome, Henrik, we've been waiting for you,' Philip Argos said cheerfully.

By his side, a little too close, Rilke was smiling her most beautiful smile.

'Here.'

Elroy put the little USB stick down on Philip's desk.

'Dejan, would you mind?' Philip nodded.

Dejan walked across the room, picked up the stick and plugged it into a laptop on the desk.

'Workless network off WASSAT . . .' he chuckled cruelly, firing a quick look at HP. 'After all, we don't want to risk any infection . . .'

The other team leaders, with the exception of Rilke, gathered round the screen. HP couldn't help glancing over at her. But she wasn't even looking at him.

He pressed the tissue harder against the cut in his forehead, but the blood wouldn't stop.

'Ooh, look at that!' Beens said, peering over Dejan's shoulder. 'Not bad at all!'

Dejan clicked the mouse, then typed in a few quick commands.

'Yes, I can only agree with Beens. Whoever put this spy program together knew what he was doing.'

He typed in a few more commands, then stood up and pulled the USB stick out.

'If the trojan had got into the mainframe we'd have been in trouble . . . Looks like it would have started sending confidential information to an external client. Customer information, user IDs, blog aliases, you name it. God knows what might have happened if he'd succeeded.'

He held the stick out to HP.

'You really did try to sink us, lad . . .' he said in a voice that sounded almost surprised.

Suddenly everyone in the room seemed to be staring at him.

He could practically feel the hatred in their eyes.

Frank took a step forward, fists clenched, but HP stood perfectly still. The blow wasn't even particularly hard, a stomach-punch that he more or less managed to steel himself against before it struck. Knees on the carpet, a sigh as the air went out of him. The guy didn't even have the guts to punch him in the face . . .

'That's enough, Frank,' Philip said curtly as Sophie and her brother dragged HP to his feet. 'I think Henrik has already realized the seriousness of his position – haven't you?'

HP nodded mutely.

'You, a convicted criminal, broke in here with a stolen passcard with the intention of stealing confidential company information.'

He took the memory stick from Dejan and waved it in HP's face.

'Aggravated theft, or industrial espionage, probably a year or two in prison, I'd guess. And I don't suppose that will do your sister's future career prospects any good at all . . .'

HP started.

'Don't involve my sister in this!' he muttered.

Philip smiled.

'So there is something you care about after all, Henrik. In other words, you're not entirely without morals . . .'

Frank, Dejan and the others grinned, but he didn't care.

'Get to the point, Philip,' he sighed. 'I've got something you want, haven't I? Otherwise the cops would be busy scraping me off the pavement by now. After all, you don't seem too bothered if you have to step over a few dead bodies . . .'

He raised his head and looked the bunch of them in the eyes for the first time. This time it was their turn to look away.

All except Philip. He gestured towards Elroy.

'Is he . . .?'

'Completely clean, no microphones or transmitters.'

'Good!'

He turned back to HP again.

'You're quite right, Henrik. I want your shares, you can sell them to me at an acceptable market rate so that no-one can claim afterwards that you were put under undue pressure. So I'm prepared to offer you twice what you managed to scrape together to pay Monika.'

He gave a sign to Stoffe, who took out a plastic folder and started to lay several documents out on the desk.

'And there are plenty of witnesses here who can testify that the purchase took place perfectly legally.'

HP nodded wearily.

'Okay, I get it . . .'

He took a deep breath, to give himself time to think.

'But I want to add one condition to the deal.'

'You're hardly in a position to make demands, Henrik, but let's hear it . . .'

'I'll sign your forms and go off into the sunset as long as you agree not to call the cops. I'm not exactly keen to do time again.'

Philip nodded.

'That sounds like it might be worth considering, doesn't it?'

He turned towards the others, but none of them had any comment.

'So what do we do about the money?' HP said.

'We've opened a Western Union account for you, the money will be transferred the moment you sign the forms.'

'No need, I've got a numbered account we can use.'

Philip met his gaze for a few seconds. Then he smiled.

'You planned for this eventuality, didn't you?'

HP shrugged his shoulders.

'In that case it would seem that I didn't entirely misjudge you, Henrik. No plan is so good that it doesn't need a backup.'

He shook his head.

'You could have gone far with us, Henrik, further than you could ever imagine . . .'

'Well . . .' HP replied. 'We'll never know, will we?'

Philip eyed him coldly.

'So, Henrik, seeing as you were prepared for this scenario, I daresay you have a price in mind? How much did you manage to scrape together to persuade Monika to sell? I offered her a million but I can imagine that she gave you a good discount. So what was it – fifty, one hundred?'

'Five!'

Philip grinned.

'So you managed to persuade my sister-in-law to sell her shares to you for a measly five thousand. Either you're a brilliant negotiator or she must really hate me . . . Oh well, we'll transfer ten thousand to your account.'

HP slowly shook his head.

'Not five thousand . . .'

He left a dramatic pause. Then he smiled.

'Five *million* . . .!'

44

The game is up

In the streets outside calm had descended and only a few lingering plumes of fireworks shot up sporadically into the night sky. He was made to wait for a while, before being bundled off to the toilet to tidy himself up. The cut over his eye wouldn't stop bleeding and he asked for a roll of tape to try to hold it together. Just as he was finished the office door opened.

'You can come back in now, Henrik . . .'

The party atmosphere seemed to have subsided somewhat. He hadn't been able to avoid hearing parts of the heated discussion while he was waiting.

'We've checked what you said,' Philip began, 'and it looks as though you did somehow manage to get hold of five million, like you said. Obviously, we're very interested to hear how that came about . . .'

'Lottery win,' HP said, cutting him off.

He saw them look at each other.

'In that case we have a proposal,' Philip said curtly. 'Six million, that's as much as we can get hold of at such short notice.'

'Seven!' HP retorted quickly.

Philip took a deep breath and from the corner of his eye HP saw Elroy shuffle his feet.

'Okay, six, then!' he said. 'As long as we can get it out of the way. But remember, no police!'

'Good,' Philip said. 'Dejan has the transfer up on the screen.'

He nodded to Dejan, who had set up a new laptop to replace the infected one.

'He'll transfer the money once all the papers are signed, then you can log in to the account yourself and double-check.'

HP nodded.

Stoffe put the papers in front of him on the desk, and he signed them, one after the other.

Then Philip did the same, before Stoffe and Frank witnessed the signatures.

'Okay, you can transfer the money now,' Philip commanded once they were done.

Dejan tapped at his keyboard, then supervised HP while he double-checked the transaction. ArgosEye's entire current account must have been cleared out.

Buying shares with the company's own money, wasn't that sort of thing illegal? But obviously that presupposed that anyone cared.

'Happy?'

HP nodded.

'Good. Then it's time for us to go our separate ways,' Philip smiled. 'You may be a wealthy man, but it will be a while before you can enjoy your money. And obviously we'll put in a serious claim for damages. I would imagine the amount will run to something like six million. What do the rest of you think?'

The others leered scornfully and suddenly everyone seemed much happier.

'Elroy, would you be so kind as to call and arrange transport for Henrik?'

'Of course,' Elroy grinned, and stepped over to the phone on the desk. 'One one two is easy to do . . .'

HP looked down at the floor. Obviously the greedy fuckers were going to shop him. You wouldn't get much of a price on the odds of that happening. But as luck would have it, he still had one ace up his sleeve . . .

'Hello, police? We've just caught a thief red-handed. It looks like he was trying to steal confidential business information . . .'

'Hold on!' Philip said, raising one hand. 'Something doesn't feel right . . .'

He gave HP a long look.

'For someone who just lost the game, you seem rather too calm.'

HP tried to avoid looking at him.

Shit!

'What were you really doing in reception downstairs?'

'Nothing,' HP muttered.

Philip looked puzzled. Then he gestured to Elroy to hand him the receiver.

'Hello, who am I speaking to? Police Sergeant Renko . . .?'

Philip started to smile.

'And what department do you work in, Sergeant, if you don't mind me asking? . . . Surveillance? I'm sorry, but the right answer was central control.'

He put the receiver down and then dialled some more numbers on the phone.

'You never cease to surprise me, Henrik!' he went on in an amused tone of voice. 'You predicted that we'd call the police, and you changed the speed dial number to one of your own. Let me guess, you've got two friends waiting in a car out there somewhere, ready to drive over and pick you up? All a bit *Ocean's Eleven*, am I right?'

HP took a deep breath.

'*Twelve*,' he muttered. 'The fake cops rescued them in *Ocean's Twelve*.'

But no-one seemed to be listening.

Philip turned to the others.

'Let this be a useful lesson to us all. Never underestimate an opponent, even when he seems to be beaten . . .'

Philip signalled to Elroy, who pulled out his mobile.

'Hello, is that the police?'

She ended the call, then looked up another number in her phonebook.

'Good evening, my dear,' the soft voice said.

'Good evening, Uncle Tage,' she replied, and noticed her heart beating a bit faster. 'I know where Henrik is . . .'

'Excellent, my dear, I'm most grateful to you. Where can I find him?'

She took a deep breath and held it for a few seconds before answering.

So the game was over.

Philip and co. had bought his shares, admittedly for rather more than they had anticipated, but still. Finally they had complete control over the company.

The champagne was no doubt flowing in the office while he and the twins waited like good little children out in reception for the cops to show up.

The real cops . . .

Shit!

He'd hoped he'd get away with it, that his bluff with the phones would work and that Nox and the Governor would show up and check him out. Then off to Arlanda with lots of nice new money in his account.

But instead he was going to get arrested for real.

A prison sentence was really the least of his problems. What worried him most was that the moment his personal details were typed into the police computer system, the warning lights would start to flash and tell the Game Master where he was.

He was actually somewhat surprised that they hadn't already found him.

That Philip and his gang hadn't already tipped them off about him. But they still didn't seem to have worked out who he was. Oh well, they'd soon find out . . .

A loud knock interrupted his thoughts.

'You were quick,' Elroy said to the two plain-clothes officers when he opened the door.

'We were just round the corner,' one of them said.

'I'd like to see your ID,' Elroy said.

The men shrugged, then pulled out their police IDs.

'I've got all the information here . . .' Elroy said, handing a plastic folder to one of the officers.

'Time, place, personal details, you'll find it all there, as well as a memory stick with the program he was trying to plant in our mainframe.'

He pointed at HP.

'Our lawyers will be in touch after the holiday with our claim for damages.'

One of the policemen leafed through the paperwork, then nodded to his colleague.

'Turn round,' he said, and HP did as he was asked.

There was a metallic click as the cuffs were put on.

'Okay, let's go.' Then, to Elroy: 'The investigating team will be in touch first thing tomorrow morning if they've got any questions . . .'

The two police officers led him out towards the lift.

'Hang on,' Elroy called after them. 'Which station will it be, in case there's anything we want to add?'

'Norrmalm,' the taller of the two officers said.

'Is that round the back of the Central Station?' Elroy asked.

'No, Kungsholmsgatan 37, we've been there a good while now.'

Elroy grinned happily.

'Just wanted to check . . .'

They took the lift down. Neither of the police officers said a word. Their car was parked right outside, a typical cop car, automatic gears and an extra internal mirror.

The taller one, who seemed to be the boss, sat in the back with HP. The car started, and as they pulled away he took out a mobile phone.

'We've got him, and are on our way,' he said tersely to the person at the other end.

'We're not going to Kungsholmen, are we . . .?' HP muttered.

But the man didn't answer.

45

Call!

'Well, my friends,' Philip Argos said. 'That's that little unpleasantness out of the way. Sometimes you have no choice but to buy your freedom, even if the price was somewhat higher than we had anticipated . . . But at least it was the solution that entailed the smallest risk in the long term. We'll put our lawyers to work on the claim for damages. It ought to be relatively simple now that we have the account number. Either way, we are all going to earn more money that we could ever have dreamed of . . .'

He raised his glass.

'To the future!'

A mobile started to ring.

'Excuse me,' Frank said.

He took the phone from the holster on his belt and left the room.

'So do we know who he was really working for? Henrik, I mean . . .?' Beens asked.

Philip shook his head.

'No, I'm afraid not. I might have my suspicions, but we'll never know for sure . . .'

'You're thinking of Anna?'

Philip shrugged.

'All the information we've managed to gather suggests that Henrik was basically working on his own. We certainly haven't been able to find any link between him and our competitors. It's possible that Anna employed him before . . .'

He gestured with his hand.

'. . . or, more likely, that her sister did, considering the whole business with the shares. But we're rid of them now, at least, the shares are ours, entirely legally and by the book, so there's no longer anything or anyone that can threaten our plans.'

Frank came back into the room. He was still holding the phone in his hand, so tight that his fingers were turning white.

'We've got a problem . . .' he said, almost in a whisper. 'That was Gitte down in the Filter. Half the fucking blogosphere seems to be buzzing about us. About us, the way we work, the trolls, the blogs, the register, you name it . . . Everything seems to have got out . . .'

He swallowed hard and pointed towards the door.

'And there are two uniformed police officers in reception wondering where our burglar is.'

Philip glanced at Dejan.

'Not a chance.' Dejan held his hands up as if in self-defence. 'The laptop wasn't connected to the net, and it was basically empty anyway. That trojan didn't go anywhere.'

'This isn't good . . .' Rilke whimpered.

'Quiet!' Philip snapped.

He turned to Elroy.

'What did he do while you were waiting out there? Did you let him near any of the computers?'

Elroy and Sophie shook their heads in tandem.

'He went to the toilet, that's all,' Sophie said. 'He had to do something about the cut he got when he . . .'

She stopped herself and glanced anxiously at her brother.

'When he what?' Philip snarled.

'. . . hit his head on my desk,' she concluded in a toneless voice.

They drove down Strandvägen, then through Diplomadstaden and out towards Gärdet – in the opposite direction to Police Headquarters.

The lights on the Kaknäs Tower were flashing through the mist off to their left, and for a few moments he thought that was where they were going.

But they passed the tower and turned off onto a little gravel track that seemed to lead out into the middle of nowhere. Hadn't there once been a shooting range out here somewhere?

'Are you real policemen?' he asked.

The man beside him shrugged his shoulders.

'Does it matter?'

'How long have you been watching me?'

'A while . . .'

'How did you know . . . I mean . . . who put you onto me . . .?'

'Who do you think, Henrik? I mean, if you really think about it . . .?'

Something in the man's tone made his heart plummet like a stone.

Philip yanked open the office door and, closely followed by the others, ran over to Sophie's desk. The computer was on the floor, but the USB ports at the front of it were empty.

'False alarm,' Beens said with relief. 'If he didn't manage

to get the trojan in somewhere, then everything going on out there is just loose gossip. He could have told his friends, arranged for them to spread the story at a particular time regardless of whether or not the trojan was feeding them information. Without any proof the story will be stone-dead in a couple of days . . .'

'Hold on!'

Dejan crouched down and picked at one of the little card-slots just above the USB ports.

A moment later he pulled out a tiny memory card, barely the size of a postage stamp.

Someone had written on the front of it: *Ykay A mofos!*

The lights from the nearest buildings were getting further and further away. The car seemed to be floating over the snow-covered ground, just swerving slightly when they hit hidden dips and potholes. For a few seconds it almost felt like being back in the desert. But that was just another of all the weird *déjà vu* moments his life seemed to have turned into.

When they finally came to a stop they were close to the edge of the forest. He could see small, flickering points of light in there among the trees, and it took him a while to realize what they were.

Cemetery candles.

They'd reached the old pet cemetery.

The men got out of the car, and the open doors let the cold night air in. Obviously he ought to try to escape. Make a mad rush for it, aiming for the streetlights on the far side of the field. But he had no energy left for running. Enough was enough.

'Is this where it ends?' he asked the men, but neither of them said anything. 'Surely it wouldn't hurt to tell me what's going to happen?'

'I thought you'd already realized,' one of the men said as he unlocked his handcuffs.

HP nodded.

'Yes, but I'd still like to hear you say it.'

The man didn't answer. Instead he pulled his jacket up and tucked the handcuffs back in position on his belt, next to his pistol.

'You can start walking,' the other man said.

He stood there for a moment, looking at them, but it was impossible to make out their faces in the darkness.

So he started to walk. The candles were flickering from inside the forest, no more than twenty metres or so away.

It was almost totally silent. Only a distant rumble and the pink sky behind him let on that the city was actually there, close by.

Suddenly he heard a bird cry in the distance. A dry croaking sound that he recognized. He couldn't help shuddering. Ten metres left to the edge of the forest. The snow crunched softly beneath his feet. He held his arms out from his sides and waited.

Five metres.

His heart was beating so hard he thought he could actually hear it.

Four.

Three.

Two.

One . . .

46

ORLY?

Suddenly he was in amongst the trees.

Surprised, he turned back towards the men. They were leaning against the car and seemed to be having a conversation.

He didn't get it.

'Keep going!' one of them called when he realized HP had stopped.

He turned round and tried to peer in among the trees. The cemetery candles were casting ghostly flickering shadows between the trunks. Then he heard car doors open and close, then an engine start up.

He took a few stumbling steps into the forest, tripped over a little, snow-covered headstone and fell flat in the snow. He got to his feet and brushed the worst of the snow off his clothes.

The car was already halfway back to Kaknäsvägen.

Were they really just letting him go?

Just like that?

He suddenly felt a sharp pain in one knee, and when he put his hand down to see he found his trouser-leg was wet with blood. It was impossible to judge the extent of the injury in the darkness, so he set off towards the candle that was burning brightest.

It wasn't until he was almost there that he realized there was someone standing by the grave.

'Welcome, Henrik,' the man said. 'We've been looking for you for a very long time. You're not an easy man to get hold of . . .'

HP opened his mouth but couldn't get a word out.

'Can I offer you a cup of coffee?'

The man raised his stick and pointed at the gravestone, which was actually a large, horizontal block of stone. On top of it, next to the large candle, stood a check-patterned flask and two cups. The man passed one of the cups to HP, who took it without speaking. The coffee was strong and scalding hot. They sipped at it in silence.

'So what happens now?' he finally managed to say.

'That's up to you.'

'H-how?'

'I have a task for you, Henrik,' the man said slowly. 'You'll have plenty of time to complete it, a whole year, to be precise.'

He put his hand inside his coat, and for a moment HP stiffened.

But instead of a gun, the man pulled out an oblong envelope and handed it to HP.

'Interesting place, this,' he said as HP opened the envelope and unfolded a sheet of paper.

'Are you aware of its history, Henrik?'

HP shook his head, he was completely absorbed in reading.

'The cemetery was started sometime in the middle of the nineteenth century by the author August Blanche, when he buried his dog out here. Other Stockholmers dutifully followed his example. Loyalty is a wonderful quality, don't you think, Henrik?'

'Mmm,' HP replied distantly.

He was halfway through the text but he had already worked out how it was all going to end.

His brain was spinning at high speed, his heart pounding in his chest. This was incredible! Completely insane!

'So what do you say, Henrik? Are you prepared to accept the task?' the man smiled. 'Yes or no?'

HP opened his mouth.

'Yes or no, to what?'

'Rebecca!' The man held out his free hand. 'How nice of you to join us!'

Rebecca stepped out of the darkness and walked slowly up to the gravestone.

HP tucked the sheet of paper away at once. What the fuck was Becca doing here? Now? Did they know each other?

'Yes or no to what, Henke?' she repeated, stopping beside him.

'Oh, I've just asked your brother for his assistance with something. It's to do with what we discussed before . . .' the man said with a smile.

'About Dad?'

'You could say that. By the way, I really am most grateful for your help in arranging this little meeting. Your colleagues acquitted themselves in an exemplary fashion.'

She nodded curtly.

HP's brain felt like it was going to explode.

Arranging?

Colleagues?

What in the name of holy fuck was going on?

'You've arrived at just the right time, Rebecca, Henrik and I have just finished our little chat.'

The man tipped the last of the coffee from the cups,

then put them and the flask away in a little camping box he'd kept hidden in the shadows beside the gravestone.

'My car is over there.' He pointed into the darkness with his stick.

'Well, it was nice to meet you both again,' he said, raising his hat in farewell. 'Goodbye, my friends!'

'But you'll stay in touch, Uncle Tage?'

'Don't worry, Rebecca,' he replied in an almost amused tone of voice. 'You'll be hearing from me again. I promise.'

A few moments later he was swallowed up by the darkness.

'Explain!' HP said as they trudged through the snow. 'Quick, before I go completely mad!'

She couldn't help smiling.

'Uncle Tage helped me with something, something important. In return I promised to help him arrange a meeting between the two of you. I've been a bit worried about you, so for the past few days a couple of my colleagues have been keeping an eye on you. They were the ones who picked you up at Hötorget. I've been keeping in touch with Malmén, the tall one, every now and then. So, didn't you recognize him?'

'Er, who?'

'Uncle Tage, we went to stay at his summer cottage up in Rättvik when we were little.'

She tucked her hand under his arm.

'The blue clogs with our names on, don't you remember? You never wanted to take them off . . .'

He just shook his head.

She emerged from the forest and headed over towards her car.

'So, what was it he wanted you to do?' she asked.

'Nothing special,' he said. 'Nothing special at all . . .'

47

Aftermath

He had almost reached passport control, and had just put his hand into the inside pocket of his coat when the men came up to him.

'Mr Argos?' the first man said, an officer in full uniform of some sort.

'Who wants to know?'

'My name is Major Erdogan,' the officer replied, without introducing the two men in suits behind him.

'Can I see your passport, please?'

He handed over his passport and the officer inspected it carefully.

'Excellent,' he said, handing the passport to one of the men behind him. 'I'm afraid you won't be granted entry to Turkey, because you are under suspicion of committing a criminal offence in another country. These two gentlemen will make sure you end up on the right flight . . .'

'Nonsense! Turkey has no extradition treaty with Sweden. You have no right to do this!'

The officer smiled and exchanged a glance with the two suited men.

'Who said anything about Sweden?' he went on. 'You're

wanted for incitement to murder in the United Arab Emirates. Dubai, to be more precise, and these two gentlemen are here to pick you up.'

The men in suits stepped up to him and the shorter one, an amiable-looking little man with glasses and a moustache, held out his hand.

'My name is Colonel Aziz,' he said in a friendly tone of voice. 'And this is my colleague, Sergeant Moussad.'

He pointed his thumb towards the other man, who was thickset and whose coarse, unshaven features were covered by a mass of small scars.

'You'll have to excuse the sergeant, I'm afraid he doesn't speak English,' Aziz went on, with a trace of a smile.

'It's good to meet you at last, Mr Argos. We've waited a long time for the opportunity to talk to you.'

'No need to get up,' she said, marching straight into his office.

'Ah, how lovely to see you,' Runeberg muttered, and slowly lowered his feet from the edge of his desk. 'So, what are you doing here, Normén? You're not due back until next week.'

'I just wanted to drop this off.'

She put a small pile of papers in front of him.

'And I'm afraid you'll also be wanting this once you've read through that.'

She dug in her pocket, then slowly handed over her police ID.

'What the hell is this, Normén?'

He sat up straight in his chair.

'You were cleared of all charges. It looks like the whole Darfur incident was a set-up, some kind of trap. And your actions probably saved the lives of all involved, but you already know that. So, why do you want . . .'

'Leave of absence?' she interrupted. 'Because I need to get away from here for a while.'

'Is this anything to do with . . . you know . . .'

'The website, you mean? Yes and no. It's mostly just about me.'

She took a deep breath.

'I need some time out of circulation to let things settle, in my own life and with my job. I've had an offer to help set up an IT security company's own personal security department . . . It's where my partner works, they've recently been bought up by a larger company that wants to expand its operations. I'll have a completely free hand, and plenty of resources . . .'

He was silent for a few seconds, then nodded.

'I understand. That sounds like the sort of offer you couldn't refuse. But you're putting me in a very difficult position here . . . We're short of people as it is. The group . . .'

'My suggestion would be to put David Malmén in charge of the group.'

He gave her a long look.

'Something tells me you and Malmén have already discussed this.'

She didn't reply.

'Okay, Becca, I'm not going to be difficult. But I want you to promise me something . . .'

'What, Ludvig?'

She allowed herself a little smile, which he was quick to return.

'That you'll take good care of yourself.'

'I promise,' she smiled.

He grabbed a pen, signed the papers, then handed her a copy.

'There, you're officially on leave of absence for a

year. Well, then, I should probably just wish you good luck . . .?'

'Thanks.'

She took the sheet of paper, folded it up and put it in her rucksack.

'Just one question,' he called when she was on her way out of the door.

'What's the name of the company you're going to be working for?'

'PayTag,' she called back, waving in farewell.

'Your telephone, Madame,' the little uniformed man said, handing her the receiver. 'I said that you were resting, but the caller insisted that I wake you.'

'It's okay, Sridhar,' she replied. 'I've been waiting for this call.'

She took a deep breath, leaned back on the sunbed and tried to collect her thoughts.

High above her a pair of birds was hovering.

Desert crows, just like in her dream.

'Hello?'

'Good evening, my dear, or is it still afternoon there?'

She raised her hand and squinted against the sun.

'Late afternoon, actually. But you're not calling to ask what time it is, are you?'

'No, quite right. I have some good news. Very good news . . .'

For a few seconds she found it hard to say anything, her heart was beating so hard against her chest that she imagined she could almost see the fabric of her bikini move.

'Did everything . . .?' she began.

'Exactly as we had hoped, even if events occasionally took a course we weren't able to predict. But of course that's one of the delights of what we do. You'll have a full report within

the next few days. Until then, allow me to wish you a very happy continuation of your holiday.'

'Okay, thank you . . .'

'No, it's us who should be thanking you, my dear. Thank you for choosing to do business with us.

'Well, goodbye, and take good care of yourself, Mrs Argos.'

The edge-of-your-seat thrills continue...

Turn over to read the first chapter of *Bubble* now!

Join in the conversation on Twitter **#gametrilogy**

1

A whole new Game?

The moment he woke up HP knew something was wrong. It took him a few seconds to put his finger on what it was.

It was quiet.

Far *too* quiet . . .

The bedroom faced out onto Guldgränd and he had long since got used to the constant sound of traffic on the Söderleden motorway a few hundred metres away. He hardly ever thought about it any more.

But instead of the usual low rumble of traffic interspersed with the occasional siren, the summer night outside was completely silent.

He glanced at the clock-radio: 03.58.

Roadworks, he thought. Söderleden, Söder Mälarstrand and the Slussen junction closed off for yet another round of make-do-and-mend . . . But besides the fact that Bob the Builder would have to be working in stealth mode, it was also slowly dawning on him that there were other noises missing. No-one rattling doors as they delivered the morning papers, no drunks shouting down on Hornsgatan. In fact hardly any sound at all to indicate that there was actually a vibrant capital city out there. As if his bedroom had been enclosed in a huge bubble, shutting the rest of the world out. Forcing him to live in his own little universe where the usual rules no longer applied.

Which, in some ways, was actually true . . .

He noticed that his heart was starting to beat faster. A quiet rustling sound from somewhere inside the flat made him jump.

A burglar?

No, impossible. He'd locked the high-security door, all three locks, just like he always did. The door had cost a fortune, but it was worth every single damn penny. Steel frame, double cylinder hook-bolt locks, you name it – so, logically, no-one could have broken into the flat. But the umbrella of paranoia wasn't about to let itself be taken down so easily . . .

He crept out of bed, padded across the bedroom floor and peered cautiously into the living room. It took a few seconds for his eyes to get used to the gloom, but the results were unambiguous. Nothing, no movement at all, either in the living room or the little kitchen beyond. Everything was fine, there was no sign of any danger. Just the unnatural, oppressive silence that still hadn't broken . . .

He crept carefully over to the window and looked out. Not a soul out on the street, not that that was particularly surprising given the time. Maria Trappgränd was hardly a busy street at any time of day.

Closed off for roadworks, that had to be it. Half of Södermalm already looked like some fucking archaeological dig, so why not go for a complete overnight shut-down? All the little Bobs were probably just having a coffee break.

Plausible – sure! But the uneasy feeling still wouldn't let go.

Only the hall left.

He tiptoed across the new floorboards over to the front door, taking care to avoid the third and fifth ones because he knew they creaked.

When he was about a metre away he thought he saw the letterbox move. He froze mid-step as his pulse switched up a gear.

Two years ago someone had poured lighter fluid through his door and set fire to it. A seriously unpleasant experience, and one which had ended with him lying in Södermalm Hospital with an oxygen mask over his face. It wasn't until much later that he had realized the whole thing was just a warning shot to remind him about the rules of the Game.

He sniffed carefully at the stagnant air, but couldn't smell paraffin or anything similar. But by now he was quite certain. The sounds had come from the front door.

Maybe someone delivering papers after all?

He crept a couple of steps closer to the door and carefully put his eye to the peephole.

The sudden noise was so violent that he staggered back into the hall.

Fuck!

For a few seconds he saw stars, and his heart almost seemed to have stopped.

Then another violent crash jolted him out of the shock.

Someone was smashing his door in!

The steel frame was already starting to bow, so whoever it was basically had to be stronger than the Hulk. A third crash, metal against metal, no bastard Bruce Banner but probably a serious sledgehammer – if not more than one.

The frame moved another few centimetres and he could suddenly see the bolts of the locks in the gap. A couple more blows was all it would take.

He spun round, stumbling over his own feet, and fell flat on the floor. Another crash from the door sent a rattling shower of plaster over his bare legs.

His feet slid on the floor as his hands tried to get a grip.

He was up.

Quickly into the living room, then the bedroom.

Another crash on the door!

He could taste blood in his mouth, and his heart was pounding fit to burst.

His hands were shaking so much he had trouble turning the key in the lock.

Whatinthenameofholyfucksgoingon . . .?

A further blow from the hall, this time followed by a splintering sound that almost certainly meant that the door frame had given way.

He grabbed the chest of drawers, and almost fell over when it glided easily in front of the bedroom door.

Fucking chipboard crap!

If the steel door out there hadn't been able to stop his attackers, then a bit of self-assembly furniture from the other side of the Baltic wasn't going to win him more than a couple of seconds at most. He leapt at the bed and fumbled about on the bedside table, which was covered with magazines and paperbacks.

The phone, where the hell was the phone?

There! No, shit, that was the remote for the television . . .

He heard rapid steps in the living room, gruff voices shouting to each other, but he was concentrating too hard on his search to hear what they were saying.

Suddenly his fingers hit the phone, so hard that it fell to the floor.

Fucking hell!

The door handle rattled, then a rough voice shouting:

'In here!'

HP threw himself on the floor, fumbling wildly with his arms.

There it was, right next to his left hand.

He grabbed the phone, scrabbled at the buttons. His fingers were twitching as if he had Parkinson's.

One, one, two is easy to do . . . like fuck was it!

A crash from the door and the Ikea chest of drawers almost fell over.

'Hello, emergency services, how can I help you?' a dry, professional voice said.

'Police!' HP yelled. 'Help m . . .'

A sudden flash of light blinded him, burning onto his retina.

Then a blow that was so strong he was left gasping for air.

And then they had him.